ROSIE: NOTE TO SELF

ROSIE: NOTE TO SELF

G.P. Taylor
with Claire Connor

Authentic

MILTON KEYNES ● COLORADO SPRINGS ● HYDERABAD

15 14 13 12 11 10 09   7 6 5 4 3 2 1

Authentic Media, 9 Holdom Avenue, Bletchley, Milton Keynes, Bucks,
MK1 1QR, UK
1820 Jet Stream Drive, Colorado Springs, CO 80921, USA
Medchal Road, Jeedimetla Village, Secunderabad 500 055, A.P., India
www.loveauthentic.com

Authentic Media is a division of Biblica UK, previously IBS-STL UK.
Biblica UK is limited by guarantee, with its registered office at Kingstown
Broadway, Carlisle, Cumbria, CA3 0HA. Registered in England & Wales
No. 1216232. Registered charity in England & Wales No. 270162 and
Scotland No. SCO40064

British Library Cataloguing in Publication Data
A catalogue record for this book is available from the
British Library

ISBN-13: 978-1-85078-833-1

Cover Design by Suzi Perkins
Print Management by Adare
Printed and bound in the UK by J.F. Print Ltd., Sparkford, Somerset

To
The Aged Aunt and my Cochon

Contents

Preface

Life.

A heady, volatile brew blending birth, class, religion, nationality, circumstance and opportunity in endless variety. One recipe, infinitely unique results. All by virtue of the secret ingredient – choice, (free will to the old-fashioned), swirling around at the bottom of every glass.

Genius.

A pinch is all that's needed: it's powerful stuff. Of course, it works differently depending on the individual concoction.

Choice.

There are some for whom choice is severely, painfully restricted to the smallest and most insignificant areas of their life. Others, meanwhile, have choices sleeting around them every day, no, every minute. So many that they cease to be aware of them, let alone appreciate what they represent. Big choices, small choices, choices that count and choices that don't. If you thought about it for too long, you'd go mad.

But here's the catch, and it's a big one: choices aren't what you think. They're fickle, dangerous things. Slippery, unpredictable. Tenacious. The big ones just don't go away. You make them once, but they keep coming back, demanding to be re-made again and again, insisting that you own them.

The truth is, only those who understand the power of choices can withstand that kind of sustained assault. Even the wise aren't immune to the deadliest kind: the mavericks, very rare and only visible with hindsight. Once or twice in every life, these tiny choices slip innocently into the fabric of an ordinary day and present themselves unobtrusively. Small enough to escape notice, powerful enough to change the course of an entire life.

This is a story about faith, courage and the power of a choice.

Chapter 1

Michaelmas

Five minutes, Rosie thought. Just five more minutes and then I'll get up. It was the first day of the new term at New York University and in the twin bedroom of a third floor studio apartment, Rosie Jacobs was dozing determinedly, the bedclothes humped up over her body so that she looked like a giant snail. Across the apartment, her room-mate tutted and switched her hair-dryer on full blast, ruffling her poker-straight blonde hair. Rosie opened one eye, squinted at Melissa, then closed it again.

Melissa Jefferies was always on time and immaculate. Rosie was usually presentable and sometimes only five minutes late. Melissa was a sorority girl who hung out at the Frat House in Chinatown, whereas Rosie was more likely to be found in the library of NYC or shooting hoops with some of the guys on the street corner. Despite their differences, the two got on well enough.

The sun had long since climbed over the distinctive Manhattan skyline and the residents of Broome Street university hall, downtown Manhattan, were up and about their business. The new students had set off for the Washington

Square campus a good hour ago, bright and shiny as new coins and eager to make a good first impression on fellow students and lecturers alike. The returning students, more worldly-wise and ever so slightly jaded, were nonetheless determined to avoid the pitfalls of the previous year and turn up on time for at least the first week. Well, most of them were.

Melissa sighed loudly. 'Rosie, come on now. Get up.'

Rosie burrowed deeper, Melissa's words no more than a muffled buzzing. She had never been a morning person and had no intention of becoming one now, not when her bed was so warm and comfortable and – 'Arrgh!' Rosie shot upright. A blast of freezing air had just invaded her little space.

'Enough already!' she pleaded. 'I'm up.' Melissa switched her hair-dryer off again and retreated to her side of the room to finish applying her make-up. Rosie yawned. 'What time is it?'

'What am I, the speaking clock?' Melissa huffed. Rosie swung her legs over the side of the bed and rubbed her eyes. Mornings were the pits.

'Do you have a ten o'clock?' she asked, half-heartedly rummaging in the pile of nearly clean clothes on the floor next to her bed.

'No, an eleven.' Melissa turned this way and that in front of the mirror, examining her profile from every angle. 'You?'

'Yeah, a ten.' Rosie began to shuffle towards the bathroom.

'Well, step on it, because it's now nine-twenty and you know they've changed the shuttle bus times this term,' Melissa warned.

'What? You're kidding?'

'I'm really not.'

For the next five minutes, pandemonium reigned. Melissa grabbed her make-up bag and retreated to her bed to complete her beauty regime, knowing from bitter experience that it was safer to be out of the way when Rosie went into warp speed. She shot in and out of the shower, barely getting herself wet, then raged around the room wrapped in her towel, rummaging desperately through her clothes and books. Melissa fielded her questions calmly, while applying mascara with a practised hand.

'Where are my jeans?'

'Bottom of your bed.'

'Oh man, I'm so, so late. Can't find my trainers.'

'In the bathroom.'

'I've lost my timetable!'

'Under the bed.'

'My hair is such a mess.'

'Clip it back. My clip's on the dressing-table.'

At last, Rosie came to a standstill in front of the mirror by the door. Her jeans were crumpled, but luckily they were mostly hidden by the floral dress she'd flung over the top. Sure, it had a few buttons missing and the lace was already trailing dangerously from her left shoe, but overall, Rosie thought, not a bad effort. She turned to face Melissa, tucking back the hair that had already escaped from behind her ear. 'Good to go?'

Melissa rolled her eyes.

Rosie grinned and took off at top speed, banging the door behind her. Seconds later, she barrelled back in.

'On the bed,' Melissa said wearily.

Rosie snatched up her book bag and timetable and sprinted off.

She jogged along Broome Street, heading west. The campus bus left from outside Lafayette, the next residence in the sequence of NYU halls peppered across Manhattan. She ran two blocks, rounded the last corner and saw the bus parked up.

'Thank God,' she panted, slowing to a walk as she approached.

In the rear window, she spotted the distinctive silhouette of George Wilder, one of her basketball buddies. His bleached Mohican bobbed up and down as he exchanged high fives with the other students on the back seat.

Suddenly, the indicator on the bus began to flash. 'Wait!' Rosie broke into a run once more. George glanced out of the window and saw her.

'Come on, Rosie!' he mouthed, waving her on.

The bus inched forward, looking for a gap in the busy morning traffic. Rosie dug deep and managed to draw level with the back wheel, her book bag banging awkwardly against her hip. The driver glanced in his mirror and caught sight of Rosie. For a split second, their eyes met, then the bus pulled smoothly away. 'Jerk!' Rosie wheezed. George elbowed his way to a window and stuck his head out.

'I'll save you a seat!' he bawled.

Rosie raised her hand in acknowledgement and collapsed against a lamp-post as the bus disappeared from view. Her lungs were on fire.

'That driver totally saw me coming,' she fumed out loud, pulling her phone from her back pocket. The screen was cracked and had been since her first year, but Rosie refused to buy a new one. 'I'll only sit on it again, Mom,' she pointed out when her mother raised the issue. 'Why waste the money?'

The time flashed urgently at her now through the distorted display. Nine-forty. Rosie squared her shoulders, took a deep breath and ran. She stumbled along the pavement, passing the Lafayette residence and Little Italy, the site of several disastrous nights out last term. A tired-looking waitress was wiping down the tables out front, but the restaurant was still asleep after the previous night's partying, its red shutters closed tightly over the windows. At last, Spring Street subway station came into view. Rosie took the steps two at a time and charged on. It was warm as usual; the air blew up and out of the tunnels towards her, bringing with it the smell of the city.

❀　❀　❀　❀

Cameron Whitton stood uncertainly on the steps of the subway station, blinking in the sunshine. He pulled a map from the pocket of his faded corduroy jacket, shook it out and stared at the unfamiliar street names. He glanced anxiously at his watch and swore under his breath. He hated being lost or being late. At the present moment, both applied. Cameron felt panic begin to creep over him. His first day on the doctorate exchange programme and he was going to be late. Not exactly the sparkling first impression he'd been hoping to make.

'Pull yourself together, man,' he snapped. 'Focus.' He frowned at the map, turned it round a few times and set off down the street.

Everyone around him seemed to be power-walking or running, which made the panicky feeling far worse. Were they all late too, Cameron wondered, or did New Yorkers jog everywhere? No one seemed to want to stop and he noticed that everyone was looking either at the pavement or the sky. In New York, it seemed, no one looked you in the face.

He stopped at the end of the block and peered at the map.

'Right,' he said in a falsely optimistic voice. 'According to this, I ought to be . . . just about opposite the campus.' He marked the spot with a finger and looked up eagerly, only to find himself staring at a grocery store across the road. The strawberries were currently half price. He loved strawberries.

Cameron took several deep, calming breaths. 'Well, that's good to know.' He tried to place the strawberry store on the map. It was now five minutes to ten. Hysteria threatened. 'Okay, start again, Whitton.' He crammed the map into his pocket and ran back down the street.

❀   ❀   ❀   ❀

The station signs flashed past as Rosie's train lurched and swayed its way uptown. 'So much for saving on travel fares,' Rosie thought glumly. She gave her purse an experimental shake and brightened at the sound. Definitely enough for a latte and doughnuts. Since she was going to be late anyway, there was no need to arrive with an empty stomach.

Rosie sat back and relaxed, closing her eyes as the motion of the train rocked her to and fro. Her mother's face drifted into her mind, triggering an unwelcome replay of one of the dreaded Kitchen Table Conversations back home in Brooklyn Park Slopes.

'Apply for a hall close to campus,' Mrs Jacobs had urged. 'Union Square, maybe. Give yourself a chance of getting someplace on time, honey.'

'Relax, Mom, it's under control.'

'I'm serious, Rosie. You're twenty-three years old. You've got to stop being late for class.'

'I'm not always late.'

'I can't believe you're lying to your own mother.'

'Mom!'

'Honey, you're always oversleeping.'

'I am not.'

'That's not what Melissa says. And while you're sleeping, your grades are slipping.'

'Mom, I'm officially exiting this conversation.'

'Okay, okay. Just remember what I said. Living closer to campus would help.'

Things would have worked out just fine, if only she'd remembered to submit the application form on time. That apartment in Coral Tower would have been in the bag instead of Broome Street, the furthest hall from campus. Melissa had wept on hearing the news. 'I should never have left you in charge of applying for accommodation,' she had sobbed.

'But Broome Street is so much cheaper. Think of all the Estée Lauder you can buy now,' Rosie replied comfortingly. 'Mascara and . . . stuff.'

Rosie was jolted from her thoughts as the train ground to a halt again. She jumped up and manoeuvred herself as close to the doors as possible.

On the platform she pushed her way through the crowds and ran towards the exit barrier. There was no queue at the doughnut stall. 'There is a God!' Rosie cried jubilantly. The businessman in front of her leapt aside in alarm, fearing he was about to be accosted by a religious fanatic.

'Oh. Um. Excuse me,' Rosie apologised.

'Idiot,' the man muttered. He looked Rosie up and down, wondering if she was a member of some new religious cult. Rosie smiled, her eyes sparkling. It was too much for the man. 'I'm married,' the man said. 'People like you disgust me . . .' Shaking his jowls like a bull terrier he hurried off, his briefcase clutched to his chest.

'Hey Marco. Mixed bag of mini-doughnuts and a large latte, please,' Rosie chirped with a shrug of her shoulders. It was what she did every time she was late. 'Five bucks, Rosie,' Marco smiled, 'But as it's you, make it three . . .'

Rosie scrabbled in her purse. The clock above the doughnut stall read five minutes to ten. 'Sorry Marco, no time!' She tipped the contents of her purse onto the counter, snatched up the paper bag and cardboard cup and took off.

'Hey!' shouted Marco as he scrambled to catch the spilling coins. 'Late again?'

'What's new?' Rosie laughed over her shoulder as she ran up the steps. 'It's all there, keep the change!'

She didn't see the man standing staring at his map and so she butted him right in the back. Rebounding, she toppled onto the pavement. Scalding liquid seeped through her fingers and the coffee cup crunched beneath her.

'Why don't you look where you're going?' she shouted, as someone grabbed her from behind and hoisted her to her knees.

'Are you all right?' asked a concerned voice in a warm and unmistakably English accent. Rosie scrambled up and found herself face to face with a faded corduroy jacket. She looked down at the brown stain spreading across the front of her dress, then up at the tall, scruffy guy, whose brown eyes were fixed anxiously on her. The man held out his hand. Rosie stared at him, her mouth open.

'Cameron Whitton,' the man said as he tried to mop the coffee stain from her dress without asking.

'Rosie . . .' she said, unable to take her eyes from his face. He was beautiful, she thought, hoping she hadn't said the words out loud. And here she was, covered in coffee. Typical.

Cameron took a step towards her. 'Are you all right?' he asked again, taking her arm. Rosie backed away, flustered.

'That coffee cost me three bucks!' she snapped.

'Goodness, that much?' Cameron replied with a smile as he stooped and began retrieving the books that had spilled from her bag.

Rosie examined the remains of her breakfast. The dough-nut bag was now a crushed, pulpy mess of paper. Custard and strawberry jam oozed across her shoes. For a moment, she considered just sitting down on the pavement and bawling.

'My dress is ruined!'

'I'm sorry. Won't it wash out?'

'Why didn't you look where you were going?'

'Actually,' said Cameron, handing her the books with an amused smile, '*You* ran into *me*.'

Rosie's temper flared. 'Don't you dare laugh at me!'

'I wouldn't dream of it.'

'I was clearly in a hurry. You should have got out of my way.'

'I had my back to you.'

'And I'm late for class!' she finished.

Cameron sighed. 'That makes two of us.' He pulled the crumpled street map from his pocket and waved it hopefully at her. 'Looking for the University. Perhaps you could help me?'

Rosie glared at him.

'Fine,' said Cameron, 'I just thought that being as you are the only person in New York who seems prepared to speak to me ...' He gave up, irritation finally overcoming his good manners. 'I'll just carry on walking round in circles all day. Thank you and goodbye!' He stalked away.

'Whatever,' Rosie muttered, as she slam-dunked the remains of the doughnuts into a nearby bin. 'Perhaps if you looked where you were going people would help you,' she shouted after him, storming off towards the campus.

After a few paces she glanced back at the Englishman, his upright figure still visible amid the stream of commuters leaving the subway. He was going the wrong way.

Rosie hesitated, shifting her weight from foot to foot and levering her now-sticky bag higher onto her hip. 'Wait!'

She dodged and wove her way along the crowded pavement. Half the world seemed to turn and stare at her, stained, dishevelled and shrieking like a harpy, but the Englishman marched on, head down, staring at his map.

'Deaf as well as stupid,' Rosie puffed. 'Why am I doing this?' Melissa's clip lost its grip on her curls and spiralled off into the crowd, leaving her hair flapping across her face with every step. She turned to grab it, but it had vanished under a thousand purposeful feet. Rosie put a hand to her side. She was getting a stitch.

'Hey, you! English guy! Wait!' Half a dozen men skidded to a halt. They looked guilty, as though being English made them criminals. This time, Cameron was one of them.

Rosie staggered up to him and doubled over, clutching her side with both hands. The crowd flowed past them like water round a stone. Cameron waited. Rosie looked up through her matted curls and pointed a shaking finger at him.

'Wrong . . . way,' she wheezed, sweat trickling down her forehead.

'Thank you,' Cameron said fervently. 'Give me your books and lead the way. Hurry.'

Five minutes later, they were on campus, Rosie trotting to keep up with Cameron's long strides. 'I can't believe we're in the same class,' she said chattily. 'Such a coincidence.' Cameron nodded, only half-listening.

'Time check,' he said tightly.

'Ten minutes past,' Rosie answered, shouldering a door open and waving him into the College of Arts. She led the way down a bright white corridor, past classrooms and lecture theatres. Light streamed in through a sequence of large bay windows set into the left-hand wall, each alcove containing a huddle of students cosied up together on the cushioned window seats. Some of them called out to Rosie and she waved a greeting as they hurried by.

'Almost there now.' She glanced up at Cameron's tense face. 'Hey, don't worry. It's just a seminar. The post-grads don't mind if you're a little late.'

Cameron's eyebrows disappeared beneath the long fringe flopping over his forehead. 'Really?'

Rosie shrugged. 'Why would they? The PhDs have to teach undergrad classes to pass their teaching module. We have to be there, but they're mostly interested in the credits, not the students.' She stopped beside a wooden door on which the number thirteen gleamed in polished brass. 'Here we are.'

Cameron swallowed hard, his face suddenly pale. Rosie frowned at him, her hand already on the door. What was wrong with this guy?

'It'll be okay. Really. Just say you slept in. The post-grads are always pumped-up jerks, but they're harmless.' Cameron looked down at her and burst out laughing. Rosie beamed at him and lifted her book bag out of his arms. 'That's better. Come on.'

She opened the door and they were instantly hit by a wall of noise. The room was filled with laughing, chatting students, sitting in groups, sprawling on desks, calling out to each other across the aisle as they caught up on all the holiday gossip. Rosie gave Cameron's arm a little pat. 'You see? We made it. Prof's not even here yet,' she crowed.

'Rosie, here!' George Wilder waved at her from the middle row on their right, his legs stretched out over the seats next to him. Rosie plopped gratefully into the chair beside him. The noise level dropped to a low hum.

'New look?' George enquired, staring at her wild hair and food-splattered clothes. Rosie punched him on the arm.

'Long story.' She looked round for Cameron, intending to offer him the seat next to her. 'Where's he got to?'

'Good morning, class.'

Rosie whipped round. Cameron was leaning casually against the front desk, hands in his pockets. She stared at him, open-mouthed. He grinned at her, his nerves apparently miraculously cured.

'I'm a third year doctoral student, here on exchange from Oxford, England,' he announced.

There was a ripple of interest at this piece of information and Cameron held up his hands for silence before continuing. 'I'll be taking your medieval literature class this semester.' He pulled a well-thumbed copy of Chaucer's *Canterbury Tales* from his pocket and waved it at Rosie.

'Do you know this guy?' George hissed.

Rosie's cheeks flamed as she shook her head. Cameron raised a neat slender eyebrow at her and she knew with a dreadful sinking feeling that there was worse to come.

'Now,' he said, still wearing the painfully broad grin, 'I have it on good authority that, as a post-grad, I ought to go by the name of Pumped-up Jerk' – there was a collective shout of laughter from the class – 'but please just call me Cameron.'

He held Rosie's gaze steadily as he spoke, his eyes twinkling. Every head in the room swivelled towards her, aware that there was some kind of joke being enjoyed at her expense. George elbowed her and sniggered. Rosie slid as low as possible in her seat, pulled her hair across her face and prayed for a grand piano to materialise and drop on the infuriating Englishman's head.

The seminar that followed was fast-paced, energetic and fun. For Rosie, mortified and furious in equal parts, it was the longest hour of her life. When Cameron finally dismissed the class she shot to her feet, head down and bolted for the door.

'A word, please,' Cameron called in a tone of irrefutable command. Everyone knew who he meant.

Rosie shuffled into a seat as the students jostled their way out, buzzing with enthusiasm. She stared at the floor. A few seconds later, Cameron's tan loafers came into view and stopped by her desk. They looked as though they'd never seen a tin of polish. 'It's Rosie, isn't it?' Rosie nodded silently, keeping her eyes stubbornly on the shoes. Unfazed, Cameron crouched beside the desk and looked up at her.

'I'm sorry. I just couldn't help myself.'

'You made me look like a total idiot.'

'They were laughing with you.'

'I wasn't laughing.'

'No,' he conceded. 'Tell me, do you ever go out for dinner with pumped-up jerks?'

'Get lost.'

Cameron's mouth twitched at the corners. He really was incredibly good-looking. 'How about dinner with a pumped-up *English* jerk?'

'I'd rather eat my own foot.'

'Okay, I'll bring dessert.'

Rosie scowled at him. 'Are you always this persistent?'

'No,' he said. 'Only when it matters.'

Chapter Two

Pearls and Posies

Rosie smiled, remembering that first meeting. And now here she was, more than two years later and three thousand miles from her home in Park Slopes, Brooklyn, about to marry the 'pumped-up jerk'.

She looked out of her bedroom window onto the three miles of deer park that made up the grounds of Carrington Hall near Oxford, Cameron's family home. The gravel drive-way alone made a magnificent first impression. It was as broad and straight as a Roman road, with an honour guard of ancient beech trees to either side. They seemed to march faithfully along the quarter of a mile from the gated archway to the Hall. The trees bowed to the east as if in homage, bent by the cold winds that blew in from the hills, and their long branches offered shelter to the deer and sheep that grazed upon the grounds. The house itself was vast, imposing, a leviathan of stone with ornate Georgian windows and carvings of cherubs above the double oak doors.

Cameron had called it 'the old barn', so of course the first time Rosie had visited she had been completely overawed. That first day, she warily approached the entrance, afraid to take hold of the door knocker for fear the bronze gargoyle head would snap at her fingers. 'What on earth am I doing here?' Rosie had said, as she stared into the green eyes of the creature that had hung on the door since the house had been built.

Inside the Hall there was a sentient quality, as though it had absorbed something of every life that had entered the house over the years. A whole spectrum of emotions had gradually seeped into the essence of the building. It reminded Rosie of St Patrick's Cathedral in Manhattan. She had often sneaked inside to escape the summer heat or winter snow of New York – well, that's what she told herself as she crossed the threshold. In reality she knew that she just loved being there. It was as if every stone had listened to every prayer that had ever been said. Faithful words calling to God had infused it with goodness.

Now, on the other side of the Atlantic, Rosie felt the same about Carrington Hall. It would be difficult *not* to belong here. No matter how she was feeling, Rosie could always find a place that echoed the desire of her heart.

Today, as Rosie watched from her window, it seemed that everything was cocooned in expectant stillness. The sun climbed lazily in the sky, casting early shadows from the spiralling stems of the Sweet Bay topiary. The garden was normally alive with birds, splashing in the cracked stone fountain or flitting busily from tree to bush, but this morning there was nothing but a solitary blackbird grubbing for food on the dewy lawn below.

Rosie held her breath, listening to her beating heart. The day she had been waiting for had finally arrived. The small chapel by the lake had been garlanded with summer buds, yew and holly branches. Outside the Hall, a vast marquee was festooned with golden balloons. A red carpet rolled out towards the chapel and gave way to an avenue of wild flowers. This was what she wanted. This was where she belonged.

Rosie turned, smoothing out the folds of her wedding dress and hoping that her mother wouldn't notice that instead of the beautiful but crippling high heels, she was still wearing her trainers. Mrs Jacobs bustled in from the small dressing-room and, with a mother's unerring instinct, homed straight in on Rosie's footwear. 'Oh *Rosie*,' she began. Luckily, at that moment there was a sudden commotion outside.

'Please, Madam, let me do that!'

'It's quite all right, I can manage.'

'I really don't think . . .'

The door opened suddenly. Rosie spun round, clutching her bathrobe to cover her dress.

Lady Mara Whitton walked forward timidly, holding a vase of enormous flowers in front of her. 'I'm so sorry, I thought you were in another bedroom!' she said, her eyes sparkling with mischief. 'I, er, wanted to be sure there were fresh flowers in all the rooms, ready for the guests,' she finished, giving the vase an unconvincing little shake. Rosie wasn't fooled.

'She isn't ready!' replied Mrs Jacobs, fussing round. Aunt Phyllis and Rosie's cousin Anna appeared from the dressing-room to see what all the noise was about, holding what looked like armfuls of veil. 'Kindly leave the flowers and remove yourself. The *last* thing my daughter needs is servants bursting in on her an hour before her wedding to adjust the décor.'

Rosie felt her cheeks flame. 'Mom, let me introduce . . .' Too late. Lady Mara extended her hand graciously. 'You're Mrs Jacobs? I am Lady Whitton. Delighted to meet you at last. *So* sorry I couldn't be here to welcome you last night.'

The colour drained from Mrs Jacobs' face, as Aunt Phyllis and Anna let out gasps of Brooklyn horror. Lady Mara's eyes twinkled. Rosie winced. Lady Mara was going to have a field day with this.

Aunt Phyllis and Anna stood nervously to one side; Anna gawping at Lady Mara while Phyllis bobbed up and down slightly as she rehearsed a curtsey. Lady Mara looked at her and then at Rosie. She gave a nod, but was obviously wondering if the curtsey was a distinct nervous tic.

Rosie watched as her mother's carefully prepared speech evaporated in the face of Lady Whitton's courteous onslaught. Mrs Jacobs dissolved in embarrassment. Rosie shook her head and groaned. This wasn't how she'd planned to introduce her mother to a member of the English aristocracy. Oh well, time for a distraction. Rosie cast her fluffy pink robe aside and coughed loudly. Lady Mara looked up and gasped.

'Oh, it's perfect!' she exclaimed, her lilting Scots accent ringing out across the room. Rosie folded her arms and waited. Lady Mara gazed at the wedding dress a moment longer, then sighed happily. She turned to Mrs Jacobs, took her hand again and held it firmly between her own.

'I'm sorry,' she said earnestly. 'Forgive me. And,' she added hastily, seeing Rosie's raised eyebrows, 'I admit that I couldn't wait to see the dress. I thought I'd burst. We will be friends and I am so glad Rosie will marry my son.'

Lady Mara swooped into a low curtsey, still clutching Mrs Jacobs' hands so that she was dragged down with her. Rosie's mother staggered, glancing desperately at her daughter for assistance. She hadn't read this in her book of etiquette. Could you curtsey to a curtsey or did it have to be a bow? Seconds passed. Lady Mara held her pose, perfectly balanced. Aunt Phyllis looked as though she might faint with admiration.

'I — that is — uh, sure,' stammered Mrs Jacobs eventually. 'Please call me Christine. We all think the world of Cameron in Brooklyn and he sure is brave, taking on our Rosie. I mean, look at her now — every inch a bride. Except for the trainers.'

Lady Mara looked down and smiled. The wedding dress brushed the floor so Rosie's feet could not be seen. 'Trainers?' she asked.

'Couldn't find my shoes,' said Rosie offhandedly. 'Had them last night — this morning they were gone.' Her tone of voice made it clear that this wasn't up for discussion.

'They'll be excellent!' smiled Lady Mara. Darting across the room, she shook hands briskly with Anna and Aunt Phyllis, then hugged Rosie carefully.

'Show-off,' Rosie murmured as Lady Mara kissed her and pulled away.

'Mustn't crush the dress, love the trainers.' Lady Mara said warmly.

Rosie grinned back, feeling her nerves ebb away. It was impossible to be cross with Mara for long. She was infuriating

and eccentric, but she radiated so much warmth and energy
that you couldn't help but be swept along by her.

'Shall we toast the beautiful bride?' Anna suggested, nodding at the champagne bucket standing on the dressing-
table.

'I'll pour,' offered Mrs Jacobs, hastening to the table and
pouring unusually generous measures into the delicate crystal flutes. The women raised their glasses in a musketeer-like
salute. Mrs Jacobs took a deep breath. 'To Rosemary and
Cameron. Health, happiness and –'

The door burst open again. A tall, dark-haired, beautiful
woman barged into the room carrying a creature that could
have been a rat wearing a collar, but was in fact a very small
dog. 'Lady Mara!' she screamed excitedly. 'Lord James, he say
that you must come ee-*med*-iately to your room.' The dog
tried to snap at her hand. 'No, no, Angelo!' The dog wriggled
out of her arms to launch itself at Rosie.

After five years in London, Valentina spoke English perfectly. It was well known that she used her Italian accent for
added dramatic effect. Rosie breathed deeply, willing herself to keep her temper, though her foot was twitching
with the urge to kick the dog or her sister-in-law, or possibly both.

For the past two years, Valentina had done nothing but
slither in and out of Rosie and Cameron's lives, leaving
effortless trails of discord oozing behind her. It was on the
Staten Island ferry that Cameron had nicknamed her the
Toxic Snail. Before the ferry had docked at the pier,
Cameron had told Rosie the story of how his twin brother
had met Valentina.

She had married Fraser unexpectedly, in Milan. They had told no one, just turned up together at Carrington Hall just before Cameron had left to work in New York. Valentina had held out her hand and shown him the wedding ring that his brother had bought for her. It glistened like a cluster of rocks on a gold reef. Now, that same ring glinted in Rosie's face as Valentina picked a thread from her dress, her glossy lips curled in an insincere smile. She patted Rosie's cheek patronisingly. 'Ah Rosie, you look ...' Valentina cast her eyes heavenwards, searching for the right word, 'Well, we must all make the best of what we have, no?' 'Compliment' delivered, Valentina turned to look for Angelo, who was causing more mayhem than Rosie would have thought possible for one small dog.

'Er, I'm kind of allergic to dogs,' Aunt Phyllis quavered, as Anna made valiant attempts to shoo Angelo away from Rosie's dress.

'Christine,' beamed Lady Mara. 'May I introduce my daughter-in-law, Valentina?'

Valentina looked Mrs Jacobs up and down before proffering an over-manicured hand in her general direction.

'*Buongiorno*,' she said without emotion, withdrawing her hand swiftly, as though she feared contamination.

'Another trick introduction?' joked Anna. 'Hey, we've already been caught out once, you can't fool us with that accent! Can we call you Val?'

'Not if you expect me to answer,' she snapped back. Rosie glanced down at her champagne flute, expecting the contents to freeze over as Valentina glared at Anna.

Angelo broke the silence by choosing that moment to sink his teeth into Rosie's dress, shaking it from side to side

and growling ferociously. Anna lunged frantically at the dog.
Aunt Phyllis began to sneeze violently into her handkerchief
and Mrs Jacobs moaned incoherently and downed her drink
in one gulp.

Lady Mara took charge. 'Thank you, Valentina, I'll come
right away,' she said, taking Valentina by the elbow, Angelo by
the scruff of the neck and propelling them firmly towards
the door. 'See you later, girls. Good luck!'

'Your dress,' Valentina hissed as she shot a disapproving
look at Rosie over her shoulder, 'is not as it should be.'

'What does she mean by that?' snapped Anna, swinging
round to face her cousin. Silently, Rosie looked down at the
dress, where Angelo's teeth marks could be seen.

'This won't ruin the day,' her mom said. 'Just hold your
bouquet in front of it. It was an unfortunate accident, nothing more. We're from Brooklyn and in the spirit of the family you must be gracious . . . charitable . . . forgiving?'

'In the spirit of family, I could cheerfully wring Valentina's
scrawny Italian neck.' Aunt Phyllis said as she swigged another
glass of champagne. 'Someone should take that dog and . . .'

Rosie's mobile phone bleeped, jerking her back to reality.
'Hello?' she said through gritted teeth.

'How's my beautiful girl?' boomed her father proudly.
'Half an hour and counting! Are you good to go?'

'Good to go, Dad,' Rosie said.

❀   ❀   ❀   ❀

Cameron had the kind of eyes you could fall into. Beautiful
deep brown, puppy-dog eyes with impossibly long lashes

that were completely wasted on a man. Rosie was thoroughly jealous of them. They twinkled mischievously now as he backed away, hands outstretched to fend off the blows from her bouquet.

'Careful, Rosemary *Ethel,*' he laughed. 'Those flowers are for throwing, not beating up your poor husband.'

'We agreed no middle names in the ceremony, you toad,' said Rosie furiously, trying to get a solid strike in under his guard. 'Cameron James . . . Rosemary Ethel . . . I saw the look on Valentina's face.'

'Ah, married bliss,' said Fraser, appearing from around the corner. He shook his head reprovingly at his twin.

'Stop grinning, darn you,' Rosie growled, whacking him in turn. 'You laughed too, Fraser.'

'It was unexpected. Ethel?' he asked disbelievingly.

'It was my grandfather . . .'

'He was called Ethel?'

'No, you fool, he was in love with Ethel Merman – the singer. From Queens?'

Seeing his chance, Cameron pounced, pinning Rosie's arms to her sides and kissing her. 'Come on,' he smiled. 'They'll be waiting to eat.'

They were the two hundred and fifty guests, most of whom she didn't know. When Lady Mara had persuaded her to get married in England, Rosie had no idea what she was agreeing to. Her close friends and family were hopelessly outnumbered by the might of the Whitton dynasty.

Some were family, business associates or James's old school friends. Valentina had insisted on bringing several work colleagues, while Lady Mara had invited two eccentric cousins, three times removed, whom even Cameron had never met and who only spoke Gaelic.

Sensing her reluctance to go inside, Fraser patted Rosie's arm comfortingly as the trio strolled up the steps towards the Great Hall. 'Relax,' he said softly. 'The hard part is over.' He wasn't kidding. A full nuptial mass had taken an hour and a half. Even the priest was sagging by the last Amen. The Whittons didn't do things by halves.

Rosie smiled at Fraser, thinking how much she liked him. He was the complete opposite of Cameron. The twins were both charming, good-looking men but Cameron's features held a kind of tranquillity that Fraser's lacked. Fraser's fast-paced city life, with its high-profile business deals and A-list parties, bore no resemblance to the sleepy rhythm of his brother's academic career. But for all Fraser's success, Cameron often worried about him.

'Fraser isn't strong,' he once confided in Rosie. 'He's terrified of failing. Almost as if he thinks we love his success, not him. Crazy.' Rosie was sceptical. Surely five years of being married to Valentina required superhuman strength and courage, not to mention patience.

'Ready, Rosie?' Fraser said as they got to the top of the steps.

'Hmm?' With a start she realised they were at the doors of the Great Hall. The toastmaster drew himself up, preparing to announce them.

'Another grand entrance,' Rosie whispered to Cameron. Her stomach churned. Ahead of them, Fraser skidded to a halt.

'Valentina, you've got to be kidding,' he muttered.

'What's wrong?' Rosie asked nervously, gripping Cameron's arm tightly. Fraser gestured at the enormous seating plan mounted on the adjacent wall.

'I'm sitting next to the dog again,' he moaned. "There are three people in my marriage and one of them is a dog.'

'And the other is called Angelo,' Cameron laughed, as he swept Rosie swiftly through the doors, forcing the toastmaster to dive ahead of them. 'Ladies and gentlemen, the bride and groom!' As the couple made their way through the throng of guests to tumultuous applause, Cameron stooped and whispered in Rosie's ear. 'If it makes you feel any better, my full middle names are Donald, Sinclair and Brice. Did you know?'

Rosie didn't care. She was with the man she loved. The evening passed in a blur of food, wine and unfamiliar but friendly faces. After the meal and speeches were over, the tables were cleared and the ceilidh began.

Watching her parents gamely trying to master the unfamiliar steps of Scottish dancing, Rosie felt a swell of pride. If this was alien to her after two years with Cameron, what must it feel like to her family, fresh off the plane from Brooklyn?

'Aunt Phyllis is a bit of a mover, isn't she?' laughed Cameron, watching as Fraser twirled her round the floor.

'Unlike the Twiglets,' Rosie said, pointing to the bar where Valentina and her friends from the modelling agency stood in a tight, skinny cluster, smoking hungrily.

'They're like a pack of summer wolves.' Cameron said.

'Summer wolves?' Rosie asked.

'So hungry they want to devour you but too frightened to make the first move,' he replied as he held her hand.

'I see Angelo got his own plate,' Rosie said sourly. As she watched, Valentina broke away from the pack, striding across the room to seize Fraser by the arm. She spoke urgently, pointing at his mobile and jabbing her finger into his chest for emphasis. Fraser backed away, shaking his head.

'What were they arguing about?' Rosie asked Cameron, too far away to hear what they were saying. From where she was standing, it didn't look good.

'Thank you, Rosie,' Cameron replied, as if he hadn't heard her question. He suddenly wrapped his arms round his wife in a bear hug that lifted her off her feet.

'For what?' she squealed, hanging on for dear life as he swung her around.

'For everything,' he said seriously, setting her down carefully. 'For marrying me. For agreeing to have the wedding here. For making my mother so happy.' He nodded at the nearby table where Lady Mara was holding court, chatting animatedly to a group of Rosie's friends. 'Even with all her contacts, Mother's list of potential daughters-in-law was getting thin,' he said with a wry smile.

'Yeah, you were almost past your sell-by date when I picked you off the shelf,' teased Rosie, recalling Cameron's numerous tales of excruciating blind dates arranged by his mother. Luckily for Rosie, Cameron refused to be pushed. 'You could have married the incredible Lady Sophie Wooster or Tanya De Veer.'

'They are nothing like you,' he replied.

'They are rich, pretty and upper class.'

'So are you,' he said as the noise of the party faded.

'I was a girl you met in New York covered in doughnuts. I dropped a book on your foot.'

'You made me smile and bought me coffee,' he said.

'But will I make you happy?' she asked.

'As happy as my Mother and Father – if that's possible.'

James and Lady Mara were everything to each other. He was the image of his sons and didn't look much older. Years spent climbing in the Alps had chiselled his frame to that of a man half his age. Lady Mara had been desperate to see both her sons married and know the joy that she had found with Lord James. She had gone to the chapel by the lake every night and knelt before the altar and prayed for her boys. She asked nothing for herself but that they would marry women who loved them.

'And what about abandoning my whole life in America and moving thousands of miles to be with you?' Rosie added. 'Don't forget that part.'

Cameron touched her cheek, gently traced the line of her jaw with his fingertips. 'I won't,' he said softly. 'Not ever. I love you, Rosie Whitton.'

Rosie hugged him fiercely, feeling like the luckiest girl alive. In a few hours' time, they'd be in the car, leaving the clamour of the party behind them. They had delayed the honeymoon until later in the summer, when Cameron had a natural break between teaching semesters. Right now, Rosie needed to look for a job and, in any case, both she and Cameron wanted time to settle into the cottage on the outskirts of Oxford that was James and Lady Mara's wedding gift to them.

A deep sense of contentment settled over Rosie as Cameron took her arm and drew her back towards the party, a vivid picture of their life together shimmering before her in the night air. 'I want seven children – just a small family – and a big home, messy and crammed with books and love,' Rosie said.

'Christmases with the Whittons at Carrington Hall; long summers visiting your family in the States . . . there is so much more to come. Rosie Whitton . . . so much more life' Cameron bawled as he lifted her from her feet and onto the dance floor. And as her husband spun her round and round to the sound of the bagpipes, Rosie prayed a silent prayer. 'Let it be so.'

Chapter 3

Trinity

'Hey! Sleeping beauty . . . come on. Wake up!'

'What?' Rosie blinked a few times before hauling herself upright. She yawned, rubbed the sleep from her eyes and tried to focus. Three cups of coffee were crammed together on the bedside table.

She leaned across and dipped her little finger tentatively into each one.

'Cold, cold, cold.' She flopped back onto the pillow.

'Oh no you don't!' Cameron sat down on the bed and began to poke her with his finger.

'Ouch!'

'Serves you right. Come on! Every single morning I bring you mug after mug and you sleep through each one.'

'That's not true.' She tried to fend off his poking. 'We – ell, OK, it is. . . a bit. . . I do take a sip, you know . . .'

'Yes, before crawling back under that quilt!' Cameron sat back and his face creased into a puzzled frown. 'Did you *always* sleep this long?'

'It's the air. In Brooklyn it smells of bagels and coffee – here it just smells of . . . sheep!'

'All right, my darling, you drink your coffee and I'll fly to New York and bring you a bagel. Then you can sniff it and feel at home.'

'That sounds like a good idea to me.'

'Really, Rosie, you've got to get up. You've only got half an hour to get ready.'

'What!' Rosie sat bolt upright. 'Why didn't you wake me?'

Her husband stood up and walked to the door. 'I'm not even going to bother to answer that. But you better get a move on, my darling.'

'OK, OK. Where are my slippers?' Rosie retrieved her slippers from under the bed and heard her husband chuckle at the sight of her backside sticking in the air. 'What time is it anyway?' she called.

'Nine thirty-five,' came the reply.

'WHAT!'

'No time for coffee now!' Cameron had left the room and his answer drifted up through the wooden floor. The cottage was so tiny you could carry out an entire conversation from different parts of the house. It was one of the things Rosie loved about it.

'Oh man!' Toothbrush in hand, she hurtled through the door and took the stairs two at a time, her bathrobe flying out behind her. She ran into the kitchen. Her gaze fell on Cameron's rucksack, standing tidily by the back door, packed and ready to go. And then she saw the kitchen clock.

'Oh, *Cam*!'

He'd grabbed the morning paper and was glancing at it.

'Why didn't you wake me earlier?' she wailed.

'I believe I tried, my darling,' he answered, not taking his eyes from the front page.

'I can't function without coffee. I just can't!' Rosie flapped around, losing precious seconds in her hunt for coffee. 'Where are the mugs? There are no mugs! What's happening around here?'

'I suspect all the mugs are by your bedside.' Cameron put his paper down with a rueful smile. 'I'll do that,' he offered, taking the coffee jar from her hand. 'You go and get dressed.'

'But I need to pack!'

'It's done. Your case is in the bedroom. Just stick your washbag in and you're ready.'

She looked at him, his kind smile, that endearing fringe flopping over his forehead. 'You are the best husband in the world, you know that?'

'I believe I do.' Cameron grinned, opened a cupboard, found a mug and then glanced over his shoulder. 'Get going. They'll be here any minute.'

Rosie blew him a kiss as she headed back upstairs.

She took the quickest of all showers and, when the water stopped, smiled to herself as she listened for a moment to the comforting sounds of Cameron pottering around down-stairs, talking to himself as he made breakfast.

'You know,' she called as she dashed between bathroom and bedroom, leaving criss-crossing water trails on the car-pet, 'I did the right thing, marrying you. There can't be many guys who could be trusted to pack for a weekend away.'

'Just as well I did,' he called back, 'or we'd be horrend-ously late . . . again.'

Rosie sighed. He was being good-natured about it, but in the first three months of married life, punctuality had been the one major sticking point between them. Cameron was never late; Rosie was still on college time, more relaxed about losing ten minutes here and there than Cameron would ever be. He had never mentioned it when they were in New York, but back in England . . . well, it was something she'd noticed. He was always clock-watching. Actually, she had come to believe that clock-watching was a national pastime in England, along with making tea and discussing the weather. It wasn't such a big deal, really, Rosie reflected. Just another of the million little things which reminded her she was a foreigner here.

Take the weird English small talk, for example. Back home, if two people met they said, 'Hi, how you doing?' or 'Great to see you!' But in England they began every conversation with a random comment like, 'Lovely day!', 'It's looking like rain,' or 'The fog will be rolling in by teatime, if I'm any judge.' Rosie had soon realised that these exchanges were deadly serious, part of the fabric of society, in fact, and it was absolutely *not* OK to laugh.

Then there was driving on the left, the infuriating way that some of the smaller local shops would close at odd times of day, leaving an unspecific sign declaring 'Back Soon'. Once, Rosie had waited and waited. 'Back Soon' had turned into an hour and still no one came.

Rosie sat down on the bed, towelling her hair dry. English people were baffling. They seemed so formal, somehow; but when you got to know them, they were warm and caring. So why the formality to start with?

'Weird,' she breathed. 'I wonder if all English people are like this, or just the ones I've met?'

She missed New York, missed its sights, sounds and vibrancy. She often wondered how long it would take to become assimilated into English culture. It was proving tougher than she had anticipated. The whole pace of life was slower here.

'Man, three cars on the village road and they'll make a radio announcement,' she muttered to herself. 'Ah, come on, Rosie, it's just teething problems.' After all, Cameron was always by her side; he'd guided and supported her through the confusion of those first weeks, his reassuring manner so rock solid. Rosie had come to rely on him in a way that she never had before and she knew that, because of this, they'd become much closer. On the whole, they were blissfully happy and, as Rosie's mother reminded her during her occasional homesick calls to the States, settling into a new place took time, no matter where you were.

Ten minutes later, Rosie lugged her case downstairs and collapsed at the kitchen table. Cameron had set out a plate of hot buttered toast and a mug of coffee so big you could practically dunk your head in it. Teacups just didn't do it for Rosie in the mornings. She knew Cameron didn't understand but he faithfully prepared what he called her 'rocket fuel' every day. As the caffeine soaked into Rosie's system, her brain finally booted up and an odd thought struck her.

'Do you suppose Fraser does this for Valentina? Or does she do it for him?' she mused.

'Do what?' asked Cameron, now up to his elbows in soapsuds at the kitchen sink. Rosie gestured vaguely around the room.

'All this, the whole morning stress-busting routine, I mean. Breakfast, the washing-up . . . you know?' she trailed off, not wanting him to think she was making fun.

'I think,' said Cameron, pulling the plug out of the sink and drying his hands briskly, 'that if Valentina told Fraser to jump through hoops and bark like a dog, he'd do it. Why do you ask, anyway?'

Seeing the sudden tension in his face, Rosie was sorry she'd mentioned it. 'Oh, I don't know,' she said. 'Maybe I'm wrong.'

'Rosie?'

'OK,' she said, 'I just saw them arguing at the wedding and Fraser looked kind of . . .'

'Under the thumb?'

'Sort of.' She sipped the coffee.

'Hmm.' Cameron frowned. 'You're not wrong. Fraser's not been himself lately.'

'Something up, you think?'

'I don't know. I tried to ask him. He told me to get back to the philosophy and leave the business to him.'

Rosie was kicking herself for spoiling the atmosphere. She decided to switch the subject to something that would lighten the mood. 'Did your father teach you to climb?'

Cameron's face brightened at once. 'Oh yes, started when we were five. He took us to the Alps. Made us walk up some hills and told us they were mountains. We've done it every year since.'

'The Whittons' great mountaineering adventure,' said Rosie. 'Isn't that what I heard him call it?'

Cameron laughed and his wife smiled. She loved to see him laugh. She walked to him and put her arms round him. 'Isn't it scary up those mountains?'

He kissed her forehead. 'It's more walking than climbing – I'll take you one day. We can get the ski lift and walk down.'

At that moment, there was the sound of a horn and, as they glanced out of the window, they saw a red Bentley convertible pull up in the drive, gravel spraying beneath its wheels.

Lady Mara, in the passenger seat, saw them at the window and waved excitedly.

Rosie and Cameron went to the door and threw it open. Valentina was stepping out of the Bentley, looking like Grace Kelly in a cream linen suit and black silk headscarf, held in place by a pair of enormous Jackie O sunglasses. A pair of black satin stilettos with ribbons tied around the ankle completed the outfit. Manolo Blahniks, unless Rosie was much mistaken.

'*Ciao!*' Valentina called and began tottering up to the door.

'Hmm. Sensible footwear for camping,' Cameron murmured into Rosie's ear and she stifled a laugh.

Valentina kissed the air either side of his face.

'You have to be the most glamorously dressed camper in the world,' he told her.

'Change of plan, change of plan. Weather forecast, he is dreadful. Champney's Spa, Forest Mere, *perfetto*.'

Rosie glanced down at her own outfit of T-shirt, jeans and old running trainers.

'Can you just give me a second?' she asked, determined to stay calm. 'I think there's something I forgot to do –'

'*Avanti, avanti*, Rosie. No time,' clucked Valentina. 'We go now, have to be there soon.'

Cameron stepped round her and stooped to kiss his wife. 'Whatever happens, promise me you'll keep your temper,' he whispered.

'What, you mean I can't drown her in the spa?'

Cameron tightened his arms around her. 'Be serious for a moment. I mean it. I know it's not exactly what you'd planned, but this weekend away means a lot to Mother.'

'Alright, alright! No fights, I promise, OK?'

'Just remember, you're worth ten of her,' he said, kissing her again.

'Yeah, I know that.'

Cameron stepped away, smiling and lifted Rosie's case into the boot of the Bentley. Rosie clambered into the back seat. Cameron's mouth twitched as he looked down at her, wedged between a faux fur leopard print holdall and a hot pink vanity case. 'I'll make it up to you,' he mouthed.

Valentina backed the car and spun the wheel recklessly.

'Yeah, you will,' Rosie muttered.

'The boys are on their way,' Lady Mara called to Cameron out of the open window. 'Have a good time and behave!' She turned to Rosie. 'I'm sorry about the camping.'

'It's OK.'

'It's the weather, you know. Valentina . . .'

'Yeah.'

'When I thought of this whole weekend away idea, I originally thought if the boys could do something adventurous, then so could we.' Lady Mara glanced at Valentina. 'But of course, we could never match the Alps . . . Perhaps it *is* more fitting to go to a spa, after all.'

'Hmm,' said Rosie.

'This weekend away with the boys means so much to James,' said Mara, conspiratorially. 'Talks about it all year and acts like a child until he's on the mountain.'

'What do you usually do when the guys are climbing the mountains?'

'Nothing much. You know, I've spent too many long years standing on the touchline at rugby matches or watching interminable games of cricket. At least now I have two daughters to share a pleasure with and if the boys can climb mountains, we can pamper ourselves.'

'Daughters . . .' Rosie was deeply touched by Lady Mara's affection. 'Still, got to admit, I'm kind of more a camping sort of person . . .'

'It will rain!' Valentina interrupted. 'I rang them – the camp-site. I tell them we are not coming. Fraser has paid for our weekend. It is my bonus.'

'Bonus? For what?' asked Rosie.

'Any man can be hard work. I just think of this as part of that.' Valentina tapped her fingers on the steering wheel.

'Yeah,' murmured Rosie. 'I kind of wondered how you'd cope with camping.'

'Rosie, you must speak up.' Valentina's eyes flashed in the rear-view mirror. 'I not hear what you said.'

'It doesn't matter.'

'Is probably your funny accent.'

'My funny . . .!' Rosie took a deep breath.

The Bentley accelerated and Rosie twisted round in her seat and looked back. But it was too late to catch a last glimpse of Cameron. Tears sprang to her eyes.

'Alright, Rosie?'

Rosie blinked a few times and nodded at Mara.

'Two days,' she said to herself. 'Don't be such a wimp . . . two days and you'll be home.'

Valentina was a crazy driver. She drove on alternate sides of the narrow country lanes as the mood took her. No creature was safe as she bore down at speed, honking her horn at any cars that had the nerve to get in her way.

Each time they overtook (on the left, the right and once on the pavement), Lady Mara waved and smiled politely at the beleaguered motorist, while Valentina gestured rudely and screeched insults in Italian.

'What fun!' Lady Mara shouted bravely.

Rosie was sending up a prayer. 'Lord, I know she's just as scared as I am . . .!' and stretched forward to put a comforting hand on her mother-in-law's shoulder. Lady Mara gripped it so hard that Rosie's fingers went white. After a while, Rosie closed her eyes and concentrated on pushing the fear away with anger as she brooded on her wasted efforts. She had gone to a lot of trouble to plan for the weekend. It wasn't as though they'd have been roughing it, not at Lady Mara's age. Rosie had found a luxury camp-site in Lyme Regis. They were to stay in pre-erected yurts, top quality airbeds with proper bedding and even a restaurant. It was perfect. In her dreams, Rosie had envisaged a weekend of leisurely country walks and sunny picnics by the sea, followed by quiet evenings in a rustic local pub, during which she and Valentina would miraculously experience a meeting of minds over a jug of beer as Lady Mara looked on benevolently.

Instead, Rosie knew she'd be spending the weekend having her lifestyle and eating habits scrutinised, virtually naked with complete strangers prodding her cellulite, squeezing her spots, irrigating her colon and wrapping her in foul-smelling mud. A meeting of minds over a seaweed wrap hardly seemed likely, but there was no way out. She had promised Cameron and she'd just have to make the best of it.

Miraculously, they arrived at Champney's Spa without accident or injury, though Rosie felt she couldn't speak for the traumatised motorists of Oxfordshire. Valentina left the Bentley on the drive with the roof down and stalked off to inform the staff of her arrival. Within a minute she had launched into a heated debate with the receptionist – they could hear her from the driveway.

It was left to Rosie to bring the luggage in from the car. Lady Mara smiled gratefully at her as she lumbered up the steps for the third time. 'Thank you so much for coming, Rosie,' she said, pressing Rosie's hand. 'I really am sorry about the camping but we'll have a lovely time, you'll see. All girls together.'

Rosie couldn't be angry with her; this elegant lady, usually so impeccably turned out, was standing there, rumpled and windswept, with great chunks of hair trailing out of her bun.

'Sure we will!' She patted her own hair, which felt like a bird's nest after the open-air drive.

The foyer was furnished in a colonial style, with over-stuffed leather sofas, oversized plants overhanging their pots and wicker chairs. Lady Mara and Rosie sat down to wait for Valentina, who was striding up and down, taking a call on her mobile, totally ignoring the receptionist's plaintive bleating about the use of mobiles on the premises.

'I wish there'd been time for me to repack, though,' Rosie said, unable to bite her tongue any longer. 'I've brought all the wrong clothes for a spa break.'

Lady Mara turned to her, bewildered.

'But didn't Valentina ring you?'

'Ring me? No.'

'I asked her to tell you . . . This is really not on. I'm so sorry, Rosie, you must be furious.' Lady Mara heaved herself up purposefully. 'I shall speak to Valentina.'

Rosie tugged her back down. 'Forget it, it's fine. Honestly, it doesn't matter. I'm sure it was mistake. She just forgot. She was busy, I guess.'

Lady Mara frowned. 'Valentina can be very thoughtless at times, Rosie.'

That was an understatement, thought Rosie, looking around for a distraction. Her eye fell on the no smoking sign. 'So anyway, no cigarettes for two days, huh? Good for you,' she said encouragingly. 'Are you going to be OK with that?'

Lady Mara's face fell. 'What do you mean?'

Rosie pointed up at the sign.

'Oh,' said Mara. 'But Valentina said . . .'

'Oh my gosh,' said Rosie.

'Impossible . . . impossible . . .' Valentine was shouting into her phone. 'You can't do this . . . no . . . please . . . I am a Whitton . . .'

Rosie felt Lady Mara's body tense as she gathered herself.

'Right,' she said. 'Come with me.'

She stormed off across the foyer. Rosie hurried after her, resisting the urge to call out that she could have smoked as much as she liked on the camp-site.

'Valentina?' Lady Mara tapped her smartly on the arm. 'Get off the phone. Valentina!'

Snapping her mobile shut, Valentina whirled round, her arm raised high. Rosie rocked back on her heels in shock. Valentina's face was livid, scarlet-painted lips peeled back in a feral snarl. A bead of sweat trickled down her face, making grimy tracks in her make-up. She looked like a wild animal, cornered but ready to fight. Her arm shook visibly and Rosie leapt between them, certain Valentina was going to strike.

Lady Mara faced Valentina calmly, suddenly every inch the lady of Carrington Hall. 'I don't know what has happened to upset you,' she said, 'but get a hold of yourself. Right now, please.'

Her voice was full of authority. At six foot, Valentina towered over Lady Mara's diminutive frame but she seemed to shrink into herself as Mara spoke. Her arm dropped limply by her side.

'What on earth,' said Lady Mara, 'has come over you?'

'Nothing.' Valentina sounded sheepish. 'Is nothing.'

'It doesn't look like nothing to me.'

'Is modelling agency. Has problem.'

'Really?' Mara put her hand forward. 'Give me my room key.'

Valentina dropped the key into Mara's hand, with some reluctance.

'Go and compose yourself. When you're ready, Rosie and I will be taking tea in the conservatory. You may join us there.'

Valentina glared at Rosie, then turned on her heel and tottered towards the elevator, mumbling under her breath.

'Room 51, Rosie. It appears we're sharing. Let's get unpacked, shall we?' Nodding graciously to the receptionist, Mara swept up the staircase to the elevator on the first floor. Rosie started after her. Evidently, there was more to Lady Mara Whitton than met the eye.

Shut into the cool safety of the elevator, Rosie gazed at her reflection in the mirrored wall. She wondered what on earth had got into Valentina. She suddenly caught Mara's eye.

'I expect it's very hard work,' said Mara, 'running a model agency.'

Rosie half-smiled. 'Mmm. Maybe she needs a rest in a spa or something.'

Lady Mara's eyes twinkled. 'Or camping.'

'Maybe we should suggest it.'

'Then again, perhaps not.' And as Mara's smile dimpled her face, Rosie caught a glimpse of Cameron in his mother.

'Oh, Cam,' she murmured, 'I am so going to miss you. But I won't murder Valentina. I promise. Not yet, anyway.'

❀   ❀   ❀   ❀

'Hey, maybe this won't be so bad.'

Rosie had avoided the dreaded seaweed wrap and was surprised to find herself enjoying her Swedish massage and session in the flotation tank. She spent an hour floating in warm, thick saline, blindfolded and listening to white noise. Her thoughts were all about Cameron. What was he doing now? She could see that floppy fringe, those brown eyes smiling, laughing, as he joked with his father and brother on the ski-lift. She thought of him zigzagging athletically down the mountain; and when she imagined him at the après ski, glass in his hand, standing by a roaring log fire . . . she so wanted to be there.

Ten minutes later, she looked in on Mara in the next treatment room. She was wrapped from head to foot in strands of thick, green kelp.

'I feel like sushi,' Lady Mara complained, and she started to giggle. 'I need to swap the seaweed for a thermal wrap, to warm my old bones.'

Rosie smiled at her affectionately. 'You know, I'm glad you're having a good time.'

'Of course I am!' Mara looked serious. 'You know, Valentina apologised to me most politely.'

Rosie murmured, 'So she should.'

'You notice the way she keeps cutting her treatments short to rush off and check her phone? I told her, we've come here to relax . . .'

'She looks awful.'

'She didn't sleep much. It's that modelling agency.'

'Oh dear,' said Rosie, trying to sound sympathetic. It didn't quite work, so she went on, 'Did *you* sleep OK last night?'

'Um . . . well, I'm a poor sleeper . . .'

Yeah, thought Rosie. And I know you spent half the night hanging out the window, smoking.

By teatime of the second day, any fun element and sense of novelty had worn off. Mara seemed tired, Valentina looked pale and Rosie was fed up.

'Well, girls, I've had a wonderful time,' said Mara, stirring her herbal tea, 'but I wonder whether you would mind if we cut our little adventure short? We could go home tonight, if you're both happy about that. We were leaving straight after breakfast tomorrow anyway . . .'

Rosie sat up straight. 'Yes! I mean . . .'

'Is good idea!' said Valentina.

Lady Mara blinked at them both. 'I hope you both enjoyed it . . .'

'Yeah, sure,' said Rosie, vigorously nodding her head.

Mara looked at her other daughter-in-law. 'Did *you* enjoy it, Valentina?'

'It was good – but not so good,' she replied, with a shrug of her shoulders.

'You should tell the office where to go,' advised Rosie, 'when you want to take a break.'

Valentina cast a scathing glance in Rosie's direction. 'Is my own business. Cannot tell them "where to go".'

'You're obviously under a lot of pressure,' said Mara.

'Is OK.' Valentina waved a hand. 'I go pack.' She stood up and tottered off towards the elevator.

'Yeah, me too.' And Rosie was soon racing up the stairs, two at a time. She didn't hear Mara's dry observation: 'Hmm. The rest *has* done her good.'

❀ ❀ ❀ ❀

'You'll come in for tea, won't you, girls?' said Lady Mara as the Bentley pulled up by the steps of Carrington Hall. 'I gave the domestic staff the weekend off and I find I miss them when they're away. Silly of me really – the house is always so empty without James.'

Rosie hesitated. It was nearly dark and she wanted nothing more than to curl up in her own bed and sleep until Cameron arrived home late the next day. Then she caught Valentina watching her sister-in-law over the tops of her sunglasses; she had to drive Rosie home, either way. That decided it for Rosie. She was too tired to deal with Valentina at the moment. Maybe tea would perk her up a bit.

'Tea would be lovely,' Rosie smiled. 'I'll give you a hand while Valentina parks up.'

The entrance vestibule was dark and smelled musty. Lady Mara fumbled with the light switch.

'The circuit's blown,' she said. They both jumped as the phone trilled. 'Oh dear, can you get that, Rosie? I'll have to go and trip the switch.'

The phone rang and rang, an insistent, jarring noise in the gloom of the long hallway. Unsure of her bearings in the dark, Rosie groped her way along the wall. She followed the sound of the dreary ring until at last her hand brushed against a table.

'Carrington Hall, hello?'

A stream of rapid French erupted through the receiver. Rosie tried again.

'I'm sorry, I don't speak French – *je ne parle pas le francais.*'

The voice spoke again, urgent but more slowly this time. It was a man and he sounded agitated.

'You got the wrong number, maybe?' Rosie said loudly and slowly.

There was silence on the line, then a different voice.

'Madame? Hello?'

'Hello. This is Carrington Hall, can I help you?'

'Madame Whitton?'

'Yes, well, one of them.' Rosie yawned. 'Oh, excuse me . . .'

'Madame Whitton?' the voice repeated.

'Yeah, but there are three of us. Which one do you want?'

'There 'as been an accident.'

It took a moment for what he'd said to register.

'What?' said Rosie, at last. 'What accident?'

'I am so sorry.'

Suddenly, Rosie wasn't tired any more. Her mouth was dry. 'What do you mean, an accident?'

'Monsieur Whitton. Bad accident, Madame. Am so sorry.'

Now Rosie was shrieking. 'Which Monsieur Whitton? Which one? Which *one*?'

'We believe they were all of that name, Madame.'

'Were . . . were *all*?' Her voice was breaking.

'It is quite terrible.'

'You mean –'

'They are dead, Madame. All three dead.'

Rosie felt as if all the breath had been knocked from her body. She fell to her knees, the receiver hanging from her hand. At that moment, the lights came on but it made no difference. The world had turned black.

'Rosie?' Valentina's voice seemed to come from a long way away.

With a supreme effort of will, Rosie raised her head. Valentina stood a little way away. As they stared at each other, Lady Mara appeared around a corner, wiping her hands on an old rag. She started as she saw Rosie on the floor.

'Darling! What's wrong?'

'Cameron . . . they're all . . . gone.'

'Gone?'

Then Rosie fainted and knew no more.

Chapter Four

Vigil

The library at Carrington Hall was small, but its limited resources were deployed with military efficiency. The neat oak bookshelves stretched from floor to ceiling in one continuous sweep around three of the four walls, breaking ranks only to allow room for a door in the second wall. Even there not an inch of space was wasted; smaller bookshelves flowed up and over the lintel to link with their stronger cohorts on either side. A small mahogany table squatted peaceably in the centre of the room, like an old campaigner flanked by the Home Guard – a mustard-coloured standard lamp standing stiffly to attention and a leather armchair; badly faded and bleeding stuffing from one arm, but still straight-backed and proud.

After all their years of faithful service, they endured. It was as if everything in the room spoke of the people they served. The British stiff upper lip . . . do not surrender your positions. A job to do. Shoulder to shoulder, facing the fourth wall as if it were the enemy, they stood their ground.

An enormous bay window looked out over the grounds. It lit the room so that on even the darkest day, reading was possible without the electric light. The shadows of the windowpane danced across the fine Persian rug. Two turtledoves sat just outside and looked in. Rosie watched them from her perch on the window seat; they billed and cooed like lovebirds, never to be apart.

She drew her eyes away from the window and looked around the room. She was unable to bring herself to sit in the leather chair. Cameron's chair. She could almost see him sitting there; book in hand, a smile on his face. This was his favourite room, she thought, as she snuggled deeper into his cardigan, as if to bring him near to her. She looked up at the mountain of books. All of them ancient, many by writers she had never heard of. Her eyes drifted along the shelves until she came to the fireplace and a peculiar stand of four books. The leather binding on each was well worn, as if they had been handled by many generations.

The first night Cameron had brought her to Carrington Hall he had taken her to this room. 'These are all you'll ever need,' he said, running his finger along the spines of the four books. 'If a disaster was to strike the world or I was cast on to some deserted island, as long as I had these, then life would be worth living.'

Rosie's gaze rested heavily on the shelf as she remembered the night. It seemed long ago. She wanted to reach out and touch the books, take them one by one from the shelf and read them, hoping to hear his voice again. Her eyes crowded with tears.

It could have been an oppressive room, but for the size of the window, which flooded the room with light in the daytime. It had heavy velvet curtains to make a cosy hibernation spot on winter evenings.

Rosie wiped her face on the cardigan's sleeve. She remembered how Cameron had first described the library to her. They were in the Tribeca Grill on Greenwich Street, where they had watched New York footballers rub shoulders with De Niro. Rosie and Cameron had compared childhoods, greedily trying to absorb the years they'd missed of each other's life.

'Nothing like this place,' Cameron had said. 'No brick walls and modern art in the library, just books, one on top of the other. It's my private window on eternity. Light and literature, complete illumination for body and soul.'

Those were his exact words. She had been still a little in awe of the research graduate from England, with his intellectual discussions and poetic turn of phrase. Much later, Cam admitted to Rosie that he'd spent hours thinking up lines like that in the hope of impressing her, but he doggedly defended the truth of that particular description until she visited Carrington Hall to see the library for herself.

They had spent many happy hours in here together, talking about whatever came into their heads or just reading in companionable silence. Cameron always in the chair; Rosie curled up like a cat on the broad windowsill, just as she was now. If she closed her eyes, he could be there.

Rosie pressed her face to the window, her tears mirroring the rain that beat steadily against the outer pane. Or was it the other way round? What did Cameron call it? Pathetic Fallacy – that was it – the weather echoing the mood of a character in a novel, like in *Jane Eyre*. Whatever! What did

Jane have to cry about, anyway? At least Mr Rochester sur-
vived. Rosie? She'd settle for them finding Cameron's body.

The rescue team had found James and Fraser after a few
hours of searching. They must have fallen at the same time
because their bodies were found lying close together.
Cameron was not with them. Experts were examining the
climbing gear and retracing the route in an attempt to clarify the details of the accident.

There would be a full report, apparently, but for now they
surmised that either James or Fraser had got into difficulties.
One had tried to help the other and both men had fallen.
That left Cameron. Either he had tried to reach the others
after their fall and his body lay not far away, perhaps a little
higher up the mountain, or he had gone on alone to fetch
help. This – said the French authorities – was the most logical course of action in such circumstances. However, since
no distress call had been received on the day of the accident,
they anticipated that Cameron's body would be recovered in
the next twenty-four hours.

Rosie thought it was such a cruel choice of word, 'recovered'. As if he would get better. She allowed herself to con-
sider the possibility that he could still be alive – somewhere
on the mountain, high in a snow cave. He could be out
there, lying weak and injured. Couldn't he? Could he? In her
heart, though, she knew that he was gone. Whatever the
authorities deemed a 'logical course of action', there was no
way Cameron would have watched his father and brother
fall and climbed on alone. Anyone who knew him knew
that. Lady Mara had dismissed the notion with a scornful
toss of her head, saying simply, 'They didn't know my boys.'

Two smaller questions remained, eclipsed by the current search for Cameron, but questions nonetheless. The French were particular about such things. Firstly, even if Cameron had taken the illogical step of trying to reach his family, surely knowing them to be dead after a fall from such height, why had he not made a distress call before attempting to do so? The alarm had been raised by the local climbing centre when the three had failed to check in at the end of the day.

Secondly, what had caused James and Fraser to fall?

Beneath her composure, Rosie sensed that Lady Mara was waiting, keeping her grief banked up inside until this was resolved. Valentina, too, seemed to need answers. Not Rosie. There were a thousand possible reasons and she didn't want to torment herself by playing them out in her mind's eye, each more dreadful than the last. It wouldn't change anything. The voice in her head told her that he was dead. She nestled deeper into his cardigan, holding the tear-dampened sleeve to her face and breathing deeply through the wool.

'Why did you do this, Cameron?' she sobbed. 'It shouldn't be like this.' One thought came to her again and again. They fell and died as they had lived . . . together. That was enough for her.

But the thought of Cam not being found terrified her. He had to come home. Surely she wouldn't be robbed of saying goodbye? Rosie gripped the windowsill and sobbed harder, feeling the life leak out of her with every tear. She didn't fear death. Everything she held dear told her it was not the end of life. When her grandmother had died, it had been Cameron who'd said that life couldn't be stopped by the final beat of a heart. Creation would be so cruel if it allowed people to be born and then die with nothing else.

Rosie had prayed since she was a child. She had just accepted everything that she had been told about God without question. Now, in the library, she couldn't understand why a loving, all-powerful God would allow the man she loved to die in this way.

'No tears, girl. It's not the English way. Chin up, press on.' She heard again her father's playful words when she had dropped her parents off at the airport after the wedding. He had pretended to be English in his best Park Slope Brooklyn accent. As the line echoed in her head they seemed to fit the circumstance.

She'd told her mother she was coping. There had been a fraught exchange on Sunday night during which her mother had insisted she was coming over right away, while Rosie argued she should wait for the funeral.

It seemed a strange thing to be keeping her family at arm's length at a time like this. Rosie was barely holding it together and knew that one hug from her mother would make her crack. What was it about mothers that made you want to cry with relief when they put their arms around you? Talking on the phone was hard enough.

There was a knock on the library door and before Rosie could speak, it opened slightly.

'I thought I'd find you here,' Mara said gently as she stepped inside.

Rosie looked at her ashen face and tight lips. She could see where she had wiped fresh tears from her face. 'I was just . . .' she tried to reply.

'It was his favourite place. When he was a boy, he spent all his time in here whilst Fraser was out in the fields,' Mara replied, watching her daughter-in-law carefully.

'I just wanted to be near Cameron and he always went on about these books.'

'You'll be near soon,' Mara said and paused. 'They'll be bringing him home with James and Fraser.' From the look on Mara's face, Rosie knew what she meant. Cameron's body had been found. He was dead.

'Will I see him?' she asked. 'I have to see him one more time.'

Mara didn't reply immediately. She had pulled the old prayer book from the shelf of four books and held the thin pages in her fingers.

'I was married with this very book. Kept it here since that day. Never thought James would be buried with it. Never thought I'd outlive my own boys. It's not right, Rosie. Children shouldn't die before their parents.'

Watching Mara gave Rosie a startling insight into the perplexing English reserve. In times of extreme emotion like this, keeping your distance and saying little enabled you to remain in control of yourself, though the breaking point would eventually come. It had worked brilliantly until Rosie had entered the library, but then, she was learning from a master.

On the night of the phone call, after the initial shock and tears, Lady Mara had swung into action, making tea and sandwiches and standing over her daughters-in-law until she was satisfied that they had eaten. Next she had made up two of the bedrooms while Rosie and Valentina called their families with the news. Then she saw both girls off to bed armed with brandy, hot water bottles and half a sleeping tablet each.

'You can't cope with a tired heart at times like this,' she had said as she bustled them upstairs. There was no question of them going home by themselves.

Once she was alone, Lady Mara dug out the guest list from her wedding file and drew up a fresh list of all the people who would need to be informed, dividing it into those who could reasonably be contacted after nine o'clock on a Sunday night and those who should be called first thing in the morning.

By midnight she had broken the news to most of the close relatives. And by the time Rosie and Valentina stumbled downstairs the following morning, Lady Mara had already informed the domestic staff and was three quarters through her list of telephone calls.

That was yesterday. Now, Mara stood in the library and held Rosie as if she were her only child. The women sobbed. Their hearts were broken.

❀ ❀ ❀ ❀

The next morning, Mara broke off from her morning phone calls to join Rosie and Valentina for breakfast and bring them up to speed.

'So, my dears, I've just been speaking to James's cousin. He's agreed to fly over to France once the three boys are ready for home. It's best he takes care of that side of things. We three need to be together to agree on ... on ...' she faltered slightly, holding back tears, ' ... the arrangements. Give them the send-off they deserve. No, Rosie,' she added gently but firmly, seeing the look on Rosie's face. 'Your being there could do nothing to speed up the process.'

Rosie swallowed hard and nodded, staring at her plate as the tears threatened.

She was saved by Valentina, who set down her espresso cup with a clatter, a crimson flush sweeping up from her throat to her hairline. 'I wish to go to France and bring Fraser home,' she said stiffly. Lady Mara watched her.

'You will have ample chance to see him once he is home,' she answered. 'I propose the coffins be kept here at the Hall until the –'

'No!' protested Valentina, half-rising from her chair. 'It is . . . there is . . . Fraser's things, his luggage . . .'

'Will be flown home intact and delivered into your hands, my dear,' Lady Mara interrupted, a puzzled frown on her face. 'What is the problem? Is there something of particular value among Fraser's belongings?'

Valentina shook her head, her hair whipping across her face. 'No, I . . .' Realising she was out of her chair, she sat down heavily. 'I stay here,' she finished.

'That's settled then,' said Lady Mara, as if the outcome had never been in doubt. 'Now, I quite understand if you want to go to your homes, but I hope you will stay here with me for the next few days at least, just while we sort things out.' She paused. Valentina shrugged but Rosie smiled up at Lady Mara, grateful for an excuse to delay returning to the cottage alone.

'Thanks, Mara. I'm not sure I can face going home right now.'

Lady Mara nodded and squeezed Rosie's shoulder as she rose from the table. 'I must get on. You know where I am if you need me. Anything at all, just ask.' And she was gone. How long Lady Mara could keep up the brave front, Rosie didn't know.

Valentina sloped off immediately, leaving Rosie alone at the table. Rosie made her way up to the library to ring her mother, wanting above all else to escape the furtive stares and sympathetic glances of the staff as they went about their business. From her vantage point in the window seat, she spied Valentina power-walking round the grounds in the pouring rain, clad in a pink velour jogging outfit with matching headband and white trainers, her head bent against the rain and mobile phone clamped to her ear, towing Angelo along on the end of his diamanté-studded leash. Gazing out across the gardens now, however, Rosie saw no sign of Valentina. Perhaps she'd gone to dry off, or defied Lady Mara after all and gone back to her London flat.

Rosie got up from the window seat and paced the room, her own mobile held obediently to her ear. She tried to pay attention to her mother.

'I'll be across tomorrow. We've booked the red-eye from New Jersey.'

'I need to see you Mom – I never thought it could be like this,' Rosie confessed as she finished the call.

Rosie had wanted to match Lady Mara smile for smile. There had just been that one time when she'd seen her mother-in-law cry. Maybe it came from being British, maybe it was just all those years of living in this cold wet place that made it all so matter of fact.

Rosie fumbled in her pocket for a tissue, trying to regain some measure of her earlier self-control. If the coast was clear, maybe she should take a walk herself, she wondered. The fresh air would do her good and she desperately needed to lift her mood. After two hours in Cameron's library, she was in danger of losing her grip on herself. She was too close to him here, as she would be in the cottage.

As Rosie moved decisively towards the door, it opened to admit Lady Mara.

'I thought you might be up here again,' she said quietly. Mara understood what the library meant to Cameron. Had meant to him, Rosie corrected her thoughts brutally. 'May I come in?'

Rosie nodded, retreating to the windowsill as Lady Mara advanced into the room. Rosie sat down again and drew her knees up protectively, flinching as Lady Mara settled herself in Cameron's chair.

'Are you all right?' said Mara, leaning forwards to get a better look at Rosie's face. Without warning, the strain became unbearable and Rosie nearly gave voice to the screaming in her head.

'All right? My husband is dead, crushed and broken on some godforsaken mountain a thousand miles from here and you sit there calmly in his chair, in his chair, and ask me if I'm alright?' Her body shuddered with the effort of containing the words. If she let them out, the grief would sweep her away. Rosie focused on her breathing, willing the moment to pass.

'Rosie?' Lady Mara was beside Rosie, gripping her knees, eyes wide with concern.

'I'm . . . fine.' gasped Rosie, forcing the words out through the internal maelstrom.

'Listen to me,' said Mara in a voice that brooked no argument. 'We're going to walk outside and then I'm locking the door, for now.' She ignored Rosie's cry of protest, steering her grimly out of the room, her face set. 'It's not good for you to be up here, Rosie, you're making yourself ill.' She slipped the key into the pocket of her cardigan and tucked her arm through Rosie's. 'Now come along. You need some air.'

Outside, the rain had eased off. The air was fresh and damp, carrying the woody scent of the trees and hedgerows. Rosie breathed it in, feeling the flare of emotions subside as they strolled through the knot garden, leaving her comfortably numb again.

Lady Mara studied Rosie closely as they followed the twisting gravel pathways past the designs of intricately woven herbs towards the central fountain, stealing sideways glances at her but saying nothing. They walked on in this way for ten, maybe fifteen, minutes before Lady Mara spoke up.

'I wanted to talk to you, Rosie,' she began carefully, 'about Cameron's will.' Rosie looked at her blankly. 'James has a will,' Lady Mara continued, relieved that Rosie showed no sign of plunging into hysterics again, 'and I believe Fraser and Valentina also have one, but I wondered whether you and Cameron had given thought to writing one before, that is, since the wedding?'

Rosie shook her head, unable to see where Lady Mara was going with this. She found it hard to picture the kind of couple who would draw up a will three months after getting married. Seeing her confusion, Lady Mara pressed on hurriedly.

'I want to assure you, Rosie,' she said earnestly, 'that everything of Cameron's is now yours. And this,' she stood still, sweeping one arm out in a wide arc to emphasise her point, 'that is, Cameron's portion of the inheritance, will pass to you when I die.'

Rosie stared at Lady Mara, completely taken aback by the scope of her generosity. Misinterpreting her silence, Lady Mara patted Rosie's hand comfortingly.

'I know that you may not stay in England now, Rosie. No one could expect it of you. But know that you have a home here. Cameron would have wanted it and so do I.' Rosie nodded and squeezed her hand. It was all she could manage, but she saw in Lady Mara's eyes that she understood.

'Ah, look.' Lady Mara pointed back towards the house, where a black Mercedes was pulling up beside the front steps. 'This is the solicitor now. I left a message for him earlier today.'

Dropping Rosie's arm, she led the way back through the garden and into the house. Old Abbot, the Whittons' butler for the last twenty years, stopped them in the entrance hall.

'Mr Thwaites is in the drawing-room, Madam.'

'Thank you, Abbot. Tea for four, please,' said Lady Mara, 'though I don't know where Valentina has got to. If you see her, send her in, will you?'

'Of course, Madam.'

Rosie followed Lady Mara obediently into the drawing-room and stood placidly, vaguely aware that Lady Mara was making introductions. Her thoughts drifted as she shook hands with the grave-faced Mr Thwaites and allowed Lady Mara to guide her to a chair. She was aware of the buttons on Mr Thwaites's pinstripe waistcoat glinting in the light from the window even as they strained across his ample girth. He sighed as he withdrew the crisp papers from his leather briefcase.

Rosie had no interest in the discussion of wills and, though she did her best to pay attention, fatigue crept unbidden through her limbs and her eyelids began to droop. Long hours spent grieving in the library had left her exhausted. Slowly, the solicitor's words, punctuated only by the occasional wheeze, began to fade to a dull drone. Rosie had no notion of when her eyes finally closed and silence slipped about her like death itself.

'NEVER!' hissed Lady Mara.

Rosie jerked awake, suddenly aware that something was very wrong. How long had she been asleep? Lady Mara sat opposite her, white-faced, two spots of colour splashed high on her cheekbones.

'James would never have done such a thing,' she declared, fury radiating from every line of her body.

Rosie looked fearfully from Lady Mara's rigid face to the solicitor's solemn expression. 'What is happening?' she asked.

Mr Thwaites shook his head. 'I'm afraid there can be no doubt, Lady Whitton,' he said quietly, holding up his hand in a placatory gesture as she opened her mouth to reply. 'I have the documents here. They have been signed by both James and Fraser Whitton, the trustees of the estate.'

'James wouldn't have signed such a document.' Mara's voice remained steady, although Rosie could see it took everything she had. 'He wouldn't have done this.'

Mr Thwaites adjusted his position. He spoke slowly. 'It was all enacted legally and is totally binding.'

'Then find the loophole, man. That's your job,' snapped Lady Mara.

Rosie stared at her, astonished. Again, the regretful shake of the head, this time accompanied by a helpless shrug. 'I'm afraid there isn't one, Lady Whitton. The deal is watertight in every respect. The substantial funding required for the joint venture was provided by United Oil, but on the basis that both parties would share the cost in the event of failure. The estate, the family trust in its *entirety*,' he stressed the last word, 'was committed to underwrite Fraser's share.'

'Fraser's?'

'Your son, Fraser, brokered the deal, but, as I said before, the documents are signed by both Fraser *and* James.'

Valentina slid unobtrusively into the room and sat down beside Rosie. Rosie shrugged in reply to her questioning glance and immediately fixed her eyes back on Lady Mara's face. Lady Mara was bolt upright in her chair, hands clasped tightly in her lap, holding her composure in a grip of iron. This time her voice betrayed her.

'The Hall?' she said hoarsely. The solicitor bowed his head for a moment, as though paying homage to the dead. Gathering his courage, he met Lady Mara's eye.

'Under the circumstances, United Oil have agreed a time for you to leave. It is very generous, but leave you must,' he said.

'Then what do I have?'

'Whatever is in Lord James's private account,' he replied.

Lady Mara nodded once. Then, with a great effort, as though forcing her way through an invisible barrier, she turned her head. Rosie shivered as the weight of that stare passed over her and came to rest on Valentina.

'You knew.' It wasn't a question. Valentina bowed her head.

Too late, Rosie leapt to her feet and watched with mounting horror as Lady Mara grew old, withered and crumpled silently to the floor.

Chapter Five

Lauds

Rosie lay on her back, staring into the dark. She pressed her fingertips hard into her scalp, searching for the off switch to her brain. If only. She glanced at the illuminated display screen on her alarm clock. Wide awake before five am. That had to be a first, she thought, kicking her way out of the covers and flicking on the lamp. Recently, sleep had become a very cruel thing. Every morning she woke up thinking Cameron would be there. She had searched for the cups of coffee on the bedside table. She had slept in his favourite jumper, doused in his cologne. And she had listened in the darkness for any sign of him being in the house, but there was always silence.

Pulling on her robe, Rosie padded across the thick carpet to the window; behind the shroud-like drapes, another day had come. She waited by the window, hoping to glimpse him outside, looking for the lights of his car in the driveway.

Tugging the curtains aside, Rosie wrapped her robe more tightly around her tired body and eased herself up onto the windowsill. Far across the grounds, the sun was just clearing the treetops. Why did it keep doing that, she thought stupidly. Rising, crossing the sky, sinking below the horizon, day after day as though nothing had changed. 'But everything's changed,' she wanted to shout. 'He's dead.' Yet all around her the world and everything in it was carrying on exactly as it had before, not knowing or caring that it had been robbed.

Rosie sighed, the rational part of her brain reminding her that in the press of humanity three lives was nothing; a snap of the fingers, a turn of the head, a solitary tear. Hundreds of people died every day, just as hundreds more were born. There shouldn't have been enough room on the planet but somehow, through some quirk of physics, the newborns didn't fill the places of the departed. They each occupied their own, new space on earth, while the spaces left by the dead remained, gaping voids in the lives of those who had loved them.

She picked up the Bible next to her. Lady Mara had put it in her bag last time they were in the library together. It had belonged to Cameron, given to him at his first communion. The pages were worn, with favourite verses highlighted and underlined. Her eyes flicked over the pages as she thumbed through. Then she stopped. The corner of one leaf was folded over. It pointed to a line of text that had been underlined twice. Rosie read the line. Psalm 34 . . . *The Lord is close to the broken-hearted and saves those who are crushed in spirit.*

Rosie slid off the windowsill, shaking her mind free of such thoughts. Things were difficult enough without thinking that God was trying to speak to her. Today of all days, it was imperative that she kept it together. She checked the clock. Five-thirty am. Time to go and check on Mara.

It was dark in the corridor. Rosie crept past the bedroom doors, not wanting to disturb the sleepers or, worse, attract the company of a well-meaning relative, all of whom were desperate to offer their condolences. They had begun arriving two days ago in preparation for the funeral, some of them unannounced. Most of the Whittons had stayed at Carrington Hall for Rosie and Cameron's wedding and it quickly became apparent to a stunned Rosie that the family assumed the same hospitality would be extended on this occasion.

Of course, Rosie admitted as she scurried up the stairs towards Mara's suite, they had no way of knowing that four days ago she had suddenly become the mistress of the Hall by unhappy default. Perhaps, had they realised, things might have been different. As it was, Rosie had found herself playing hostess on top of everything else, a role for which she felt horribly ill-equipped.

'Life will go on,' she had been assured for the fourth time yesterday. 'You'll find someone else.' Rosie had smiled as graciously as she could and had not tipped boiling coffee in to the lap of Simon Coltrane, the effete publishing cousin who followed her around the house at every opportunity. He reminded her of a game-show host with his fake tan, Patrick Cox shoes and red socks.

In the wake of Mara's collapse, the first wave of phone calls from relatives announcing their imminent arrival times had caught Rosie completely unaware. The information sank without trace in her overloaded brain, already swamped by concern for Mara and a thousand small decisions that now clamoured for her immediate attention.

Donations to charity in lieu of funeral flowers? A choir to accompany the organist? Who should be invited to the family get-together after the funeral? Should the funeral be postponed if Mara didn't improve? The staff hovered expectantly, but Rosie was too preoccupied with overseeing the arrival of the coffins to notice.

After a few hours of waiting for orders that never came, Abbott and the senior domestics had ridden to her rescue, assuming total responsibility for the guests and loyally maintaining the illusion that they were acting under Rosie's direction. Faithful Abbott had positioned himself at Rosie's elbow as she stood in the entrance hall to greet each arrival, discreetly murmuring names and essential details as the maids glided back and forth, offering refreshments and showing people to their hastily prepared rooms.

Things would have been impossible without Abbott's knowledge, Rosie reflected as she rounded the final corner. Apart from the practical support, she knew he'd been shielding her from all the questions about the Hall. Naturally, the staff had been informed, though they had kept the details vague. Valentina argued against it but Rosie insisted they be given time to look for new positions.

The relatives were trickier. Somehow, Abbott had contrived to disperse the news among them without giving the full details. He then made it his business to intercept anybody trying to 'get to the bottom of things', as he put it, before they reached Rosie. The gallant old man continued to dismiss Rosie's halting attempts to express her gratitude. 'It's my job, Madam,' he said stiffly, inclining his head as he backed away. His deference made Rosie uncomfortable. Abbott was more than three times her age and far more worthy of respect than she was.

Deep in thought, Rosie failed to notice the figure standing at the door to Mara's suite until she was a few feet away. Cursing silently, she pulled up short, all hope of fading back into the shadows gone as the figure turned. 'Who's there?' The woman's voice shook slightly.

Rosie advanced cautiously. 'Mom?'

'Rosie, thank God. You frightened me.'

What are you doing here?'

Mrs Jacobs clutched her robe, half-defensive, half-defiant. 'I – didn't want Mara to be alone and I thought, I hoped, you'd be resting.'

Rosie nodded, hearing what her mother didn't say; that Rosie had shut her out at this most desperate of times and so, needing to help, to be useful in some small way, she had come here. Not for comfort, certainly. Mara was beyond that. But just to be there, to show solidarity. 'How is she?'

'The same. The nurse gave her another shot around four.'

'Mom, you've been here all that time?'

'I couldn't sleep.'

'Me neither . . . Dad?'

'Out like a light. Too much whisky after dinner last night. He's not used to it.'

They smiled at each other in the half-light of the corridor, a dangerous moment of intimacy bridging the protective gap that Rosie had created. 'Rosie . . .' Mrs Jacobs began, reaching a tentative hand out to her daughter.

'Thanks, Mom. Go back to bed now, get some rest.' Rosie moved swiftly towards the door, trying to cut the conversation dead, but it was too late.

'Rosie, wait!' Her mother's hand closed on the sleeve of her robe, pulling her back. 'You've been avoiding me.'

Rosie shrugged, keeping her eyes fixed on the carpet. It was true enough. With the best of intentions, her parents had been trying to corner her, desperate to coax a decision out of her. Grief, responsibility for the Hall and the pressure of covering for Mara had so muddled Rosie's brain that she hardly knew day from night, let alone what her future plans might be. All she knew for certain was that she wasn't ready. Seeing the panic in her eyes, her Dad had backed off a little, but her mother was unshakeable.

'Look at me,' said Mrs Jacobs. Unwillingly, Rosie dragged her gaze upwards to meet her mother's, bracing herself for the onslaught. 'Honey, the funeral is today, you can't put off your decision any longer.'

Rosie took a deep breath. 'Mom, there's been so much to think about,' she began. 'The Hall, Mara, all the legal stuff. I – I can't handle it, I need more time to . . .'

'Which is *exactly* why your father and I want you to come home!' cried Mrs Jacobs, pressing her hands to either side of Rosie's head, forcing her to maintain eye contact. 'You need time to recover, of course you do,' she continued, 'but what better place to do that than back home, surrounded by the people who love you?'

'I – I –' *Cameron loved me.* Rosie felt the tears welling up and twisted her head to the side, trying to free herself from her mother's grip. 'But Mara –'

'Mara may need professional care,' said her mother quietly.

'Don't – don't say that!' gasped Rosie, her breath coming in heaving gasps. 'She's going to be OK, she's . . .' Tears trembled dangerously on her lashes. She willed them back. *Not now! Stay strong.*

Mrs Jacobs tilted her daughter's face up, gently pressing her advantage. 'Sweetheart, it's the truth.' Rosie shuddered as a single tear tracked down her cheek. 'This is it,' she thought as a terrible pressure began to build in her chest, 'I'm losing it.' Sensing victory, Mrs Jacobs pressed on.

'So how about it, honey? You're already selling the cottage; the Hall will be gone in a matter of weeks. How would you manage? Come home, Rosie. You've got your whole life ahead of you.'

'NO!' With a scream, Rosie tore herself free, hands raised in fierce denial of her mother's words. 'No, Mom!' Mrs Jacobs fell back, helpless in the face of Rosie's anger. Rosie stared at her mother, but it was Cameron's laughing face that filled her mind. 'Don't you get it?' she said. 'I don't *want* my whole life ahead of me. I want the old one, here, with him. I can't leave him here . . .'

She backed away, fumbled for the door handle and fell into the room, firmly shutting her mother out. She had to stay strong. She had to.

Alone in the corridor, Mrs Jacobs lifted both hands to the door as if to force her way in, then thought better of it. She trudged slowly back to her room, arms hanging at her sides. Why couldn't Rosie see sense?

Rosie leaned back against the door, listening to the sound of her mother's retreating footsteps. Released by her mother's words, suppressed grief rose up from the pit of her stomach and attacked again, threatening to consume her. Fists clenched, she fought it, forcing it back. She remained where she was for several minutes, breathing slowly and deliberately, not daring to move until she was sure of herself. Finally, she approached the bed and sank quietly into the low armchair that had been dragged to the bedside from its usual place by the dressing-table.

Mara was sleeping but even in repose her body seemed taut, the skin stretched too tightly across her face, so that her characteristically gentle features looked skeletal, grim. Her hair lay loose on the pillow, but Rosie saw that someone – her mother? – had tucked it neatly behind her ears and straightened the bedclothes. Her spectacles lay on the bed-side table beside a tumbler of water and an embroidered handkerchief, all untouched.

Rosie gazed at this impostor, so unlike her strong, elegant mother-in-law, while the questions buzzed like mosquitoes about her head.

To stay in England seemed both futile and impossible. Her part-time job at the local library wasn't enough to make ends meet and the mere thought of living at the cottage without Cameron was so painful that she had already put it up for sale. Part of her longed to go home with her parents but ... Rosie shook her head. She couldn't rebuild the life she'd had before; it would be like pretending Cameron had never existed. To leave England would be to accept that he was gone forever. Her whole being recoiled from the finality of that departure. Yet there was nothing to keep her here any more. Whether she stayed or not, Cameron was never coming back.

Then there was Mara. What would become of her? Whatever happened, Rosie had already resolved to give her most of the proceeds from the cottage sale, but how far would that go? Once the Hall changed hands, her mother-in-law would be homeless. Who would take care of her? Certainly not Valentina, who hadn't set foot in the Hall for three days. Another relative, then? Most of those Rosie had met were at least as old as Mara. Ought she to offer herself?

Hours passed as Rosie sat there, one hand plucking fretfully at the bedclothes as she kept watch over Mara, praying for answers that would not come. 'The Lord is close to the broken-hearted and saves those who are crushed in spirit.' The words echoed again in her mind, as if being whispered just for her.

A light tap on the door brought Rosie crashing back to the present. She rose awkwardly from the chair as the nurse entered the room, one of the maids following discreetly behind her. 'We need to prepare Lady Whitton now,' said the nurse, crossing to the bedside and stooping to check Mara's condition. Without a word, Rosie moved towards the door, her slumped shoulders betraying her exhaustion.

'Madam?' Rosie turned, one hand on the door handle.

'What is it?' she asked wearily.

Mara's maid looked steadily at her, an unbearable mix of pity and compassion in her eyes. 'It will be all right,' she said.

Rosie nodded, her eyes bright with unshed tears, and fled. The most burning question of all seared at her mind. She reached her own room, her jaw set. Only a trusted few knew and no one else must find out, not until they were sure. There was a chance – the doctor had said – a chance that it was just the severity of the shock, that Mara would come back to herself in time. But would she make it through the funeral? Would the other mourners see through the disguise of perfectly coiffed hair and smart black suit and guess the awful truth – that behind the eyes shrouded by the delicate veil and pillbox hat, Mara's mind had snapped?

❀ ❀ ❀ ❀

Rosie heard the gravel crunch. She drifted over to the window in time to see a chic black trouser suit almost entirely obscured by a wide, low-brimmed hat hurrying across the drive. Valentina? It had to be. Rosie smoothed down her black pencil skirt and returned to Mara's side. Mara was dressed in a black Yves Saint Laurent suit and was being held up in a straight-backed chair. It was the first time she'd been out of her bed and dressed in days.

'Madam, Mrs Whitton is here,' Abbott wheezed as he opened the door.

Valentina swept in. Rosie felt self-conscious as Valentina's critical gaze swept over her, pausing with clear disdain at the black ribbon in her hair. Turning to Mara, she carefully lifted her huge hat and bent down to bestow her customary air kiss greeting.

'Sit down please, dear.' With a trembling hand, Mara indicated the chair beside Rosie. Valentina blinked. Rosie had become accustomed to their mother-in-law's quavering voice, but to Valentina, who hadn't been back to the Hall since Mara's collapse, it would sound completely alien. Slowly she sank into the seat.

'I want you both to go home,' Mara managed.

Rosie leant forward grasping the older woman's hands. 'How can we leave you like this?' she said tearfully. 'You're all alone, you're sick. We want to take care of you.' Beside her, Valentina said nothing.

Mara shook her head and tried to speak, but the words took a long time to come. 'I am . . . grateful,' she began. 'But – home. You m-must . . . go. Thank you,' she added, before slumping back in her chair, apparently exhausted. Rosie was distraught.

Valentina shrugged and smiled, patting Mara's hand kindly. 'It is probably for the best, no?' she said. Rosie glared at her.

❀   ❀   ❀   ❀

They endured the funeral in silence, Mara propped up between Valentina and Rosie in the foremost pew. Rosie found it hard to listen. Despite the lengthy eulogy on the qualities of the Whitton men, it felt like it had nothing to do with the Cameron she knew. As her mind wandered, she began to feel guilty about her feelings towards her sister-in-law. After all, they had both lost a husband. During the final hymn, she prepared a smile of solidarity and looked across Mara to Valentina. Valentina, however, had chosen that moment to check her watch. Rosie wanted to throw up. Even as they followed the coffins out of the church, Rosie detected Valentina's impatience at having to match Mara's slow pace down the aisle.

They sat rigidly in the funeral car on the way to the family gathering afterwards. As it pulled up at the hotel, Rosie rushed out to assist Mara. She wasn't used to wearing heels and in her hurry, she lost her footing and staggered, arms flailing, into Valentina.

'Oh! Sorry! Excuse me.'

The clutch bag spun out of Valentina's grasp, scattering its contents across the car park.

'Just leave it!' Valentina lunged. But Rosie was already dropping to her knees to scoop up the lipstick, wallet, powder compact, plane ticket, passport . . . Rosie stared up at Valentina in disbelief. The Italian shot a nervous look at the car where Mara sat waiting, oblivious. She snatched her things back and began to cram them roughly into her bag, avoiding the challenge in Rosie's eye. They both rose to their feet.

'You're leaving?' Rosie glanced towards Mara.

'As she told us to,' Valentina shrugged, turning to enter the hotel. Rosie blocked her way.

'But this ticket is for today, this afternoon,' she hissed. 'You'd already booked it. You were going anyway, weren't you?'

'Today, tomorrow, what difference does it make?'

'What difference does it . . .?' Rosie bit the words off, staring blankly around the car park. Valentina laughed and threw back her hair. 'You want to play the doting daughter?' she spat. 'Be my guest!'

Rosie pulled back from the shoulder and slapped her as hard as she could across her face. Valentina squealed. Rosie stood her ground and watched as the elegant Italian swallowed hard, whipped round and stalked off, clutching her bag. She almost collided with a tall man in a suit who had just emerged from his car. Swearing in Italian, she pulled her hat down to cover her scarlet cheek. The man watched her disappear. His eyes locked with Rosie's for a second before she turned back to Mara, for once grateful for her mother-in-law's condition.

Rosie didn't see Valentina again. She assumed she must have booked a taxi to the airport and vanished. She spent most of the afternoon at Mara's side, shielding her from the more persistent relatives. It had been a long day and Rosie could see that Mara needed to get back to the Hall to rest.

'I'll just be a minute, Mara. I need to settle up with the hotel. Then I'll take you home, OK?'

Leaving Mara for a moment, Rosie went in search of the reception. She felt suddenly exhausted. She dipped into the restroom to splash her face with cold water. As she retraced her steps, snatches of conversation floated towards her. '. . . be willing to find you a position in the household. And your daughters-in-law, of course. As you know, there's plenty to be done on the estate.' Rosie rounded the corner.

It was the tall man from the car park and another shorter man that she hadn't seen before. Mara looked between them, confused. 'As a last resort,' the tall man continued, 'the Dower House is vacant.'

Rosie marched up to them and threw her arm around Mara protectively. Her face felt hot as anger flushed into it.

'That won't be necessary. Mara and I will be just fine, thank you.'

Rosie didn't notice their reaction, just Mara's slight protestations.

'No Mara, I've made up my mind. I'm staying.' Rosie turned.

'Gentlemen, have a safe journey.'

Chapter Six

Bitter Tears

Rain flung itself against the windscreen as Rosie pulled out of the short stay car park and onto the road that would take them away from the airport. She gripped the steering wheel, leaning forwards to get a better view. The thick cloud and driving rain made it seem later than it was. Headlights of other motorists flashed through the torrents. Rosie squinted into the almost darkness and tried to keep in her lane.

She heard another plane pass by overhead and wondered if it was her parents up there, winging their way back home without her. She fought off a ridiculous urge to look up in case they were waving and, instead, forced herself to focus on the road ahead. If she wrote the car off, it would have to be sold as scrap and they needed a better price for it than that.

Rosie glanced in her rear view mirror. Mara sat silently in the back seat, head resting back, hands folded neatly on her lap. Rosie had whacked the heating up to full blast and wrapped her snugly in a tartan rug, the kind normally used for picnics and garden parties, but Mara continued to shiver. It was that kind of a day.

'OK, Mara?'

Silence.

Rosie tried again. 'We'll be home soon,' she said brightly. Mara closed her eyes. 'Good idea, take a little nap, keep your strength up,' Rosie finished, hating the way she sounded, 'but keep your seatbelt on, OK?' It was like talking to a small child. She switched her gaze back to the road in time to see a silver Mercedes launch out from a slip road into the space directly ahead of her.

'Dammit!' she shrieked, stamping viciously on the brake and thumping the horn. The Mercedes owner gestured at her as he cut across to the fast lane and roared off.

The funeral reception was already replaying in her mind, causing the bubble of anger in her stomach to expand, swelling up and out until the car was engulfed by it.

It wasn't the fact that Valentina had gone back to Italy. Rosie hadn't truly expected her to stay in England, any more than Mara had. If she was honest, she'd been torn about what to do for the best as well. Hadn't Mara given Rosie her blessing twice on the matter of leaving, once as they walked in the garden and again on the day of the funeral? And on top of that, her mother had applied enough pressure to snap even the strongest resolve. Rosie could have left with her head held high and nothing but good wishes from all concerned, as could Valentina. They'd both had the same free choice.

Rosie probed deeper into the bubble, trying to pinpoint the core of this unfamiliar rage. It definitely wasn't the fact that Valentina had gone. That didn't make her a villain, any more than staying made Rosie a saint. No, it was the *way* she'd gone. Valentina hadn't waited for Mara to tell her it was OK, hadn't asked if Mara needed her or questioned how she

would manage alone. She'd just gone right ahead and
booked her flight without so much as a word to anyone.
There had been no trace of love, no sense of duty, not even
the faintest acknowledgement that Rosie, Valentina and
Mara were family. Not blood relatives, sure, but they'd been
bound together by law and marriage. Death didn't change
that.

Rosie's cheeks flamed as she recalled the scene. She
shouldn't have slapped Valentina, but finding the plane ticket
like that and booked for that very afternoon! Her mind had
frozen but her body reacted instantly, her hand shooting out
before Rosie knew what she was doing. Oh, Valentina
deserved it all right, but cat fights weren't Rosie's style.
Cameron would have been mortified. Yet, Rosie couldn't
quite bring herself to regret it.

There had been just one moment of shame – that feeling of being caught – when the man appeared out of his
car and stared. Rosie had felt his winter-grey eyes on her
back as she returned to Mara and the whole time they had
walked slowly together all the way across the parking lot
and into the hotel – like he was challenging her to face
him. Well, she'd certainly done that later on. The guy had
nerve, offering Mara some kind of shepherd's hovel and
employment 'only as a last resort', as if she was a social par-
asite looking for a quick buck and an easy gig. And *then* he
turned out to be a relative, Mara's second cousin or something, come down from the north with his sidekick! Hugh
Thornprick, or was it Fenwick? Unconsciously, Rosie dug
her fingers into the gear stick, her nails gouging the soft
leather casing.

At least he offered, her conscience whispered traitorously. *No one else has.*

With a start, Rosie realised it had got dark. She switched the headlights on and turned the heater down a notch. Her eyes were prickling with fatigue and she didn't want to fall asleep at the wheel. An exit junction flashed by on the left and she checked the number on the sign. Eight more junctions before their exit. Outside was the intermittent hum of fast-moving traffic as cars whipped past, splattering each other with mud and rainwater. Inside, she could hear the sound of Mara's gentle breathing and the rhythmical flick-flack of the wipers across the windscreen, keeping the rain at bay.

He offered. No one else has.

Rosie switched the radio on and fiddled irritably with the tuning dial, but it was no use. The truth sat there, an unwelcome presence squatting determinedly in the passenger seat. Apart from her parents (whose increasingly desperate suggestions she found impossible to accept), no one had offered to help. Rosie's eyes widened in shock as the full extent of her decision hit her. Valentina had scarpered; her parents had gone home; the cottage was sold; and a property developer with big ideas was poised to take possession of the Hall, courtesy of United Oil.

As for the Whittons, once the loss of the Hall could no longer be concealed, the extended family ties that had seemed so strong had begun to disintegrate. The family severed any ties of responsibility to the ageing matriarch who had presided so graciously over them. She was, after all, Scottish and therefore a foreigner, albeit one who had lived among them for the past thirty years or more. It hadn't both-ered Rosie – there was no one whom she knew well enough to trust with Mara in any case – but she had minded for Mara's sake. Her parents' departure made it official; she and Mara were on their own. Rosie tightened her hands on the wheel and put her foot down.

❀ ❀ ❀ ❀

It was past midnight. Rosie lay in her bed – at least the bed at the Hall that had become hers after Cameron's death. It was the room they had stayed in together when they had vis-ited in the weeks after their marriage. She'd finally given up trying to sleep. Her parents would be halfway home now. She began re-running the horrible conversation they'd had that morning. She'd been doing that a lot recently – reliving conversations. It was her way of holding on to the past, she supposed.

'This is madness, Rosie!' her mother had finally snapped over breakfast.

'Not now, Christine.' Dan put a hand on his wife's arm, but she flung it away.

'When then, Dan? Tonight? Tomorrow? When we're back home and Rosie's here, no job, nowhere to live, nothing –'

'I am in the room, Mom,' Rosie scowled.

'I know, honey. It's just that you don't seem to be thinking straight. It's not your fault – it's the grief. You're grieving.'

Rosie had fumed, silently. Her mother could see she was losing ground, but that just made her more desperate.

'I know you want to look after Mara, honey. And I admire you for that – I really do. But you can't do it on your own. That poor woman – she may never recover.'

'You don't know that.' It was Dan who intervened, saying the words that stood silent on Rosie's tongue. His wife glared at him.

'It's 'cause I love you, honey.' Christine continued. 'I don't want you to make the wrong decision just because – because you're not thinking straight.'

The clock in the adjacent room struck ten.

'Your flight's at five thirty so you'll need to be ready to leave here at two,' Rosie said, before standing and leaving the room.

'I'm real proud of you, honey,' her dad had said to her retreating back.

It was this that had nearly broken her. She'd spent a long time in her room after that, letting the tears flow. Angry at her mother, angry at herself for losing it, angry at her dad for nearly making her change her mind. Once she'd composed herself, she'd checked on Mara. Her skin was cold to Rosie's touch. Rosie was closing the window when she heard her parents just underneath on the drive. She couldn't see them from where she was, but she could hear the tears in her mother's voice

'Do you think she'll be OK?'

'Rosie's tough,' she heard her dad say. 'She'll come through it.'

She pulled away from the window. She hoped he was right.

Abbott padded slowly up the stairs, stoically ignoring the pain in his arthritic knees. He had always been a firm believer in mind over matter but time was catching up with him. Today he felt old. Behind him, the visitor moderated her pace considerably. She knew where she was going but accepted the old man's courteous guidance. Abbott paused as they reached the top, wheezed slightly, then plodded resolutely on.

'This way, madam.' Halfway down the corridor, he stopped beside some ornate double doors and turned. 'If you're ready, madam?' The visitor inclined her head, signalling for him to proceed. Abbott knocked twice before opening the door part way. 'Dr Hepworth, Madam?'

'Thanks, Abbott.' Rosie nodded at him to send her in.

Dr Hepworth smiled at the old butler as he stepped back to usher her through. She swept into the room, shook hands with Rosie and set her bag down on the floor. Lady Whitton was propped up on a cluster of pillows, but the doctor turned first to Rosie, scrutinising her. 'Good morning, Rosie. How are you?'

'Just fine, thanks.'

Dr Hepworth nodded, noting the slump of Rosie's shoulders and the rings beneath her eyes, so dark they resembled bruises. 'Are you having trouble sleeping?'

Rosie shrugged. 'A little, I guess.'

'I could easily prescribe something to help you.'

'Thank you, but there's no need.'

Dr Hepworth nodded. 'If you change your mind . . .' She turned her attention to the frail figure sitting in the bed. 'How are you feeling today, Lady Whitton?'

'Perfectly all right, thank you.' Mara smiled and nodded, but her eyes seemed vague and unfocussed.

'May I sit down for a moment?' asked the doctor. Mara inclined her head and Dr Hepworth perched on the edge of the bed, rummaging in her leather bag. She took Mara through a series of minor checks, temperature, blood pressure, reflexes, all of them a smoke-screen for the real examination. From the opposite side of the bed, Rosie watched intently.

'Just pop this under your arm, please. What day is it?'

'Er, Tuesday, I believe.'

'Lovely. Roll up your sleeve for me while I check your blood pressure, that's it. Do you mind me asking how old you are?'

'Sixty-five.'

'And your birthday?'

'March the third.'

'Blood pressure seems fine. Keeping busy, are you? What have you been doing this week?'

'Well, I . . . we . . .' Mara looked at her in confusion. 'I've been . . .' Flustered, she looked to her daughter-in-law for reassurance. 'I can't remember. Why can't I remember? What's going on?'

Rosie hurried forwards and took Mara's hand, a bright smile pasted onto her face. 'It's OK, it's OK. We've been so busy with this and that, it's no wonder you can't remember. We've had lots of visitors and the last ones have just gone, haven't they? Remember?' Mara clutched Rosie's hand, staring at her. Rosie held her gaze calmly and Dr Hepworth observed in silence as the panic faded from Mara's eyes. Mara sank back against her pillows, nodding slowly.

'Yes, yes, that's it. I remember now, of course,' she said, the peace of ignorance descending on her like night-fall as she closed her eyes. Dr Hepworth waited. After a minute or so, Mara opened her eyes and smiled brightly at the doctor. 'Was there anything else?'

Dr Hepworth smiled and stood up, closing her case with a purposeful snap. 'No, that's all for today, Lady Whitton. Everything's fine, you just need a little more rest.' Mara nodded obediently and immediately shuffled down the pillows. Dr Hepworth quietly withdrew to the corridor as Rosie fussed over the covers, tucking Mara in like a little child.

❀   ❀   ❀   ❀

'Milk and sugar?'

'Just milk, please.'

The two women faced each other across the low coffee table in the blue lounge. Mara had tended to use this room to receive visitors and Abbott saw no reason to deviate from tradition, even now. He hovered in the background, ostensibly to replenish the tea, but in reality to be on hand if Rosie should need his support. Neither of them had been sure how this meeting would go.

Rosie sipped her tea delicately, eyeing Dr Hepworth over the rim of her blue-white china cup, trying to gauge her thoughts. The doctor's face was unreadable. They sat in silence for a while, until finally Dr Hepworth put down her cup and sighed.

'Rosie, Mara isn't well. You know this. There's no improvement.'

Rosie felt her jaw stiffen. 'It's just the shock,' she said stub-bornly. 'Who wouldn't react after something like this?'

'Who indeed?' thought the doctor, watching the almost unnatural display of composure from the young woman. 'You don't look so well yourself behind that mask.' Aloud she said, 'You're right, it is the shock. Physically, Mara is in good health, apart from her lack of appetite. Mentally . . .' she spread her hands wide in an open gesture, 'she may come back to herself, she may not. Grief manifests itself differently in everyone.'

Rosie looked down at her hands. 'Where is she?' she asked. Dr Hepworth hesitated, searching for the right words.

'Mara is shielding herself,' she began carefully, 'shielding her mind. Her brain can't deal with the trauma and so it has simply shut off the information. You've noticed that her long-term memory is fine? That's because in her mind, it's safe to remember things from the past. It's the recent past that she has locked away.'

Rosie gazed searchingly at her. 'What can I do to bring her back?'

The doctor shook her head. 'Nothing. It's all down to her,' she continued hurriedly as Rosie began to protest. 'I'm not an expert in this area. Mara will need a psychiatric assessment to confirm what I'm saying, but off the record, I believe there are three possibilities. She may deteriorate into old age from this point, mentally and physically; it may be that fragments of the truth come back to her over time; or something could happen to trigger off the memories – though what that could do to her . . .' Dr Hepworth saw the flash of fear in Rosie's eyes and broke off. There was no need to spell it out.

Rosie struggled visibly for a moment, gathering her strength. From the corner of her eye, the doctor noticed how the elderly butler stepped protectively towards the sofa, but Rosie quickly shook her head and looked up. 'Mara is strong,' she said. 'She just needs time and care. I can give her that.' Her voice held a note of utter certainty, but whether her conviction was justified or simply borne of desperation, Dr Hepworth couldn't tell. Her faith in Lady Whitton was incredibly admirable, but realistic? Professionally speaking, it was highly unlikely.

'Where will you live?'

'That's my business.'

Dr Hepworth sighed. 'I'm not the enemy, Rosie. I'm trying to help you.'

Rosie hesitated, glancing at Abbott. He made a tiny movement that might have been a nod. Rosie bit her lip. 'We're going to rent in town, Mara and me. We haven't fixed on a place yet.'

'Good. Very good. So you'll keep up Mara's regular appointments?'

'I will.'

'Excellent. For now, keep her medication as it is. The sedatives will control any agitation or undue anxiety. If she shows signs of improvement, we will reduce the dosage.' Dr Hepworth rose, extending her hand to Rosie. At the front door, she turned back. 'If you need some support, there are people who can help. Day care centres, temporary respite, that sort of thing. I'll get you the phone numbers of a few places.'

Rosie gave her a tight smile and closed the door gently. She leant against the cool wood and listened until the sound of the car engine faded away. She and Abbott stood shoulder to shoulder in the hallway, listening to the miserable silence pervading a house that had hummed with life and activity for so many years.

'Our last day,' Abbott said. It was the first time Rosie had ever known him venture a comment unrelated to his responsibilities. This was their last day. Rosie sensed the memories all about them, falling soft and thick like the winter snow she loved back home. 'Strange how life can change. But in all this sadness there is one good thing.' Rosie looked at him as if she didn't know what he was talking about. 'You ... Miss Rosie. I am glad the Lord brought you to us – a true gift. Lady Mara needed someone and here you are. Thank you Miss Rosie, thank you.'

'No, Abbott,' she answered softly, as the tears coursed silently down the old man's face. 'Thank *you*.'

Chapter Seven

The Dreaming Spires

Number fifty-four Sitwell Street had, in its glory days, been a majestic town house with ample room for a large family, live-in domestic staff, an aspidistra and even a pet or two. Its wide corridors and high-ceilinged rooms had echoed with the sounds of children's laughter, the centre of its wooden staircase worn smooth by countless journeys to the upper floors. From there, the more daring boys would mount the old mahogany banister rail for the treacherous but exhilarating slide back down to the entrance hall, egged on by the screams of their sisters.

Wonderful parties had been hosted in the drawing-room, especially in the winter, when the roaring open fire was stoked to draw the guests in and the smell of mulled wine and freshly roasted chestnuts wafted out onto the street. A grand piano had nestled into the curve of the great bay window that overlooked the street, carefully positioned to showcase the talents of its players to those uninvited passers-by, who gazed enviously in at the scenes of warmth and merriment before they hurried home, shoulders hunched against the elements.

Now . . . times had changed.

Number fifty-four had long since been carved up into one-room studio flats, housing both ambitious students and impoverished intellectuals. Downstairs, the drawing-room had been partitioned into two flats, currently inhabited on one side by a second year Classics student with an unhealthy interest in recreational drugs and on the other by a Japanese exchange student who worked late into the night and lived in perpetual anxiety that her grades might slip. The corridors were silent now, the staircase grubby and untended.

To the rear of the house was Flat 3, which used to be the scullery. It was the smallest flat in the house, consisting of three main rooms that served as a lounge, bedroom and kitchenette, with a small built-in bathroom cubicle tagged on. The letting agent referred to it as 'charmingly compact'. It was clean at least, but the bare white-washed walls, stained beige carpet and sparse furnishings created a Spartan atmosphere throughout.

Pip . . . Pip . . . Pip. 'You're listening to BBC Radio Four . . .' The clock radio blared into the silence. Rosie jolted awake in an instant and immediately rolled over, groping for the off switch.

'. . . The time is seven o'clock . . .' several items were dislodged from the bedside table, scattering across the carpet in Rosie's haste to kill the alarm before it woke Mara.

'. . . Here are this morning's headlines . . .' The bed creaked as Mara rolled over, mumbling and reaching out her hand. In desperation, Rosie rolled right out of bed onto her hands and knees and ripped the plug straight out of its socket.

Silence. Rosie raised her head and peered cautiously over the edge of the mattress. Mara was still asleep. Thank God. Scrambling to her feet, she pattered across the threadbare carpet to the bathroom cubicle, panicked and furious. What was it with that alarm clock, anyway? She'd *definitely* set it for six, no question about it. How could it be seven o'clock?

Rosie squeezed into the cubicle. To call it cramped would be a gross understatement. It was smaller than her old closet back home in the States and she was obliged to leave the door open to create a bit of elbow room on one side. She peered into the tiny mirror above the sink. Her face looked back at her, tired and puffy-eyed, a spider web of tiny cracks in the glass distorting her reflection like the cheap, trick mirrors at old-fashioned funfairs. The lines spread crazily across one eye and carved up her cheeks, matching the premature marks lately appearing on her skin. A new one every day, it seemed.

Rosie touched the tips of her fingers to her face, silently naming the lines and furrows as she traced them one by one. This one was grief; that one, fear. She drew one hand across her forehead; these were worry. Finally, (the *pièce de résistance* in this year's autumn/winter wrinkle collection), she drove one index finger hard into the short vertical slash between her brows. Anger, the deepest of all. Only her eyes held a fragile spark of hope, staring out through the cracked looking-glass with fierce determination. As Rosie watched, they filled with tears. She dropped her gaze immediately to focus on the chipped enamel basin.

'Mirror . . . mirror . . . Snap out of it, you're late already,' she muttered, shaking herself out of the moment like a dog just out of the water. She twisted the taps briskly. They were tarnished and coughed out a sickly dribble of rust-tinged water but, hey, at least it was cold. Rosie hastily splashed her face and neck and scrubbed herself dry with a grimy hand towel, cursing herself for oversleeping even as another part of her brain noted that a trip to the launderette was well overdue. She shook her head. There were too many balls to keep in the air.

Generally speaking, she needed an hour and a half to get everything done in the morning and be at work for seven-thirty. Mara was slow and needed incessant prompting in order to be dressed, fed and settled by the time Rosie left and then the buses were often delayed, their drivers sleepy and unapologetic. But today – Rosie scooped up her wristwatch from the carpet – she'd be lucky to make it to work by eight. Lurching dangerously as she tried to hop into her sweat-pants, Rosie jumped her way over to the kitchenette and wrestled a slice of bread out of its plastic packaging with her free hand. She chewed furiously and washed it down with the dregs of yesterday's apple juice, swigging straight from the carton. Then she wriggled into her regulation sweatshirt, jammed her feet into her trainers and trapped her unwashed hair beneath a baseball cap. Finally, she snatched up her mobile and switched it on. OK, she was ready.

She strode to the door but paused with her hand on the doorknob, casting one last look around the room as she made frantic mental calculations. If she could get through by 10 am, she could pop home to check on Mara and still make it back in time for the lunchtime rush. Maybe. If the buses were on time. But that would mean extra bus fare. Perhaps she could bring the bike if her boss turned a blind eye. If, if, if.

Rosie chewed her bottom lip anxiously as she gazed at Mara, finally sound asleep after her restless night. She'd be OK for a couple of hours, wouldn't she? Rosie crossed the room, grabbed a used envelope and pen from the worktop and scribbled hurriedly. Choosing the best apple from the tired selection in the fruit bowl, she laid the envelope on the pillow and balanced the apple on top. That would have to do. Easing the door shut behind her, she risked a quick glance at her mobile phone. Seven twenty-five, the display pulsed ominously. Rosie shoved it into her pocket and ran.

Around nine thirty, Mara awoke. The morning sun seeped in through the cheap, unlined curtains, its light piercing her closed eyelids. She raised one hand to shield herself from the unwelcome glare and rolled wearily onto her side. A green apple lay on the adjacent pillow. Mara regarded it with mild curiosity, noting the smooth curve of its outline and the tiny irregular dimples that pockmarked its flesh. After several minutes of careful deliberation, she decided it was a Granny Smith. It seemed important to clarify this point before touching it. Satisfied with her diagnosis, she freed one age-mottled hand from the duvet and picked up the apple, clearing her line of vision. The room came into focus, sending a jolt of panic through her. Mara struggled to raise herself up onto her elbows, gazing round at the bare white walls and the cheap, mismatched furniture. This wasn't her bedroom. And where was Rosie?

Mara sat up with difficulty and saw that the bed was pushed right up against the wall. Slowly, she inched her way across the mattress until she reached the spot where the wall gave way to a window. She pulled the flimsy curtain aside and gazed out, not at the grounds of her beloved Hall but on a completely unfamiliar street. Cars were crammed into tight parking spaces, bicycles chained to railings, people rushing along, heads down.

Utterly bewildered, she gripped the apple, staring at its polished surface as though it were a crystal ball that might magically reveal her whereabouts. The skin remained as blank as her mind. Where was Rosie? Mara lay down, pulling the covers up to form a protective cocoon around her.

She was vaguely aware of feeling disconnected from her body, as though she was looking out through her eyes from a long way back inside her head. She felt that she ought to recognise this place; the knowledge was there, whispering at the edges of her mind, but each time she reached out, it fell silent and fled. Frustrated, Mara turned onto her side again, dislodging the envelope from its place on Rosie's pillow. Ah, a note. She grasped it eagerly. This would explain things, surely.

Gone to work. Back soon. Rest up, have some breakfast. Love, R x

Mara read it twice. She had no idea where Rosie worked, but the breakfast part made sense. She lay back on her pillow, nodding sagely. No doubt Abbott would be along shortly with her breakfast tray. Lady Mara waited.

❀   ❀   ❀   ❀

Two miles away, Rosie was pedalling through the streets of Oxford on an old-fashioned grocer's bicycle. Her manager's sarcasm was still stinging her ears half an hour after the telling-off. Solene Pullman, proprietor of Angel Cakes, was not a woman to be crossed. Rosie had missed the bus and found Mrs Pullman waiting pointedly at the door when she finally stumbled over the threshold, panting and dishevelled, at ten past eight.

'Has anyone explained to you that we run on Greenwich Mean Time here in England, Rosie?' Mrs Pullman had snapped in her best English accent, chopping off the end of each word neatly to emphasise both her displeasure and her absolute command of the language. Parisian born and bred, Solene Pullman had to be the only Frenchwoman alive who wanted to be English. Not just any old English either. She'd married an Englishman and harboured stupendous delusions of grandeur.

Benjamin Pullman, a gentle, mild-mannered man, was head groundsman at one of the Oxford colleges and highly unlikely to be knighted for his services to grass-cutting and the eradication of lawn diseases like pythium, rust and snow mould.

But Mrs Pullman didn't let a tiny glitch like that get in the way of her ambition. As far as she was concerned, an English business and an English husband with links to a prestigious intellectual establishment was a good place to start. The only way was up. Rosie occasionally flirted with the idea of telling Solene she was related to the aristocracy just to see the look on her face, but knew she wouldn't stand up to the subsequent interrogation. Prying questions were the last thing she needed right now.

Mrs Pullman had sneered when Rosie stood mutely before her, refusing to rise to the bait. 'When you move to another country you have to re-set your watch,' she continued in a patronising tone. 'It might be half past seven in the morning in New York but here in England it most certainly isn't. If we are running a business then we have to be on time.'

Rosie remained silent. She remembered what Sir James Whitton had said on the first night she had ever met him. They had been talking about the intricacies of football and the World Cup. They had sat watching it on TV. The commentator had said that Paris was hosting the final that year. In his deep, dry voice, Sir James had quipped that the only thing the French should be allowed to host was an invasion.

Tired and stressed, Rosie felt her temper rise. 'Now listen, Solene, I –'

'Whatever happens, keep your temper. She isn't worth it.' She stopped dead as Cameron's voice surfaced in her mind. Almost his last words to her, standing in the driveway of their cottage with Valentina.

'I'm really sorry,' she finished lamely. 'I overslept.' Solene had arched her brows and continued to stare at Rosie, drumming her fingers on the door jamb. 'It won't happen again,' Rosie said finally through gritted teeth, forcing herself to look meekly at the floor. Mrs Pullman twisted her thin lips in a sour imitation of a smile and nodded at the wicker basket on the counter.

'Hurry along then, Rosie. We at Angel Cakes guarantee a prompt service to our customers. Here in England, punctuality counts!'

Rosie had lugged the basket out the back to the waiting bike, silently vowing that if Mrs Pullman uttered the words, 'Here in England', again in the next thirty seconds, she'd punch her lights out and to hell with the job. Perhaps the woman sensed this as she followed Rosie out because she simply leaned on the wall and watched without further comment as Rosie clipped the basket onto the handlebars with considerable difficulty, mounted up and pushed off.

Rosie pumped the pedals hard now, trying to make up a bit of time. She was halfway through her regular delivery route but still well behind schedule. At this rate she wasn't going to make it back for Mara and still manage the lunchtime deliveries on top. Fear spurred her on and she picked up her pace again, crunching the gears. The bike was one of the old grocery models with sit-up-and-beg handle-bars, made in the days before suspension and padded saddles. The large basket on the front made steering impossible and the narrow seat dug in to all the wrong places.

To take her mind off her aching backside and pass the time, Rosie had developed a game called 'Mrs Pullman Is . . .' The rules were simple. Every day she chose a letter and thought up as many words as she could, beginning with that letter, to describe her. It wasn't kind, but summoning up the lists helped Rosie to bite her tongue whenever Mrs Pullman decided to tear a strip off her.

Today's letter was P. Rosie indicated left and swung onto a side street. 'Mrs Pullman is . . .' she puffed. 'Pretentious. Preening.' The bike rattled over cobblestones, sending mini shock waves all the way up from Rosie's feet to her teeth. 'Petulant. Pathetic.' She stood up on the pedals, swerving to avoid a careless pedestrian. 'Proud. Promiscuous?' Her conscience whined. OK, so she didn't know her well enough to choose that one. 'Prudish, then.' That was safer. Rosie hit the brakes, jumped clear and ran alongside the bike for a few steps, steadying the basket with one hand as she brought the bike to a stop beside Brown and Tibbett's Book Emporium. She kicked the bike-stand down, grabbed a packet from the basket and dashed in.

'Morning Phil,' she gasped to the tubby man in his late thirties who appeared smiling from behind a stack of musty-smelling books. She held the packet out. 'Sorry I'm late.'

Phil Tibbett laughed and patted his midriff, where his shirt buttons strained to keep his paunch in check. 'Hardly wasting away, am I?' he chuckled affably. 'But come on Rosie, this isn't your usual grand entrance.'

Rosie sagged against the counter. 'Phil, don't make me. Not today.'

He wagged his finger at her. 'The formalities must be observed,' he insisted cheerfully. 'Come along now, out with it.'

Rosie groaned. 'Good morning, Angel Cakes delivery. Our baking is legendary, it tastes just heavenly.'

Phil sighed happily. 'That's more like it. Got time for a brew today?'

'No.'

'Madame Horror giving you a hard time, is she?'

Rosie nodded.

Phil came out from behind the counter and looked closely at her, noting the tension in her face. He was no fool and had realised early on in their acquaintance that

Rosie was concealing some kind of trouble in her life. The little American usually covered it with a bright smile and friendly banter but today the mask had slipped. 'Anything wrong?' he asked tentatively. Rosie nodded, unable to meet his eye.

'Everything.'

He laid a hand on her shoulder. 'Can I help?'

She shook her head, aching to trust someone. 'I just need to get back.'

'Best get on then,' he said with a genuine concern.

'Yep. See you later, Phil.'

He crossed to the window and watched as Rosie pedalled off unsteadily. For all her determination, she was a fragile thing, he thought and he wished she had confided in him. He might have been able to help and realised with a sudden shock how much he wanted to. There had been various women in Phil's life over the years, but he'd never really bothered too much. But Rosie – there was something different about her, a kind of joyful spontaneity despite her mysterious troubles. It was a quality that was sadly lacking in his life. Outside, Rosie reached the end of the street and disappeared from view. Phil shook his head and turned away.

Mara shifted irritably, twisting this way and that on the lumpy mattress. What time was it? Where was Abbott? She couldn't lie here all day waiting for her breakfast to arrive, for heaven's sake. She threw back the covers and swung her legs over the side of the bed, feeling for the floor. Her foot knocked against a bottle of pills, part of the debris from Rosie's fight with the alarm clock. The bottle rolled out of sight beneath the bed.

'No slippers either,' Mara tutted, levering herself carefully to a standing position. There was something different, something out of place but she didn't know quite what. It was as if every memory echoed in her head, every thought chasing the other.

A sense of unease blossomed in her mind as she stood there, staring around the bare room. There was something she ought to know, she realised; something she *did* know, something important . . . She felt sharper today, as though she'd been walking in fog and was at last beginning to emerge on the other side. It was . . . Mara clicked her tongue impatiently against the roof of her mouth as the answer slipped away again. There must be a new maid, she decided, crossing the room and unhooking her raincoat from its peg behind the door. No matter. She'd track Abbot down and get things straightened out. But first, she needed breakfast. Mara threw the door open and strode purposefully down the dingy hallway, where the front door stood invitingly ajar.

Rosie pedalled hard, puffing and blowing as she reached the brow of the hill. The road quickly levelled out and she slowed down, cycling one-handed as she fished in her pocket for her mobile.

Ten forty-seven. Right. Rosie did some quick mental calculations. She'd be home by 10.50. That gave her fifteen minutes with Mara, five minutes to call the doctor about possible day-care centres, twenty minutes to get back to Angel Cakes for lunchtime deliveries. She coasted into Sitwell Street, offering up a silent prayer that Mara was OK.

'*You're worrying about nothing,*' she told herself. '*Mara has probably woken up, made a cup of tea and settled down to watch daytime television.*' She knew the routine, even if Rosie hadn't been there to lead her through it. So maybe she wouldn't be dressed and she hadn't had her tablets –

'Her tablets!'

Rosie leapt off the bike and took the steps two at a time, leaving the bike sprawled on the pavement behind her. A volley of thoughts shot across her mind as she sprinted down the hallway, like bolts slamming home on a cell door. She hadn't given Mara her sedative. The doctor said she wasn't ready to come off them yet. Mara might be frightened, hysterical. Would she have found the note? Rosie burst into the flat.

'Mara? Mara!'

The room was empty. Mara had gone.

Chapter Eight

Revelation

'Open up! It's an emergency!' Rosie ran back and forth down the hallway, banging repeatedly on the doors of the other ground-floor tenants. The Japanese student, who would not fully have understood but would very politely have tried to help anyway, was at a lecture. The Classics student was still wallowing in an alcohol-induced sleep from the previous night and heard nothing.

Rosie sprinted up the stairs and hammered at every door on the first floor. She knew she was clutching at straws. Everyone would be out and about at this time of day.

Abandoning the idea abruptly, she clattered back down the staircase and stopped, realising the front door was still swinging wide. Of course. It had been that way when she had got home. She forced herself to stand still, though tears of fright were streaming down her face and the adrenalin pumping through her body clamoured for her to run. She lowered herself onto the bottom step, breathing slowly and deliberately.

In, hold it . . . and out. In, hold it . . . and out. 'All right now,' Rosie said aloud. 'You left the door open; someone else could easily have done the same. Mara's wandered out and got herself lost. So . . .' she trailed off. So what? She didn't want to call the police in, not yet. Mara could be just around the corner for all she knew, but Rosie needed to find her fast. She needed help. Pulling out her mobile, Rosie hit the speed dial and waited. 'Come on, come on!' Her foot tapped an urgent rhythm on the floor as she counted the rings. '*Be* there, please be there.'

❀   ❀   ❀   ❀

On the other side of Oxford, an elderly man was locking his front door. He settled his sun hat firmly on his head and turned to leave. At that moment, the phone began to ring inside his shabby apartment. 'Drat,' he muttered, fishing in his pocket for the keys. As he lifted them to the door, his hand cramped without warning and they slipped from his spasming fingers.

'Bother it!' He sat on the doorstep and methodically massaged his hand and forearm until the worst of it passed. He hoisted himself up and put the key back in the lock. The phone stopped.

'Typical,' the man grunted and set off for the second time. Three strides down the path, the phone rang again. He sighed and made as if to go back. But it was pension day and he wanted to avoid the afternoon queue at the post office. 'They'll ring back later if it's important,' he said to himself, swinging the battered wooden gate shut and heading briskly towards the city. If only his knees weren't giving him so much gyp, he could have cycled and been there in half the time, thought Abbott ruefully.

Alone in the stairwell of fifty-four Sitwell Street, Rosie hurled her mobile to the floor in frustration. She paced up and down, trying to calm her thoughts long enough to make a decision, but the anxiety was suffocating. She had to act. Where could she find help?

'To hell with it, I've got no choice.' Rosie slammed the door behind her, leapt onto the grocery bike and pedalled off, calling Mara's name as she steered her way towards the city centre.

The weather veered between warm and cold in the way that only the English climate can. It was like a charming but inde-cisive party host trying to please as many guests as possible. A strong breeze spliced through the August heat, buffeting the trees that lined the road and thoughtfully shepherding stray flocks of clouds across the sun at regular intervals. Mara glanced up at the sky and shivered as the sun vanished again. She belted her raincoat more tightly around her.

Something was definitely wrong.

Judging by the ache in her feet, she'd been walking for quite some time now. Mara still felt sluggish but the odd, foggy feeling in her head seemed to have lifted a little, revealing that she hadn't the faintest idea where she was going. There was no problem with that side of things; a good walk cleared your head, everybody knew that. One didn't have to be *going* anywhere, as such. No, the difficulty was that

behind this so-called fog lay a significant number of other
mental blanks and this was very troubling. Mara pursed her
lips. Old she may be, but senile she certainly was not.
Something was definitely wrong.

'And that's another thing,' Mara said to no one in particular, irritation causing her to speed up despite her sore feet,
'people are staring.' It wouldn't do at all. Spotting an empty
bus shelter on the opposite side of the road, Mara decided
the sensible thing was to sit down for five minutes, catch her
breath and approach the problem logically. She stepped off
the pavement into the road.

❀   ❀   ❀   ❀

Solene Pullman stood behind the counter of Angel Cakes,
staring furiously at the clock mounted high on the opposite
wall. It was parchment coloured with a wide, gold rim. A
ring of Botticelli-style cherubs chased round and round the
inner clock face, endlessly pursuing the black filigree hands.
Most people would find the clock unnecessarily large, even
intimidating. To Solene, it symbolised British Punctuality, the
adopted quality she prized above all others. The clock's artificial heart beat rhythmically into the ominous stillness
pervading the shop. Even the cakes seem to wait in quiet
obedience under Solene's glare.

The phone sliced abruptly through the silence, causing
Solene to jump. She snatched at the receiver, not taking her
eyes from the clock. 'Hello Angel Cakes, our baking is legendary, it – yes, I do apologise – no, we have your lunchtime
order, but we are experiencing a temporary hold-up and I –

really, there's no need to cancel – if you could just . . . hello? Hello?'

Madame Solene threw the receiver back onto its cradle and released a stream of very unladylike French at the clock. The cherubs smiled forgivingly. Solene ground her teeth. 'Thirty-eight minutes late,' she hissed, prowling from the counter to the door and back again. 'Thirty-eight minutes, Rosie Whitton. And counting. Make no mistake about *that*.'

At the other end of the line, Phil Tibbett forced himself to put the phone down gently. What he really wanted to do was bounce it off the ceiling a couple of times and finish off with a drop-kick through the front window of the Emporium, but he could see British Telecom taking a rather dim view of the manoeuvre. He could just imagine the conversation with the repair engineer.

'Are you able to describe the nature of the fault, Mr Tibbett?'

'Er – complete connection failure?'

'And when did you notice the problem?'

'Shortly after I ripped the phone from the socket and booted it through the window.'

'Ah. I see. Unfortunately sir, cathartic temper tantrums aren't covered in the terms of your line rental agreement.'

'Could you just double-check that with your supervisor?'

'I'm afraid not, Mr Tibbett.'

'How about if I beg?'

'Please don't, sir.'

Phil sighed heavily, trying to ignore the ache in his belly. What did he care about the sandwich order? There were half a dozen cafés within a five-minute radius of the book shop and most of them delivered. He shouldn't have lost his temper with Mrs Pullman, but he was worried when Rosie failed to turn up. He felt a fierce protective surge in his chest at the thought of the little American.

If that woman has upset her, I'll . . . I'll cancel my account permanently – oh. Damn. He puffed his cheeks out. *I've just done that, haven't I.* Phil struck his head with the palm of his hand. *Idiot! Now she'll get it in the neck because of you! And she won't be popping in twice a day now either.*

It was just as well that a young beautiful American woman wouldn't look twice at a fat old bookseller, Phil thought despondently. Otherwise he'd just have blown his chance big-time. He leafed miserably through a stack of Shakespeare plays waiting to be categorised and shelved. 'Where are you, Rosie?' he sighed as if it were the Amen of a prayer.

'Phil!'

Rosie crashed through the door, wild-eyed and dishevelled.

'Good grief!' Phil jumped backwards in fright, bumping into the shelf behind him and dislodging a couple of war poetry compilations.

'I need your help.'

'Anything.'

'Do you have a car?'

'Yes, it's out the back, I can –'

'Lock up. Let's go.'

She turned and ran towards the door. Phil stared after her, awestruck. Rosie glanced back and saw him standing motionless beside the counter. '*Now*, Phil!'

'Yes. Right. I'll just, er –' He realised he was dithering. 'Coming!'

Phil revved the engine on his battered Audi, trying to warm it up so it wouldn't stall every twenty feet. He glanced at Rosie, scrunched and tense in the passenger seat. She leant forward, hands clenched in her lap. The tired leather seat set her auburn hair off perfectly. This was it – his chance to play the Knight in Shining Armour, show her what he was really made of. *Say something, man.* Phil cleared his throat nervously as the car rolled forward, edging out into the traffic.

'I . . . you . . . that is –'

'What is it?' He felt himself wilting under the pressure of her gaze.

'You . . . don't have my sandwich on you, by any chance?'

'Excuse me?'

'My lunch order, you know . . .' he felt the blush burn its way from his collar right up to his eyebrows. 'Forget it.' He cleared his throat again to fill the excruciating silence. 'Where are we going?'

'I don't know yet. Just drive, will you?'

'Right.'

❀ ❀ ❀ ❀

Upon reaching the bus shelter, Mara found that it wasn't empty after all. A trio of teenage girls were huddled in one corner, taking it in turns to practise smoking. They jumped guiltily as Mara appeared and sat down beside them. The tallest girl snatched the cigarette from her waif-like friend and threw it to the ground.

'What d'you do that for?' whined the third girl, a dumpy character whose mother had made the ill-advised choice of a pleated skirt from the approved school uniform list. 'What's an old bag lady going to do?'

Mara eyed them closely for a few seconds, sizing them up. Bag lady, indeed! Who did these little flibbertigibbets think they were? She reached into the pocket of her raincoat.

'Oh *great*,' hissed the leader, 'she's going to report us now, you idiot.' The girls had removed their ties as a precaution against public denunciation, but it wasn't a fool-proof method. They shifted from foot to foot, preparing to run.

Mara smiled and calmly withdrew not the mobile phone they feared, but a lighter and a packet of cigarettes. She flipped the lid open, extracted a cigarette and lit up in one fluid movement. 'Gitanes,' she said, sitting back and exhaling a series of perfect smoke rings. The schoolgirls' eyes widened. Mara proffered the box towards them.

'Smoking's bad for you,' the waif muttered, in a ridiculous attempt at denial.

Mara nodded happily. 'Quite right. Sticks of sin, my mother called them.' The dumpy girl edged closer and cautiously took a cigarette.

'Can you teach me how to do that?' she asked, nodding at the smoky halo still hanging in the air.

Mara's eyes gleamed. 'Gather round.'

After a few minutes of intensive instruction, a companionable silence descended on the bus shelter, broken only by occasional bouts of coughing as the girls discovered that Gitanes were considerably stronger than Marlboro Lights. Mara sat propped against the back of the shelter with her eyes closed, swinging her legs to and fro. There was something she ought to be doing, she mused, but she couldn't quite remember what. Anyway, she hadn't had this much fun in years. Beside her, the waif fidgeted and made polite excuse-me noises.

'If you don't mind me asking – where are your shoes?'

'Hmm?' Mara opened her eyes.

'Your shoes,' the waif repeated. 'Why aren't you wearing any?'

Mara looked down at her feet in surprise.

'I – I don't know,' she said, staring around as though seeing her surroundings for the first time. 'Where are we?'

The girls exchanged anxious looks.

'Oxford,' said the tall girl.

'Oxford?'

❀   ❀   ❀   ❀

Abbott limped along the road, heavily favouring his left leg. His right knee had been throbbing for the last mile. 'Should have taken a taxi,' he grimaced. 'Damned arthritis.' Rounding the corner, he spotted a bus stop through the trees ahead. 'No, you can make it, man,' he coaxed himself. 'Keep going.' He struggled on for a few steps before reluctantly conceding defeat. 'Bus it is, then.' Abbott puffed into the bus shelter and sank gratefully onto the hard plastic seat.

At the other end of the shelter, some teenage girls were clustered around a mad-looking old woman. The poor creature had no shoes on and was evidently distressed but Abbott was hot, tired and in no mood to assist. He decided to ignore the unfolding drama. At that moment, one of the girls turned and looked at him in mute appeal. They were out of their depth. Abbott groaned inwardly. He levered himself slowly to his feet and hobbled over.

'Can I be of any assistance?' he asked politely. The girls stood back and the wild-haired woman lifted her head.

'Abbott?'

'*Madam!*'

❀   ❀   ❀   ❀

The Audi had been doing laps of the city for half an hour. There had been no sign of Mara. Phil drummed the fingers of one hand idly on the dashboard and cleared his throat noisily for the umpteenth time. It made Rosie want to scream. She clenched her teeth and focussed on scanning the street. Phil finally plucked up the courage to ask the question that had been trying to jump off his tongue from the moment Rosie careered into his shop.

'Rosie?'

'Yes?'

'Who are we looking for?'

'My mother-in-law.'

'I – didn't realise you were married.' His heart sank.

'I'm not, really.'

'Right.'

'It's complicated, OK? I can't explain.' She smiled crookedly at him, her eyes suddenly full of tears. 'I'm sorry, Phil. I'm being awkward and mean.'

'Don't apologise. I want to help,' he said, trying not to sound like a freak.

Rosie leaned across and laid a hand briefly on his arm. 'Thank you.'

'Hey, look, there's Angel Cakes,' Phil said, trying to change the subject. 'Wonder what Madame Horror's doing, eh?'

Rosie leaned even further towards him and, despite what she'd just said, Phil had the crazy notion that she was going to kiss him. Then he realised she was peering out of his side window at a black taxi pulling up at the kerb. An old man in a suit climbed gingerly out, his straw sun hat askew on his head. He stooped and reached back into the taxi. Rosie dug her fingers into Phil's arm.

'Ow!'

'Stop the car. Phil, stop the car!'

Rosie wrenched the door open and threw herself out. Phil braked hard as she ran straight into the road, heedless of the traffic. Her eyes were fixed on the unkempt woman emerging from the taxi. 'Mara!'

Mara clung to Abbott's arm as he hauled her upright. She turned at the sound of her name. The world slowed, everything blurring except the sight of Rosie, her Rosie, running full tilt towards her.

'Noooooooo!'

Abbott made a grab for her but Mara was already moving, launching herself from the pavement. There was a screech of brakes, the unnatural impact of flesh against metal, then the awful sound of nothing. Just silence, a car and a body in the road.

Chapter Nine

Exodus

At that very moment, Hugh Fenwick was sitting at an old mahogany writing desk in his study. It had belonged to his mother and to his grandmother before her. The heavy, ornately carved legs remained sturdy and the surface of the table carried the glossy sheen of fresh polish. Its age was only betrayed by the brass inkwell sunk into the wood in the style of an old school desk. Hugh used it to store paper clips.

The desk was piled high with correspondence and paper-work from the estate. One tenant had a grievance against another regarding boundary fences, last month's accounts needed verifying, harvest was almost upon them and a prompt yet accurate estimate of the yield was vital. They needed to be sure there was sufficient storage space if the weather broke. Hugh rubbed a tired hand across his eyes. There was some essential maintenance work waiting to be approved on several of the farms. He really ought to deal with that today.

After three years of running the estate, he still felt his father's shadow over everything. Hugh knew that he did a good job; it was just that his father had been so capable, so experienced. So loved, not least by Hugh. At forty, Hugh's black hair still displayed no hint of grey. Yet inside, there were days when he felt grey from head to toe, as though life had leached the colour from his soul.

He strode to the French windows and stood for a while, looking over the garden to the rolling Northumbrian hills beyond. He loved the family estate at Earleside and the wild, unfettered countryside of Alnwick. There were places where the land had grudgingly allowed itself to be shaped to human specifications, like the manicured rose garden beneath the window, but it would never truly be tamed. Hugh felt a sudden impulse to fling open the doors and slip out of the garden through one of the side gates. From there it was a short jog to the local riding stables. He could be out on the hills within the hour, riding wherever the mood took him. Nothing to contend with but the land, the horse and the wind, carrying with it the faint but ever-present tang of the sea. Freedom. Hugh glanced at the mounds of paperwork and groaned. He could force his body to sit at the desk, but it would do no good while his mind roamed the moor.

The door opened silently and a matronly housekeeper entered carrying a bundle of letters. She studied the man by the window with a kind of exasperated fondness, tutting inwardly at his patched brown cords and crumpled cotton shirt. He'd been the same as a lad, she remembered, always looking as though he'd just come in from the fields and somehow getting away with it. A man of his standing ought to dress more smartly, in her opinion, but there was a peculiar sense of rightness about Hugh. While you ought to see a scruffy man with tousled hair, you simply saw Hugh and knew instantly that he couldn't be any other way.

You'd have more chance of stealing the moon than making Hugh Fenwick be anything but himself. As *certain people* should have realised, the housekeeper thought darkly, stumping across the wooden floor. A lot of heartache could have been avoided. That was all forgotten now, perhaps, but forgiven? Not by her, not by a long chalk. Loyalty was deeply embedded in the Fenwick household.

'More work for you,' she grunted, slapping the letters down on the table. Hugh jumped.

'Mrs Drummond! I didn't hear you come in.'

'Didn't want to interrupt you,' sniffed the housekeeper, pointedly addressing the empty chair, 'since you're hard at work and all.' Hugh raised his hands defensively, but his grey eyes were mild.

'Just a short break.'

'And the rest, Shuggie.' He smiled at the childhood nickname, but didn't dare retaliate.

'Is that the post?' he asked, stretching a hand out hopefully.

'Aye. And you needn't get excited. If there was anything that looked like news, I'd have run all the way and you know it.'

Hugh scuffed a hand through his hair and dropped into the chair with a sigh. 'I know,' he said softly. 'I handled it all wrong.' There was a moment's silence. Mrs Drummond patted his arm awkwardly.

'You offered,' she said gruffly. 'That's what matters.'

Neither of them believed it. This cryptic exchange was the closest they'd come to discussing Hugh's cousin Mara since the funeral. There had been no word from her since, though Hugh had written fortnightly to repeat his offer of help. Mrs Drummond was well aware of that. She'd posted the letters.

'Better get on. Lunch at one o'clock sharp.'

'Thank you, Mrs Drummond.'

Hugh plucked a document from the desk and made a show of studying it as Mrs Drummond left the room, but as soon as he was alone again he tossed it aside and rested his head in his hands. His thoughts went spinning southwards, crossing the long miles to hover over the plundered shell of Carrington Hall. His conscience ached like a rotten tooth.

Rosie lay curled on her side in the narrow space between consciousness and oblivion. This had to be the most uncomfortable bed she'd ever lain in, she thought drowsily. She was cold and the pillow felt as if it were driving hundreds of tiny needles into her cheek. Somewhere close at hand was a persistent buzzing noise, like a badly tuned radio. Rosie couldn't make out what was being said, but neither could she shut the sound out. It was infuriating. She really ought to sit up and switch it off, but for some reason she was unable to move. Her body pressed down on the mattress, which dug painfully into her bones.

Suddenly a hand shot out of the darkness and fastened on her arm, gripping it tightly. Pain jolted through Rosie's body like an electric shock and she screamed in agony. The hand immediately released her but the pain remained, coursing up Rosie's arm in waves. Her eyes flew open. A few inches from her face, a pair of deep brown eyes stared intently back at her.

Cameron?

'You can't take her. Not Rosie, too. Not Rosie, too.' A woman's voice repeated the phrase over and over again, like a mantra.

'Mara?' Rosie's mouth felt rusty. There was blood on her lips.

Tears toppled from the brown eyes as the mantra changed. 'You came back. Thank you, thank you, Lord.'

Other voices cut in, clinical and detached. 'Move back now. This one onto the stretcher first.' Rosie cried out in pain as more hands took hold of her.

'Sedative please. Move back, sir. Move back.'

Rosie felt herself falling backwards, away from the scene of the accident. The brown eyes followed her into the darkness, tear-filled but candle-bright, holding on to the very last moment. In the instant before she passed out, Rosie knew that for better or worse, two people, not one, had come back that day.

Phil trudged through the corridors of the hospital, balancing three cups of vending machine tea on a tangerine-coloured plastic tray. He glanced anxiously at the tea. It already looked well on the way to being stewed, but he daren't speed up for fear of spilling the lot. Two hours after the accident his hands were still shaking.

'If it really is good for shock, I'll go back and buy up the entire stock,' he muttered as the liquid slopped dangerously close to the rim of the flimsy cups.

Phil was torn. He desperately wanted to go home, but didn't want to leave without seeing Rosie. It was clear he was intruding on very personal matters, though exactly what, he didn't know. Clearly an outsider, he felt like a stage-hand stumbling into the spotlight among the actors. Desperate to be of use, Phil had dived gratefully into the cultural safety net peculiar to British etiquette – whatever the occasion, whatever the problem, a cup of tea is always appropriate.

For the first time in his life, Phil found himself wondering what the equivalent action to 'a nice cup of tea' was elsewhere in the world – did a German mother, on seeing her teenage daughter burst through the door in floods of tears, reach calmly for a bratwurst and a hanky? Phil laughed aloud and immediately looked round guiltily. How could he be larking around while Rosie was lying unconscious?

'Shut up, you clown,' he said sternly. A passing doctor caught his eye and frowned. Phil wheeled round in panic. 'I didn't mean you!' he called to the man's retreating back. There was no reply. Phil's shoulders slumped. 'Just keep your mouth shut and deliver the tea,' he instructed himself. He reached the door of the private room and hesitated, listening for voices. Satisfied that he wasn't interrupting, he edged the door open with his hip and manoeuvred his way in.

'Hey, I'm the one who brings refreshments,' said Rosie weakly. 'Are you after my job or something?'

'You're awake!' Phil set down the tray and hurried to the foot of the bed, grinning like a fool. Rosie smiled up at him, flanked on either side by the elderly couple from the taxi. The woman seemed in a worse state than Rosie, but she sat determinedly upright in a wheelchair, clutching Rosie's hand as though to prevent her from wandering off.

'You'll live then?' Phil asked, taking in the cuts and bruises on Rosie's face and the heavy plaster cast encasing her left wrist.

'Oh, yes, it's nothing. Bit of a headache, that's all. It's my job I'm worried about.'

'You're not going back,' the frail lady said quietly.

'Absolutely right, Mrs . . . er...' Phil looked nonplussed. Rosie steeled herself for the introductions.

'Phil, Lady Mara Whitton, my mother-in-law,' she began. Mara inclined her head graciously. 'And this is Abbott, who was our butler. Abbott, Mara, this is my friend Phil. He runs a bookshop in town.' Abbott half-raised himself from his chair and made a slight bow. They waited politely but Phil simply stood there, choking on his reply.

Finally he burst out, 'Tea in a plastic cup?'

Mara smiled. Rosie rolled her eyes.

'I'm still me. Sit down.' She patted the bed.

Phil edged forward and lowered himself onto the edge of the mattress, his thoughts churning. *Lady Whitton*? She'd been in the press a couple of months ago, hadn't she? Something about a loss of assets – had there been a bereavement? He couldn't remember and it hardly seemed appropriate to ask. He'd have to look it up later on the net. Lady Whitton! Did that make Rosie a lady too, or a lady-in-waiting or something? Why was she selling sandwiches?

Rosie saw the distress in his eyes. 'Phil, relax. It's okay,' she said gently. 'They're just people.'

Phil nodded, still unable to speak.

Rosie turned her head carefully towards Abbott, trying not to wince. 'Now, getting back to what we were discussing earlier – there's no need to rush into anything. We're not going to pack up and ship out in a hurry just because of a little accident. We can still manage.'

'One-handed on a bicycle?' queried Abbott mildly. 'In any event, Miss Rosie, two months' thinking time is hardly rushing.'

'It's not just that. I turned the offer down.' Rosie's face twisted as she remembered the horrible encounter with Mara's cousin. 'The guy didn't mean it. He was just paying lip service, doing his sworn family duty or whatever. You weren't there, Abbott. It wasn't a genuine offer, believe me.'

'Four written invitations seems fairly genuine to me,' Mara murmured.

'You've told her? Today?' Rosie accused Abbott. 'Without asking me first?'

Abbott shrugged. 'The circumstances are somewhat altered,' he answered. 'You were indisposed, Miss Rosie and Lady Whitton . . . was not,' he finished, avoiding any direct reference to Mara's health.

'That's not the point!' Rosie spluttered. 'I asked you to filter the forwarded mail at the post office, not to – to –'

Abbott raised one eyebrow. 'Not to what? Furnish Lady Whitton with details of the correspondence directly addressed to her? Concerning matters directly relevant to this discussion?'

Rosie glared at him, but realised she was on dangerous ground and subsided.

Mara spoke up. 'The question is not whether we will accept, but when,' she said. 'We are going.'

'We're not welcome,' Rosie maintained.

'I don't agree,' replied Mara. She drew herself up, her chin lifted in the old way. 'But I make no claim on you, Rosie. I can go alone. You've done so much for me and this –' she gestured roughly at the hospital bed, her voice starting to rise, '– this is your reward? You're injured and unable to work and I – I . . .' Without warning, Mara's agitation peaked and the crippling confusion reasserted itself on her features. Abbott sat forward, instantly alert. Mara rallied, clawing her way back to lucidity. '. . . I want to go home. My real home,' she finished. She slumped down in her wheelchair and covered her eyes with one hand.

Phil remained quiet, a spectator to what should have been a private affair. He had observed the whole conversation like a tennis rally and saw a final silent exchange pass between Abbott and Rosie. He knew Abbott had won the point. Rosie stretched out her good arm and gently stroked Mara's hair.

'Where you go, I go,' she said. 'That was the deal.'

Mara made no reply. Clearly, all was not yet well.

Phil stood up, suddenly imbued with an uncharacteristic sense of purpose. 'Lady Whitton, allow me to escort you back to your room.'

'Thank you,' said Mara, her voice faint with exhaustion. Phil grasped the wheelchair and steered it towards the door.

'How will we get there?' asked Rosie. The question was addressed to Abbott, but it was Phil who answered.

'I'll take you. I don't care where it is or how far,' he said over his shoulder, not yet ready to say goodbye. 'Just tell me where and when.'

'Northumberland. Next week, if the doctors allow it,' Abbott replied swiftly.

'Done,' said Phil, his heart breaking at the utterly dejected look on Rosie's face.

'But my job!' she protested.

'I'll take care of it,' Phil said and closed the door before she could change his mind.

'It's settled then,' said Abbott. Rosie turned her head away, closing her eyes in defeat.

Later that day, Mrs Drummond left her work in Earleside's kitchen and went to inspect the new girl's handiwork in the adjacent staff office. No longer able to do the heavy cleaning work herself, she wanted to be quite sure her standards were maintained. She peered at the carpet, then ran a finger along the shoulder height mantelpiece. It came away covered in dust. Mrs Drummond frowned.

'If you want something done,' she moaned, making her way over to the desk to examine the wood. 'Looks clean enough, but . . .' she bent over the surface and gave an experimental sniff. 'No polish.' As she braced both hands on the table and prepared to push herself upright, a flash of red caught her eye from beneath a sheaf of papers. Mrs Drummond lifted them aside and found the office answer machine. 'Oh. One of *them* things,' she thought suspiciously.

Mrs Drummond didn't trust answer machines on the grounds that you didn't know who you were talking to. You could leave a message for someone and for all you knew, any Tom, Dick or Harry could listen to it at the other end. It was like inviting someone to eavesdrop on you. Mrs Drummond hesitated. Euan, the estate manager, had taken the day off so she ought to answer it. She pressed a few buttons on the machine at random. Nothing happened.

'Stop winking at me,' she told it and gave it another prod. There was a click and a disembodied voice spoke into the room. Mrs Drummond stood very still. When the machine clicked off, she reacted as though hearing the starter's gun in a race. All thoughts of polish and cleaning were abandoned as she ran down the corridor at full steam, bellowing as she went. 'Mr Fenwick! Fetch Mr Fenwick!'

On the day of the exodus, Rosie wore her defeat like a fashion statement. It was tightly wrapped around her closed face like a scarf, trailing across her slumped shoulders to tangle about her dragging, reluctant feet. She sat hunched over her broken wrist on the bottom step of number fifty-four, staring at nothing. Sitwell Street was quiet that morning. The Audi gleamed by the kerb, freshly washed and valeted for the occasion. An old trailer had been attached to the tow bar, its contents covered with a frayed tarpaulin. Not ideal, but the best Phil could come up with at short notice. He emerged from the house with the last few odds and ends from the flat. Rosie watched as he half-climbed into the back of the car, stowing them haphazardly on the back seat. They were leaving so much behind.

Phil backed out awkwardly and joined her on the step. They sat in silence for a few moments as Phil rehearsed his speech. With the help of Google and a few back copies of the local newspaper, he'd found out an awful lot in a short space of time. Not everything, but enough to make sense of Rosie Whitton and her tragic situation. He took a deep breath.

'You don't want to go, do you?'

'No.' Rosie stared straight ahead.

'Your mother-in-law seems to be on the mend.'

'Yes.'

Phil gathered himself, knowing there was little hope but driven to speak anyway. 'You don't have to go.'

'I know that.'

'I mean, you could stay here, with me. If — if you wanted.'

There was a note of desperation in his voice. It punctured Rosie's brooding thoughts. Too late, she realised the danger and turned to him, aghast. It was too late. He leaned towards her and unexpectedly kissed her on the lips. It was clumsy and awkward like a teenage first time.

'Oh Phil, I — if I've given you the wrong impression . . . I can't . . . it isn't . . .'

Mortified, he cut across her. 'No, it's fine. Absolutely fine. Just wanted to, you know, make the offer. I realise it hasn't been long since . . .' He focused his gaze on a small hole in the left knee of his jeans. 'Not a problem . . . always seem to get it wrong . . . just read too many books.'

Rosie's cheeks were burning with shame.

'Have I led you on?' she asked as the words stuck in her throat.

'No.' Phil stumbled awkwardly on the word. 'You've been great. Best sandwiches I have ever had.'

She turned to face him and tried to smile.

'Phil, listen to me. I have to be with Mara. She needs me and – and – she's all I have left.'

'Of your husband?' He said as he raised his head and looked her in the eye.

Rosie flinched but didn't look away. 'Maybe that's part of it, yes. I've nothing to offer, Phil.'

'You've got everything to offer. Your whole life ahead of you . . . Rosie, it's not all over.' The words echoed in her heart. It was as if Cameron was speaking to her.

Rosie shook her head, her green eyes bright with emotion. They stared at each other in silence. It was Phil who looked away first.

'I just wish . . .' she said, as the breeze blew about her feet.

He stood up with a sad smile and offered Rosie his hand. 'Friends?'

'You bet.' She grasped his hand and hauled herself to her feet.

'Better get this show on the road, then, eh?'

'Sure thing.'

Rosie trudged to the car, her jumbled feelings twisting into a tight knot in her chest. Her wrist throbbed and she was glad of the distraction. Abbott appeared in the doorway with Mara. Rosie watched as Phil hurried up the steps to take her other arm. Dear, sweet Phil. She felt cruel and wretched at the same time.

Above all, she hated goodbyes.

Abbott settled Mara into the front seat and crouched down, speaking a few quiet words of farewell. He clasped Mara's hand in a gesture that said much more than his words. He stood up with painful care and shuffled round to face Rosie. She groped for the right thing to say, something that would tell how much she owed him. Nothing came.

'Thanks for everything, Abbott.'

'It was nothing, Miss Rosie.'

Rosie was too tired to argue the point. She reached for his hand. Abbott jerked it back and rummaged in his jacket. He withdrew a small package, clumsily wrapped in brown paper and string. 'This belongs to you. An oversight with the packing.'

Rosie accepted the parcel without comment and stuffed it into her bag. She squeezed Abbott's hand and turned away hastily. 'Goodbye, then. Take care.'

'Madam?' For the first time ever, Rosie heard a note of anxiety in Abbott's voice. She paused, one leg already in the back of the Audi. 'Don't be angry with me. This is for the best, you know.'

Rosie's throat burned with the effort of containing her tears. 'It's not you, Abbott. I'm angry with myself.' She ducked into the car and pulled the door shut. 'Go, Phil.'

The Audi hiccoughed into life at the third attempt. 'Come on, old girl.' Phil revved the engine madly. 'Oh – not you, Lady Whitton.' Rosie's wrist gave a sudden, sharp twinge. She pulled the package out of her bag and tore off the paper. Four slim volumes spilled out and slid across the seat as the car moved off. Rosie burst into tears.

'Stop the car. Phil, stop the car!'

The brakes squealed. 'Not again. Watch where you're going!' shouted Phil as Rosie threw herself out of the car and pelted back down the road. Standing alone by the steps of the house, Abbott watched her running towards him. Rosie skidded to a halt and flung her good arm round the old man, crying into his shoulder.

'Cameron's desert island books. Thank you.'

Abbott patted her back uncomfortably. 'Miss Rosie, my suit . . .'

Rosie stood back, laughing through her tears. 'Will you do one last thing for me?'

'Of course,' Abbott replied.

'Tell me your name.'

'My name?' He looked at her in confusion.

'Your real name.'

Abbott gave a tiny shrug. 'It's Titus.'

'Well, then.' Rosie stood on tiptoe and kissed him on the cheek. 'I love you, Titus Abbott.'

The old butler's face creased in a smile of pure delight. He raised a hand to his cheek and held it there, taking the memory of the kiss into his fingers as Rosie jogged back to the waiting car.

'Goodbye, Madam,' he whispered, as the car pulled out of sight. 'God speed.'

Chapter Ten

Nunc Dimittis Servum Tuum

The countryside flashed by in a green blur as the Audi battled with the Friday afternoon traffic, made worse because it was the end of the school holidays. People carriers accounted for at least half of the other vehicles, driven by haggard-looking parents, their children's faces pressed up against the windows, amid a sea of sleeping bags, toys and badly packed suitcases.

'They look like they're drowning,' Phil said, swerving suddenly to avoid a lorry. The trailer lurched and swung out behind the Audi, almost wobbling into the fast lane. Dozing in the back, Rosie struck her head against the window with a resounding crack. Mara and Phil winced.

'Ow!' Rosie sat up groggily, rubbing her temple.

'Sorry about that,' Phil said cheerfully. 'Shouldn't lean too hard against that door, by the way. The catch isn't very secure.' Rosie loosened her seatbelt and edged further across the back seat. She heard an ominous rattling noise and glanced apprehensively out of the rear window, but the trailer was still there, one corner of the tarpaulin flapping around like a broken wing.

'Where are we?' she asked Phil.

'A little way past Newcastle.'

'Not far now,' added Mara, craning her neck round the head-rest to smile at her daughter-in-law.

Rosie smiled back at her, taking careful note of Mara's appearance. She looked tired and older than her years, but the hospital doctors had said she was 'on the road back to health'. There had been a marked improvement in the week following the accident – the periods of confusion were undoubtedly reducing as Mara's memory returned. The psychiatrist had spoken very positively about Mara's recovery, but tempered her words with a sobering forecast of 'difficult periods and temporary relapses' as the grieving process began in earnest. 'Just take it a day at a time,' she had advised, signing the hospital discharge papers and handing Rosie a bundle of prescriptions.

It was going to be a long, hard road back in more ways than one. Rosie stared blindly out of the window, no longer registering the picture-postcard landscape. In her mind she saw again the little country church where James Whitton had been a chorister in his youth. The intimate, well-tended graveyard reaching around either side of the church building like two great arms, so that the dead appeared to embrace the living. Rosie stood once more in the shade of a great sycamore tree overhanging the low boundary wall, as Mara knelt beside the three closely grouped marble headstones. Abbott watched from a respectful distance.

Rosie had looked on as Mara's body shook with the knowledge of her newly-awakened grief. She dug her fingers into the fresh turf beneath her as she wept, then slowly closed her hands and raised them to her face. Rosie approached then and knelt silently beside her. Mara began to rock to and fro, fists pressed forcefully against her eyes. 'Mara?'

'It's over,' Mara whispered, uncurling her fists to stare at the handfuls of earth cupped in her palms. She splayed her fingers, letting the soil trickle away through the cracks. 'They're gone. How can life hold anything but bitterness for me now?'

Rosie shook her head adamantly. She took Mara's filthy hands in hers and reached for the words she knew Mara needed to hear. 'It's not over, for them or for us. One day –' she faltered, but willed herself on, '– one day we'll see them again. That's what your faith teaches. But we must go on. I'll always be your daughter.'

They had knelt together on the damp grass as Mara drew strength from Rosie's courage. Strength enough to stand, to be led gently from the graveyard. Strength enough to say goodbye. As they walked away, Rosie felt as if she was sinking into the ground with every step, bent under the weight of her own hypocrisy. Even as she held Mara tight and spoke words of comfort and hope, she cast one, anguished look back over her shoulder to the place where her own heart was buried.

'The Lord is close to the broken-hearted and saves those who are crushed in spirit.' Rosie said, remembering the words of the psalm.

Life *was* bitter and her words were empty of meaning. Rosie didn't believe in anything much any more. There was no room for a loving God. He had been silent for too long, hiding in the shadows of her grief, kept out by the sadness and anger.

'Rosie?' Phil's voice summoned her back. He was watching her in the rear view mirror, his chubby face tight with concern. Rosie wiped away her tears and swiftly ordered a smile onto her face.

'Right here.'

'Do you need anything? A stop, or . . .?'

'No, I'm fine. You watch the road, I'm enjoying the scenery,' she said. 'Beautiful, isn't it, Mara?'

'Wait until you see the real Northumberland,' Mara replied. Rosie was pleased to hear the eagerness in her voice. The further north they drove, the more Mara's spirits seemed to lift.

Maybe this is for the best after all, Rosie thought, rubbing her hand where the plaster cast had begun to itch. She'd have to swallow her pride for now but once her arm was fixed, she would make sure they were independent. Rosie didn't intend to rely on this Mr Fenwick and his grudging charity a minute longer than absolutely necessary. There were bound to be plenty of jobs in the area. She conjured up an image of Cameron and held it before her like a battle standard. In her mind, she saw his old, confident smile and heard his teasing words.

'You go, Brooklyn girl.'

'I won't let you down, Cam,' she whispered.

Hugh Fenwick roved aimlessly about the kitchen, waiting for the kettle to boil on the Aga. After a while, he began to measure his steps across the worn flagstones. Twenty paces from the Aga to the pantry door at the far end of the room. Quarter-turn. Surely they would arrive soon. Nine paces to the back door. Quarter-turn. Twenty paces to the fridge. Perhaps they'd got lost? Turn, nine paces back to the Aga. Check the kettle. Start again.

The door opened a crack and an attractive woman with a sleek blonde bob stuck her head into the room. 'Hugh!'

'Hmm?'

'How long does it take to make a cup of tea? We've been waiting quarter of an hour upstairs.'

'Sorry, Charlotte. I forgot to put the kettle on.' Hugh sat down at the long pine table in the centre of the room.

'Where's your housekeeper anyway?'

'Sorting out the Dower House for our guests,' he mumbled. The kettle began to whistle. Hugh jumped up. Charlotte grabbed his arm and forced him back down.

'Stay there. I'll do it. And stop that,' she added as Hugh ran his hands distractedly through his hair. 'You're making yourself look like a wild man from the hills.'

Hugh laughed, his face transformed by his smile.

'But that's exactly what I am, Charlotte,' he said.

'Well. Perhaps,' she allowed. 'But we don't want *them* thinking that, do we?' She loaded up a tray with teapot, biscuits and tea-cups and handed it to Hugh. 'Come on. Alastair will think we've fallen into a black hole at this rate.'

Hugh followed her out into the hallway and up the stairs. Charlotte's cream kitten heels tapped an efficient staccato on the wooden floor as she marched in the direction of the drawing-room, her navy trouser suit rustling. Charlotte and

Alastair Alderson were his best friends. He'd met Alastair at prep school and remained close to him over the years. When Charlotte burst onto the scene she had slotted right into the friendship. Most of Hugh's limited free time was spent with them.

Charlotte held the door open and ushered Hugh into the drawing-room, which was decorated in delicate blues and creams. Alastair was sunk deep into an armchair, his tan brogues casually kicked off.

'What kept you?' he complained. 'A man could die of thirst in here.'

'Don't whinge, Alastair,' said Charlotte as Hugh set the tray down onto a low glass-topped coffee table. 'We've got important business to discuss.' She poured the tea, handed it round and settled onto the couch.

'Now ... Mara we know. This place was like home to her, once upon a time. No problem there . . . But the young widow, the American girl.' Charlotte raised an eyebrow, 'You say she's a bit volatile?'

Hugh nodded, the memory of Rosie punching Valentina at the funeral still fresh in his mind.

'Definitely. And very proud, I think. Easily offended.' He rested his elbows on the table, cupping the delicate teacup in both hands. 'What do you think?' he asked anxiously. Charlotte sipped her tea reflectively.

'Mmm. Well, they've had a bad time of it. They'll need their space. Don't crowd them.'

'Right.' Hugh said.

'But you want them to feel welcome . . .' interrupted Alastair between noisy slurps of his tea.

'Absolutely,' agreed Hugh.

'So don't embarrass them,' said Charlotte. 'They won't want charity.'

Hugh frowned. 'But they're practically destitute. They *need* my help.'

Charlotte rolled her eyes. 'Yes, but think, Hugh. When you've got nothing, dignity is everything. It's all that's left.'

'You're right.' Hugh sat back, gazing up at the ceiling. How could he give help that didn't look like charity and give them space while making it clear that he was there if needed? Be close, but distant at the same time? Suddenly it came to him. 'Euan!'

Alastair raised an eyebrow. 'Turnbull?'

'Yes. He can look after them. And – and they can work on the estate. That way . . .' Hugh paused, his mind working through the implications, '. . . they'll earn their keep and it won't look as though I'm playing the great and generous Lord of the manor.'

Charlotte looked doubtful. 'It might work, I suppose, if you put it to them in the right way. It could only be a good thing. But go carefully, Hugh. Euan can be . . .' she tried to think of the source of her uneasiness. Nothing specific came to mind. She looked to her husband for support.

'Well. He isn't you,' said Alastair lamely.

'That's exactly the point,' replied Hugh. 'He's the estate manager, my deputy. It's the perfect solution.' He drained his teacup and stood up. 'As a matter of fact,' he said, 'I think I had this notion at the funeral. I may even have mentioned it to them at the time.'

Alastair's jaw dropped. Charlotte's hand froze halfway to the biscuit plate and a look of incredulity passed between them. '*At the* . . .? And, err, what did they think of the idea?' she asked carefully, a custard cream teetering in mid-air.

Hugh shrugged. 'I can't remember. To be honest, I'd forgotten all about it. Listen, I'm going to find Euan right away. Make yourselves at home.' He strode off.

Charlotte stared at his retreating back in disbelief. 'Men,' she scoffed, pouring herself a fresh cup from the teapot. 'A bit volatile, indeed! Lucky she didn't knock him out.' She glanced at her husband and saw that he was still speechless. She reached across the coffee table and tapped him on the knee. 'Close your mouth, darling, and drink up. We need to be off.'

❀   ❀   ❀   ❀

The Audi stopped at a lonely crossroads on a country road. Rosie and Phil got out and spread the old map over the bonnet. 'Right,' said Phil, poring over the faded paper. 'If we're *here*,' he jabbed a finger at a minuscule spot on the map, 'then it's got to be left.' Rosie leaned across him, tracing the route with a finger.

'Phil, I really don't think it can be.' Rosie pointed at the left hand road. 'Check it out. It's nothing but a dirt track.' She crossed the road to examine the old wooden signpost, but it was so weather-beaten that the writing was illegible.

'Trust me, Rosie,' Phil called. 'It's left.'

'Why don't we ask someone?' she countered.

'OK, those sheep look rather helpful – what about them?'

'Well, what do you suggest?'

'We go left.'

'It's not left!'

Mara leaned out of the car window to get a better view. 'I think I recognise this spot,' she said thoughtfully. They turned to her expectantly. 'Left,' she said firmly.

'Ha!' Phil smirked at Rosie and began stuffing the map back into his jacket.

'Whatever,' Rosie grumbled as she slouched back to the car.

They drove along the track for quarter of an hour, jolting from one pothole to the next. 'This is wrecking my suspension,' Phil said as the Audi bounced over a stray rock and ploughed straight into another puddle. Rosie bit back a sarcastic reply. They were all tired and hungry.

'We're almost there!' Mara cried excitedly. 'Just look at the rhododendrons, Rosie. Northumberland's famous for them. Stunning, aren't they?' Rosie could barely hear her over the noise of the trailer crashing along behind them. They rounded a bend and saw an old, rambling house looming up against the skyline. 'There it is!'

Rosie squinted through the glare of the afternoon sun. There was nothing of the form and beauty of Carrington Hall in this place. The various buildings and outhouses straggled to either side of the main house, seemingly at random, as though they'd been flung from a giant catapult and taken root wherever they fell. It looked beautiful and yet barren. So different from Oxford, so different from New York. The sky was deep blue and cloudless.

Rosie felt an impulse to claw the door open, sprint back to the crossroads and hitch a lift from the first person who stopped. Destination: anywhere but here.

'Get real, Rosie,' she muttered under her breath. 'You'd starve to death waiting. Note to self – learn to speak Sheep as soon as possible – there's going to be no one else to talk to round here.'

On top of everything else, she'd have to turn vegetarian. Come to think of it, they hadn't even passed a sheep for a while, let alone anything else. Rosie turned to look out of the rear window and wailed in horror. 'Phil!'

❀   ❀   ❀   ❀

Hugh found his estate manager in the old barn, where the hay bales were stored at harvest. Euan Turnbull looked up as Hugh approached him. 'Just reviewing the storage space,' he said cheerfully. 'Something wrong?'

Hugh tried to relax his shoulders and leaned against the wall. He'd been so delighted when he'd first thought of Euan as the answer to his problem that he hadn't even considered how to put the idea across. The pair of them had regular meetings but never one of this kind. Hugh considered how to reply.

'Well – not wrong, exactly. Actually, I have a little job for you.'

'I'm listening,' Euan said.

'Well, as you know, my father's cousin and her daughter-in-law will be arriving shortly. Remember, you met them at the funeral,' he began. As Hugh went on to explain the needs of his guests, his recent conversation with Alistair and Charlotte and finally his proposal for Euan, he didn't notice the other man's blue eyes narrow, nor how his freckled face darkened with displeasure.

'So what do you think?'

Euan looked distracted. 'What do you think, Euan?' Hugh repeated.

'Look, Hugh,' Euan sighed. 'It's harvest time and, quite frankly, I'm up to my eyes. We all are. I'm sorry for them and all, but I haven't got time to spend holding their hands when there's work to be done. I've enough on with the tenants, you know that.'

'I appreciate that, Euan. But this is a very delicate situation. I guarantee it would only be for a few weeks. They'll soon find their feet. And anyway,' Hugh continued, 'I can take on some of your work. The harvest ball, perhaps?'

'I don't need any help, thanks,' Euan replied, an angry flush making his complexion clash unattractively against his cropped red hair. 'I'm on top of it.'

'So what's the problem then?' Hugh asked, folding his arms.

'I'm just saying it's not reasonable to expect –' Euan broke off as a loud bang reverberated around the yard, followed by a tremendous clattering. 'What the hell's that?'

Hugh ran to the barn door to find the yard buzzing with noise as staff appeared from every direction, seeking the source of the commotion, Mrs Drummond was first to shoot out of the double-fronted oak doors of the house. A rust-coloured Audi juddered through the gate, back-firing repeatedly. Silence fell as it came to a stop in the centre of the yard. All eyes were drawn to the wounded trailer lagging behind. The tarpaulin sprawled on the ground, held on by one remaining knot. A ragged assortment of clothes and possessions bled in a steady trickle back along the track as far as the eye could see.

Shading his eyes with one hand, Hugh thought he could see a pastel blue dressing gown impaled on a bush at the point where the track dipped out of sight behind the hill. On the gate was a large pair of pink pants, comfortable, but certainly not for display. They hung from the latch, swinging like a flag. Someone tittered and before Hugh could speak or move to stop it, laughter was rippling through the watching crowd.

The car door was thrown open and Rosie clambered out in her faded jeans and crumpled sweater. Hugh gave a start at the sight of her injured arm. He wondered whom she must have punched to get such an injury.

The laughter was quickly hushed behind raised hands as Rosie tossed her hair back and stared around the yard, her eyes defying anybody to mock her. She looked magnificent, beautiful and so out of place.

Hugh strode forward, glaring at his staff.

'All right, everyone. You've got a lot of work on at the moment. Don't let me keep you.' He turned towards Rosie but Euan cut in ahead of him, suddenly all smiles and hand-shakes.

'Euan Turnbull. Good to see you again, Rosie. I'll be helping you to settle in. Anything you need, just come to me. My door's always open.' He nodded at the dispersing crowd. 'And don't worry about that lot. Everyone goes about in flocks here – it's the country way.' Rosie laughed. 'That's better,' Euan grinned. 'Now, you look tired – how about a cup of tea? Then I'll show you round, if you like. What happened to your arm? How's the other fella?'

Rosie looked over at Hugh, her eyes hard; he hadn't changed since the funeral. He stepped forwards and opened his mouth to speak, but Euan was already ushering her towards the house.

'Euan!' Hugh called, but Euan kept walking and twisted one hand behind his back to give Hugh the thumbs up. Rosie didn't look back. Hugh stared after them irritably. What was that all about? The way she'd looked at him . . .

'Hugh?' Mrs Drummond was beside him, one arm around Mara.

'Mara,' Hugh shook her hand warmly. 'How are you?' Mara smiled sadly and gave a little shrug, as if to say, 'What do you expect?' Hugh could have kicked himself.

'Hugh, Mara's tired,' said Mrs Drummond quickly. 'I'll take her straight to the Dower House.'

Hugh stood back. 'Of course. Thank you.' The yard was nearly empty now. Hugh shoved his hands in his pockets and kicked angrily at a loose stone. It hadn't gone how he'd planned.

'Err, hello there?' Hugh spun round and found himself face to face with the driver of the Audi, a fat, kindly looking man. 'Phil Tibbett,' he said, pumping Hugh's hand vigorously. 'Friend of Rosie's from Oxford.'

'Pleased to meet you,' Hugh said mechanically, staring up at the house. He ought to go and introduce himself properly. Phil looked back down the track and sighed.

'Suppose we'd better make a start on collecting that lot up, eh?' he said. Hugh looked blank. 'The luggage,' Phil added, indicating the half-empty trailer. 'It's not as bad as it looks. I think we only lost the tarpaulin on the last half mile or so. Pot holes are like craters here, aren't they? Hop in. I'll drive.'

'Right, right. I'll, err . . .' Hugh looked about for assistance, feeling slightly panicked at the thought of retrieving his cousin's underwear from the roadside. It felt inappropriate. But the estate staff had obediently vanished and Phil was already coaxing the Audi back to life. Hugh gave up and got in the car. Introductions would have to wait.

Chapter Eleven

Threshing

The sitting-room of the Dower House was not a pleasant place to spend an evening. If you looked carefully, there were signs of a recent spring-clean – the curtains had been washed, the rugs beaten and the fireplace swept out – but cobwebs trailed from the cornicing and the scuffed floorboards bore the hasty tracks of a broom where the dirt had been pushed into the corners.

In every alcove the wall-mounted light fittings were shrouded with tasselled lampshades in dusky pink. They illuminated suspicious-looking damp patches on the faded floral wallpaper. The mismatched furniture had been covered with multi-coloured crochet blankets and plaid throws in an effort to smarten the place up. It could have been vintage chic, but it was more like a junk shop jamboree. There was also a peculiar smell, as though a large rat had died after being wrapped in mothballs. The electricity was off until the morning, apparently. This was an oversight but Rosie liked the charm of several candles in every room – even one perched precariously on the cistern of the loo.

In the candlelight, Rosie knelt on the home-made rag rug by the fireplace, coughing fitfully. Her throat felt coated with dust. She bent cautiously towards the fire, prodding at the glowing lumps of coal with a poker. When Euan had done this earlier the effect had been immediate, but Rosie's attempt produced nothing but a brief shower of sparks from the embers. 'Argh!' She rocked back on her heels, shielding her face.

The poker struck the hearth with a clang as clouds of smoke billowed into the room. Rosie glanced anxiously at the ceiling, but there was no sound from the little bedroom upstairs. She stood up, dusting the ash from her jeans. 'Well, you're freezing to death but at least Mara's asleep. Count your blessings, Rosie,' she told herself. The fire smouldered and the smoke refused to escape up the chimney. Rosie bent down and peered up the flue. There, in the shadows, she was sure she could see something stuck. It looked like a rolled up bedspread or bundle of papers. Taking the poker, she prodded the blockage until it moved.

There was a sudden black avalanche that spilled out of the chimney, dousing the fire in soot and covering Rosie. It crackled and filled her nose and ears. She sighed.

Hand on hip, Rosie surveyed the dismal surroundings.

'I just want to go to bed,' she said out loud, dusting the soot from her face. But she was full of nervous energy, still wired from the stresses of the day. When she had cleaned up the mess, she pulled a crocheted blanket off one of the armchairs and wrapped it round her shoulders, tucking the corners awkwardly into the collar of her T-shirt to keep it in place. That would have to do.

Rosie wasn't used to a house that made so much noise. What wind there was whistled across the chimney as the floors creaked above her. The back door rattled on its hinges. It shook as if someone was outside trying the latch. She hated feeling so insecure – even with the bolts on the door.

The back door rattled again. Rosie jumped.

'Is someone there?' she called.

There was no reply. Rosie heard soft footsteps outside in the dark. They scraped on the stone step. The door moved. Someone was pushing against it. Rosie picked up the poker and crept towards the door, her heart hammering. She listened at the door, sure she could hear someone breathing painfully on the other side. It was as if they were wheezing. Then came three long, deliberate, loud taps at the door. It was like the banging of stone against the wood.

As she reached for the doorknob, something heavy bumped against the other side of the door. Rosie stifled her squeak of panic and leaned the poker quietly against the wall.

She grasped the doorknob and began a silent countdown. *Three . . . two . . . one . . .*

'Who's there?' she bellowed, flinging the door open, brandishing the poker threateningly in the air. 'Stay where you are!'

Something large and stinking butted her in the stomach, knocking her to the floor. It towered over her and then licked her face.

'Goat?' Rosie murmured as she pushed the beast away and out of the house. 'You've got to be kidding me.' She peered out into the darkness and saw a herd of frightened goats cowering against the wall. Rosie sank onto the doorstep and laughed, taking in great gulps of night air. 'We're being burgled by a goat? Mom will never believe this.' She leaned against the door frame, her laughter giving way to tears. It was all too much. The goat trotted up and butted her companionably on the shoulder. Rosie flapped her hand at it. 'Go on, go home. Find a field.' The Nubian looked up at her with huge, stupid eyes. 'I mean it. You're not coming in here.' She rose from the step and gave the creature a little shove. It bleated and ambled away. Rosie stood for a few moments longer, trying to breathe herself calm.

'Rosie?' Rosie took a step backwards to see Mara's face at an upstairs window. 'What's going on?'

Rosie waved. 'It's okay Mara, go back to sleep. I'm just taking a look around,' she called. Mara opened the window and gazed down, her eyebrows arched.

'Oh, really? Dressed up as Superman's Granny?' Rosie looked down at herself and laughed. She did look pretty odd, armed with a poker and wearing the crochet blanket like a cape, the remnants of soot like a Zorro mask on her face. On the other hand, explaining would make her look even more ridiculous.

'OK, I'm coming in now. Goodnight.' She started up the steps.

'And Rosie?' Mara leaned out of the window.

'Yes?'

'Don't talk to the goats, dear. You don't know where they've been.'

'I'll keep it in mind.' Rosie locked and bolted the door, listening to Mara chuckling to herself upstairs. She smiled as she worked her way about the room, pulling curtains and blowing out the candles. It had been worth the fright just to see a flash of Mara's trademark wit — a good sign.

As she drew the curtains on the last window, Rosie caught sight of a distant torchlight bobbing along the track. 'Probably a shepherd looking for that dumb beast.' She felt her way across the room to the stairs and climbed wearily up to bed.

Hugh stopped at the dry-stone wall that encircled the Dower House's small garden. He dipped his torch so that the beam struck the house at its base. The lights had gone out while he was still some distance away and he knew he'd missed his chance again. No matter. He hefted a large wicker basket in one hand and set it down on the doorstep. After a moment's thought, he pulled a scrap of paper from his pocket, scribbled a few lines and wedged it into the side of the basket. 'That should do it. They'll find it in the morning,' he mumbled. He made his way quietly back to the track and set off on the half-mile walk home.

❀   ❀   ❀   ❀

The following morning, Rosie woke up cramped and stiff after a restless night. Her bed was made up in the old-fashioned way with sheets and blankets, half of which had slid onto the floor as she tossed and turned in her sleep. She dug her watch out from beneath the lumpy pillow.

'Seven o'clock? Practically the middle of the night,' she moaned. Sunlight poured insistently through the window, putting paid to any hope of a sleep in. Rosie pulled on an

old hooded sweatshirt and grumped her way down the stairs
to put the kettle on.

With only one hand in use, even the simplest tasks mush-
roomed into a full-scale operation. It reminded her of the
hideous team-building challenges from her Girl Scout days:
get six people across a river using only a lemonade bottle, a
ball of string and a packet of crisps. Usually there turned out
to be a perfectly decent bridge you could have used in the
first place.

Miraculously the electricity was working; all the sitting-
room lights had switched themselves on over night. Rosie
was just inspecting the meagre contents of the buzzing
refrigerator when someone thumped on the door.

'What's wrong with these people? Doesn't anyone sleep
around here?' Rosie complained, fumbling with the bolts.
She pulled the door open and found Euan Turnbull bending
over something on the doorstep. 'Hello?'

'Oh, hello there,' Euan straightened up hastily, shoving his
hands into his coat pockets. He smiled up at Rosie. 'How did
you sleep?'

Rosie grimaced. 'Terribly. A bunch of birds decided to
have a party right outside my window at four in the morning.'

Euan laughed. 'The dawn chorus is incredible out here.'
Rosie glared at him, intensely irritated by his cheery tone.

'Yeah, a real riot.' She really, really needed a coffee. 'Listen,
Euan, it's kind of early and I'm really not a morning person,
so . . .'

Euan held his hands up in apology. 'Of course. You'll
be needing this.' He handed Rosie a large wicker basket

covered with a checked cloth. 'Just a few home comforts. Be up at the house for ten-thirty. I'll meet you there.'

He gave her a cheeky wink and sauntered off, tossing a balled-up piece of paper nonchalantly from hand to hand.

'Hey, thanks!' Rosie called after him.

Half an hour later, Mara entered the living room and found Rosie cross-legged on the floor, an empty coffee cup at her side and a plate of half-eaten toast balanced on one knee. She was surrounded by food. 'Mara, hi!' Rosie beamed at her and gestured at the array of packets and tins. 'Check it out.'

'What is all this? Are we expecting a siege?'

'Supplies. Euan brought it first thing.'

'How thoughtful.'

'And look –' Rosie rummaged in the basket and came up waving a packet of biscuits. 'Oreos. My absolute favourite.' She clasped them to her chest and sighed rapturously.

'I'll leave you to it,' said Mara and shuffled off to the kitchen.

At eleven o'clock, Rosie staggered through the gates of the main house, half-leading, half-carrying Mara. She slumped against the gatepost, her good arm clamped around Mara's waist to prevent her from falling.

'Can we get some help here?' Her shout echoed around the yard. Mrs Drummond came hurrying out of a side door and rushed to their side, flapping and clucking like a frightened hen.

'Good heavens, you've never walked up? In this heat? In your condition?' Rosie wasn't sure which of them she was addressing. She pushed back the strands of hair plastered to her forehead and nodded. 'But it's uphill all the way!' blustered the housekeeper.

'I know,' said Rosie pointedly, taking a firm grip on her rapidly slipping temper. *Talk about stating the obvious.* 'Mara insisted – said she was up to it – done it before . . .'

Mrs Drummond gave her an odd look, as though she'd read Rosie's mind. She deftly shouldered Mara's weight and began walking her slowly across the yard. 'Let's get you inside. You need a nice cup of tea and a sit down.'

'Don't fuss me,' said Mara. 'I'm quite alright. I've walked that track a thousand times.'

'Well, forgive me for saying it, but that was a good few years ago, Madam.'

'I'm three years younger than you, Ellen, and I'll thank you to remember it.'

'Some people never change, Madam.'

'And don't call me Madam. We've known each other too long for that kind of nonsense.'

Rosie watched in astonishment as the pair bickered their way into the house. It hadn't occurred to her that Mara would know any of the staff here, not after, what, forty years away? And not just know them, but on first name terms as well. Abbott *always* called Mara 'Madam'. 'What's the story there?' she wondered. 'Mrs Drummond must have been here, like, forever. Wow.'

Rosie straightened up and rubbed her aching shoulder, unsure what to do next. She felt lonely and out of place without Mara. What was she supposed to do here?

'I guess I should look for Euan,' she decided, making a mental note to thank him for the food hamper. Maybe he'd be in one of the barns, doing farmy things. 'You're totally out of your depth, Rosie,' she sighed out loud, trudging towards the nearest outbuilding. She peered into the shady barn. 'Nothing but a heap of hay in there.'

She turned away to continue her search when there was a sudden rustling noise and a flicker of movement at the edge of her vision. Rosie whirled round, peering into the gloom. There was nothing to see, but she knew someone was there. 'Hello?' A dark shape moved furtively behind a bale of hay. Rosie's heart thudded wildly. 'Who's there? Euan?' The rustling sound came again. Probably kids fooling around. 'It's not funny. Just come out,' said Rosie firmly and moved towards the hay bale.

Then, before she could move, several things happened at once. A black dog detached itself from the shadows and leapt at Rosie with a ferocious growl. Euan appeared in the doorway. He threw himself forwards with a shout. Rosie ran blindly out into the yard, screaming with fright. She struck something solid, heard a yell and looked up to find a horse rearing over her. She narrowly avoided a flailing hoof as she flung herself aside, instinctively shielding her head. The cobbles struck her injured arm as she hit the ground.

Rosie lay face down in the dirt, her breath coming in shuddering, uneven gasps. Close by, the horse whinnied and snorted and its rider answered in low, soothing tones.

'Rosie!'

Euan emerged from the barn, holding the snarling dog by
its collar. A restraining hand dropped onto Rosie's shoulder
and gripped hard.

Hugh lifted Rosie to her feet and turned her to face him.
'Are you all right?' he asked. Her arm and shoulder
throbbed, but she nodded and managed a small smile. Hugh
glared at her. 'Don't ever – *ever* – run at a horse like that
again. Understand?' His fingers dug painfully into her shoulder. Rosie twisted away from him but he held on, forcing
her to look at him. 'Do you understand?'

'You're hurting me!'

Hugh released her and stepped back, running a hand distractedly through his hair. 'I'm sorry. But you shouldn't have
. . . it's incredibly dangerous.'

'And a howling mad dog isn't?' Rosie challenged.

He frowned. 'That's not what I. . . the horse could have
been badly injured.'

'The horse could have been injured? The *horse* could
have?' Rosie took a step towards him, her chin jutting forwards aggressively. 'You ass. You callous, jumped up twerp!
This yard was empty a minute ago, totally deserted. That
horse came out of nowhere.' Her hand balled into a fist at
her side. 'I get knocked to the ground and you think of the
horse? I ought . . . I ought to –'

Hugh saw the fist and stepped back.

'Rosie, are you okay?' Euan arrived panting at her side,
full of concern. She rounded on him, shaking with anger.

'Sure, no problem. I got attacked by rabid dogs practically every week back in Brooklyn. If it weren't for my arm
I'd have ripped its throat out with my bare hands.'

'I'm so sorry.' Hugh said, sure she was going to punch him.

'Oh, well that makes it all OK then, doesn't it?' Rosie spat at him. All the pent-up anxiety and frustration of the past weeks seemed to be pouring out of her and she was too far gone to care what she said. 'I'm minding my own business when Rocky the friendly Rottweiler tries to savage me and you're sorry?' Euan stared at her, his mouth working silently. 'And you −' Rosie hissed, jabbing a finger viciously at Hugh, 'You practically trample me to death and all you care about is whether that mangy old nag is OK! What's *wrong* with you people?'

'We care about our animals,' Euan said defensively.

Rosie smacked herself dramatically on the forehead.

'Oh, I get it. I'm just a person, so I don't matter. You can't sell me at the cattle market, right? Or is that next up on the agenda?' Her voice rose to a shriek.

'Enough.' Hugh cut in. He marched over to his horse and swung himself up into the saddle. 'No one was hurt. Euan, take her with you. Show her what she needs to know. There's work to be done.' He nodded stiffly to Rosie, snapped the reins and cantered off.

Rosie stared after him. He would be good-looking − if he didn't make her so mad. Hugh had a rugged face, weather-lined but still attractive, with steel grey eyes. Her chest heaved as the fit of temper burned itself out. Euan stood a few feet away, eyeing her warily.

When the blood stopped pounding in her head, Rosie looked up at him and gave a little shrug, something between an apology and 'What did you expect?'

Euan pointed to the path running between the outbuildings and they fell into step beside each other. Rosie breathed
deeply, already regretting her outburst. It had been a long
time since she'd lost her temper like that.

They left the cobbled path and passed through a five-bar
gate, heading into the bright patchwork of fields beyond.
Rosie kept her head down, picking her way with care
through the assortment of wild flowers and thistles clumped
among the long grass. Euan looked sideways at her, judging
whether it was safe to speak.

'So,' he began cautiously. 'Are you always like that?'

Rosie shook her head. 'Not at all,' she said earnestly. 'I just
– have this temper and sometimes it . . . well, you saw.'

Euan gave her a lopsided, charming grin.

'I certainly did,' he chuckled. 'You know what? I think
I'm going to enjoy having you here.' Rosie smiled up at him
in relief. 'And by the way,' he said casually, leading her
towards a battered Range Rover parked by the boundary
hedge. 'Stella isn't a Rottweiller, she's a Collie-Lurcher cross.
Very friendly once you get to know her.'

Rosie snorted. 'Yeah, right. And I'm the Queen of
England.'

Euan gave her a little shove with his shoulder and she
shoved him back. They climbed up into the car and drove off
across the field. On the summit of a nearby hill, Hugh reined
in his horse and watched them go.

Chapter Twelve

Lucernare

'So, the Harvest Ball,' said Charlotte, her voice crackling down the phone line. 'What arrangements have you made for your guests?' Hugh shrugged, dislodging the handset wedged between his left ear and shoulder. He caught it clumsily, knocking the letter he'd been drafting off the desk.

'Damn. Sorry, lost you there. Erm, arrangements are pretty much the same as last year. Food, drink, band, dancing, carriages at midnight.' He laughed. 'Same as every year, come to think of it. Can't break with tradition, there'd be a full-scale uprising.'

'No, Hugh, your *guests*,' replied Charlotte with exaggerated patience. There was a bewildered silence. 'Your cousin Mara and . . .' she said impatiently.

Hugh frowned. 'Ah, yes. They're invited, of course, but it's unlikely Mara will come. She's still quite frail. I imagine Rosie will be there.' He hesitated. 'Actually, Lottie, do you think you and Alastair could . . .?'

'Look after your cousin-in-law once removed, or whatever the technical term is?'

'Second cousin by marriage, isn't it?'

'Heavens, *I* don't know, Hugh. But listen, you'd be a better chaperone than us, surely? We haven't even met.' Her voice sharpened. 'Are you bringing a lady friend? You sly . . .'

'No, no.' Hugh back-pedalled furiously, glad that Charlotte couldn't see him blushing. 'I just don't think I'm the best person for the job. With all the meeting and greeting and so on. Anyway . . .' Hugh hesitated, 'she's as mad as cheese and I always get the feeling she wants to punch me.'

'What have you done?' she asked bluntly.

A picture of Rosie flashed across Hugh's mind, red-faced and yelling at him in the yard.

'Nothing, nothing at all. I haven't seen her for a week, in fact, with all the work I've got on.'

Hugh had been actively avoiding Rosie since the horse incident, but he wasn't about to tell Charlotte.

'Hmmm,' Charlotte drawled, clearly unconvinced. 'Well, don't worry, Alastair and I will take care of little Rosie.'

'Thanks, Lottie,' said Hugh gratefully. 'And I'll get Euan to collect her and drop her off, save her walking in the dark.'

'Always the gentleman,' she said fondly. 'See you later, Sweets.'

'Bye, Lottie.'

Hugh let his breath out in a long, slow cloud of relief, glad to have escaped a full-on grilling. Charlotte didn't often let him off so lightly. He stretched, every muscle in his back protesting from the long hours of desk work he'd been putting in lately. He pushed his chair back and moved to the window.

The large field that Euan had allocated for this year's ball was just visible through a gap between two outbuildings.

Even by Hugh's standards, it was an impressive sight. Where three hours ago the field had been empty, several dozen staff swarmed busily around a massive marquee which would comfortably hold three hundred guests.

Hugh shaded his eyes against the sun. Even at this distance, he could identify the various teams; a human chain passing armfuls of planks from man to man for the interlocking dance floor, a group circling the marquee to secure the external guy ropes, a knot of household staff scurrying to and fro with decorations. An enormous bouquet of helium balloons bobbed towards the marquee on a pair of disembodied legs, their owner invisible behind the mass of floating blue and silver globes.

'Fantastic work,' Hugh commented.

'Thanks.'

Hugh jumped, stifling a shout. Euan was standing right behind him.

'For God's sake, Euan,' Hugh gasped, clutching the windowsill for support. 'You nearly gave me a heart attack. How long have you been there?'

Euan grinned. 'Couple of seconds,' he said. 'I was always light on my feet. It's all the boxing training when I was a kid.' He feinted left and threw a mock punch at the heavy curtain drapes. 'You like it then?' he asked, nodding at the window.

'As I said, fantastic,' Hugh replied. 'You've done a great job.' They stood side by side, watching the distant workers. 'Where's the catering tent going to go?'

'You can't see it from this angle, there's an awning at the back for the mobile kitchen.'

Hugh clapped him on the shoulder.

'You've thought of everything. I really appreciate it, Euan.'

Euan beamed, lapping up the praise. 'Anything else need dealing with today, Hugh?'

'Actually, yes. I've a favour to ask you.'

'Oh?' Euan sensed what was coming.

'Could you bring Rosie up to the ball tonight and take her home later on? If you take Duchess and the old trap, you'll still be able to have a beer or two.'

'No problem,' Euan smirked. 'You won't hear me complaining with a firebrand like that on my arm all evening. I might even get my fingers burned.'

Hugh felt a strange and unexpected surge of anger and hurriedly turned his head away.

'Don't worry, Euan,' he said coolly, his gaze fixed on the horizon. 'Some friends of mine have offered to chaperone Rosie for the night.'

Shoulder to shoulder with Euan, he felt the muscles bunch in the younger man's arm.

'Just the chauffeur then, am I?' Euan said. 'Shall I wear a uniform?'

Hugh took a deep breath. This was ridiculous. What did it matter if Euan Turnbull had designs on Rosie?

'Come on, Euan,' he said, trying to inject a friendly note into his voice. 'It's not like that at all. I didn't want to ask too much of you. After all your hard work, I felt you deserved a proper night off.' Euan gave a non-committal grunt. Hugh sighed. 'Besides, I didn't want to assume you were available. You usually have a date lined up for the ball.' He glanced at

Euan's face and decided to risk it. 'Sometimes more than one, if I remember rightly.'

A few years ago, Euan had mistakenly invited two girls to the ball. While he had been perfectly willing to share, the *ladies* in question had not. After several glasses of ceilidh punch, a rather violent disagreement had erupted during the meal, lending a whole new meaning to the term 'bun fight.'

Euan chuckled in spite of himself. 'What a night that was.'

Hugh smiled as the tension ebbed from his estate manager's face.

'Look, I'll do the taxi run for Rosie,' Hugh offered. 'There was no offence intended.'

Euan shook his head. 'No, it's fine, really. I over-reacted. Bit on edge today, I suppose.' He leaned forward, eyes narrowing as he stared at the marquee. 'Talking of Rosie, isn't that our little American over there?'

Hugh followed his gaze to a patch of open grass beyond the marquee. A figure was running about, zig-zagging from left to right with one arm pointing to the sky.

'Yes, but what's she doing?'

'No idea.'

Both men stared, utterly mesmerised, as Rosie zoomed around the field. Suddenly she dived into the marquee, then reappeared, dragging a reluctant man behind her.

'What the . . .?' breathed Hugh.

Euan pressed his face to the window.

'Is he carrying a ladder? He is, look, she's making him set it up out there. It's in the middle of nowhere.'

'Now she's climbing up it and waving her arm around again.'

'What is she . . .? She's going to be off that in a minute if she isn't careful. She's already got one broken wrist.'

'No, it's OK, that chap's holding it steady at the bottom.'

'I can't stand it,' Euan declared. 'I've got to see what she's up to. Catch you later.'

'Right. Thanks again, Euan,' Hugh called as the door swung shut. He turned his attention back to the tiny figure atop the ladder, hair blowing round her face in the breeze. He'd never seen such odd behaviour. What *was* she doing?

Rosie clung to the top of the ladder with her knees.

'Please come down now,' begged the man at the foot of the ladder. 'The wind's getting up.'

Rosie twisted round to look down at him, brows knitted in concentration.

'Sorry – be down in a minute,' she mouthed. The man smiled anxiously and took a firmer grip on the metal frame. 'Mom? Can you still hear me?' Rosie shouted. Her mobile phone signal was cutting in and out, making conversation difficult.

'Yes, honey, don't shout,' came Mrs Jacobs' voice. 'Did you hear what I said about Mrs Feltz's cat?'

'Yeah, awful. Poor thing.'

'Personally, I always check the washing machine before I switch it on.'

'Mom, you don't even have a cat!'

There was a polite cough from below. 'Mrs Whitton, I really need to get back to work.'

'Listen, Mom, I have to go soon.'

'But you haven't even told me your news.'

'There isn't any really. Mara's OK, I'm working on the farm.'

'That's disgusting! You've got a broken arm.'

'It's just my wrist, Mom. I can still work. I'll find a proper job soon.'

'Miss? Could you come down now?' said the man below as the ladder began to sink into the soft earth.

'I can hear people, where are you?' asked her mother.

'Up a ladder in a field.'

'Miss . . . you're on my head . . .'

Rosie looked down and, seeing she had inadvertently rested one foot on the man's head, swiftly moved it.

'Did he say you were on his head?' her mother asked.

'I'm not now, Mom,' Rosie replied as the ladder sunk deeper into the ground.

'What about the accident report from the French police? Have you chased that up?' Rosie's stomach lurched at the mention of it. She swallowed hard, tasting bile in her mouth.

'I have to go.'

'Rosie? Have you heard from France?'

'You're breaking up – bye, I love you.' Rosie hit the End Call button, leant over the side of the ladder and retched. She felt as though she'd been punched in the stomach.

'Rosie? What's going on?' Euan was standing at the foot of the ladder. He stretched up and caught hold of her leg. Rosie shook him off.

'Let go, I'm coming down.'

She thanked the disgruntled ladder man, a smile pasted on her face, and turned to Euan. 'Hey, what's up?'

Euan laughed out loud. 'What's up? What's up is you climbing ladders to nowhere like a madwoman. What were you doing up there? Looking for heaven?'

Rosie waved her phone at him.

'Just calling home,' she said calmly. 'The signal is terrible.' *Like everything else round here.*

'And you thought standing on a ladder would make a difference?' Euan roared with laughter.

'It did,' Rosie insisted, stung by his reaction. Euan wiped his eyes with a corner of his shirt.

'You're a one-off, Rosie, you know that?' He slung a companionable arm across her shoulders. 'Come on, you crazy Yank. There's still a lot to do before Cinderella can go to the ball.'

Rosie carefully shrugged him off as they strolled back to the marquee. She didn't want to be touched.

'I can hardly wait.' Her grimace was hidden behind her windswept hair.

❀   ❀   ❀   ❀

Mara gazed into the grimy wardrobe mirror that was edged in carvings of holly and ivy leaves. 'Beautiful,' she said softly. Rosie stood beside her and stared miserably back at herself.

'I look like an ageing Prom Queen,' she stated flatly.

'No,' Mara protested, settling the satin layers more smoothly over Rosie's net underskirt. 'No one needs to know you wore this to your school prom.'

'But *I* know,' Rosie pointed out. 'I never thought I would have to wear it again.'

'Never mind,' Mara replied firmly. 'It's a classic style and it still fits you like a glove. What a good job you kept it.'

Rosie looked down at the dress.

'I'm hardly going to blend in wearing electric blue, am I?'

Mara placed her hands on Rosie's shoulders and glared at her.

'Listen to me. The function of a ball gown is not to help you blend in. It is to make you stand out, like the jewel in a ring. Look at yourself.' Rosie glanced half-heartedly at the mirror. The empire line sash felt too tight against her ribcage and the short chiffon sleeves emphasised her slumped shoulders. Mara gave her a little shake. 'Stand up straight and look properly. There, you see? The colour contrast with your hair is stunning, dear. You look beautiful.' Rosie bit her lip.

'Yes, but —' she cut the words off, her eyes filling with tears. *Cameron isn't here to see it, so what's the point?* Mara smiled sadly at Rosie, her own eyes brimming in response.

'But nothing,' she said quietly. 'Look beautiful for you, Rosie. Cameron would want that.'

Rosie sat down heavily on the bed and began twisting a length of hair round her fingers. 'I don't want to leave you here alone,' she said, keeping her eyes on the coil of hair.

'Don't worry about that,' Mara assured her briskly. 'Mrs Drummond is coming down to do a bit of cleaning and keep me company.' Rosie started on another section of hair. Mara watched her with a mixture of anxiety and tenderness. 'I can't ask this of you,' she said suddenly. 'We'll go together.'

'No way,' Rosie said quickly.

'I'm well enough,' Mara protested. 'It would be ungracious not to attend.'

'No Mara, absolutely not. I'll be fine.'

They stared at one another, each wordlessly challenging the other's lie. It was Mara who dipped her head. 'We'll just show our faces, then. An hour or two is enough for courtesy's sake. Hugh will understand.'

Rosie snorted. 'He'll be too busy playing Lord of the Manor to notice. I don't care what he thinks of me, anyway, the man's a pompous ass.'

'I'll let you finish getting ready in peace,' said Mara diplomatically.

Fifteen minutes later, Rosie walked awkwardly down the stairs, her feet unused to the high court shoes pinching her toes. Mara had stationed herself by the window, perched high on a kitchen stool. 'Perfect timing,' she said, letting the curtain fall. 'They're here.'

Rosie took a deep breath and squared her shoulders. 'I'll give your apologies to the landlord,' she promised, 'but I'm not curtseying or anything.' Mara smiled and kissed her goodbye.

'Hugh is a good man, Rosie,' she replied, 'and he improves on closer acquaintance. Bear that in mind.'

Mara stood on the threshold and watched as Euan leapt from the driver's seat and made a great show of handing Rosie up into the trap. The dappled old grey stood patiently in her traces, tail swishing languidly at the last of the summer flies as Euan fussed over Rosie. They made a handsome couple, he in his dinner jacket, she with her hair trailing in loose curls down her back, her gown vivid in the evening light.

Looking distinctly under-dressed in her cardigan and slacks, Mrs Drummond clambered down unaided and stumped into the Dower House.

'Evening, Mara.'

'Good evening, Ellen.'

'Have you had your medication?'

'Don't be tiresome.'

'Well, have you?'

'Yes! Have you brought the whisky?'

'What do you take me for?'

'A bringer of single malt, I hope . . . I am so much better. Nearly back to my old self.'

Rosie gripped the wooden seat of the trap with both hands as Euan unhitched the pony and tethered it loosely to the fence a short distance from the catering tent.

'It'll be quieter for her over here,' he called. 'Do you need a hand down?'

Rosie shook her head. The swell of noise from the marquee had rooted her to the spot. She hadn't been to a party by herself for a long time. *I'm not sure I can do this.*

Euan walked back to the trap and looked up at her expectantly. 'Come on then,' he said.

'In a second.' She felt alone . . . alone with a capital A. There was no Cameron to lead the small talk she so hated. No Cameron to make her laugh with his appalling dance moves. No Cameron to keep track of her purse, hold her drink or give up his jacket when she got cold. No Cameron . . .

She was on her own. Now she realised it more than ever. A great chasm opened up inside her even as she swallowed her panic and tried to relax her grip on the seat. 'Just tell me again, what's the point of this party?' she croaked.

Euan looked irritated. 'Weren't you listening when I explained it? Traditionally, it was an annual occasion for the tenants to renew their fealty to the Lord. Now it's just a party but nobody ever misses it. It's one of those unspoken rules, like going to church on Christmas Eve.' He glanced at his watch. 'Come on, or we'll miss the start of the ceilidh.'

Rosie gave a start. 'It's a ceilidh?' She panicked – *just like my wedding.*

Euan ground his teeth. 'Yes! Oh, for goodness sake!' Before she could react, he grasped her by the waist and plucked her out of the trap. 'Loosen up, will you? And try and get into the party spirit,' he said, propelling her briskly towards the marquee. 'It'll be a great night, OK? You look amazing. You have nothing to worry about – you're the girl who punches people and climbs ladders . . .'

Rosie blinked back tears as she stumbled along, her heels snagging in the turf.

The noise inside the marquee was deafening. The tent was festooned with swags and bows of flowers and evergreens. Lanterns hung from the bows and at every post that held up the cavernous roof were neatly stacked columns of pumpkins and first fruits. A huge crowd milled around on the dance floor as the ceilidh band made last minute tuning adjustments in preparation for their opening set.

Large circular tables were arranged in a sweeping arc around three sides of the dance floor, the fourth side open to allow access to the bar. A knot of women surrounded a large display board, trying to decipher the colour-coded seating plan. As Rosie looked about in bewilderment, a man emerged from the heaving mass on the dance floor and waved eagerly at Euan.

'Just coming,' Euan shouted. He dropped Rosie's arm. 'Got a few people to say hello to,' he said. 'Have to keep the tenant farmers sweet, you know how it is. You're sitting with some of Hugh's friends. They'll be along in a minute, I expect.' He smirked, misreading the look of terror on Rosie's face. 'I'm sure they're not that bad. I'll be back for a dance, OK?'

Rosie's mouth went dry. 'Euan, please, I –'

Euan's lips pressed over her words with a quick kiss that just grazed the corner of her mouth. Instantly, Rosie pulled away, her body rigid.

'Don't worry, I'll find you,' Euan promised with a sly smile and melted into the crowd.

Rosie remained where she was, her thoughts in turmoil. *He had no right. It was accidental. I don't want it.* She scrubbed at her cheek and mouth with the back of her hand trying to erase the invisible stain that seemed to cling there.

Several people brushed past her in quick succession. Rosie realised she was in the way. She moved towards the entrance, stopped, completely disorientated. It was way too soon to leave. Where should she go? Her head began to throb.

'Rosie?' Hugh seemed to materialise before her out of thin air.

'Hi,' Rosie said faintly, trying to drag herself back to the moment. 'Mara sends her apologies.' She kept her head down, her brain vaguely noting that Hugh's dress shirt had come untucked at the front and that he was missing a cuff link. Hugh was talking to her, she wasn't listening.

'. . . so pleased you came,' Hugh finished. 'Cameron was a good man. I know how difficult this must be for you.'

'You do?' Rosie raised her head and let the mask slip, just for a moment. Hugh stepped back in shock at the desolation contorting her face.

'I . . . er . . .' he fumbled for the right words as he grabbed a glass of red wine from a passing tray and held it out for Rosie. 'Perhaps . . .'

'Fine . . .' Rosie said as she reached for the glass.

The glass tipped as Hugh was buffeted by some guests on their way to the punch. His hand threw the drink forward. Anyone watching might have thought he'd done it on purpose.

'Oh, hell,' Hugh said as he tried to mop the stain from the front of her dress. 'Rosie, I'm sorry.' He beckoned urgently to a woman in a sparkling purple gown. 'Lottie, get her out of here.'

'Hugh . . . what have you done?'

'He ran me down with a horse and doused me in wine,' Rosie replied.

'A horse?' Charlotte asked incredulously.

'It wasn't like that . . . she ran in to me and the horse knocked her over and she fell in the mud . . .'

Rosie allowed herself to be hustled away.

'You missed a great party,' Euan slurred as the old pony plodded along the path. 'I kept looking for you for a dance,' he added accusingly. 'Where were you?'

Rosie clung to the seat as the front wheel dipped into a pothole.

'With Charlotte and Alastair Alderson. Keep your eyes on the track,' she answered.

'Duchess knows where she's going,' Euan said. He sat back in the driver's seat and put his feet up, the reins slack between his fingers. 'See?' He watched her through half-lidded eyes. 'What were you doing all that time?'

'Just talking. I was a bit upset. Hugh tipped wine down my dress. Look, shall I drive?'

'What for?'

'You don't seem . . . quite yourself.'

'Are you saying I'm drunk?'

'Yes.'

'So what if I am?'

'Let me take over, it's not far now.'

'I thought we were going to be mates.'

'What? We are. I'm only saying –'

'You avoided me like the plague the minute someone better came along.'

Rosie stared at him. 'Hey, you're the one who ran off and left me.'

'By order of the gentry,' Euan muttered. 'He didn't want me hanging around with such a beautiful girl. I think he wants you for himself.'

'What are you talking about? Please watch where you're going.'

'Just because you married money, it doesn't make you better than me.'

'My husband is dead.' Rosie's voice was little more than a whisper, but every word vibrated with rage. Euan fell silent.

Completely indifferent to the mood of her passengers, Duchess ambled on, past the dry-stone wall, through the open gate and stopped alongside the Dower House. Euan turned to Rosie, remorse plain on his face. She was already moving, jumping lightly to the ground, her shoes dangling from one hand.

'Rosie, wait,' Euan pleaded. 'Don't go like this.'

Rosie made for the door.

'I'll send Mrs Drummond right out,' she said over her shoulder. 'Thanks for the ride.'

'Rosie! Do you cook breakfast?"

'You've known me a week, Euan. One week. Back off!'

Behind her, Rosie heard the sound of a boot striking wood as Euan gave vent to his frustration. She didn't look back.

The lamps were lit in the sitting-room, but the fire had burnt itself out. 'Mrs Drummond?' There was no reply. 'Mara?' Rosie discarded her shoes on an armchair and went swiftly upstairs, bunching her dress in both hands. 'Mara?' she called again. There was a scuffling sound before Mara answered.

'In here, Rosie dear.' Rosie entered the bedroom and found the two women sitting casually at opposite ends of the bed, like bookends. Too casually.

'What are you guys doing?' she asked. 'Mara, I thought you'd be asleep.' Mara smiled innocently.

'Well, I'm in bed, dear, as you see, but I couldn't sleep. Mrs Drummond and I have been chatting.' Mrs Drummond nodded vigorously, listing dangerously to one side at the foot of the bed.

'Uh-huh.' Rosie scanned the room, taking in the pack of cards protruding from the pocket of Mara's dressing-gown and the bottle of whisky clearly visible underneath the bed. 'Well, Euan's waiting outside,' Rosie said sweetly, after the briefest of pauses. 'Thanks so much, Mrs Drummond.'

'Of course. Goodnight Madam, Rosie.' The housekeeper smelt of single malt. She squeezed clumsily past Rosie, her pockets jingling with loose change.

Rosie listened for the sound of the front door closing, trying to select a sensible thought from the weird parental clichés her brain was churning out, *What have you got to say for yourself, young lady? I won't have you gambling and drinking under this roof! You're up way past your curfew.*

In the end, she settled for 'We'll discuss this in the morning.' Mara laughed to herself as she slid down under the covers without a word and Rosie swept from the room in a flurry of indignation.

Rosie wrestled her way out of her dress, kicked it into a corner of her bedroom and pulled on her pyjamas. 'Why are you getting so worked up?' she muttered, shaking out the blankets in search of her woolly bed socks. 'So she had a couple of drinks and played a few hands of cards. It's not a crime.' She threw the bedclothes aside and dropped to her knees to search under the bed. 'Where are my socks?' She pulled out her suitcase and felt around behind it, trying to tame the fierce emotions clawing at her. She felt angry, angry at Euan, angry at Mara, angry with Hugh for his unexpected kindness. And, she was angry with herself – just for being angry.

Rosie sat back on her heels, reaching for the heart of it all. It was . . . it was . . . With a sudden movement, she wrenched open the suitcase and pulled out the four books, still in their paper and string parcel. She stared at them as though seeing them for the first time. 'It's you, Cameron,' she said, tears of disbelief blurring her sight. 'I'm angry with you.' She rocked backwards and forwards on the cold floor, hugging herself as she wept.

Only when her legs grew stiff with cold did Rosie wipe her eyes on the sleeve of her pyjamas and drag herself up onto the mattress. She took a candle and matches from her bedside table and struck a light with shaking fingers. With great care, she placed the lighted candle on the narrow windowsill. 'I'm sorry,' she whispered.

Then she switched off the lamp and lay in the dark, watching the tiny, flickering flame. The bedroom door creaked open and Mara padded noiselessly into the room. She climbed into the bed, lay down and wrapped her arms around Rosie like a mother cradling a nightmare-stricken child. Long after they had fallen asleep, the candle continued to burn steadfastly in the window, as if to light the way home to travellers lost in the dark.

Chapter 13

Autumn

Mara sat at the long pine table in the centre of the kitchen and basked in the warmth of the Aga. It gave off a gentler, more constant heat than the open fire. Best of all, it didn't eat three pine logs every hour, nor did it have to be stoked and tended.

A collection of pots and pans hung in an orderly row along one wall, their burnished sides appearing to glow with reflected heat. Brightly coloured mugs nestled between cake tins and storage canisters on the thick wooden shelves that filled the wall from the Aga to the sink. The house appeared to have grown in cosiness while she sat there. It had become warmer and more welcoming with every hour. Mara felt at home for the first time since leaving the Hall.

Everything about the room exuded a sense of comfort and security that Mara remembered from her childhood. It was like stepping into the past. Mara slid off her shoes. Even the flagstones beneath her stockinged feet seemed to have lost some of their chill. She pulled a copy of a kitchenware catalogue towards her and began leafing through the pages of the autumn–winter collection. The array of weird and wonderful gadgets was astonishing. She wondered why on earth anybody would want an electronic egg slicer or tea warmer. It was quite beyond her.

There was a sudden blast of cold air as the door opened. Mrs Drummond shouldered her way into the room, carrying a large tray piled high with cutlery.

'Found anything you like?' she enquired, setting it down on the table with a clatter.

'Just browsing,' Mara shrugged, pushing the catalogue away. 'It's amazing what people will buy these days.' She used the table to lever herself up and went to close the door. 'Chilly today,' she remarked.

'Mmm. Autumn's here, right enough.' Mrs Drummond ducked into a floral-patterned apron and struggled to fasten the ties around her middle. Rolls of fat bulged on either side of the thin fabric strips as she pulled the knot tight, creating a silhouette like a tube of toothpaste squeezed in the middle. She looked appraisingly at Mara. 'How are you feeling?'

'Fine, fine. A little tired.' Mara eased herself down onto a chair. 'And before you ask about my blasted medication, the answer is yes.'

'I was about to offer you a cup of tea, actually,' sniffed Mrs Drummond, indicating the kettle on the Aga.

'Liar.'

'I was!'

'Yes to that, too, then. One sugar.'

Mrs Drummond fetched a teapot and busied herself at the Aga, pouring and straining with her usual efficiency. Mara rested her chin on her hands and gazed through the window at the grey clouds scudding across the October sky. Every day seemed so long and yet, while she had been occupied with the hours and the minutes, whole weeks had crept by.

Now autumn was upon them. She remembered how much her beloved James had adored this time of year. The trees were clad in their red-gold finery and the smell of almost-Christmas lingered in the air. Mara couldn't recall ever liking the season. It was a contrary streak in her otherwise bright nature. To her, autumn signalled the onset of decay and darkness closing in. This year she loathed it more than ever.

'What's the trouble then?' Mrs Drummond asked abruptly, her back still turned. 'Something's eating at you. Apart from, you know . . .' she shovelled a heaped spoonful of sugar into each mug, added a measure of whisky to her own and stirred them vigorously to cover her embarrassment. Mara said nothing. Mrs Drummond set the drinks down, rattled various tins in search of biscuits and finally fussed her way back to the table. The women faced one another silently. Mara pulled one mug towards her and cupped it in both hands, staring at the dark liquid.

'Rosie has gone to look for a job,' she said at last.

Mrs Drummond looked baffled. 'I thought she'd gone for a day trip to Newcastle,' she said. 'Didn't Euan drop her off at the station?'

'Yes,' said Mara, 'but she's stopping off in Alnmouth on the way home. She's determined to find work off the estate.'

Mrs Drummond raised an eyebrow. 'In Alnmouth? She'll be wasting her time. Anyway, it's Wednesday. How does she intend to get home?'

Mara held up her hands in defeat. 'I tried to tell her,' she said, 'but Rosie needs to discover things for herself. She can

be impossibly stubborn and if she sets her mind to something, she won't be told.'

'Like someone else I could mention,' Mrs Drummond
muttered into her tea. Mara favoured her with a look of regal
indifference and reached for the biscuit tin.

Mrs Drummond cleared her throat. 'Changing the subject, what happened after the night of the ball?' she asked
curiously. 'You never did get round to telling me.'

'Oh, Euan was on the doorstep the next morning. I think
there'd been some kind of argument,' Mara said. 'Rosie sent
him off with a flea in his ear but, from what I gather, they
soon made it up. Storm in a teacup.'

'No, not that little episode,' said Mrs Drummond. She set
her mug aside and pulled the tray of cutlery towards her. 'I
meant us, Rosie busting our poker game. Pass me a polishing cloth, will you? Left of the sink, second drawer down.
Was there a terrible row?'

Mara obediently got to her feet. 'Well, she tried to make
me have a lie-in the next day, on account of staying up so
late.' She took two cloths from the drawer and passed one to
Mrs Drummond. 'Mind you, I think she had plenty more to
say about it but she bit her tongue.' She grinned wickedly at
her friend. 'Just as well we weren't smoking.'

They sat in silence for several minutes, dividing and sorting the cutlery into piles ready for polishing. Mrs
Drummond had noticed that tasks like this had a thera-
peutic effect on Mara, so presented them as often as she
could. No doubt the novelty would wear off in time but,
for now, it took Mara's mind off her troubles for a little
while. Mrs Drummond picked up a knife and began

polishing it vigorously. 'Rosie doesn't find our acquain-tance . . . odd, then?' she pressed.

'Of course – you are terribly inappropriate, Ellen. How dare you call me anything other than "Madam"! Your inso-lence is astounding. Not only that . . . corrupting me with whisky and poker! I simply must be treated with the respect befitting my station – you . . . you wench!'

'I'm serious.'

Mara chose a soup spoon and held it up to the light, examining her bulging reflection in the convex surface. 'I suppose Rosie might find our friendship strange, but she hasn't questioned me about it.'

'The staff are talking,' Mrs Drummond informed her.

Mara waved her cloth dismissively. 'Staff do. There's no harm in it and they're none the wiser.' She looked sharply at Mrs Drummond. 'Are they?'

Mrs Drummond grinned slyly. 'Still embarrassed about it after all these years, Mara?'

Mara blushed. 'Don't be ridiculous. For your information, Ellen Drummond, I don't mind whom you tell.'

'You made me swear to keep it a secret.'

'We were ten years old.'

Mrs Drummond pointed the gleaming knife-tip at Mara. 'A promise is a promise,' she said sternly. 'I've told no one and never will.' She put the knife down and started on a row of forks. 'You can, though, if you want to. Rosie might like to hear about it.'

'Perhaps,' Mara acknowledged. 'But the tale of my stupidity and your heroics will keep for now.' She gave a sudden snort of laughter. 'Rosie has more than enough on her plate for one day.'

'You're right there,' said Mrs Drummond. 'How many miles from Alnmouth to the estate, do you reckon?'

'At least ten,' Mara guessed.

'So we'll send Euan to rescue her?'

'If she's not back by dark, certainly,' Mara agreed. 'But not Euan,' she added. 'Send Hugh.' She glanced out of the window at the gathering clouds. 'Although I think she'll manage, if the rain holds off,' she said thoughtfully. 'She's a resourceful girl.'

'You're a hard woman, Mara Whitton,' Mrs Drummond said reprovingly. 'More tea?'

❀   ❀   ❀   ❀

Rosie wandered through the streets of Newcastle, feeling the heartbeat of the city pulsing around her. It was small compared with New York but still, it felt like a little piece of home, with the roar of the traffic, the incessant pounding of feet on the pavement, snatches of a hundred different conversations rising like steam in the air as she threaded her way among the crowds in the shopping precinct.

There were no wild hills or great empty spaces exposing her grief to the open sky; here, she was hemmed in by life. The strange Geordie accent was undiluted, more foreign than anything Rosie had heard before. A thread of laughter was woven into the strident, upbeat cadences of the chatter surrounding her. If a smile could have a voice, thought Rosie, it would sound like this.

Newcastle felt friendly, but not intrusively so. There was an occasional nod or smile from a passing shopper, even an apology from a man who bumped her shoulder, but nobody looked at Rosie too hard or for too long. No one fixed her with a look of pity that said, 'I know,' or gave her a clumsy pat and mumbled, 'Poor lass,' when they thought she could not hear them. After weeks of feeling stared at, she experienced a blissful freedom in the fleeting companionship of strangers. She realised that she was genuinely smiling for the first time since . . . since . . . Somewhere close by, a clock struck three. Rosie turned regretfully towards the train station with a silent promise to return as soon as she could.

This was a great way to spend her day off, even if she was almost broke. Now it was time to find herself a job.

An hour later, Rosie got off the train at Alnmouth. It was the smallest station she had ever seen, consisting of just two open air platforms. A small waiting-room stood proudly on one, the other had only a bus stop type of shelter. It did, however, have a free-standing local map and some open-air benches dotted along the concrete strip. Evidently, the architect had tried to be fair in this respect. The decorators had also done their best – every roofing girder, bench or metal pole had been painted a gaudy kingfisher blue and some potted shrubs dotted along both platforms lent an encouraging sign of life to the place.

Currently, the shrubs were the only sign of life. Rosie stepped through the exit and looked around. Alnmouth was like a ghost town. 'Where is everyone?' she asked aloud as she trudged along the little high street. There was nobody to answer her. It was eerie. Every shop window was dark or shuttered, each door proclaiming 'CLOSED' in dark letters.

Rosie found herself wondering whether she'd missed a tragedy, or some great world event. 'Maybe they've all been abducted by aliens?' She shivered. Surely somebody had to be around. She just needed to keep looking. Suddenly she caught sight of a lit window up ahead. She hurried towards it.

Through the thick old-fashioned panes she found herself face to face with a variety of merchandise, from elastoplast to the little bottles of party bubbles Rosie remembered from years ago, lit from above by the strip light that had originally led her to the window. An arrangement of packet mixes was artfully propped up with jumbo packs of toilet roll beside a towering pyramid of tinned soups. It looked like one of the re-enactment shops that museums create to bring history to life for children. Rosie looked up at the faded sign above the peeling paintwork, half-expecting it to read *Shop From Wartime Britain*. Instead, *Alnmouth Post Office & General Store* introduced itself in no-nonsense block capitals. Rosie stepped inside.

The elderly shopkeeper's head was just visible above the counter-top, her spectacles balanced on the end of her nose, engrossed in a newspaper. Rosie approached the counter and waited politely. The lady leaned closer to the paper, her mouth framing the words as she read. Rosie tried a little cough.

'Well I never,' said the lady, shaking the paper out and turning the page.

'Excuse me?' Rosie said loudly. The lady shot up from her stool with a squawk of surprise.

'Oh, you gave me a fright there,' she babbled, clutching the paper to her chest as she steadied herself against the counter. 'I was about to close up for the day.' She straightened her spectacles to get a better look at Rosie. 'What can I get for you, dear?'

Rosie offered up a silent prayer. 'Actually, I'm looking for a job.'

The old woman stared at her as though she'd sprouted a second head. 'In Alnmouth?'

Rosie nodded. 'Do you know of any vacancies?'

The woman sucked in her cheeks and shook her head. 'I'm afraid not.'

'What about here?' Rosie suggested. 'I'd love to work in a store like this. Maybe you could use some help, with Christmas coming up and all.'

'What difference does Christmas make?'

'Well . . . the Christmas rush?'

'In Alnmouth?'

Rosie plunged her hand into her jacket pocket and pulled out a folded brown envelope. 'Here,' she said desperately, pushing it across the counter. 'My resumé. I do have experience of customer services and I'm very efficient.'

The lady shook her head.

'We don't have the trade,' she explained, not unkindly. 'This is Alnmouth.' She handed the envelope back to Rosie, who stuffed it into the pocket of her jeans.

'I guess it is pretty quiet,' Rosie admitted, looking out at the silent street. 'Where is everyone?'

'It's Wednesday.' The lady looked pityingly at Rosie. 'You're not from round here, are you.' It wasn't a question. Rosie looked blank. 'Half-day closing.'

'Half-day . . .?' Rosie grappled with the idea. 'But the shops can't just close. What if people urgently need something in the afternoon?' The nine to five hours of Oxford had felt restrictive, but this – this was something else.

The old lady pinched the bridge of her nose and shut her eyes while she took a deep breath. 'Well,' she replied, speaking very slowly and clearly, 'if that happens, they come here. I'm still open, see?'

Rosie was incredulous. 'Where I come from, some of the stores stay open twenty-four hours a day.'

'When do they sleep?' the shopkeeper asked, not waiting for an answer. 'It's just the same in England,' she continued. 'Ridiculous ideas have spread but thankfully, not this far.' She smiled at Rosie as she hobbled to the door and flipped the sign over from Open to Closed. 'Some people are all "Me-me-me" and "Now . . . this minute".' Well, let me tell you, even the bairns hereabouts know how to wait for something. Patience is a virtue.' The woman stopped for breath and eyed Rosie up and down as if she knew something about her. 'Life isn't about doing, but being. It's about thinking and knowing where you are going.' She opened the door and gave Rosie a serious look. 'I'm closing up now. Get yourself home before the rain sets in.'

Rosie shuffled to the door, feeling like a naughty child unable to grasp the scope of its error. 'Which way is the bus stop?' she asked forlornly.

'Bus stop?' the woman half laughed. 'Wednesday half-day closing,' she repeated. 'No buses after 1 o'clock. Do you have far to go?' The shopkeeper saw Rosie's expression and drew her own conclusion. 'Wait here,' she sighed and disappeared behind the counter, returning with a yellow and brown flowery umbrella that looked fifty years old. She thrust it at

Rosie. 'Take this,' she said. 'Save you getting drenched. There's a taxi rank about five minutes from the station, *if* you can afford it. Mind how you go.' The door closed and the window blind rolled down with a snap.

Rosie couldn't afford it.

It took ten minutes for the rain to set in and another five for it to soak right through Rosie's clothes. She strode on, clinging grimly to the flimsy umbrella. After thirty minutes the light began to fade and the pavement petered out. Rosie climbed the grass verge, pressed herself into the hedgerow and walked on. The spokes of the umbrella caught in the sharp spike of the hawthorn. Rosie turned up the collar of her jacket and trudged away, leaving the sorry contraption stranded amid the leaves like a giant artificial flower.

She pulled out her mobile and saw that an hour had passed. Her determination began to fade. In all that time, no more than three cars and one tractor had driven by. The road was deserted. She wiped the tiny screen with a sodden cuff and pressed a couple of buttons. There was no signal, naturally.

Clenching her teeth to stop them chattering, Rosie did some quick calculations.

'One hour . . . three miles. Two more hours to get home.' She brushed against the bushes at the roadside, heedless of the twigs digging into her arm. 'I'm going to drown.' The wind blew a fresh scattering of raindrops onto her face, mingling with her tears. It was now dark. Rosie stumbled on. 'Hot coffee,' she mumbled, forcing her numb lips to move. 'Toasted bagels . . . roaring fire . . . woolly blankets . . .' There was a rumble of distant thunder. Rosie stopped. It wasn't possible. Not on top of everything else. There it was again. She turned her face up to the sky, squinting into the driving rain. 'God . . . why won't you help me?' she yelled.

Suddenly, a car rounded the bend and bore down on her, its headlamps blazing.

'Here!' Rosie screamed as she leapt forwards from the hedge, waving her arms frantically and jumping up and down.

It didn't stop. The car ploughed through a deep puddle and swerved out of her way. A tidal wave of muddy water sprayed high into the air. Rosie was helpless and took the full force of the tsunami in the face. She staggered back, spluttering with shock and spitting out dirt. Before she had time to recover, the car braked hard, flipped its lights onto full beam and reversed towards her at speed. Fearing she was about to be run over by a madman, Rosie screamed and dived towards the bushes. There was another squeal of brakes. The passenger door was flung open.

Rosie half lay in the wet leaves, soaked and sobbing. *This is it. I'm about to be kidnapped, or stabbed. Maybe both. I'm such an idiot.*

The driver leaned out.

'Get in, quick,' said Hugh.

Chapter 14

Magnificat

Hugh Fenwick drove carefully along the unlit country road. He knew its twists and turns by heart. The road surface was running with water as the squall raged closer. Soon the storm would be directly overhead.

Hugh could handle these things. Thunder – lightning – storm – hail, the hurly burly of the heath and the dark of night. What he couldn't handle was the strange girl crouched in the seat beside him. For the last five miles, she had still not said a word.

The important thing, he decided, was to stay calm. A strong side-wind buffeted the car, tugging his attention back to the road. He slowed down to drive through the deep puddles that filled the road like a river. *Concentrate man,* Hugh thought, as he willed her to speak.

Rosie had drawn her knees up onto the seat, her body angled away from him. In the dimness, Hugh couldn't tell whether she was hiding her face or trying to blow some life back into her frozen fingers. Her auburn hair hung in rain-dark ribbons over her shoulders, twigs and leaves caught among the curls. She reminded Hugh of a wounded animal, poised to lash out at anyone who came too near. He glanced across at her as he changed gear and saw that she was shivering violently.

He reached into the back seat of the car. 'Here,' he said gruffly, thrusting a tartan picnic rug at her, 'get this round you.'

'Thanks,' Rosie said in a constricted voice. She pulled the rug awkwardly round her body and closed her eyes. Of all the people who could have rescued her, it had to be him. With no one but the two of them there, he might try to broach the subject of the Harvest Ball, or even Cameron. The thought filled her with panic. She wasn't currently on speaking terms with her Cameron-memory, never mind talking *about* him.

Rosie forced her body to relax. Of all the people God could have sent as an answer to prayer, it was Hugh Fenwick. Perhaps if she feigned sleep, Hugh would let her be.

'You must be frozen,' Hugh offered, his voice softer. Rosie took several deep look-I'm-asleep breaths. Hugh cleared his throat. 'I said, you must be frozen,' he repeated loudly. Rosie opened one eye and shot him a look so loaded he could almost hear her thought. *No kidding, Einstein.* He hurriedly groped around on the back seat once more and found her a Thermos flask. 'I think there's still some tea in there,' he said. 'That ought to warm you up a bit until we get home.'

Rosie didn't want tea. She wanted whisky, brandy, gin; something potent that would shoot fire through her limbs. Coffee would have been great. Hugh kept glancing over so she sat up and fumbled with the flask. She wedged the plastic lid that doubled as a mug between her knees, slopped a decent amount into the mug and took a swig. The tea was tepid and cloyingly sweet. She swilled the liquid from cheek to cheek until she could bring herself to swallow it.

'Thanks,' she said.

Her hands started to throb as blood forced its way back into her icy fingers.

Hugh took a deep breath that sounded like a sigh. It was so difficult to have a conversation with this prickly girl. To him, she was all attitude and monosyllabic replies. He felt like a father trying to tease information out of a rebellious teenage daughter. People were supposed to grow out of that, for goodness sake.

'Did you enjoy your visit to the city?' he asked, raising his voice above the thunder.

Rosie nodded, still occupied with the onerous task of emptying the mug. It was making her feel sick. The tea dribbled down her throat like a bleeding nose.

A flash of lightning momentarily lit her face and Hugh glimpsed her sour expression and the twist of her mouth. He found himself bridling at her surly manner. If anyone had a right to be cross at this juncture, surely it was him.

'What were you doing in Alnmouth?' he asked as lightly as he could.

'Trying to get a bus home,' Rosie answered.

'That's all?' he replied, hoping she would go on.

'Yes.'

So . . . she wasn't even going to admit it. Hugh began to seethe.

'Mara . . . Mara tells me you are looking for a job,' he said stiffly.

'Did she?' Rosie replied, wondering why Mara should say that to him.

'Perhaps you'd like to explain.'

Rosie took one last swallow and carefully screwed the mug back onto the flask before replying. It seemed to take a long time.

'Not really,' she said at last, looking warily at Hugh. He seemed offended, but why? Rosie couldn't fathom it out. She felt cold, tired and embarrassed by the whole experience. All she wanted was to sleep.

'But Mara said . . .' Hugh gripped the wheel tighter and accelerated, taking the next bend faster than he should. Rosie fell hard against the passenger door.

'Hey, steady,' she protested. Hugh didn't apologise. Rosie began to feel uneasy. 'Listen,' she said, trying to sound as friendly as she could. 'Obviously I'll still do my bit on the estate but it's not as if you actually need me and I need a job that pays proper money.' Hugh stared straight ahead through the rain-spattered windscreen. A muscle twitched in his cheek. Rosie gave up. 'I didn't find a job today, anyhow. Alnmouth was closed . . . Not that it's any of your business.'

'Not my . . .?' Hugh's head jerked as though she'd struck him. 'You plan to tramp round all the local villages for God knows how many miles around, telling anyone who will listen that I don't pay you enough and that's none of my business?' His voice grew louder with every word. 'Do you realise how insulting that is? Do you?'

He stabbed the accelerator again. The engine roared and the car lurched forwards, skidding dangerously in the wet.

Rosie threw the Thermos flask into the foot well. 'Insulting? I'll tell you what's insulting, Hugh Fenwick,' she gulped, hardly able to get the words out. 'Insulting is working for nothing but a roof over my head and one hot meal a day. Insulting is accepting a basket of groceries from the kitchen staff every week when I have no means of paying for it. Insulting is having to be grateful all the time and – and being indebted for *every damn thing*.'

She spat the words out as though they were poison.

'If you needed money, why didn't you come to me?' Hugh growled. 'I don't pay you enough? Ask for a raise. I'm a fair man, Rosie. I don't make you glean the fields . . . Don't bad-mouth me the length and breadth of Northumberland. I have a reputation, damn it!'

He thumped the steering wheel and the horn blared as his fist connected with it. Rosie jumped. Hugh was starting to frighten her, but there was no way she was backing down.

'*If* you don't pay me enough?' she said shakily. 'Hugh, you don't pay me at all.'

'Don't give me that,' scoffed Hugh. 'Your wage envelope is there in the office pay day tray every month, just like everyone else's. I even asked Euan to put yours through as cash until you get your bank account moved.'

'You did?'

The car rolled to a stop, almost of its own accord. Hugh pulled the handbrake up and flicked on the overhead light. They stared at each other.

'Rosie.' He leaned towards her, his face earnest. 'You have been collecting your wages, haven't you?'

Rosie bit her lip. 'Nobody told me,' she mumbled. 'I thought – the accommodation, the free groceries. Payment in kind.' Now that she had said it aloud, it sounded ridiculous.

'But what have you been doing for money?' Hugh asked, suppressing his frustration. Rosie turned her face away from the pity in his eyes.

'Our old butler has auctioned some things for us. He sent a little money up.'

'Not your husband's things?' Rosie's face crumpled. Hugh swore quietly. 'Oh . . . Rosie. What a cock-up.'

'It's no big deal,' she lied. 'The stuff had to be sold in any case. We couldn't keep everything.'

'I'm so sorry . . .'

Hugh had a sudden impulse to reach out and hold her, but something prevented him. Instead, he put a hand on her shoulder and squeezed in what he hoped was a comforting way. Rosie shook him off, her face slamming shut against his sympathy. Anger couldn't touch her but compassion could fell her defences with a single strike and she wasn't going to break down in front of him again. She scrabbled behind her for the door handle.

'Thanks for the lift. And the wages. I can walk from here.'

'What?' Hugh was completely thrown. 'We're still a mile from home.'

'The rain's almost stopped, look.'

'It's torrential!' he said as he made a grab for her arm.

Rosie dodged and tumbled out of the car. She put her head down and set off into the storm, following the beam of light from the car's headlamps.

Hugh sat clutching a fistful of picnic rug, completely con-
founded. What the hell was he supposed to do now? Wrestle
her back into the car? Follow her home like a seedy kerb-
crawler? He peered through the windscreen. Rosie had gone
beyond the headlamps' range. The storm had swallowed her
up.

'Damn it!' Hugh leapt out of the car and sprinted after
her.

Within seconds he was drenched. Raindrops rebounded
off the road as he ran, stumbling through potholes and puddles in the dark. Water seeped through his brogues and up his
trouser legs.

'Rosie!' He grabbed her by the collar of her jacket.

'Get off me!' Rosie screamed, twisting this way and that.
Hugh tightened his hold on her collar and took a firm grip
on her upper arm.

'This is insane behaviour!' he bawled. 'Come back to the
car.'

'Go away!' A deafening thunderclap broke right above
them. Forked lightning flickered across the sky. Rosie tried
to wriggle out of her jacket. Hugh redoubled his grip. There
was nothing for it. He bent his head and shouted into
Rosie's ear.

'I promised Mara I would bring you home. I'm keeping
that promise.' He stooped, hoisted her over his shoulder in a
fireman's lift and strode back to the car, ignoring the punches landing on his back.

Rosie found herself unceremoniously dumped in the passenger seat with the door slammed and locked behind her.
Hugh dived into the driving seat and had the car moving well

before his own door clicked shut. Even Rosie wasn't mad enough to throw herself out of a vehicle moving this fast.

'What on earth,' Hugh panted, his face shiny with sweat and rain, 'was that about?'

Rosie refused to look at him.

'I just wanted to walk, OK? Get home under my own steam. I needed some space. It's not a crime.'

'You are the oddest person I have ever met.'

Rosie turned her back on him. 'Maybe you should get out more.'

Lord, give me strength. Hugh clamped his mouth shut and drove.

❀   ❀   ❀   ❀

That night, Rosie dreamt about New York. It was a Sunday morning. Someone was hammering on the door of her room in Broome Street. Rosie crawled out of bed to answer it, wearing her duvet like a cloak. Cameron was lounging against the wall outside her room.

'Come on, gorgeous,' he said, holding out his hand. 'Rise and shine. I'm taking you away from all this.'

'But it's soooo early. I haven't even had a coffee,' Rosie moaned.

'Rocket fuel ready and waiting.' He produced a steaming polystyrene cup from behind his back and wafted it beneath her nose. 'Come on, get dressed.' How could she say no, with Cameron standing there all cute and hopeful in his scruffy jeans and grey Aran sweater, all muffled up in his dorky Oxford college scarf?

The dream went on. Cameron took her to St Patrick's Cathedral, where they lit candles and listened to a visiting choir perform. Then they took the subway over to The Shark Bar and sat in the window seats, drinking Irish coffee from tall glass mugs and watching the world go by. Cameron reached across the table and laid his hand over Rosie's. 'Do you know something?' he said. 'I think . . .'

'Rosie? Rosie, wake up.' Mara's voice boomed across the bar. What was she doing there? Cracks appeared in the cosy scene. 'Wake up.' Rosie struggled to hold on but the picture was disintegrating rapidly now, a bright morning taking its place. 'Rosie!'

'What's wrong? Is it still morning?' She sat up, confused and disorientated.

'The clocks have gone back. You've had an extra hour's sleep.' Mara replied.

Rosie rubbed her eyes. 'You woke me up to tell me that?'

'No, silly.' Mara switched the light on and sat down on the bed. 'There's going to be a church service this morning.'

'I've already been,' Rosie mumbled, her brain still in the New York dream.

'No, you haven't,' said Mara. 'There's a rota for occasional services in the little chapel and there's a priest coming today.'

'I didn't even know there was a chapel,' Rosie yawned.

'Oh, yes,' said Mara. 'Been there for years and years. It's out on the land a little way. Now come on.' She stood up and tugged the bedclothes back. 'We don't want to be late.'

Rosie's heart sank. 'I'm not sure I can. I'd be a hypocrite, Mara. God and me haven't been on real speaking terms . . .'

'Don't be silly. I'm sure He won't hold a grudge!'

'I'm sorry Mara, it's not just that – I've already made plans for this morning.'

'Oh?' Mara looked disappointed and a little cross. 'What plans?'

Rosie racked her brains for a plausible excuse. She didn't want to be face to face with God. She didn't want to be face to face with Hugh. Rosie didn't want to lie but the words just dropped from her lips.

'Um . . .' *I can't go. It will remind me of Cameron and New York and being happy.* 'Euan,' she said. 'Yes. Euan is taking me out for lunch.'

'But Euan's coming to pick us up,' Mara objected, wondering why he hadn't mentioned it to her.

'That's fine,' Rosie said, improvising wildly, 'I expect we'll go straight on from there.'

Mara seemed put out. 'The service will be finished in plenty of time, Rosie. The chapel is lovely and everyone will be there. Surely you could come and then go on?'

Rosie reached for her dressing-gown. 'The thing is . . . he's made a booking. He won't want to be late.'

Mara wasn't buying it. 'But it's only half past eight. Where on earth are you going . . . Holy Island?'

'Um, I don't exactly know. It's a surprise,' Rosie said, cringing as the lies deepened. 'He just said it was a long way. A very long way.'

This time she thought that Mara appeared to swallow the lie.

'Well, I hope you enjoy your day,' she said with a sigh. 'But I'd love you to see the chapel another time. James proposed to me there, you know.'

'Mara, I didn't know.' Rosie felt like a real low-life, but it was too late. She'd stitched herself up with her own story.

'Never mind,' Mara said, moving back to let Rosie climb out of bed. 'There'll be other opportunities.' She couldn't quite hide her disappointment. 'No doubt Hugh will escort me home afterwards.'

'Yes,' Rosie agreed, a sour note colouring her voice. 'I'm sure he will. He's good at that.'

Mara gave her a sharp look but let it go.

'You and God . . .' Mara said in a whisper. 'It's not His fault and you can't blame Him. There will always be unexpected tragedies.'

'It helps to blame someone.'

'Faith was the one thing that James and I cherished in our life. Every night we would pray together and give the day to God. It's the only time when three in a marriage works. God was the glue that kept us together. Now James is dead, talking to God brings me closer to him.'

'I'm not at that place, Mara. If I went to church, I . . .' Rosie gasped. She thought of Cameron and their wedding day.

'You're going to have to face Him one day – best get it sorted out,' Mara smiled. 'I'll pray for you.'

Rosie took hold of her hand and squeezed it gently.

'I love you, Mara . . .'

'You'd better look lively, dear, or you'll have us both crying. Euan will be here soon.'

'Five minutes and I'm good to go. Promise.' Rosie said, heading towards the bathroom.

When the knock on the door came, Rosie sprinted down the stairs.

196 *Rosie: Note to Self*

'I'll go!' Mara was already there.

'Good morning,' Euan said cheerfully. 'Ready for church? Should be a sociable do, lots of folk there.'

'Yes,' said Mara. 'What a pity to be missing it.'

Euan looked taken aback. 'You're not coming, then? Are you poorly today?' he asked politely.

'Not at all,' Mara assured him. 'I'm certainly going. It's you I'm talking about.'

There was an uncomfortable pause. Euan cleared his throat.

'I . . . er . . .' he stuttered. His eyes strayed to the foot of the stairs, where Rosie was pointing from herself to him and making exaggerated chewing motions, a mime that he couldn't decipher at all. Mara smiled kindly at Euan.

'I'm not criticising, Euan, not in the slightest. I'm sure you'll have a lovely time with Rosie. Where are you taking her?'

Rosie saw the whites of Euan's eyes and quickly intervened.

'Don't ask him in front of me, Mara,' she scolded, sweeping their coats up and dashing to the door. 'It's a surprise, *isn't it, Euan?*' Rosie glared at him, willing him to play along.

'Yes . . . A surprise . . .' Euan latched on to the idea and clung to it. 'I know how Rosie loves surprises. And Rosie . . .' he plunged his hand into the pocket of his bomber jacket and produced two brown envelopes. 'Here. I'm sorry – it was *my* fault. Hugh was furious with me.'

'Thanks a lot.' Rosie slid the little packets swiftly into the pocket of her jeans and hustled Mara into her coat, ignoring her quizzical stare. 'I'm totally fine about it.

Misunderstandings happen. I'm sorry Hugh was mad at you.'

'No worries.' Euan gave her his crooked smile.

Rosie was so relieved she couldn't help grinning back.

Mara was waiting by the car, tapping her foot impatiently. 'Would anybody else like to apologise for something, or can we go?' she said. 'You may as well drop me up at the house. I can go on from there with the staff. Anything's better than watching you two gurning at each other,' she added under her breath.

'So tell me,' Euan said a short while later, one hand on the wheel as he bounced the old Range Rover carelessly down the track, heading away from the house to the main road. 'Where *are* we going?'

'Well, I told Mara you were taking me for lunch,' Rosie admitted, slightly shamefaced at her own cheek. 'But we don't have to,' she added quickly. 'We can do whatever you like.'

'Really?' Euan's smile widened, his eyes glinting mischievously.

'Within reason,' Rosie replied primly.

'Still gives me plenty of scope.'

She hated it when he got suggestive, but she figured he was like that with everyone. Rosie knew that when it came to women, Euan was a shark. Still, there was something a bit crass about his reply. Cameron would never have used a line like that.

'I'm out of the game, Euan. You know that.' She felt awkward at having to spell it out.

Euan laughed. 'In that case, lunch it is. In fact, it's perfect. I couldn't have planned it better myself. There's a pub I want to visit and it's quite a drive, as it happens. We're a bit ahead of ourselves, mind. How about a coffee in Morpeth first?'

'Sounds great,' Rosie said. She watched the sun climb up even higher over the distant sea. Her stomach felt like lead. It had been selfish of her not to go with Mara, but she just couldn't face it. God was . . . well, was He even there? Life seemed pretty arbitrary from where Rosie was sitting. 'I feel really bad about lying to Mara,' she murmured.

Euan dropped his hand briefly onto her knee as he changed gear. 'Don't let it worry you, Rosie. What's a little white lie between friends, eh?'

Chapter 15

Te Deum

Christmas . . . Just hearing the word spoken aloud used to send a thrill of anticipation shooting through Rosie. Now the thought of it made dread bubble up in her stomach like vomit. She fetched a hot water bottle to cuddle and folded herself into one of the garish armchairs in the sitting-room, her slim legs dangling over the arm. It was lunchtime and she'd chosen to come back to the Dower House, exchanging food for privacy.

On her lap was one of Cameron's desert island books. Rosie gently stroked the cover and traced the illuminated title with her finger. Every so often she fetched one from the trunk beneath her bed, but she never opened them. Holding them seemed enough. It was like touching a piece of him. For a brief time, Rosie would tap into a hidden niche where she was still capable of feeling, like an underwater air pocket. Then she would cry, shout, laugh, or simply sit in calm silence until she locked the book and herself, away once more. Today it was Shakespeare.

It was one of those volumes where the pages were thick with minute print. Like all of his books, it was well thumbed. It had a stiff spine and felt solid in her hands.

She eyed the rickety coffee table between the chairs. Though it was too unreliable to hold coffee cups, empty or full, she didn't like to throw it out. Not that it was hers to dispose of. On a good day, it managed a plate of biscuits with supervision. Currently, the little table was giving the performance of its life, balancing a bumper pack of Christmas cards on its sloping surface. Mara had brought them home and produced them with a brave smile a couple of weeks ago, but lacked the conviction to follow through. They had been on the coffee table ever since.

Rosie reached over and extracted a few cards from the transparent packaging. A polar bear in a striped scarf threw snowballs at a penguin, trails of glitter marking their trajectory through the bright blue air. On another, a sober-faced Holy Family gazed at the abnormally white lamb presented by a troupe of shepherds in their Sunday best. A deranged donkey stood by the manger looking as if it were about to eat baby Jesus. Then there was a particularly unimaginative yellow star with gold edges stuck in the centre of a midnight blue background. The final design depicted a Father Christmas squeezing his torso into a snow-dusted chimney, oblivious to the toys cascading from his over-stuffed sack across the roof.

It was the kind of selection that catered for all tastes, or lack of. The verses inside weren't much better. *Have a holly jolly Christmas . . . tidings of comfort and joy . . . love and bear hugs this Xmas . . .* and (possibly the worst pun she'd ever seen) *have a wholly holy Christmas.* Rosie tossed the bundle aside.

For the first time, her favourite season felt like nothing more than a gigantic global manipulation. 'Tis the season to be jolly . . . let nothing you dismay . . . eat, drink and be merry . . . these were imperatives, not suggestions. There might as well be Christmas police patrolling the streets, barking out commands and threats to festive dissenters. 'It's Christmas, be happy! Have fun! Get that tree trimmed! Stock up on eggnog!' That would be more honest than all this subliminal pre-programming, Rosie thought.

It was insidious. How had she failed to notice it before? Try as she might, she couldn't get the slogan 'Christmas is a time for family' out of her mind. So where, amid this outpouring of gaiety and merriment, did she and Mara fit in? Rosie slid onto the carpet and wedged some of the cards under the dodgiest leg of the coffee table. She scooped up the rest and threw them into the coal scuttle. 'Let that warm our hearts this Christmas,' she said.

Though Rosie didn't know it, Mara was struggling with similar anxieties. She escaped from the kitchen, where Mrs Drummond was regaling her with the latest titbits of local gossip, collected her coat and wandered outside. It was cold and bright and the wind was cutting its winter teeth on the bare trees. Back-endish weather, Mrs Drummond would call it. Mara vaguely thought of going for a walk, but her feet carried her to the little cowshed where Duchess lived.

Her primary concern was not Christmas itself, but where to spend it. Mrs Drummond was going to her niece in Gateshead and had offered to ask if Mara and Rosie could join them. Mara wasn't at all sure she could cope with being a house guest, with the obligation of having a good time, or at least putting up a good pretence.

The staff would be on holiday, of course and Hugh was visiting his sister's family in the Highlands. Not that it made any difference, since Rosie seemed unable to hold a civil conversation with him. 'Perhaps Oxford?' she wondered. But to whom would they go?

There was only Abbott. He certainly would have made arrangements with his usual quiet efficiency, but a hotel would be soulless and expensive. Mara had been fretting at the problem for weeks now, round and round, finding herself back at the same conclusion every time – Christmas would be just the two of them, alone at the Dower House, with the ghosts of Christmas Past pressing in around them. She gave an involuntary shudder. It was the only sensible option but a dismal prospect nonetheless.

Mara was surprised not to find Duchess' head poking out over the stable door, watching the world go by and begging snacks from the farmhands. Unusually, there was no sign of the little pony, though the top of the stable door was open. Mara tugged at the bolt on the bottom door and entered quietly. She stood just over the threshold for a few moments, letting her eyes adjust to the gloom. It smelt of hay, manure and sweat: wholesome country smells that took her back to her childhood days of rising at dawn to muck out the stables with her brother and feed their ponies before breakfast. 'Beauty,' Mara murmured. 'Yes, that was her name.' Robert had teased her for months about that.

She moved further into the stable and saw Duchess in the corner, as far away from the door as she could get. 'Hello, old girl,' Mara said. 'Keeping your ears out of the wind today?' Duchess whickered and dipped her head. Mara smiled and stretched out her hand. 'Very sensible,' she said, rubbing the long grey muzzle and letting Duchess snuffle at her palm. The pony pushed forwards and began to nose in Mara's pocket. Mara laughed and patted her on the neck. 'Did you think I'd forgotten?' she asked. Duchess flicked her ears and crunched through the little bag of sugar lumps Mara had brought from the kitchen, paper and all.

Mara ran her hand over the pony's withers and pursed her lips. 'Looks like someone's done half a job on you here,' she said, spotting a grooming kit hanging from a nail in the wall. She opened the cloth bag, took out the brushes and tentatively set to work. First the dandy brush to get rid of any dried mud or dirt on the coat. Next she took up the body brush and curry comb. Three strokes with the brush, then a pause to clean the bristles with the comb. Part of her was astonished that she remembered the technique after all these years. Duchess gave a lazy stamp and turned her attention to the feeding trough.

Mara relaxed into the rhythm of the job. It was soothing and gradually she felt her anxiety subside as she moved fluidly through the routine. The smell of the pony's coat overpowered her, carrying her back to happier days.

She remembered racing Robert over the fields, neck and neck to the finish line. Robert's pony was the superior jumper, but no one could beat Mara and Beauty in a race. 'Hunter,' she mumbled, seeing again the Welsh cob cantering beside her and hearing her brother's shouts of excitement as he urged his mount on. Tears started in her eyes at the memory. Mara felt a pang of longing for that old, easy companionship and the days when they rode bareback across the land with their arms outstretched, trying to catch the wind. She laid her cheek against the soft coat and breathed in the scent of the past.

Hugh found her like that, one arm flung over the pony's back. Her eyes were closed and she was smiling, but her cheeks were wet. He approached quietly, wondering if she were unwell.

'Mara?'

'Hmm?' she came to slowly, as though waking from a deep sleep and looked about her. 'Oh, Hugh. Hello. Do you need me?' Hugh took her hand.

'I came to finish grooming Duchess, but I see you've beaten me to it. I didn't realise you knew horses.'

'Oh yes,' replied Mara. 'I knew them, once. I never walked if I could ride.' She gave a little chuckle, recalling a time when she and Robert had tried to take their ponies to church with them one Sunday, claiming they grew anxious if left alone all day. The vicar gave them short shrift, of course.

Hugh was watching her, waiting for an explanation, but Mara only handed him the grooming kit and said, 'Just the hoof picks left to do.' Hugh worked quickly, lifting each hoof in turn and deftly prising the earth and stones free as Duchess stood placidly. He hung the bag back on its nail and turned to Mara.

'Come with me,' he said impulsively. Mara guessed his intentions and a spark of excitement lit her eyes. She grasped his hand. 'I will.'

❀ ❀ ❀ ❀

Rosie hauled herself up off the floor, picked up the Shakespeare and set off up the stairs, intending to return it to the trunk. She was halfway up when she heard her mobile beep.

'Shoot.' Rosie clattered back down to the sitting-room and dug it out from the armchair cushions.

She read the display screen and steeled herself as she flipped the handset open. She had been expecting this call for days. 'Hold on, Mom. I'm just – oh – just *hang on!*'

Rosie pounded back up the stairs to the bathroom, banged the toilet lid down and stepped up onto the seat. She braced her plaster cast against the overhead cistern and put the phone to her ear. 'Mom? I can hear you now. Start over.'

'Rosie – I can hardly hear you.' Mrs Jacobs squawked. 'Your father wanted to know if . . .'

Rosie gazed out of the narrow window, focusing on the gentle rise and fall of the fields and farmlands towards the hills. Her mother's pleading filled her ears.

'I know it's Thanksgiving next week but it's too far for Mara right now, Mom,' she said. More pleading followed. 'No, I'm not going to leave her.' The pleading became cajoling. The cajoling became tears.

Rosie was immovable, letting her mother sob into one ear while the cistern gurgled into the other. Thanksgiving was one celebration she could avoid with ease. Finally, in desperation, Mrs Jacobs played the patriotism card.

'Thanksgiving is a national holiday, a sacred institution for the United States of America, Rosie,' she said, her voice ringing down the line like a bugle call. 'We join as a family to give thanks for the birth of our great nation. God preserved the first settlers through famine and hardship and it is your patriotic duty to recollect and give thanks.'

This was too much for Rosie. 'Oh, come *on*, Mom,' she said scathingly. 'Yes, it's a big holiday, but don't give me all that first settlers' fairy tale. It was you who taught me the real story, remember? How the Native Americans saved the Pilgrims from famine and when winter was over, the settlers shot them all? Hallelujah!' Rosie waved her arm madly and almost toppled from her perch. She grabbed the toilet chain to save herself, setting off the flush. 'I bet God was real pleased about that, huh?' she said over the noise. 'Give me a break.'

'*Rosie . . .*' Mrs Jacobs dissolved into tears again.

'Mom, I'm sorry,' Rosie said.

'I'll be sure to send you some Thanksgiving cookies,' her mother sobbed. 'We love you so much, Rosie.'

'I love you too, Mom. Mom?' The line had gone dead. Rosie jumped off the toilet and kicked the bath hard.

She crossed the landing, put the Shakespeare safely back in her trunk and stalked downstairs. Then she threw her jacket on and left the Dower House, tangling her scarf awkwardly around her neck as she went. Lunch break was over.

By the time Rosie trudged into the estate office, stamping the cold from her toes, it was half-past one. The walk had taken longer than she expected today. Euan was on the phone. He looked up from his desk and mouthed, 'How's it going?' as she approached.

'What have you got for me?' she asked. Euan rolled his office chair along the carpet, stretching the phone cord to its limit.

'Uh-huh. Yes, I'll tell Hugh. Two am, Kielder. Full hunting party, is it? We'll be there. Some of the tenants might come as well.' He grabbed a file, rolled back to his desk and scribbled something on it in pencil. Rosie hovered awkwardly. 'Yes, you're right. It's always worse at this time of year,' he said. 'The poor deer don't stand a chance. Still, more poaching, more chance of catching them red-handed, or at least scaring them off, eh?' He passed the file to Rosie and blew her a kiss, grinning as she caught it and mimed a drop-kick into the bin.

'He's like a dog with a bone,' she muttered, heading off to find the Range Rover.

Rosie threw the file onto the passenger seat and sighed. More inventories. Hugh was scrupulous about maintaining the tenant farmhouses and several tenants had requested repairs or replacement items of furniture. It all needed checking and gave Rosie the chance to see the lie of the land, quite literally. It took her out of herself, which she supposed was a good thing. Euan's note made Rosie smile. *Sunday lunch – the Anvil?* She hadn't heard of that one.

Euan was going out of his way to show her around the area and Rosie was fast becoming a connoisseur of the English Sunday roast in all its varieties. It was sweet of him. She found a pencil in the glove compartment and drew a thumbs-up sign beside the messy writing, knowing Euan would check the file for her reply. Which reminded her . . . Note to self, Rosie: find out who was on the phone.

Hunting poachers sounded daring and dangerous. Rosie had heard of Kielder Forest but no one had mentioned a deer population. She pictured herself stealing through the woods in the dead of night as part of a crack hunting team, setting traps for the dogs and laying concealed nooses on the forest floor, ready to hoist unwary poachers by the ankle.

A thrill ran down Rosie's spine. Maybe if she worked on Euan, they'd let her go along sometime. She could certainly do with some excitement. She sighed, opened the file and scanned the first page. 'Leaking roof at the Old Granary,' she read. 'Approval required for repairs.' OK. Haven't been there before. 'Tenants Ged and Harriet Lucas.' She punched the postcode into the Sat Nav system and the Range Rover lurched off with a horrible crunching sound. As usual, she stalled the engine several times before making it through the gates. Life would be so much simpler if everybody drove automatics, Rosie thought, wincing as her wrist twinged. The engine screamed as she mangled the gears again. 'Hope you're having a better day than me, Mara,' she sighed.

❀   ❀   ❀   ❀

Mara was leaning against a fence at the local riding stables, watching a riding lesson. She felt strange in her borrowed boots and jodhpurs and the back protector Hugh had insisted on was going to be a nuisance. Apparently everyone wore them these days. Three staid ponies plodded around the paddock, doing their best to keep their young riders on their backs. The instructor turned slowly in the centre of the circle, shouting directions. 'Heels down, Jessica,' she called to the youngest pupil, a blonde girl with long plaits whose hat had tipped down over one eye. 'Relax your grip.' Jessica nodded fearfully and clung on even tighter. Mara chuckled.

'Ready, Mara?' Hugh walked across the courtyard, leading a solid-looking black Dales pony with feathered fetlocks and a beautiful dark brown horse. Mara looked admiringly at it.

'Irish Draught?'

'Irish Draught cross Thoroughbred,' Hugh replied. 'You really do know horses.'

'I said so, didn't I? What are their names?'

'This is Merlin,' said Hugh, patting the thoroughbred. He handed the pony's reins to Mara. 'And this little fellow is Jet.' He led Mara to a mounting block and handed her up, then swung himself up onto Merlin's back and looked down at Mara. 'Sure you don't want to be on a lead rein?' he asked anxiously. Mara gave him a withering look.

'I was riding before you were even born, Shuggie,' she said. Hugh grinned.

'Go carefully, then. After you.'

It was an incredible feeling, being on horseback again after twenty years out of the saddle. Still, Mara rode slowly along the bridleway that skirted the fields by the riding stables. Despite her bold claims, she was wary of falling. Hugh rode a little way behind, keeping a close eye on her.

At Mara's age the whole idea was lunacy, but as he watched her jogging along, straight backed, calm and completely attuned to the pony, he knew his hunch had been a good one. When she glanced back at him he saw colour in her cheeks and mischief in her eyes, as though she had reached through time and struck a bargain with her younger self to trade places for the afternoon.

The bridleway veered to the right, taking them across some pastureland. Mara reined in and sat her pony quietly

while Hugh dismounted to open the five-bar gate. Mara
guided Jet through and leaned out of the saddle to speak to
Hugh.

'We've warmed up now,' she said brightly. 'Let's ride.'

It was all the warning Hugh received. Mara snapped the
reins, dug her heels in and Jet responded instantly, stretching
into a canter in a matter of seconds.

Mara threw her head back and whooped, her hair streaming out beneath her riding hat like a silver pennant in the
wind.

'What on earth?' Hugh dragged the gate shut and flung
himself into the saddle. 'She'll break her neck!' Clods of earth
flew up from beneath Merlin's hooves as Hugh set off in
pursuit. Sheep scattered right and left as the horse thundered
along the bridleway. *'Mara!'* he roared. 'Stop!' Mara didn't
hear, or didn't want to. Her sheer recklessness took Hugh's
breath away. At any minute the pony could catch its hoof and
stumble, or Mara could lose her balance and tumble from its
back. With greater power and speed, Merlin gained rapidly
on the pony until the riders were level. 'Stop!' Hugh
ordered. Reluctantly, Mara slowed to a trot, then a walk. She
shot a reproachful look at Hugh.

'I was going to stop at the next gate,' she said. 'There was
no need to panic.'

Hugh swallowed hard, forcing his heart back to its proper
place in his chest. 'If you try that again,' he rasped, 'I'll have
you banned from the stables.'

Mara's eyes flashed. 'I told you I could ride.'

'And I believed you. But not like that, Mara. Not now. You
might have been thrown, or worse. Then what would I tell

Rosie?' They reached the gate and Hugh dismounted. 'I'm not opening this until you promise to go steady. Walk or trot, no more.'

Mara glared at him. Hugh wouldn't budge. 'Oh, very well,' she huffed. 'I promise.'

Hugh slid the bolt back on the gate. 'You gave me an awful fright, Mara.'

Mara's face split into a huge grin. 'But it was worth it.'

Chapter 16

Thanksgiving

On the morning of Thanksgiving, Mara got up early. She felt her way across the dark landing and crept down the stairs. Under normal circumstances, it would take a small fireworks display outside the bedroom window to wake Rosie, but Mara liked to adhere to form. Creeping around was an essential component of surprises. Besides, it added to the fun of it all.

Mara clicked the kitchen light on and tiptoed around, fetching various items from their hiding places and arranging them on a large tray. She hushed the frying pan when it dared to sizzle and pounced on the whistle kettle at the first sign of a peep. Humming under her breath, she scurried happily to and fro, enjoying the anticipation. Plates were warmed in the oven, cutlery polished and the single linen napkin, specially starched by Mrs Drummond, was folded into the shape of a peacock. Mara had spent a whole morning under Mrs Drummond's strict tutelage to learn the skill and was delighted with the results.

When everything was ready, she lifted the *pièce de résistance* from the fridge and placed it delicately on the corner of the tray. On a whim, she covered the tray with two white tea towels to hide the contents and stood back to examine her handiwork. The cafetière looked a bit peculiar, spiking up beneath the tea towel like a snow-covered Statue of Liberty, but the overall effect of the mysterious humps and bumps was very pleasing.

Mara took a deep breath and picked up the tray. At the foot of the stairs, she stopped and stared up. The tray wobbled slightly in her hands.

'One flight,' she reminded herself. 'That's all. Eighteen steps. You can do this.' The veins stood out on the backs of her hands as she renewed her grip and began the ascent. Halfway up her arms began to tremble but she held on and gained the upper landing, dumping the tray on the washing basket in the nick of time.

Mara leaned on the banister while she got her breath back and took a quick peek under the tea towels. There were a couple of small spillages and one of the teaspoons had bailed out due to turbulence, but the important things were still in place. Silently, she opened the door to Rosie's bedroom before she lifted the tray and braced herself for the final push. Suddenly she froze. Her mind had gone blank at the crucial moment. 'Come on,' she whispered. 'You know it.' The cutlery started to rattle as the tray turbulence returned. Mara knew she couldn't hold on much longer. Only one thing came to mind.

A horrible wailing noise penetrated the warm, dark cave Rosie had fashioned from her sheets and blankets. As the weather grew colder she had started experimenting, creating a kind of den from the bedclothes each night. The trick was to leave no part of herself exposed to the air. It was stuffy but warm and, despite a high risk of suffocation, was proving an effective strategy.

Rosie woke with a start as the wailing grew louder. Even shielded by layers of bedclothes, it was a dreadful sound.

'Mara?' she called, scrabbling around as she searched for a way out. The wailing was right beside her now, punctuated by a sudden crash close to her head. Rosie yelped with fright. 'Mara? I'm coming!' She surfaced from the tangle of blankets and saw Mara at her bedside, waving a tiny flag on a cocktail stick.

'*Con*found their politics, *frus*trate their knaaaaa-vish tricks,' she bellowed. 'God save us all. May he sedition hush and like a . . . torrent rush, Rebellious . . . Scots to crush . . . God save the . . . Queen . . .'

This is one of those surreal dreams, Rosie thought. The ones where you think you've woken up but in fact you haven't. Any minute now a walrus will come in wearing a tutu and tell me I've won the lottery. I shouldn't have had that cheese last night.

Mara finished with a flourish and a sharp salute.

'Lovely . . .' Rosie lay still, wishing God would save her from her own warped imagination.

'Happy Thanksgiving!' Mara cried and collapsed on the bed, crushing Rosie's leg.

'Ouch!'

'Sorry, dear.'

Rosie edged away from her. 'I'm . . . I'm awake,' she said faintly, trying to make the necessary psychological adjustments in her brain. 'So . . . this is kind of weird.'

'I've brought you breakfast in bed,' Mara beamed. 'Your special Thanksgiving treat. Come on, sit up.'

'What's with the singing?' Rosie asked.

Mara blushed. 'I'm sorry about that. It was meant to be *The Star Spangled Banner* but I forgot the words. Had to make do with ours. I've got the right flag, though.'

'Great,' said Rosie, trying not to laugh. Five minutes into the day and already it was the oddest Thanksgiving she'd ever had. She hiked herself up and propped her back against the wall. 'So what's for breakfast? It smells good.'

Mara bustled over to the bedside table and set the covered tray on Rosie's lap.

'It's a bit unusual,' she said. 'Symbolic. I'll explain as you go along.'

'I couldn't be any more surprised than I am already,' Rosie said, lifting off the tea towels. She was immediately hit by an overpowering smell of salt and fish. 'OK, I take that back.'

'Craster kipper,' Mara said proudly. 'A local speciality, representing the harvest of the land, or sea in this case.'

'And this?' Rosie pointed at a small, individually-sized cheesecake.

'New York cheesecake, of course.'

'Of course.'

'The base is made with the crumbs of the cookies your mother sent from America,' Mara continued. 'They didn't survive the journey but I thought it would be a terrible shame to waste them. It was Ellen's idea. A Thanksgiving Cookie cheesecake.'

Rosie lifted another plate. 'And American pancakes, representing . . . America?' she guessed. Mara nodded. There was something intriguing hanging from the side of the cafetière. It looked like several locks of hair tied to a piece of string. 'And this?' Rosie asked pointing to it.

'Scalps. I wanted to find a Native American recipe to symbolise their aid to the first settlers, but there wasn't time. Didn't Thanksgiving have something to do with scalping the natives?'

Rosie breathed a sigh of relief.

'It's perfect as it is,' she said. 'And coffee and orange juice to wash it all down.' She looked at the crammed tray and felt a surge of affection for Mara, seeing how much thought and effort had gone into the surprise, however wacky the result. She touched the napkin, admiring the crisp concertina folds of the peacock fan. 'Did you do this too? It looks incredible.' Mara beamed.

'All my own work,' she said. 'And I've got a present for you. It's . . .' Rosie arranged an excited look on her face and prayed for something normal, '. . . an extra day off. Hugh agreed straight away.'

'Very kind of him,' Rosie said graciously. She hugged Mara close. 'But not as kind as you.' Mara was delighted.

'Eat up, eat up,' she urged, flapping her hands at the tray. 'Your kipper's getting cold.'

It was ten o'clock by the time Rosie had ploughed her way through breakfast and got dressed. She had snapped up Mara's suggestion of a day of hiking and couldn't wait to get going.

'Are you sure you'll be all right going off by yourself?' Mara called up the stairs.

Rosie swallowed her initial response, recognising her own protective instinct reflected back at her. It was a natural response to their situation, but wearing to be on the receiving end. Getting a little space would be no bad thing, she realised. They couldn't keep each other wrapped up in cotton wool forever.

'I'll be fine,' she called back. 'I've got the map and my mobile.' No need for Mara to know how unreliable the signal was. 'I've even got a compass.' With any luck she might remember how to use it.

Downstairs, Rosie found Mara pacing about in the sitting-room, clutching a blue knapsack. 'I've packed your lunch,' Mara said, tripping over the words. 'And there's a flask of coffee and some biscuits as well.'

'Any more surprises I should know about?' Rosie joked. 'No fanfares when I open the bag or anything?' Mara swiped at her with the knapsack. 'I will be fine, you know. I know the estate pretty well now.'

'By road, but you haven't been cross-country before,' Mara fretted. 'It's easy to get lost.'

Rosie rolled her eyes. 'So I'll ask somebody. It's hardly uncharted territory. This was your idea, remember?'

'I remember,' Mara sighed. 'It seemed good in theory.'

'It is good,' said Rosie. 'Newcastle will be heaving today and I heard they've got all the Christmas lights up already. I'm not in the mood for that. This is a much better plan. I'll be back before you've even missed me.'

'By teatime,' Mara reminded her.

'It's a promise.'

'And if it rains . . .'

'I'll get wet. Stop worrying. I was a Girl Scout, I can do countryside.'

Mara stood on the doorstep, waving Rosie off as though she were setting out to conquer Everest.

'Don't forget to thank Hugh if you see him,' she called. Rosie nodded half-heartedly. She turned at the bend in the track and gave Mara a big wave.

'See you,' she called, cupping her hands round her mouth.

Mara waved back and closed the door. Rosie hoped Mrs Drummond had an extensive list of distracting jobs lined up for Mara today. She settled the knapsack more comfortably on her back and walked on, swinging her arms in time. She glanced down and flexed her newly liberated wrist in a little wave, just because she could. This was going to be fun.

For the first hour, Rosie followed the track away from the house, with the intention of getting up to the main road. There was no fixed plan.

It felt good to be able to wander along without needing to check the time, or think about where she ought to be. The open spaces frightened her less now that she was getting to know the area. Or perhaps it wasn't that. With a sudden insight, Rosie saw that it was the lack of people that had made the countryside feel so empty. Once she'd started to look at the landscape in terms of what was there, rather than whom, the place began to feel crowded. Life was bursting out on all sides in Northumberland, even in winter.

Rosie trailed a stick idly along the thinning hedge as she walked, dislodging a few leaves. She couldn't come this way without recalling Phil and the trailer incident when they had first arrived. It had never been mentioned, well, not to her face, but neither was it the sort of thing people would forget. If she looked hard enough, there'd probably be a bunch of sheep wearing her missing beanie hat and half a dozen of her socks. The thought made her laugh.

Phil had sent her a card a couple of weeks after they'd arrived in Northumberland. Rosie hadn't replied, unable to find a suitable platitude to fall back on. Thanks for the lift? Thinking of you? Having a lovely time? None of it would have been true. She wondered how Phil was getting on and felt ashamed that the thought had only just occurred to her three months down the line. Cutting contact was probably for the best, she reasoned, fishing a biscuit out of her knapsack. It would be unfair to give him false hope.

'Rubbish!' Rosie startled herself imagining what Cameron would have said to that idea. She had spoken in her head to him before, even allowed herself to hear what he might reply, but never the luxury of a conversation. Perhaps she had been protecting herself – scared that if she allowed herself to drift fully into a discussion with the memory of her husband, she may never want to return to the present. But here, alone in the Northumberland wildness . . .

'I've missed you, Cam. It's been a long time.' Rosie savoured the first words of her imaginary dialogue. 'Why haven't I done this before?'

'You were too angry before.'

'Right now I am,' she objected. 'I just dropped a good biscuit.'

'Sue me.'

Rosie laughed. 'Your honour, I'd like to bring a case against the voices in my head? You're not even here. You're just a . . . a . . . I don't know. A manifestation of my grief, or something.'

'A shadow of my former self?'

'Very funny.' She dug out a second biscuit and took a bite. 'Apparently it's really common. People talk to their deceased loved ones as though they're still there.'

'In a way, I am. Heaven is all around.'

Rosie flung her stick over the hedge. 'Whatever that means.'

'How do you explain my replies?' the voice in her head asked curiously.

'I always said you spent too much time at the Oxford Debating Society. I know you, Cameron. I know what you'd answer – if you were here . . .'

'So I'm like your Jiminy Cricket?' Hearing his voice – even if it was in her imagination – was precious. She didn't care if she was mad with grief. She didn't want it to end.

'I guess.' Rosie replied, knowing she was speaking to herself. 'I'm not sure of heaven . . .'

'You don't think all I was in life just died on a French mountain do you?' the voice said softly as if it were no longer in her mind but next to her. 'Something must go on . . .'

'If only,' Rosie sighed. 'But then, isn't that wishful thinking – just like God and angels?'

'How long does this, erm, this stage of grief last?' the voice asked, sounding more like Cameron.

Rosie shrugged. 'No idea. Until I move on? In which case, never.'

Cameron's voice was calm. 'You'll get there.'

'Maybe I don't want to.'

'But you will.' The voice faded, but the note of conviction resonated in Rosie's mind.

There was a public bridleway signposted left and Rosie decided to follow it. The hedge had been cut back from the wooden stile to allow safe passage into the field. Rosie climbed through and wandered on, berating herself for her strange behaviour. Talking to herself was one thing, but talking to herself and pretending it was Cameron? Conjuring up his voice? Grief or no grief, that wasn't a normal way to behave. Maybe she needed help.

'It's official,' she informed a fat, passing sheep. 'I'm cracking up.'

Rosie traipsed along for another hour, enjoying the crisp air and fading colours of autumn. She pushed all thoughts from her mind and tried to be fully present in the moment. Only the last leaves lingered on the bare trees, the rest made up a crunchy carpet on top of the decomposing vegetation. The ground had hardened beneath an early frost, trapping most of the moisture underground. A few boggy patches remained. Rosie looked down at her muddy boots. She seemed to be treading in all of them.

The sun was bright but offered no warmth. Rosie didn't care. She found the cold invigorating and could avoid getting chilled, provided she kept a reasonably fast pace. Mostly she followed the paths and bridleways in a random fashion, occasionally checking her position against the map.

Getting lost wasn't a consideration. There were enough landmarks for her to recognise roughly where she was in the greater scheme of things. After a while she began to play old childhood games to pass the time, puffing her breath out in front of her like a baby dragon, spotting shapes in the twisted silhouette of a tree, hunting for pine cones and the last of the conkers. What clouds there were formed animal shapes in the sky. As she walked, Rosie watched them change, both hopeful and afraid she might hear Cameron's voice again.

Since waving to Mara, she hadn't seen another soul but Rosie knew that was to be expected. Hiking was a weekend pastime. What kind of a person went out in the hills on a freezing Thursday in November?

'Mad dogs and Englishmen go out in the midday sun, but not in November,' she quipped to a robin that followed her from tree to tree for a while, clearly on a human surveillance mission. She spent the next mile trying to devise an equivalent idiom for Americans in winter, but couldn't make anything fit.

Eventually, Rosie remembered the lunch Mara had packed for her. Looking ahead, she saw that the path slalomed back and forth up a long, slow climb. 'The view will be great from up there,' she murmured, shading her eyes as she stared up at the hill. 'Food at the top.' Half an hour later, she panted over the final rise and stopped short. Someone was there before her.

A man with bushy white hair was sitting with his back to her on a large, flat outcropping of stone set into the grassy summit. He sat comfortably with one leg casually thrown out to the side, revealing a stout walking boot and a bright red gaiter encasing the leg to the knee. This was no amateur.

Rosie hesitated, wanting to claim her chosen lunch spot but sensing a quality of stillness in the scene that she was loathe to shatter. She stood there for a long time before turning away. Her foot dislodged a stone and the man turned at the sound.

'Hello there,' he called jovially. 'I didn't hear you come up.' Rosie mumbled something about passing through and made to leave, but the man brushed her words aside. 'Why don't you join me? It's a marvellous view.' He patted the stone beside him. 'Plenty of room for two.'

'Thanks.' Rosie approached the rock and sat down, feeling inexplicably shy. 'I've disturbed you,' she said awkwardly.

'Not at all, not at all,' he said affably. 'I was half asleep, actually. Good job you came when you did. Another five minutes and I'd have rolled right off the edge. So *I* should be thanking *you*.'

Rosie smiled and unhooked her knapsack. 'I've got some food here,' she said, fumbling with the fastenings. 'We could share. It's not much, but . . .'

The man shook his head. 'Far too much flesh on these old bones,' he said dolefully, patting his stomach. 'You carry on, my dear. You carry on.'

'Oh. Um, OK then. If you're sure.' Rosie eyed the long, lean legs and spare frame. Was this one of those weird English jokes where people kept a straight face and deliberately said something really dumb? His face gave nothing away.

She unpacked her sandwiches and began to eat, casting around for a suitable topic of conversation. To her surprise, the man seemed quite content to do nothing but sit there beside her. After the initial urge to fill the space with the flimsy small talk she hated, Rosie felt herself relax into the silence, letting it wrap around her as she absorbed the beautiful view from the hilltop. It was oddly comforting.

When she had eaten the last crumbs of her lunch, Rosie produced the flask and showed it to her companion. 'Coffee?'

His eyes lit up. 'Yes, please. Hang on, I've got just the thing here.' He unzipped a pocket and held out a small hip flask. Rosie looked mystified. 'Whisky,' he prompted. 'Irish coffee?'

'Wow. That's a treat,' Rosie said, holding out the plastic mug. He poured a generous measure and watched as Rosie added the coffee. 'You first,' she said, handing him the mug. He gulped it down, poured another shot of whisky and passed the mug back with a satisfied smile.

'I'm Aelred,' he said, pressing one hand to his chest.

'I'm sorry?'

'Aelred,' he said again. 'And don't be sorry. It's a bit of a shocker, but I've grown used to it over time.' He heaved a mournful sigh and made his face droop, but his eyes gave him away.

Rosie smiled, sure of the joke this time. 'I'm Rosie,' she replied. Aelred leaned forwards, resting his arms on his knees.

'Rosie,' he repeated, testing the word on his tongue. 'What brings you here, Rosie?'

Rosie looked into his eyes and felt a sudden certainty that she could talk to this man. Really talk. Why him, why now, she didn't know. Perhaps because he was a stranger. Maybe it was his simple act of accepting her silence and not pressing her to talk at all that made her choose to speak. Whatever the reason, Rosie sat beside Aelred on the cold stone, stared out at the horizon and let it all come tumbling out.

Every so often, she would glance from the horizon to his weathered face. It was ageless, the type of face that carried time well. Rosie could tell he was old – as old as Mara at least. Yet there was something about the man that made him different. His sharp blue eyes and tanned skin framed a face that always welcomed a smile. The old man looked strong for his age, as if he walked the hills each day, his white hair blowing in the wind.

Whilst she talked, Aelred listened without saying a word. He smiled occasionally and nodded in affirmation of what she was saying, but Rosie knew he was hearing every word. It was the first time she had opened her heart. She felt no fear, no concern. It was as if everything was being scoured from her soul. The hills were her cathedral and the sun her light.

It was a long time before she ran out of words. Afterwards, they sat in silence for a while. Then Aelred leaned over and squeezed her hand.

'Thank you,' he said. 'It was brave of you to share that with me.' Rosie looked about her and realised with a shock that it was getting dark.

'What time is it?' she gasped, scrambling to her feet.

'Four-thirty,' said Aelred, slightly bemused by the swift transition from tranquillity to panic.

Rosie began stuffing the debris from lunch into her knapsack.

'I promised I'd be back in time for tea,' she gasped. 'It's a two hour walk. Mara will be frantic. I have to go.' She wrestled her arms into the shoulder straps, incoherent with panic. 'It was – thank you, I – we should . . .'

'Calm down.' Aelred got to his feet and adjusted his gaiters.

'You don't understand!' Rosie burst out, knowing she didn't want to walk in the dark.

'After all you've said, I think I do,' he replied. He took a red woollen hat from his pocket and pulled it on. 'There's a decent road ten minutes walk from here. I'll take you.'

'I can't hitch a lift!' Rosie spluttered. 'I could be waiting all night.'

'My car is parked there,' Aelred said patiently.

'Car?' Rosie gasped

'What?' he laughed at the outraged look on Rosie's face. 'You thought I'd hiked for hours and fought my way to the high ground, like you?'

'Well, yes,' said Rosie, pointing at his boots and gaiters.

'It pays to look the part, my dear,' Aelred grinned. 'I can hike all day in the summer months but not at this time of year. Perish the thought. In the winter I drive up here for the peace and quiet. Plus,' he gave her a conspiratorial wink, 'it's a great place to meet women.'

Rosie laughed.

It took just over half an hour to reach the Dower House. Aelred stopped the car but kept the engine running.

'I won't come in,' he said. Rosie thought he looked almost shifty.

'Thanks for a great day,' she said. 'I feel a lot better.'

'I'm up at the viewpoint most Thursdays,' Aelred said casually. 'We could start an open-air coffee club.'

'I don't always get Thursdays off,' Rosie explained.

'An open-ended invitation, then.'

'That sounds perfect.' Rosie climbed out of the car and stood at the gate to wave him off. A strange thought struck her. In the space of one afternoon, she'd told this man everything about herself, keeping nothing back. He had received it all like a gift and calmly driven away.

All she had was his name.

Chapter 17

Yuletide

Hugh awoke on Christmas Eve after three hours' sleep, feeling anything but festive. He stumbled downstairs in yesterday's clothes and made his way to the staff office. He passed by the kitchen and ordered a late breakfast. Euan was sprawled across the desk in the office with his head resting on his arms.

'I wasn't expecting you in today,' said Hugh.

Euan didn't raise his head. 'Few things to tie up,' he groaned. Hugh dropped into a chair.

'I felt sure we'd catch someone last night.' He yawned, running his palm over the fresh crop of stubble on his face. 'The conditions were perfect for poaching. It was the heaviest cloud cover we've had for weeks.'

'And their last chance for a kill before Christmas,' Euan added. 'Venison will make a mint on the black market at the moment. There's plenty of places wanting to stock up for the festive season but it won't be so easy to flog come January. Easier to trace locally, too. They'll ship out and sell it on elsewhere.'

'No doubt about that,' agreed Hugh. 'What I don't understand is why they weren't out there. Six months this racket has been going on and we've never even come close.'

Euan propped his head on his hands. 'Unless . . . no.'

'Unless what?' asked Hugh. 'Go on.'

'Unless there's a mole in the hunting party,' said Euan. 'Someone who could alert the gang when we plan a watch in the forest.'

Hugh ran a hand through his hair, making it stand on end.

'It's possible, I suppose.' He frowned. 'But who? Half of the team are police and the rest are landowners, tenant farmers or forest rangers.' He ticked them off on his fingers. 'Mark Graham, Ben Armstrong, John Whitfield . . . They all want to see the poaching ring broken.'

'True,' Euan admitted. 'But it wouldn't have to be one of the group. It could be a friend or relative, even a neighbour. The volunteers don't keep their involvement a secret, do they? Anyone close enough to have a friendly conversation could ask a few leading questions and find out everything they needed to know.'

'You're right,' said Hugh. 'It's time we tightened up on what we say.' He stretched his arms up over his head, trying to loosen the tension in his shoulders and upper back. 'I'll raise it at the next meeting.'

The door opened and Mara trundled in with a tray. Her confidence and steadiness, had increased since the Thanksgiving success. She had been in the kitchen when Hugh ordered breakfast and had insisted on bringing it through herself. Euan pushed his paperwork aside to make room for it on the desk.

'Look at the state of you both,' Mara tutted. She handed them each a large mug of tea. 'You look like the walking dead.'

'So would you if you'd been out hunting deer poachers from midnight until seven in the morning,' protested Hugh. Euan raised a cautionary eyebrow. 'Don't be ridiculous,' Hugh said. 'You can't possibly suspect Mara of passing information to a poaching ring. Apologise.'

'No offence intended,' Euan said, bobbing his head at Mara, 'but you see how easy it would be?'

'No doubt,' Mara smiled. 'I'm guilty of many things but poaching isn't one of them.' She reached out and plucked a twig from Hugh's hair. 'Have some food and go back to bed.'

'I can't. I'm leaving for my sister's at two o'clock and I haven't packed,' Hugh said. 'Or wrapped the children's presents.'

'If you're planning to drive to Scotland, you could do with some more sleep, Hugh.'

He smiled. 'It's so good to see you looking well. I'm glad you came to live here . . . Merry Christmas.'

Hugh kissed her on the cheek as he squeezed her hand. It was more than a seasonal display of affection. Mara stood back and looked at him.

'It saved my life. I didn't know what I was going to do when James and the boys died . . . but you came to the rescue . . . for Rosie too.'

'And I've got to finish up here and drive to my Gran's in Berwick,' Euan interrupted, crunching through a slice of toast. 'No rest for the wicked.'

'It's supposed to be a holiday,' Mara laughed.

'Try telling that to Josie's brood,' Hugh grumbled as he thought of a house full of his sister's children.

Mara ruffled his hair. 'You'll have a lovely time.'

'Are you sure you'll be all right here?' Hugh asked.

Mara picked up the breakfast tray. 'Oh, don't worry about us,' she said lightly. 'We've got our own plans.' She left the room quickly with her head down. Hugh looked at Euan, who shrugged as if to say, yes, it's sad, but what do you expect me to do about it?

Mara hid her tears in the kitchen. It was her first Christmas without James. If she could manage 'all right' it would be a miracle.

In the Dower House, Rosie tried to put her own plan into action. The sitting-room was a mess of torn wrapping paper, cards and long strips of tangled crepe paper laid out in lines of red and green. Rosie squatted on the floor looking harassed, several dressmaking pins clenched between her teeth. She took stock of the situation. The surprise decorations were not going well.

At home, her mother decorated the walls with Christmas cards hung on lengths of ribbon or crepe paper. Rosie was trying to copy the technique using the cards Mara had bought – those that had escaped the coal scuttle She couldn't remember how her mother attached the cards to the crepe strips and, after sacrificing too much sellotape, she had decided to pin them instead. Her fingers were covered with spots of blood where the pins had jabbed her as they pushed up through the cards, but she had succeeded in making a prototype.

Rosie spat the pins out and stood up. She fetched a stool from the kitchen and towed the strip of cards across the floor. She pressed a lump of Blu-Tack into the top of the strip and pushed it firmly onto the wall as high as possible, so that the cards hung in a vertical line to the floor. The effect was pretty. More importantly, it was low key. No frills, no fuss. Just a few of these dotted about the room to acknowledge Christmas without going over the top. Rosie glanced down at the remaining strips of crepe. One down, four to go.

There was a sudden, urgent knock at the door.

'Coming!' Rosie jumped down from the stool and picked her way to the door. Charlotte Alderson stood on the step beside a fat Christmas tree.

'Have you got one already?' she asked, trying to peer past Rosie into the sitting-room.

'No,' said Rosie, 'we didn't get around to it.'

'Oh, good. Alastair, take the tree in,' Charlotte commanded, 'while I fetch the rest of the stuff from the car.' She trotted off without waiting for a reply. Rosie wondered whether anyone had ever said no to Charlotte Alderson. Alastair's head appeared from behind the branches of the tree.

'Resistance is futile, just do what she says . . .' he murmured with the resigned smile of a man who had accepted the fact a long time ago. 'Definitely futile.'

'So I see,' Rosie replied. 'This is, um, really kind of you.' She stood aside to let him through. Charlotte whirled in carrying two large cardboard boxes.

'Goodness me!' she said, surveying the floor. Rosie blushed. 'Have you been burgled?'

'Excuse the mess. I was trying something out.'

'Not to worry, we'll soon have it cleared up,' Charlotte said as she balanced on one leg and pushed the front door shut with her heel. It closed with a bang. The strip of cards fell from the wall as though hit by enemy fire and played dead. Alastair approached the unmoving heap and prodded it gingerly with his toe.

'I think this one's carked it,' Alastair pronounced as if he knew what was to come.

Under Charlotte's direction, the Dower House was transformed in less than an hour. The result was extravagant, professional and completely impersonal. The tree was trimmed with silver and blue baubles, snowmen and reindeer perched on the windowsills and plump hearts in checked blue and cream fabric hung on ribbons from every doorknob. There was even a miniature nativity set, with the stable and crib at one end of the mantelpiece and the three kings plodding along at the other.

'They can't arrive until Epiphany, remember,' trilled Charlotte. A delicate angel with gilded wings watched graciously over everything from the top of the tree. Rosie found its fixed smile unnerving and hoped her own looked more realistic. It matched the bemused look of baby Jesus, who was remarkably large for a newborn babe. Her attempts at home-made decorations were brushed aside and ruthlessly binned.

After they'd gone, Rosie shunted the kings over to the stable and swivelled the angel's head round to face the dreadful wallpaper. But there was no getting away from it. Christmas was now in every corner of the room.

There was a second knock at the door. Rosie instinctively ducked out of sight behind a chair. What if the Aldersons had found another box of decorations in the car? Euan's face appeared at the window.

'Rosie? Are you there?' She breathed a sigh of relief and opened the door. Hugh stood there with a large turkey cradled in his arms. Rosie felt her stomach cramp at the sight of its pallid, pimply flesh. Cameron had always taken care of the fleshy aspects of cooking. She liked eating meat, just didn't like seeing it dangling. Hugh's face fell.

'Have you got one already?' he asked.

'No,' said Rosie, backing away from the door. Euan muscled in beside Hugh, brandishing a bottle of sherry in one hand and a box of mince pies in the other.

'Here you go, sweetheart,' he grinned. 'This'll warm your cockles.' Rosie gave a sickly smile. Euan began strolling around, exclaiming over the decorations. 'Hey, these are fantastic,' he said, picking up a particularly saccharine trio of singing snowmen. He flicked a switch and they broke into a tinny rendition of Jingle Bells.

Rosie looked at the fire and wondered if molten plastic emitted toxic fumes. Hugh emerged from the kitchen, wiping his hands on his jeans.

'Have you enough coal?' he asked quietly.

'Plenty, thanks.' An awkward triangle formed as Euan joined them in the centre of the room. Rosie looked from one to the other, noticing that both men looked wrecked. The dark circles beneath Euan's eyes stood out like bruises on his skin and his clothes were creased. Hugh always looked crumpled, but he was unshaven and his face was drawn with fatigue. What was wrong with them?

'Merry Christmas, then?' said Euan.

'Er, yes. Merry Christmas,' Rosie replied automatically, her eyes still on Hugh. Euan coughed expectantly. Rosie forced her attention back to him. He was waiting for something. 'And a happy new year?' she tried. Euan stared pointedly at the ceiling, then back at Rosie. She glanced up and saw a sprig of mistletoe dangling innocently from the patterned lampshade. Euan's grin widened.

Hugh cleared his throat loudly as their eyes met. 'I need to get going. Long journey. Merry Christmas.' Rosie followed him to the door.

'Hugh, wait.' He shook his head and walked quickly to his car before she could thank him. Rosie felt embarrassed and frustrated. Nothing was working out for her today. She held the door open and beckoned to Euan. 'You'd better go too. I don't want to make you late.'

'Not without my kiss,' he said, advancing towards her with his lips puckered. Rosie pecked him on the cheek and propelled him out of the door.

'You'll give in eventually,' Euan smirked. 'They all do.'

Rosie rolled her eyes at him and shut the door. She heard him laughing as he walked away.

She wandered into the kitchen and opened the fridge. Hugh had managed to cram the turkey in by adjusting the height of the shelves. Rosie hoped Mara would know what to do with it. There was no way she was going to chop off its head or stick her hand up its back end, even if it meant eating crackers and cheese for Christmas lunch.

When the third knock on the door came, Rosie pressed her forehead to the cool surface of the kitchen table. 'I can't take much more of this.'

She dragged herself to the door and opened it a crack.

'Sorry, Rosie. I didn't have a spare hand for the door,' said Mara, indicating the carrier bags in each hand. 'Mrs

Drummond insisted on buying presents for us.' Rosie threw the door open.

'Thank goodness it's you,' she said fervently.

Mara's face changed. 'What is it?' she said fearfully. Rosie shook her head and ushered Mara inside. There was a thud as Mara let the bags fall. 'My word,' she breathed. 'What happened here?'

'Charlotte and Alastair,' said Rosie. 'There was nothing I could do.' Mara seemed to be struggling for words. 'We've been invaded by Christmas I'm afraid.'

'It's very . . . very modern,' Mara finally managed. 'How kind. I suppose we ought to leave them up.'

'I suppose,' Rosie said reluctantly. 'Oh and there's a dead bird in the fridge courtesy of Euan and Hugh,' she added, wrinkling her nose. 'I can't go near the thing.'

'You've had quite a day,' said Mara. She put her arms around Rosie's waist. 'I sense that now may not be the right time to tell you that we're invited to the Aldersons' dinner party on New Year's Eve,' she murmured, her voice trembling with laughter. Rosie dropped her head onto Mara's shoulder.

'There would never be a good time to tell me that.'

Mara steered her towards the kitchen.

'Why don't we put the kettle on and I'll fill you in on the latest gossip. Hugh was out all night, you know.'

'I think I might need a small sherry,' said Rosie weakly.

'Push the boat out, have two,' chuckled Mara. 'It's Christmas.'

The rest of the day dragged interminably. Mara had been offered a lift to midnight mass in Morpeth by one of the tenant families. She took herself off for an afternoon nap so that she could stay awake later.

Left to her own devices, Rosie was at a loss. There was no work to do. She tried to read a book but couldn't settle. The tree angel seemed to have eyes in the back of its head and there was just too much tinsel. Even the Baby Jesus seemed to be grinning as if he knew something she didn't. Rosie set the book aside and drifted into the kitchen.

She turned on the old radio, took some carrots and onions from the tiny pantry and put on a wipe-clean red apron advertising Vermouth, '*The cook's choice!*' Soon the stock was bubbling on the hob, filling the room with the smell of her mother's favourite soup. The radio crackled as the opening bars of a familiar tune floated across the room, causing Rosie to stop dead, up to the elbows in hot, soapy water. Bing Crosby crooned the lyrics of White Christmas and the music wrapped itself about her like enfolding arms. Rosie closed her eyes and heard Cameron's voice rumbling the harmony. A tear tracked down her cheek. Outside a flock of wild geese arrowed across the sky, going home to roost.

After supper, Rosie and Mara sat by the fire, talking and dozing. At ten-thirty there was a knock at the door. 'I'll go,' Rosie yawned. 'You get your coat on.' Danny Hardy, the eldest son of the family from Lowdale Farm, was waiting on the doorstep, well wrapped against the cold. He grinned shyly at her.

'Hi Rosie,' he said. 'Is Mrs Whitton ready?' He jerked his thumb at the blue people carrier waiting on the track. 'Everyone's in the car.'

'She's just coming, Danny,' said Rosie. She leaned out of the door and waved at the car. 'Tell your folks Merry Christmas from me and thanks. I know coming here is out of your way.'

'It's no trouble,' he assured her. Mara appeared at the door.

'Good evening, Daniel. Shall we go?' Danny held out his arm and escorted Mara to the car with exquisite politeness. Rosie smiled. All four Hardy children were lovely but there was something about Danny that made him stand out, a kind of natural gentility combined with formidable intelligence. Northumberland wasn't going to hold him forever, she thought, waving them off into the dark.

Rosie locked the door and plodded to the kitchen. She made herself a mug of cocoa and took a mince pie from the packet Euan had brought, stuffing a second into her pyjama pocket to ward off the midnight munchies. She paused at the foot of the stairs and looked around. Rosie wondered what Mara was doing and in her own way envied her. She felt she didn't have the courage to meet God just yet, even if He came as a child.

Despite the razzmatazz of the decorations, there was a peculiar quality of stillness to the room. It was almost peaceful. 'Merry Christmas, Cam,' she whispered. 'I miss you. Please, God, keep him safe.'

Chapter 18

Hogmanay

Charlotte ran back and forth between the kitchen and the lounge, her burgundy cocktail dress shimmering in the intimate lamplight. Well, *ran* wasn't the right word, Rosie decided. It was more of a fast glide, her legs powering along while her upper body remained beautifully composed. Rather like a duck, in fact. Rosie snorted into her goblet of mulled wine.

'Are you all right?' Alastair asked politely, pausing in the act of offering round a tray of mixed canapés and vol-au-vents.

'Fine,' Rosie choked, regretting her unkindness immediately. It was generous of the Aldersons to invite them and, in truth, she was in awe of Charlotte's flawless hostess skills. Rosie could manage a three-course meal for two people if the first course was soup and the third course was coffee and mints. She sat back in her chair and tried to make herself as unobtrusive as possible.

It wasn't difficult in a room like this. The Aldersons' lounge was a large, rectangular room with a comfortable array of leather and walnut furniture. A traditional log fire blazed within a carved fire surround that climbed up to a mantelpiece at shoulder height. An ornate mirror hung above the fire and reflected light across the room, its heavy gold frame matching the tasselled tiebacks on the wine-coloured curtains draped over the French windows. It was the kind of decor that was described in her mother's beloved *Good Homes* magazines as 'opulent', yet Charlotte had contrived to add a homely note with a cluster of family photos mounted together in clashing, mismatched frames.

Mara and Rosie knew no one except Charlotte and Alastair, who were both fully occupied with their roles as hosts. Mara at least was a natural when it came to polite conversation and she was deep in discussion with an elderly gentleman, an Alderson relative of some description with hairy nostrils. Rosie, however, was out of her depth. To her, small talk was nothing but slow torture in a socially acceptable form.

To make matters worse, most of the guests appeared to be related, which lent a certain exclusivity to the banter flowing around the room. This was all very well unless you were the one excluded, thought Rosie as she eavesdropped on the chatter to her left.

A portly middle-aged woman in a peacock blue pleated skirt and satin blouse was excitedly relaying details of 'Sylvie's new fiancé' to her companion, a younger woman with cropped black hair in a stylish tuxedo jacket and killer heels. Apparently Sylvie was onto husband number four.

'Between you and me,' said the portly lady in a conspiratorial tone, 'I think our Sylvie is a bit of a gold-digger.'

Killer Heels laughed. 'You've got a suspicious mind, Madeleine,' she said. 'Maybe she's just unlucky in love.'

'Can I get you anything, Rosie? Canapé? Top-up?' Alastair bent down and waved his refreshments tray under Rosie's nose. Rosie recoiled from the smell of mushroom vol-au-vents.

'No thanks,' she said.

'Actually, I can't bear them either,' Alastair confided in an undertone. 'Don't worry, we'll be eating soon. Just waiting for a last-minute arrival.' He straightened up and cocked his head on one side. 'Ah! Speak of the devil,' he beamed. 'I think that's him now. Would you mind?' He handed her the tray and bounded off to answer the door.

Rosie got to her feet and drifted around the room, bestowing vacant smiles and vol-au-vents on the other guests. Her heels clip-clopped over the wooden floor in a satisfying rhythm until she caught her toe on the edge of the Persian rug and nearly dropped the tray in an Alderson's lap. Charlotte's duck-glide was harder than it looked. Rosie knew that wherever he was, Cameron would be laughing at her. It did nothing to improve her state of mind. Mara waved her over.

'Why don't you take that through to the kitchen?' she suggested. 'I think everyone is saving themselves for dinner.'

'Good idea,' said Rosie gratefully. She retreated to the safety of the hallway. The front door stood at one end, with the other downstairs rooms branching off at various points. It was cool, softly lit and quiet. Rosie leaned against the wall while she tried to get her bearings. She had already embarrassed herself earlier by walking into the coat cupboard. *Maybe I'll just stay here.*

The door at the far end of the hall was slightly ajar and she caught a glimpse of a tall white fridge. Rosie moved towards it, overhearing snippets of a conversation as she drew nearer. 'Might just crash out upstairs, Lottie,' a man said. Presumably this was the late arrival. Rosie paused and tried to manoeuvre the tray onto her hip so that she could push the door open.

'Stay up for the meal, Sweet,' Charlotte said. 'See how you feel.' *Sweet? What kind of a name is that?*

'Let him be, Lottie,' said a third voice. Alastair. 'He's had a long drive and it's New Year's Eve. You know the score.'

'No, no,' said Sweet. 'She's right. I'm being a killjoy. It's just dinner. I can manage.' The voice was tantalisingly familiar. Rosie pushed the door, giving her a clear view into the kitchen.

Charlotte and Alastair were seated on tall stools at a breakfast bar with their backs to the door, each with an arm around the guest between them. His head was bowed and droplets of melting snow sat on the shoulders of his overcoat. Rosie realised with horror that she was intruding on an intensely private moment. Luckily, they hadn't seen her yet. Holding her breath, Rosie reached for the door handle and began pulling the door towards her, inch by inch. The hinge creaked and Alastair's head whipped round.

'What are you doing?' he said sharply. Charlotte's arm tightened protectively about the man. Rosie had no choice but to enter the room.

'I . . . I just came to bring this,' she stammered. 'I didn't mean to intrude.' Alastair walked over and lifted the tray out of Rosie's hands.

'Much obliged, Rosie,' he said more calmly.

Rosie opened her mouth to apologise again, but the man at the breakfast bar turned and fixed her with dull, expressionless eyes, as though the effort of feeling anything had become too great. Rosie tried to speak but the greeting stuck in her throat. He looked vulnerable, haunted and hard-faced all rolled into one. She recognised the expression. After all, she saw it every day in the mirror.

'Hello, Rosie,' he said gruffly. Rosie swallowed hard, her feet carrying her forward without conscious thought.

'Hugh,' she said, 'what's wrong?' Before she could place her outstretched hand on Hugh's shoulder, Charlotte moved swiftly between them, physically blocking Rosie's path.

'Time to eat,' she said briskly. 'Alastair, could you and Rosie get everyone seated? Hugh will help me serve.'

The meal passed in a blur of noise and laughter. There was good food, excellent wine and the mood around the table was relaxed and convivial. Hugh sat on Charlotte's left with his head down and ate in silence as the talk flowed around him.

Evidently, he was well known to the extended branches of the Alderson family. His arrival had been greeted with cries of welcome and a flurry of handshakes, but from that moment on, his presence was completely ignored by every guest, as if by common agreement. Rosie watched him surreptitiously and saw that he wanted both the comfort of inclusion and the privacy of his sombre isolation. No one could understand that contradiction better than her. *But why? What's happened to him?*

The question pounded in Rosie's head until it became an effort to keep the words from spilling out. Hugh was hardly recognisable as the man who had stood on her doorstep on Christmas Eve. Mara deflected her questioning looks with a

tiny but definite shake of the head. She seemed to understand what was going on. All the guests did, Rosie realised.
Except her.

As the last crumbs on the cheese board were being
devoured, Hugh got to his feet.

'I'll do the First Foot,' he said.

'It's only half-past eleven,' Alastair yawned.

Charlotte dug him in the ribs with her elbow. 'Fetch the
coal. I'll get the spoon.'

Five minutes later, Hugh left the room carrying a lump of
coal, a fifty pence piece and a pinch of salt cupped in the
palm of one hand. Rosie looked from one face to another,
seeking a reaction to this insane behaviour, but everyone
appeared to think it normal.

'He'll be all right in a bit,' Charlotte said. 'He's done very
well.' There was a general round of head-nodding and mumbled agreement from the assembled guests. Emboldened by
two glasses of Chianti, Rosie spoke up.

'Will somebody please explain what is going on here?' she
demanded, her voice coming out louder than she meant it
to. The room fell uncomfortably silent. Everyone stared at
her. The peacock-skirt lady cleared her throat uncertainly.

'Well,' she began, 'First Footing is an old Scottish tradition
we have at New Year in the North. Just before midnight, the
men − or man − leave the house with a twist of salt, a piece
of silver and a lump of coal.' Rosie glanced up to see
whether the enormous flashing question mark was visible
above her head.

'They represent . . .' the woman screwed up her face, trying to recall the correct order.

'Health, wealth and prosperity,' chorused the other guests.

'That's it,' said the woman. 'Now, they take the old year out with them and when the clock strikes midnight, they bang on the door and we let them in. They bring the New Year with them, do you see?'

'Yes,' said Rosie. 'But that wasn't what I meant.' The room fell silent again. 'I think I need some air . . .' She pushed her chair back and headed for the door. Alastair made as if to follow her but Mara laid a hand on his arm.

'Let her go,' she said.

'Yes, but —'

'Let her go,' Mara repeated. 'Rosie will understand.'

It was cold outside. The snow had stopped, but the sky was heavy with more. Hugh was leaning against the wall of the house.

'It's bad luck for a woman to first foot,' he said as Rosie joined him. 'Especially if you're American.'

'I'm hoping for some good luck next year,' Rosie answered. 'Maybe I'll buck the trend.' Hugh didn't reply. 'I thought you were in Scotland for the holiday,' Rosie said.

'I was.'

'Why did you leave early?'

'My sister's a terrible cook.'

'That doesn't explain why you look so awful.' Hugh shrugged. He pulled out the coin and began flipping it in the air and catching it on the back of his hand. Rosie watched as it came down. Heads. Tails. Heads. Heads.

'Tell me what's wrong,' she said, moving round to face him.

'Why?' He wouldn't meet her eye.

'Because . . .' *because whatever it is makes you act like me. We're the same.'* . . . because I might be able to help?' Rosie said aloud.

Hugh laughed unpleasantly. 'Not possible.'

The coin began to spin faster, end over end in the air. It flipped out of his grasp and struck the snowy ground, sending a puff of white dust into the air. As Hugh stooped to retrieve it, Rosie stepped forwards and covered the coin squarely with her shoe. He glared up at her and for a moment she was afraid of the look in his eyes. Abruptly he turned his back and stared up at the starless sky.

'I was supposed to get married on New Year's Day,' he began in a low voice. 'Fifteen years ago. I was about your age, twenty-five. She was beautiful, intelligent, funny. Everything I wanted. Our fathers were old school friends. I was so in love . . . it was like . . . like a drug. I couldn't get enough.' His voice was rough with pain.

'Did she leave you?' Rosie asked gently. Hugh gave another bitter laugh.

'If only . . .' he muttered to himself. 'I left her,' he said louder. 'Called the whole thing off the day before the wedding. The guests had arrived, everything was paid for. She was devastated.'

'Why did you do it?'

'I realised it wasn't me she loved, not really. It was all the things I could give her.'

They stood in silence for a long time, their faces upturned to the night sky. Rosie was sure she could see the glint of tears in his eyes.

'Where is she now?' The question came out of nowhere. It was sudden and stupid.

'She's dead.' Hugh made an awful choking sound and buried his face in his hands. For a few seconds, Rosie was rooted to the spot, then she reached out and slipped her arm through his.

'I'm so sorry,' she whispered. 'I understand, I really do.'

'No, you don't,' Hugh said thickly. 'It's not the same.' He lifted his head and met her gaze, his eyes so dark they were almost black. Rosie took a step back. 'It was my fault. I as good as killed her.'

Behind them, the door was flung open and a collective shout rang out.

'Happy New Year!'

Hugh stood a moment on the path, his expression so full of anguish that Rosie couldn't bear to look at him any longer, then turned and vanished into the night. Rosie, left alone in the garden, awkwardly met the astonished gaze of the rest of the party. 'I think I need another drink,' she muttered, pushing past them into the house.

'What on earth did he mean by that?'

Mrs Drummond gawped at Mara across the table, their Thursday afternoon card game temporarily forgotten. Mara calmly laid her hand of cards face-down on the pitted wood.

'That he blames himself for Rowena's suicide, of course.'

Mrs Drummond thrust her hand into the pocket of her apron and pulled out a packet of Old Holborn and a box of cigarette papers.

'Give me a light,' she said hoarsely, fumbling with the loose tobacco. Mara flicked her box of matches across the table.

'I thought you'd given up,' she observed.

'I'm in shock.'

'So was poor Rosie.'

Mrs Drummond struck a match and began sucking furiously on the cigarette. Mara gathered up the cards, shuffled and dealt. Mrs Drummond exhaled slowly. 'So what happened?' she asked.

'Well, Hugh charged off goodness knows where, leaving us to explain his behaviour. Rosie was quite shaken up about it. I don't know what he was thinking.'

Mrs Drummond sighed. 'That man is his own worst enemy,' she said, scanning her cards. 'But as for what he was thinking, Hugh is always unpredictable at New Year. You haven't been here since it happened, Mara. He relives it every time.'

'It seems to me that he's rearranged the facts to fit his guilt. He had no way of knowing the poor girl would take it so badly. Her death was not his fault,' said Mara.

'Well, guilt is a funny thing. It takes people in different ways,' Mrs Drummond said wisely. She removed the cigarette from her mouth and stared glumly at it. 'How long is it until Lent? Maybe I could give up giving up.'

'Trust you to find a loophole, Ellen.'

'It would still count,' argued Mrs Drummond. 'Technically.'

'Your talents are wasted on housekeeping,' murmured Mara. 'You should have been a politician.'

'Or a priest?'

'I've got better things to worry about than Hugh,' Mara said. 'Euan keeps taking Rosie out for lunch.'

'I hope she knows what she's getting into then. He's a lovely lad, but a bit of a heart-breaker by all accounts,' replied Mrs Drummond.

'Well, he certainly seems taken with Rosie,' Mara said, 'but she's never shown any sign that he's more than a friend. I hope she lets him down gently. We don't need another one moping about the farm.'

The back door opened suddenly and Hugh ducked into the kitchen, his head grazing the low wooden lintel. He looked tired and restless.

'Are you busy, Mara?' he asked.

Mara indicated the playing cards with a wry smile. 'Rushed off our feet.'

'I'm going for a ride if you want to come,' said Hugh.

Mara and Mrs Drummond looked at one another. It was bitterly cold outside. Mrs Drummond hastily scooped up the cards and got to her feet.

'Good idea, Hugh,' she said, stowing the cards and tobacco pouch in the Welsh dresser. 'Mara could do with a bit of air, couldn't you, Mara?'

'Er . . . yes. Of course,' said Mara, casting an anxious look at the darkening sky.

'I'll wait in the car,' said Hugh.

Mara glared at Mrs Drummond and followed Hugh outside.

Chapter 19

Lent

'So he didn't kill her?'

'No.' Rosie replied as she rubbed her hands together.

'Then why did he say so?'

'Because he blames himself.'

'Ah.' Aelred refilled his mug with coffee from the Thermos and took a long drink. They were sitting in the Range Rover, parked as close to the viewpoint as the road allowed. They had met every Thursday that Rosie had been able, with the exception of the last three weeks when Aelred had been away. She'd kept their meetings secret, even from Mara. This was her time, her place. He was the grandfather she never had: wise, funny and unafraid to tell the truth in love. She never asked much about his life and didn't know what he did or where he lived. Rosie thought some friendships were better that way. Aelred saw Rosie glance at her watch. 'You all right for time?'

'Half an hour,' she replied. 'I have to be at Lowdale Farm for three.' She bit into an Oreo and offered the packet to Aelred. He shied away from it.

'Ugh, no thanks. Give me a ginger nut any day.' Rosie laughed and helped herself to another.

'What was her name?' asked Aelred.

'Rowena.'

'And it was definitely suicide?'

'Apparently so.' Rosie cast him a sidelong look. 'Do you know something I don't?'

'No, far from it,' Aelred said. 'It was before my time.' He sighed mournfully. 'It's typical. I go away over the New Year for one measly month and miss all this excitement.'

Rosie scowled at him. 'It's not funny, Aelred,' she said.

'I know,' said Aelred, his grin fading. 'Poor man. Still punishing himself after all these years. People like Hugh are their own worst enemy, Rosie. They can forgive others, but never themselves.'

'I guess that's true,' replied Rosie thoughtfully. 'I never looked at it that way before.' No wonder Hugh was always so grim and distant. It made sense now. 'Fifteen years, though. He should cut himself some slack.'

Aelred shot her a look that was both amused and exasperated. 'He's not the only one. You might try taking your own advice.'

'Me? I'm fine,' said Rosie, suddenly intent on the view through the mud-spattered windscreen of the car. She loved the countryside like this; sparse and desolate with the colours stripped back to earth and root beneath a frost-bitten blue sky.

'This little episode has really set you back, hasn't it?'

'I don't know what you mean,' said Rosie, deliberately obtuse.

'Yes, you do.'

'It was a shock, that's all. Anyway, it's none of my business.'

'Rosie,' said Aelred bluntly, 'I've not known you long but, since your husband died, you've got along by bottling things up. Ever thought about talking to God?'

'I talk to you.'

'Yes,' Aelred agreed, 'but we've talked facts, not feelings. We haven't even begun to scratch the surface there.' Rosie bent her head and began plucking at a loose thread in one of her gloves. She felt like a rabbit in the road, caught in the glare of unwelcome scrutiny. Aelred was careful not to look at her. 'The problem is,' he continued, 'you've been hoping the pain would go away if you ignored it for long enough. Seeing Hugh still hurting a whole fifteen years after his fiancée's death shows you that doesn't always happen. Sometimes, Rosie, when we can't do things in our strength, we have to rely on the strength of others.'

'What's your point?' Rosie gave the thread a yank. The thumb of her glove began to unravel.

'You're terrified of becoming like him,' said Aelred simply. 'Terrified you'll be like this forever. But you're not ready to let go either. And,' he added with a quick glance at her, 'probably feeling guilty about the small part of you that wants to move on.' He rested his hand gently on her shoulder. 'Am I right?'

'Are you a shrink or something?' Rosie said suspiciously, looking up at him through the curtain of her hair. She made it sound like an insult. He was either perceptive or this was obvious to everyone – everyone except her.

Aelred gave her a little pat. 'No,' he chuckled. 'Just an old man who's seen a lot of life. Believe it or not, I have walked in your shoes.'

'What?'

'Lost someone very close. Didn't speak about it. Felt I was going to explode.'

'So what did you do?' Rosie asked.

'I found the hills . . .' he paused and looked at her eye to eye. 'And I began to talk to the One who made them.'

'God?' Rosie found it hard to say the word.

He smiled.

'I remember when I was a child,' she began. 'I would pray every day thinking God was a cross between Santa and the tooth fairy. But then . . . things happened and now . . .' She forced herself to continue, 'Now, there's just too much pain for me even to think about it.'

'I felt the same. Except, that as I got older the only thing I felt I had left was that thing people call God.'

'I don't want to talk about it any more,' Rosie said. 'I mean, I do but – I can't. Not yet.' The old feeling of panic rose in her, the fear of losing control. She felt as though Aelred had casually stripped off her internal bandages and was pressing on the open wound. It was horrible.

'There's no hurry,' said Aelred soothingly. 'Grief is a long journey, Rosie. But it is a journey and there will be an end. Remember that. I've a book that might help, if you're interested. Perhaps I'll drop it off later.'

Rosie nodded, swallowing her nausea. 'Great. Thanks.' She detested self-help books, with their buzzwords and upbeat platitudes disguised as wisdom. A five-step plan was not going to bring Cameron back. God was not going to bring Cameron back. Nothing would. Death was death. She felt her spirits plummeting and quickly changed the subject. 'Where did you go on holiday?'

'The Canary Islands,' said Aelred enthusiastically. 'Fantastic place. I always take the whole of January off to recover from the Christmas rush. I'm dead on my feet by New Year.'

Rosie pounced on this piece of information.

'How come?' This was the first time Aelred had made any allusion to a job. Somehow the topic had never come up and she had begun to assume he was retired.

Aelred flapped his hand vaguely. 'Oh, er . . . this and that,' he said, looking strangely wrong-footed. 'It's a busy time for everyone, isn't it?' He buried his nose in his coffee mug.

Rosie had no intention of letting this go.

'You've never mentioned a job,' she said, glad to angle the spotlight away from her. 'We always end up talking about me. I talk . . . you listen. Come on, tell me what you do.'

'Well . . . I'm not sure how to describe it really.' He smiled at her, his eyes alight with mischief. 'Shepherd is as good a label as any, I suppose. Semi-retired now, but I help out where needed.'

Rosie narrowed her eyes. 'You're a shepherd? No way. You're not even a local.' Aelred's accent was polished, every vowel and consonant emerging pure and whole, untouched by regional slurs. Even Rosie knew that.

Aelred laughed at her expression.

'Well, there are shepherds elsewhere in the British Isles,' he pointed out. 'We're not confined to the north. I can't help my southern roots, you know.' Rosie scanned his face, freshly tanned and well weathered. Aelred was clearly at home in the outdoors and he was certainly very fit for his age. That would go with being a shepherd. It kind of fitted. Kind of.

'How old are you, Aelred?' she demanded as she looked at his neat, trimmed fingernails without any sign of sheep dip, frostbite or whatever else shepherds had on their hands.

'Seventy-three.'

'And where do you live?'

'This is like twenty questions,' Aelred complained. 'Talking about you is far more interesting.' He held out his mug. 'It'll cost you. Fill her up.'

'You've had two already,' Rosie objected. 'There's only a bit left.'

'Take it or leave it. You've got those sorry excuses for biscuits to keep you going.'

'OK, OK.'

Aelred waited until she had shaken the last drops of coffee from the Thermos. 'I have a little place at Alnmouth, not far from here.' He tipped his head back and poured the coffee down his throat. 'I also have a strawberry birthmark shaped like France on my left shoulder blade and two ingrown toenails. My mother's name was Margery and I'm a firm believer in the health benefits of full length thermal underwear.' He wiped a dribble of coffee from his chin and grinned at Rosie. 'Anything else you want to know? Favourite television programme? Inside leg measurement?'

'Yes,' said Rosie coolly. She pointed at his face. 'What's that scar on your cheek?'

Aelred looked out of the car to the far hills as he waited to reply. The Lenten wind blew from the north bringing the first clouds of a far away storm.

'Shrapnel wound, I was in the Royal Marines in my youth.'

'Really?'

Aelred fingered the raised mark on his face. 'Yes. I got this on manoeuvres in the New Forest. Took on three hundred men with my bare hands,' he laughed as he cracked his knuckles dramatically. 'Taught them not to tangle with Faulkner. Ow!'

He cringed as Rosie landed a double punch on his arm.

'A real Iron Man,' she said dryly.

'You've given me a dead arm.'

'Serves you right.'

'Fair enough. But the rest was true.'

'I believe you.'

'Is my interrogation over for today?'

'Yes.' Rosie snapped the plastic mug back onto the Thermos and stowed the biscuits in the foot well. 'But I'll get to the bottom of it.' She gave him a quick hug. 'Thanks for the pep talk. Now hop out. I've got somewhere to be.'

'Thank goodness.' Aelred opened the passenger door and unfolded his long legs. 'See you next week. I'll bring some proper biscuits.'

'Get lost,' Rosie grinned.

'Think about what I said, Rosie. God has a delicate touch on the soul.'

She watched him jog over the frozen ground to his car. A thought occurred to her belatedly. What kind of a Christmas rush could shepherds have? It certainly wasn't lambing season.

Rosie returned Aelred's cheery wave as he shot off in his battered Ford Escort. His story didn't hang together. Rosie's mobile phone bleeped a warning. There was no time to puzzle over it now. 'Late again, Rosie.' She shook her head and swung the car into a three-point turn.

❀ ❀ ❀ ❀

'Rosie!' Kate Hardy answered the door at Lowdale Farm, her welcome as friendly as her smile. 'Come in, come in. Thanks for dropping by at short notice.'

'No problem,' smiled Rosie, stepping directly out of the cold into the warm farmhouse kitchen. All around was the debris of a happy family. Chalk pictures littered the walls, pinned with horse-riding rosettes. Flour was strewn across the long table, paper holders for cupcakes huddled waiting in baking trays. It made Rosie envious of what she saw. The wood-burning stove beamed its dry heat. Here was the out-pouring of happiness.

'You'll have to take us as you find us, I'm afraid,' said Kate, wiping flour from her hands with a dishcloth. 'I got started on a mammoth baking session and the twins have got friends over from school, so the whole place is upside down. You know what boys are like.' She raised her eyes to the ceiling as a thump sounded from the floor above. 'The Lord alone knows what they're doing up there.'

Rosie grinned. 'Sounds like fun, whatever it is.'

At ten years old, Callum and Joel were a pair of rogues, but definitely loveable.

'It will be easier once the weather improves and they can run off some energy outside,' Kate replied philosophically. 'Roll on summer. Do sit down.' She bustled over to the kitchen table and pushed a bizarre-looking mess of newspaper and paste to one side. 'Lucy decided to make a papier-mâché cow, of all things.'

There was a howl from under the table. 'It's not dry!'

Rosie squatted down and lifted a corner of the wipe-clean checked tablecloth.

'Hi Lucy.' The youngest Hardy fixed her with a killer stare, enormous dark eyes embedded in a porcelain face. 'Don't worry, I won't touch it,' Rosie assured her.

'Pwomise?'

Rosie held up her hand in the Girl Scout salute. 'Promise,' she said solemnly.

'Take your thumb out of your mouth when you're talking, Lucy,' said Kate from the depths of a cupboard. Her head and shoulders had completely vanished. 'Teabags are in here somewhere . . .'

Lucy pulled her thumb out of her mouth. 'It's a lion, not a cow,' she said sulkily, twisting a strand of long dark hair round one finger.

'I could tell that right away,' Rosie lied. 'From the mane.'

'Humph . . .' The thumb went back in but from the contented sucking noises Rosie judged that dignity had been appropriately upheld. She chose one of the rickety spindle chairs and sat down.

'Actually Kate, coffee would be great,' she said, as Kate emerged red-faced and empty-handed from the cupboard, her glasses askew. 'I'm not so keen on tea.'

'Good,' said Kate, pushing her thick fringe off her forehead, a crop of grey hairs visible amid the black. She looked too young for them. 'Coffee we have. Can I tempt you to a slice of banana bread?'

'I'd love some,' Rosie smiled. Lucy crawled out of her makeshift den, climbed up Rosie's leg and curled up on her lap in a no-nonsense fashion.

'Sorry, Rosie. She's worse than a cat.'

'I don't mind at all.' Rosie smiled as she cradled the comforting weight of the child on her knee. This place was more than homely, she thought, noticing the pile of wellies stacked higgledy-piggledy by the door, the line of random socks drying on the radiator. She'd dreamed of just such a home as this, once upon a time. Kate set two mugs and a plate of the banana bread on the table, with a beaker of juice for Lucy. She picked up the third mug and a generous slab of bread and started towards the door.

'Help yourself Rosie. I'll just take this up for Danny. He's busy on some A-level coursework. All that boy does is study these days. He's applied for medical school, you know. My son . . . a doctor . . . I'll die of pride.'

'That's great,' said Rosie as Kate disappeared up the stairs. She turned to Lucy, 'And how about you? Would you like to be a doctor someday?'

'No,' said Lucy scornfully as she picked a piece of banana bread and smeared it on Rosie's coat. 'I'm going to be a farmer like my daddy.'

'Well, that's pretty cool too.' Rosie hid her smile in her coffee. They ate in companionable silence until Kate reappeared and scooped Lucy off Rosie's knee.

'Come on, poppet,' she said. 'Run upstairs and see what your brothers are doing. Mummy has to talk to Rosie now.'

'Stinky work,' said Lucy, scowling up at her mother. She trailed out of the room. A few seconds later they heard her plodding up the stairs.

'What a character,' said Rosie.

Kate laughed. 'Oh, yes. A force to be reckoned with, our Lucy. Never a dull moment with our motley crew.' She took a slice of banana bread, broke a piece off and dunked it in her coffee. 'Sorry,' she said. 'Disgusting habit.'

Rosie pushed her own plate away. 'So what's the problem? Euan said you needed to put in an application for another maintenance job.'

Kate looked embarrassed. 'Yes. I'm sorry, so soon after the last one . . .' Her fingers crumbled a chunk of bread, scattering crumbs on the table. Rosie dug the file out of her satchel and flipped through the records.

'Is it the front door again?' A few months back, the wood had swollen so much in the autumn damp that the farmhouse door had stuck in its frame, requiring superhuman strength to open or close it fully.

'No,' said Kate. 'It's the guttering this time. We've tried to manage but it's getting worse. I'm so sorry to bother you; I feel we're always on the phone about something or other. Hugh is so good about everything; I don't want him to think we're not taking care of the place.'

'I'm sure he wouldn't think that,' said Rosie, who was not at all sure. 'It's a family home, there's bound to be wear and tear.'

Kate flushed. 'Well, that's just it,' she said awkwardly. 'George caught the twins climbing around on the roof just before Christmas. They'd helped themselves to the ladders and were having a fine time up there pretending to be Father Christmas. Nearly broke their necks. The damage might have been done by them, in which case we ought to pay.'

'Let's have a look.' Rosie was well aware that money was tight for the family. She followed Kate upstairs to the main bedroom, passing Lucy in full sulk on the top step.

'Just here.' Kate led Rosie round the old wooden sleigh bed piled with worn blankets and a faded eiderdown.

'Oh Kate! This won't do.' There was a large circle of damp on the ceiling, close to the window. As Rosie watched, it spat a large drop of water into a black bucket on the carpet. 'How long has it been leaking like this?'

'A couple of months,' Kate confessed. 'The sound of it drives George stir crazy at night. It's worse than a ticking clock.'

'Well, we must get that sorted,' said Rosie briskly. 'I'll get a quote straight away.'

'But the twins . . .'

'. . . are ten years old. Even if they caused the problem, it was an accident . . . Nobody needs to know.'

Kate sat down on the bed, her relief evident. 'That will be such a weight off our minds, Rosie. George felt sure Euan wouldn't approve the repairs.'

'Why?' asked Rosie, puzzled by the remark.

'Oh, we had a run-in with him once,' Kate said dismissively, picking at a spot of crusted cake mixture on the leg of her jeans. 'Danny got a home chemistry set for his birthday and went a bit overboard with an experiment. We ended up with a huge burn mark on the dining room ceiling, ruined the plaster completely.'

'And Euan wouldn't put the repairs through? I can't believe that.'

'Believe it,' Kate grimaced. 'And fair enough, I suppose. It's his job to see that Hugh isn't ripped off by his tenants. Danny was ready to sell everything he owned on eBay to pay for the damage.'

'So what happened?' She was a stranger to Euan's ruthlessness.

'Luckily for Danny, Hugh came by on a different matter and saw the state of the ceiling. He said exactly the same as you and was back the very same evening. He and Danny replastered the ceiling together.' She smiled at the memory. 'Hugh said working as his assistant decorator was punishment enough. Danny's worshipped the ground he walks on ever since.'

Rosie was still trying to take in what Kate had said about Euan when an unmistakable smell of burning wafted through the open door. Kate clutched at her head and leapt up.

'The cakes!' They galloped downstairs and skidded into the kitchen, Rosie in the lead. Four boys stood in a human chain, passing trays from the oven to the table in a calm, organised manner. Callum pulled his head out of the oven and shook an oven-gloved hand at Kate.

'S'alright, Mum. We've managed to save the muffins. Joel's had to bin the malt loaves though.'

'Yeah, Dad won't be happy,' said Joel from his post at the table. He took a hot tray from his friend and began flipping the cakes onto a wire cooling tray with a metal spatula. Kate ruffled his hair fondly.

'Well, he'll have to make do,' she laughed. 'Well done, boys.' The four boys beamed, then hurriedly tried to recover their pre-teen cool.

'Yeah.'

'OK.'

'Whatever.'

'No sweat, Mrs H.' The lads slouched out, swiping a hot muffin apiece as they went.

The women waited until the boys were out of earshot before laughing.

'Such a funny age,' Kate said. 'And they say girls are ten times worse. I won't cope.'

'Oh, I don't know,' said Rosie, collecting her satchel and jacket from the back of the chair. 'I was pretty easy going.'

'I can believe it,' said Kate. She hugged Rosie impulsively. 'Thank you. Will you come for dinner with Mara sometime? We'd love to have you.'

'That would be great.'

When she drove away, Rosie felt happier than she had in a long time. That's what a home should be like, she thought, with a pang of longing for what might have been.

'There's still time,' said the familiar voice in her head that she thought was Cameron.

'Not for me.'

But just to be part of it for a while, to enjoy the warmth and love of a family was an unlooked-for blessing.

'Life is not about doing . . . but being . . .' the voice said.

Rosie felt a tear trickling across her cheek. All the way back, she thought of Kate and her family and all they had. Not much money, but plenty of love.

Love . . . it gave her hope. She dried the tear as a dark storm cloud lifted from her heart.

Chapter 20

Poachers' Quarry

The café on Narrowgate was crowded as usual. Hundreds of jars and tins of exotic food lined the walls and the air was thick with the smell of coffee and chocolate. Hugh had always thought it was out of place in Alnwick – Chelsea, perhaps: Alnwick – definitely not. It was the sort of café that you would never tell anyone about for fear it would become more popular.

'Do be careful, Hugh,' drawled Charlotte, mopping up the spilled water on the café tablecloth. 'We'll be soaked right through at this rate.'

'Why do we always have to meet for lunch here?' grumbled Hugh, dabbing at his jeans with a paper napkin. 'There's no room. I feel like Gulliver.' His legs were wedged painfully under the table and if he sat back in his chair, his head struck the wall.

'Because it's bijou and adorable and the mezze is to die for. You love it really.' They were squashed round a tiny table for two. It was set onto a raised wooden platform, in the shop window in lieu of a display. Fine for your exhibitionist types, but it wasn't Hugh's cup of tea at all.

'It's not even a café,' he argued. 'It's a specialist food shop with one table stuck in the window to provide entertainment for the passing tourists.'

'Not exactly, sir,' said the teenage waitress arriving to take their food order. 'We also have twelve tables and seating for sixty downstairs.' Hugh's mouth fell open.

'But it's much nicer up here,' said Charlotte swiftly, giving the waitress a withering look. The girl's blush was obvious even through a thick layer of ill-chosen foundation. Hugh threw down his napkin.

'I don't care,' he said, climbing out of the shop window. 'Six months you've been squeezing me in here to be gawped at like a chimpanzees' tea party at the zoo when there's an entire restaurant downstairs. I'm going down there.'

Charlotte folded her arms.

'Don't be difficult, Lottie,' said Hugh impatiently. The waitress looked anxiously from one to the other, her blonde ponytail swishing to and fro.

'Next time we'll eat downstairs,' said Charlotte. She glared at the waitress. 'We'll have the mezze platter to share, please.'

'Lottie, this is the last time I'm sitting here,' Hugh warned, folding his legs back under the table with difficulty. 'No wonder you never bring Alistair,' he added under his breath. 'This place is certainly not made for the fatter customer.'

'Pardon?'

'Nothing.'

The waitress scuttled off, fearful of being caught in further crossfire.

A sullen silence descended on the little table. Hugh stared moodily out of the window. A pair of old ladies pointed and

tittered as they passed. This is what it must be like to be a
nude mannequin, he thought. Hugh bared his teeth at them
and hoped the wheels would drop off their tartan shopping
trolleys. His expression turned to horror as a small child
buried his face in his mother's coat and burst into tears. She
mouthed something that Hugh couldn't make out through
the glass and towed the weeping toddler away.

'No doubt about it,' said Charlotte waspishly. 'You're a real
crowd-pleaser.'

Hugh bit back his retort as the waitress galloped up the
stairs.

'Mezze . . .' She set the platter down between them and
beat a hasty retreat before they could ask for anything else.

'How's Rosie getting on?' asked Charlotte, changing the
subject. 'I dropped in for a cup of tea at the Dower House
last week. She's blossoming out here in the countryside,
don't you think?'

'She's a decent worker.' He tore himself a generous strip
of bread and dolloped some hummus onto his plate. 'As for
the rest, I wouldn't know.'

'There's no need to be so cold. She's a lovely person.'

'So I'm told. Euan certainly has no complaints. Personally,
I can't make her out.'

'You're still smarting from New Year,' Charlotte said.
'Rosie was very gracious about that. And very concerned for
you, incidentally.' A dull flush spread over Hugh's face at the
mention of New Year.

'She pushed too hard,' he growled. 'So I gave her the
truth.'

'Your version of it.'

Hugh stabbed an olive with his fork. 'I'm not discussing this.'

'You should give her a chance.'

'A chance for what?' Hugh made another jab at the olives and sent them scattering across the table like marbles. 'I've given her a job and a roof over her head. We don't have to be best friends. She's just a kid and a foul-tempered one at that.'

'That's why you avoid her?'

'I don't avoid her.'

Charlotte studied him over the rim of her glass. 'Well, you spend time with Mara. Why not Rosie?'

'Stop trying to psychoanalyse me, damn it,' Hugh said as he tried to collect up the rolling olives to the entertainment of the two old women who had come back to have another look.

'There's no need to overreact,' she replied with infuriating calm.

'I don't need this.' Hugh pulled out his wallet and wedged some notes under his side plate. 'Listen. Rosie's had a hard time and she's good to Mara. I'm sure she's a very nice person and all the rest of it. We just don't get on. It's not a crime.' He wrestled his arms into his jacket and stood up, banging his elbow on the wall again. 'I'm going.'

Charlotte half-rose from her chair. 'Hugh ... please ...'

'No, Lottie. Give it a rest.' He stormed out of the café into the path of the old ladies. 'Satisfied?'

Later that day, Rosie and Euan drove to eat at the Black Bull in Wooler, the nearest town to the estate. Euan tried to teach her how to play darts but after half a pint of Black Sheep beer Rosie couldn't even hit the board, never mind the bull's-eye. It was just past midnight when he dropped her home and drove off, still laughing at her clumsiness.

'Next time pool!' Rosie called after him.

'I'll wipe the floor with you.' Euan shouted back, waving out of the open window as the car disappeared towards Earleside.

Rosie let herself into the Dower House and locked the door. It was nice to get out now and again but she was equally glad to be home. Euan was easy company, but his constant flirting was becoming harder to deflect. 'No' didn't seem to be a word he understood and conversation was an unknown territory. It would be a pity to spoil the friendship, though. She left her shoes on the doormat and padded towards the stairs in the dark.

'Did you have a nice time?' said a hollow voice from the shadows.

Rosie shrieked and snapped the light on. 'Mara,' she panted, her heart thudding wildly. 'I thought you'd be in bed. What are you doing sitting down here in the dark?'

'Waiting for you,' replied Mara. 'I had the fire going but it burnt out a while ago.' She was sitting in her chair by the hearth, ready for bed in dressing gown and slippers, a finely knit shawl pulled snugly round her shoulders. The ashtray by her feet was overflowing. Rosie knelt down beside the armchair and took her hands.

'You're freezing. Come on. I'll make a cup of tea and bring it up to your room.'

Mara withdrew her hands and took an envelope from the pocket of her dressing gown. 'I'll make the tea,' she said, handing it to Rosie. 'You need to read this. It's the police report.' Rosie instantly pushed the envelope away.

'I don't need to read that.'

'Read it,' ordered Mara. She shuffled into the kitchen and closed the door.

Rosie looked at the envelope for a long moment. Her hands shook as she fingered the paper inside. *Do I really want to know how he died*? Would it help, or would it just supply macabre fodder for her imagination?

'Oh God – what do I do?'

Rosie searched her feelings and felt a decision form in her mind. She didn't want to know but there was a strange sense of obligation. The envelope held the truth to the most painful thing she had ever known. Even if she never told a soul and the facts died with her, the truth demanded a hearing. She unfolded the documents with trembling fingers and leaned towards the embers of the fire. The dying glow illuminated the contours of her face as she read. She scanned the first page, flipped to the next, then back to the first. She read the words again and again. They didn't make sense. They couldn't. It didn't happen that way. Never . . . Rosie screwed up the document, fed it to the fire and bolted for the door.

'Rosie?' Mara came in to the room with a tray of tea.

'I'm going out!'

Mara didn't get a chance to reply. Rosie was gone. She pounded along the track, tripping and stumbling in the darkness, no idea where she was going, simply obeying the impulse to run. To run and keep on running until she had exhausted the adrenaline surge pumping through her body.

'*I shouldn't have read it. Shouldn't have read. Shouldn't have read.*' Rosie screamed the words that thundered in her brain. Every letter beat in rhythmic counterpoint to the slap of her shoes on the ground. 'It can't be true. . . not that way. . .' Rosie shouted into the dark night. Her body shook as wave after wave of sobbing grief overwhelmed her. She gritted her teeth and ran on.

Hugh locked and bolted the front door of Earleside and stuffed the oversized bunch of keys into the pocket of his wax jacket. He was dressed in dark-coloured walking gear and carried a powerful hand-held flashlight. A small rucksack was hooked over one shoulder. Euan was waiting for him at the foot of the steps, similarly clad in khaki trousers, jacket and thick gloves.

'All set?' he asked, jigging from foot to foot.

'All set,' echoed Hugh. 'Shall I drive?'

'Whatever.' They climbed into the Land Rover. Hugh switched the heater on and put the lights on full beam. The car crawled towards the gate, Hugh keeping the revs low until they were clear of the house.

'Good night for it,' Euan remarked as Hugh put his foot down.

'The best,' agreed Hugh. 'Low cloud cover, no moon. And it's been raining. That tends to force the deer out into the open.'

'And the poachers with them,' grinned Euan, smacking his palms together. 'Sooner or later they've got to slip up.

Maybe – look out!' Hugh slammed the brakes on and swerved, driving the nose of the car into the hedge. Euan flung his door open.

'Rosie?'

Rosie hobbled over and climbed into the back of the car. Hugh and Euan swivelled round to stare at her.

'Where are you going?' they asked in unison. Rosie stared right back at them, her face haggard but set.

'With you,' she said through lips numb with cold.

'You don't know where we're going,' Hugh said.

'You're not wearing the right clothes,' Euan pointed out.

'I don't care,' said Rosie. 'I'm coming with you.'

Euan glanced at Hugh. 'I don't know about this,' he muttered. 'It's no place for women.'

Hugh considered the options. 'We've no time to take her home,' he decided. 'Let her come. I've got a spare jacket in the boot.'

'Hear that, Rosie? You're going hunting with the big boys.' Euan's tone was patronising but Rosie didn't care. Action was what she needed.

They drove for over an hour. Rosie dozed off in the back and was woken none too gently by Hugh.

'Here.' He thrust a large coat at her. 'Put this on.' She tried to get out of the car but he lifted an arm and blocked her way. 'Wait a moment,' he said, keeping his voice low. 'This is a dangerous, unpleasant business. Stay close to me or Euan. Do exactly as you're told. Ask no questions. Is that clear?' He sounded like an army sergeant drilling a new recruit.

'Understood. Now get out of the way, Hugh.'

'Is that clear?' he repeated in a harsh whisper.

'Yes! Let me out.' Hugh walked away.

Rosie slid out of the car, blinking as her eyes adjusted to the darkness. They were parked on a chalk track with several other vehicles, including two police cars. The tall black trees were tightly packed on either side but there was a large clearing ahead, dominated by an old, ramshackle house.

'Kielder Forest,' Rosie realised. No one replied.

They were a long way from home. Hugh was standing with a group of men on the track. As Rosie started towards them, they moved away from her, heading for the house. Hugh looked back and jerked his head at her. She ran to catch up.

The house was run down and had clearly been uninhabited for a long time. Rosie felt her way along the hall, following the sound of voices into a large reception room. There was a swirling draught coming from somewhere. Rosie looked around for the source and saw the gaping mouth of a ruined fireplace in the central wall. She huddled deeper into Hugh's jacket and joined the men at the back of the group. With hats pulled low and collars upturned, it was impossible to recognise faces, but Rosie recognised one voice.

'George?' she whispered. The man beside her turned, his eyes widening in surprise.

'Rosie? What brings you here?'

'If I could have everybody's attention?' said the man at the head of the group. There was no time for explanations. Rosie smiled reassuringly at George and tried to look as if she knew what was going on.

'Car watchers, on your way,' the man continued. 'You know the routes to be covered. Any sign of a dodgy vehicle, radio in the registration, location and direction of travel immediately.' Three pairs detached themselves from the group and left the room. 'Stalkers, three groups. You've got your co-ordinates. Groups One and Three, fan out, loop round and join up with Two at the halfway point. We'll work our way back together.' He raised his wrist. 'Time 0130 hours. Rendezvous at the halfway point 0330 hours, back here at 0430 hours. Let's go.'

One by one, the men dropped their rucksacks and kitbags by the hearth and trooped out, each armed with a high-powered searchlight. Euan left the room without so much as a glance at Rosie. She began to wish she'd stayed at home. A hand gripped her arm.

'Come on,' said Hugh. 'And keep quiet.'

Hugh towed her across to two men, one with a map, the other a compass. Rosie knew neither of them. Euan and George had disappeared into the night.

'Ready?' The men asked Hugh. He nodded and, as one, they switched on their flashlights. They left the track and struck out into the trees. It was hard going. The ground was rough and uneven underfoot, sinewy tree roots tangled among the undergrowth.

Rosie was at the back of the group, constantly being whipped in the face by twigs and branches springing back into place after being pushed aside by the person in front. With no flashlight she could hardly see her hand in front of her face and after half an hour, she was seriously lagging behind.

There was no sign of the other men, or of any poachers. Not that she could have seen them in any case. Rosie bit back a scream as Hugh's face loomed up out of the darkness.

'Are you all right?' he whispered.

'Fine.'

'Then keep up.' Rosie gritted her teeth and stumbled on. It had been a mistake to come. Thoughts of the police report kept going through her mind. Cameron's death and all its details became an echo she could not shut out.

A little while later, the thought occurred to her that they might actually encounter a poacher. An armed poacher? Her thoughts ran wild. Did anyone in the group have a gun? Rosie didn't think so. In America everyone carried a gun. Even her uncle Julian kept a pistol in his man-bag and he was gay, blind, lived in the Hamptons and was not a particularly good shot.

Anxiety began to build in her chest and she picked up her pace. There would be dogs. In her mind's eye she saw Euan's dog hurling itself at her in the barn, all teeth, claws and brutal eyes.

'Hugh?' she whimpered. There was no answer. She was alone. Rosie broke into a jog, lurching and tripping from one tree to the next. Where were they? She must have gone off course. 'Hugh?' Rosie veered off to the right and plummeted through the trees. Faster and faster the sounds of imagined pursuit closed in behind her. They drew near in the darkness. In her panic she invented the growl of a dog, the click-click of a rifle being reloaded . . .

'Aaaargh!' Rosie's shoulder smacked into something dense and heavy. She stumbled to a stop. The shapeless mass swung back towards her like a hanged man. It struck her a second time as it dangled on the twisting rope. She pushed it away. A foul stench filled her nostrils. Rosie gagged, staggering forwards into a hidden copse.

She turned on the spot, staring about her in terror. She was vaguely aware of several more shapes hanging in the darkness. The smell was overpowering. She lifted her hands to cover her mouth and nose, and discovered something tacky was clinging to her face . . . Blood! She had run right into the remains of a poacher's kill. She doubled over and vomited. Her hands and knees squelched as she knelt in the gore of slaughtered deer. Dimly, she was aware of figures crashing through the trees. The poachers were coming.

'Take her back,' said a voice. Strong arms lifted her and carried her away.

Some time later, Rosie came to. She lifted her head groggily. 'Put me down.' She thrashed in Hugh's arms, but he held her easily. 'I said put me down. I can walk.'

'Rosie, hold still. We're almost there.' Hugh shouldered his way through the door of the dilapidated manor house and carried her into the room where the briefing had taken place. He put her down and went to switch on the portable lamp left in the corner. 'OK?' he asked, breathing hard from the effort of carrying her so far.

Rosie tried to focus on the beam of light to stop the room from spinning.

'I'm fine,' she said faintly. Hugh was just in time to catch her as her legs buckled.

He lowered her gently to the ground, stripped off his coat and folded it onto the floor behind her. 'You're in shock. Lie down. Raise your legs if you can.' He fetched one of the kitbags from the pile by the hearth and shoved it under Rosie's knees. 'There, you can rest on that.'

'There's nothing wrong with me,' Rosie argued, trying to prop herself up. 'This is ridiculous.'

Hugh pushed her back down. 'Look, Rosie. Why must you always be so difficult? You're covered in blood, you're shaking like a leaf and you can barely stand. It's shock. Now shut up and do as you're told. I'll fetch a blanket.'

Rosie lay down; her teeth were chattering so much that her jaw began to ache. Perhaps she was in shock, but the gutted deer weren't the half of it. The lamp threw a pool of light onto one wall, emphasising the darkness throughout the room. She heard Hugh chuntering as he rustled around among the kitbags.

'Are we back at the house?' she murmured.

'I've got a Thermos of tea in here as well. Just the job.'

Rosie began to cry. It felt strange to be tipped over the edge by something as mundane as a hot drink.

'Rosie?' Hugh scrambled to her side and peered anxiously at her.

'No tea,' she choked.

'It's good for shock.' Rosie's sobs grew louder at this pronouncement. 'All right, all right,' said Hugh hastily. 'No tea.' He tucked the blanket round her as best he could and patted her hand. 'You'll – you'll be OK in a bit,' he said uselessly. The sobs became howls.

'Oh, hell.' Hugh gathered her up and rocked her to and fro like a child. Rosie buried her face in his neck and wept until his collar was soaked. Hugh stroked her hair and kissed her forehead, overcome with tenderness at the fragility in her. When her tears eventually subsided to shuddering sighs, he said tentatively, 'I know it was terrible finding the carcasses like that, but . . .'

'It's not the deer,' Rosie said into his collar. 'I mean, not just the deer.' She pulled away from him and sat up. 'The police report on the climbing accident arrived from France.'

Hugh met her gaze calmly.

'Tell me.'

Rosie looked into his face and recognised that, of all people, here was someone who would truly understand.

'Fraser,' she began haltingly. 'Cameron's twin. After they – after the accident, we found out that he'd brokered a huge deal and it backfired. That's how we lost everything.' Hugh nodded. This part he knew already. Rosie took a deep, shaky breath. 'The report said it wasn't an accident. Fraser committed suicide, but it went wrong and James – his dad – fell too.'

'There's no doubt?'

'They found a note. Addressed to his wife and his parents. James was ill when Fraser convinced him to sign the papers for the deal. He didn't know he was signing the Hall away. After it all went wrong, Fraser knew they would lose everything, he couldn't live with himself, so . . .'

'It's taken them this long to let you know?'

Rosie tried to smile. 'French bureaucracy.' Her head drooped. 'They say it looked like Cameron tried to climb down, to reach their bodies, but . . .' she left the words hanging.

Hugh was silent as he digested the information, his face hidden in shadow. Then he opened his arms wide and drew her back in, wrapping them both in the blanket. Rosie settled her head on his shoulder and relaxed into his embrace.

'You have had a terrible time,' Hugh whispered against her ear.

'I knew you'd understand,' she whispered. Hugh tilted her chin up and studied her face as though seeing her properly for the first time. Rosie closed her eyes.

'What the hell's going on?' Euan stood in the doorway, tired and dishevelled. Hugh and Rosie sprang apart.

'Rosie's in shock,' Hugh said stiffly.

'She's not the only one.' Euan strutted into the room, his chin jutting forwards aggressively. 'I didn't have you down as a sugar daddy, Hugh.'

'Don't be stupid, Euan,' said Rosie hotly. Hugh rose without a word, collected his coat from the floor and crossed to the pile of kitbags. He swung his bag onto his shoulder and strode to the door, forcing Euan to step aside.

'I'll be ready for your apology tomorrow,' he said bluntly. 'I won't presume to speak for Rosie. In the meantime, get over yourself. And find a ride home.'

Euan waited until he had gone before turning on Rosie. 'Did he try it on?' he demanded.

'What? No!' Rosie shook her head, bogged down with tiredness and confusion. She wasn't entirely sure what had happened, or what would have happened had Euan not appeared when he did. She scrambled to her feet. 'Forget it. Are we done here?'

'We're done and it looks like you got what you wanted after all.'

'I just want to go home, Euan.' Rosie went ahead of him, feeling the heat of his stare on the back of her head as he followed close behind.

Chapter 21

Spring

Rosie awoke early on the cold April morning. She lay still for a long time. There was no point staying in bed all day, no point at all, but the thought of getting up and presenting her face to the world felt even more futile.

This must be how condemned soldiers felt in the war, she thought, when forced into line before the firing squad. Their past gone, their present fixed and their future fading into oblivion. Prisoners of fate.

'Come on, Rosie,' she told herself. 'Don't be a drama queen. Do the British thing – stiff upper lip. It's just another day.'

It wasn't, of course, but there was nothing she could do about it. She kicked herself free of the bedclothes and forced her feet onto the wooden floor.

She found Mara in the kitchen, made up and smartly dressed with her hair neatly rolled into a chignon. There must be a Sunday service on at the estate chapel, Rosie realised, for her to go to so much trouble.

'Sit down,' said Mara, busy at the little stove. Her cheeks were prettily flushed from the heat rising out of the frying pan. The table had been set with napkins and the unchipped crockery. A little posy of clipped red carnations peeped over the rim of a milk bottle beside a jug of fresh orange juice.

'Thanks, Mara,' she said, pulling out a stool.

'I thought I'd make American pancakes for us,' said Mara brightly. 'A little taste of home for you.'

'Great.' Rosie forced a smile, but her voice was flat and emotionless.

'Coffee's brewing.' Mara thumped a large cafetière down on the table.

'There's enough for six people there.'

'Well, it'll set you up for the day then.'

'That's for sure,' said Rosie weakly. They ate the plump American pancakes drizzled with golden syrup. It was much thicker than maple syrup and the treacle welded chunks of batter to the backs of their teeth.

'Delicious,' said Rosie, swilling orange juice round her mouth in an effort to dislodge the debris.

'Good.' Mara poked her finger into her own mouth. 'But it's playing merry hell with my dentures.' Rosie's face broke into a smile. Mara pressed her hand affectionately. 'That's my girl.' She swept the plates from the table and dumped them in the sink. 'Toast?'

'I'll get it.'

'No. . . no. Have another cup of coffee.' Mara slotted two slices of white bread into the dented steel toaster and started to hunt for the marmalade. 'What are you doing today?' she asked, sliding the tins and packets back and forth in the cupboard.

'No plans,' said Rosie, picking at the remains of her pan-cakes.

'Why don't you come with me to church?'

'No thanks.'

'Euan will be there,' said Mara. 'He's giving me a lift.'

Rosie shrugged listlessly. She had no interest in going to church and this was not the day to see Euan. On the other hand, she had to find something to pass the time or the day was going to drag unbearably. She already felt as though she'd been up for hours and it wasn't even ten o'clock.

'You did say you'd come along sometime to see where James proposed to me,' Mara reminded her gently.

'That's right, I did. OK, why not?'

It may as well be today, she thought resignedly. There was a kind of symmetry to it. Mara knew, of course, but said nothing. Neither did Rosie. The memory was lodged between them on the back seat of Euan's car as they drove to the chapel. Its presence was carefully ignored, like a noisy drunk on the New York subway. Rosie shifted along the seat to avoid getting too close to it.

The estate chapel was built on a patch of high ground, three miles from the main house. Of solid stone and wood construction, it had weathered many winters. There was an aura of resilient permanence about the place, as if to say that times may change, but this place would not.

Set beneath a crooked weather vane, the old bell tolled rhythmically. Several cars were parked on the main track, jacked up on the grass verge to allow passage to other vehicles. The last quarter of a mile had to be made on foot, approaching the chapel via a narrow path that wound cross-country over the fields splashed with bursts of yellow as the daffodils and primroses came into bloom.

'Cheer up, Rosie,' Euan said, nudging her with his elbow as they joined the line of people filing along the path. 'My dog looks more cheerful than you today and she's shut up in her cage at home.'

I'm in a cage, only no one can see the bars. Rosie didn't bother to voice the bleak thought. Euan wasn't to know.

'Come on, I'm kidding,' he laughed, putting his arm round her shoulders in a proprietary gesture. Rosie didn't have the heart to repel him today.

Mara moved ahead of them, her mouth thinning with disapproval. Just occasionally, there was something about the man's manner that grated on her.

'Good morning, Lady Whitton,' chirped a voice behind her. She turned and smiled at Danny Hardy.

'Good morning, Danny. Any word from UCAS?'

'Not half,' said his father proudly, striding over to clap his son on the shoulder.

'Three offers now, is it, son?' Danny nodded mutely, ducking his head to avoid Mara's gaze.

'That's wonderful news,' Mara said. 'Congratulations. You must be so proud, George.'

George beamed at her.

'First of the family ever to go to university. And not only that – but to medical school.' George was unable to contain his pride. 'Not bad going for a farmer's lad.'

'Indeed. Just the exams to sit now,' said Mara. Danny gave her a nervous smile and ran on to join his siblings.

Inside, the chapel smelt fusty and old. It reminded Rosie of viewing houses for sale in Oxford that had been left unoccupied for too long. They had that same damp, abandoned smell. The chill of last winter rolled off the walls in waves. Here though, the smell came not from neglect, but from age and a lack of central heating.

The chapel was obviously well tended. The pews were clean, the tiny stained-glass windows bright with morning sunshine. Two carved wooden statues flanked the altar, dwarfing the metal-framed votive candle stands stationed at their feet. A few tiny candle flames flickered feebly in the draught, marking the prayers and petitions of the faithful.

Rosie squinted at the lettering carved into the heavy plinths. Bede and Cuthbert, the two great northern saints. It figured. Euan steered her into a pew towards the back of the chapel. Mara sat on her other side, chafing her hands together.

'Keep your coat on,' Euan advised. 'It won't warm up for a while.' Rosie's feet bumped against a fabric-covered kneeler. She looked down and saw that it had been sewn with some form of religious motif in a tapestry style.

'Those were all handmade and embroidered by the ladies of the house for generations back,' Mara murmured. 'There'll be some initials on there if you look closely.'

'Did you make one?' Rosie whispered, intrigued by such an odd custom.

Mara smiled wryly. 'I tried. Let's say needlework wasn't my forte. I believe Hugh's mother made several in later years.'

A little bell rang from within the sacristy and the congregation rose as one, feet shuffling and hymn books rustling as they searched for the right page. A thin, reedy organ piped out the opening bars of *The Lord is My Shepherd*. Hugh scooted down the aisle and slid into the front pew, red-faced and out of breath.

The priest appeared and began a slow procession round the chapel, preceded by two grinning altar servers clad in black cassocks and lace-trimmed cottas that were far too short. The angelic effect was somewhat tempered by their matching silver Nike trainers with flashing red lights set into the soles.

Only the Hardy twins could get away with that. Joel carried an enormous candle while Callum was wielding what appeared to be a smoking metal ball and chain to deadly effect. Clouds of incense spewed out as he swung the thurible vigorously, prompting a spate of coughing from the pseudo asthmatics in the congregation.

The priest wore the rich purple vestments of Lent and a matching stole that bore intricate Celtic eternity knots worked in gold thread. His hands were joined in a prayerful attitude, his head bowed in contemplation so that his face was partially obscured by the high cowl neck of his robes.

Rosie looked away in sudden irritation as the little procession passed her by. The pomp and ritual struck a jarring note in the simple setting of the country chapel. What was the point of flouncing around? It hadn't been like this in the chapel at Carrington Hall.

Sadness welled up in her at the memory and she dug her nails into her palms to stop the tears. She set her jaw and focused on the vivid purple of the priest's vestments as he trod slowly up the sanctuary steps and moved to the lectern.

The priest stood patiently, still bent low in prayerful posture. Callum diligently covered him in a cloud of incense before bowing semi-respectfully and backing away to join his brother on a small wooden bench on the far side of the sanctuary.

Rosie saw Joel nudge Callum and point at the thurible as he mouthed, 'My turn next time.'

Callum gave a grudging nod as the service started.

'The Lord be with you,' said the priest in a unexpectedly familiar voice.

'And also with you,' chorused the congregation. Rosie's gaze snapped across to the lectern. The priest had straightened up to his full height to address the people.

'And I must say, it's lovely to be here with you again,' beamed Aelred.

Rosie sat down with a thump. A surge of panic filled her body. She wanted to run. It couldn't be. Not him . . . not Aelred . . . not a priest . . .

She stood up to have a second look and sat down immediately, her heart racing. It was. She'd been duped.

❀ ❀ ❀ ❀

The service was not as bad as she thought it would be. There had been no bolts of lightning, no voices of God and no tears. Rosie actually felt good to be among her friends. Aelred had smiled at her as he preached and despite her shock at seeing him there, his words were comforting. He made it sound so simple – finding God in stillness and beauty, letting go and moving on.

'The winter is over . . . spring has come . . . it is a time for rejoicing . . .' Aelred had said as he gave the benediction.

Were these words for her? Rosie didn't move from her seat. She sat in silence looking at the brightly painted altar. Mara took Euan to the door on the pretext of feeling unwell. She wanted to leave Rosie to think. On this day it was good for her to be in this place.

It was several minutes before Rosie moved. Most of the congregation had departed, all shaking Aelred by the hand and exchanging pleasantries at the chapel door. She waited until the church was empty, then marched up to him, eyes blazing.

He smiled broadly and held up his hands. 'You've rumbled me.'

'You lied to me.'

'My dear Rosie . . . not a bit of it . . .' said Aelred. 'Priests are shepherds of people.'

'You didn't tell me you were a priest!'

'Would it have made a difference?'

'You know it would.'

'So you like me less for knowing?' he asked quietly, his words echoing in the stillness of the chapel.

'I – no.' Rosie felt exasperated. How could she? Whatever else he might be, he was still Aelred. Lovable, quirky, wise old Aelred. 'You shouldn't have tricked me.'

'Then, find it in yourself to forgive me,' said Aelred, enveloping Rosie in an enormous hug, his vestments folding round her like wings. He smelt of coffee and tobacco and aftershave, just like a father.

'You're still you, I suppose,' she admitted when he released her. 'Anything else I should know while we're on the subject? You don't moonlight as a jazz player, spy or anything?'

Aelred grinned. 'There is one small thing. I took a new name when I made my vows to the Order.'

'So, Aelred's not your real name?'

'Not my birth name,' Aelred corrected. 'It's a bit like a woman changing her surname when she marries. I've been Aelred for forty-two years.'

Rosie's brow furrowed with the effort of following this. 'So what *is* your name?'

Aelred looked sheepish. 'Bernard,' he whispered.

'*Bernard?*' Rosie spluttered.

There was a shout of laughter behind them. They turned and saw Hugh standing beside Mara, his face creased with mirth. Rosie had never seen him look so animated. From the amusement on their faces it was obvious that they'd observed the entire exchange. Hugh walked forwards and clapped Aelred on the shoulder.

'You kept that one quiet, Father. I'd stick with Aelred if I were you.'

'It's not that bad,' said Aelred huffily.

'Could have been much worse,' said Mara kindly. 'Not much, though.' She began to chuckle. One by one the others joined in, Aelred last.

'It *is* pretty awful,' he admitted, wiping his eyes on the sleeve of his alb. 'We can still have our date on Thursday?'

Rosie nodded.

'Now, I must lock up this chapel. If you dear people will excuse me?'

'I'll help you, Father,' said Mara, trotting after him.

Hugh took Rosie to one side. 'I have business in Alnwick this afternoon,' he said quietly.

'On a Sunday?'

'No such thing as a day of rest for me,' he said ruefully. 'But look. There's a place I think you'd like to visit. You could spend a couple of hours there and I'll collect you on my way home. If you like?'

'I could do with a couple of hours to myself . . .' Rosie hesitated. 'It's my wedding anniversary today.'

'I know. Mara told me.'

'She did?'

'In confidence, of course,' Hugh said earnestly. 'I hope you don't mind?'

Rosie looked up at him, hands shoved into his trouser pockets and hair blowing wildly in the breeze. 'No,' she said, surprised to find that it was true.

'Ready to go?' called Mara from the chapel porch.

'I think Euan's gone without us,' Rosie called back.

'I'll give you a lift,' said Hugh. 'And I'll pick you up at two.'

Rosie smiled gratefully at him. 'Thank you.' Mara smiled triumphantly as the pair strolled off down the path through the fields.

'Is this the beginning of something?' enquired Aelred, offering Mara his arm.

She winked at him. 'If there is a God in heaven then this is one prayer I would want Him to answer.'

'Doesn't it say somewhere that God always has a place in His heart for love and a perfect plan for us all, Mara?' Aelred replied.

❀   ❀   ❀   ❀

'I'll pick you up in two hours,' said Hugh as Rosie clambered out of the car in Alnwick. 'I need to be home by five.'

'You're still not going to tell me what this place is?' she asked.

Hugh shook his head. 'No. But I will say this – you get free refills of coffee and there's an open fire and you can sit for as long as you like.'

'Wow. That's my kind of place.'

'I thought so,' he smiled. 'It's on your right as you go round the corner. Four o'clock.'

'Four o'clock.'

She walked round the corner and stopped dead when she saw the sign emblazoned on the side of what looked like a warehouse. 'Barter Books,' she read. 'One of the largest second-hand bookshops in Britain.'

She couldn't help feeling it was an anti-climax. Bookshops with a café were nothing new. Plus she didn't have the money to splash out, even if the books were second-hand. Although, it was a sweet thought on Hugh's part, she supposed.

Rosie trudged through the steep car parking area and found the main entrance round the back. From this angle, the building looked more like a village railway station than a warehouse.

Inside the main entrance was a small porch area, its walls filled with bookshelves from floor to ceiling, with several additional freestanding shelves dotted across the stone floor. This gave onto a larger room via an archway, where there were more shelves and a row of computers. The till was on the left behind a long saloon-style counter, staffed by a bright-eyed man wearing the kind of holey grey cardigan favoured by a certain breed of middle-aged male.

A giant framed poster in pillar-box red ordered everyone to 'Keep Calm and Carry On.' Closer inspection revealed it to be an original propaganda poster from World War Two.

As Rosie took in the scene, a whirring sound made her look up. A miniature train whizzed smoothly past overhead, its tracks resting on the tops of the bookshelves. It circled the room and disappeared through a stone archway.

'Hey, that's cool,' Rosie exclaimed. The man behind the counter chuckled.

'Follow it through,' he said excitedly, nodding at the archway.

'There's more?'

'See for yourself.'

Rosie did as she was told. She found herself standing in an ancient library. Towering bookshelves stretched the length and breadth of a high-ceilinged oblong room. Large arched windows with leaded panes filled the left-hand wall.

Happy browsers were scattered among the shelves, all wrapped in hats and scarves to ward off the chill rising from the concrete floor. The place hummed with quiet activity. In addition to the clockwork train, wooden runners had been fixed to the top of each bookshelf, travelling across the gaps in the aisle to meet the neighbouring shelf. Each runner was inscribed with a literary quote so that you walked beneath a bridge of words as you passed down the central aisle.

'Cameron would have loved this,' Rosie breathed. 'I can't believe all these books are for sale. There must be thousands.' Through a gap in the shelves, she glimpsed a room on the right filled with wooden tables, long benches and the open fire Hugh had promised her. The sign above the door read Waiting Room.

'It *is* a train station!' she cried. A woman in a flowing tie-dye dress paused as she tottered past, the large stack of books in her arms wedged in place by her chin.

'Of course it is,' she said. 'See that?' The lady indicated two thick parallel lines in the concrete, which ran the length of the central aisle. 'That's where the well for the tracks was filled in. This was the outgoing platform. And look behind you.' Rosie turned around and saw words etched into the stone high above the arched entrance. It was a memorial to the railway staff. Tears sprang to her eyes as she read the inscription.

Alnwick Station 1887 – 1968
'Their voices and those of others now unknown,
once filled this station,
along with the sound of the steam trains they served
so well,
both in times of war and of peace.'

'And those of others now unknown,' Rosie mumbled, fumbling in her pockets for a tissue. The assistant eyed her strangely and moved on without further comment.

'Choose a book,' Rosie urged herself. 'Get a coffee, curl up by the fire. Enjoy this.'

Rosie located the children's section and dug around until she found two of her favourite books, *Anne of Green Gables* and *Swallows and Amazons*. She wanted comfort today and to immerse herself in a childhood time of safety: a time when there was nothing that couldn't be made better with a hug and forever only lasted until next week.

At half past four Hugh got fed up of waiting and tracked Rosie down to the old waiting room. She was sitting close to the fire on a long pew-style bench, her back propped against the wall and her legs stretched out. Her shoes had been kicked onto the floor.

The fire crackled protectively, like a guard dog. Rosie was utterly absorbed. Hugh approached and stood before her. It seemed a shame to call her back from her other world to the here and now, but it had to be done.

'Rosie?' he said softly. Rosie's only reaction was to turn the page. Her jaw tightened. She must be at an exciting point. Hugh waited a few moments before he tried again. 'Rosie?' Still nothing.

'Taxi for Whitton,' Hugh said loudly. Rosie jumped and dropped her book.

'Hugh, hi.' Rosie was pleased to see him.

'You were miles away,' he smiled, stooping to retrieve the paperback from the floor.

Rosie had the confused look of a sleepwalker who wakes to find herself in a completely unexpected location. 'Yes,' she said vaguely, staring around the room. 'I was.'

Hugh crouched down so that their faces were level.

'Put these on,' he said gently, handing Rosie her trainers. 'It's time to go.'

'Am I late?' she asked anxiously, stuffing her untied laces into her shoes.

'It would seem strange if you weren't.' He held out his hand. 'Come on. Let's get you home.' Rosie allowed him to pull her to her feet and lead her to the door.

In the car she turned to him. 'Thank you, Hugh. It was just what I needed.'

'Good. You must come again.'

'Maybe you could come too,' she said.

'Maybe I could.' As they drove home, each was aware of a new quality to the silence between them.

Chapter 22

Beltane

Hugh was working in the estate office, trawling through the pile of overdue letters and payments, yet again. Already, it was past lunch and he had achieved nothing. The windows were wide open and a fresh breeze rustled the papers carrying in the scent of the fields. It was pleasant, but reminded Hugh that he would rather be elsewhere on such a beautiful day.

Elsewhere – with someone. Hugh groaned and shook the thought from his head. It was impossible. The age difference . . . the history . . . the entire situation. Everything was stacked against him. Except, for the first time in fifteen years, his heaviness had lifted . . . Could it work? He wondered. Could they both start again? No – the whole idea was ridiculous.

He felt a light touch on his shoulder and looked up into sparkling green eyes. His careful rationale promptly evaporated.

'Hi,' said Rosie. 'Where's Euan today?'

'Rang in sick this morning.' He suddenly realised he was grinning like an idiot and tried to pull his mouth in. 'Poor bloke sounded really bad.'

'I hope he's OK.'

'Just a touch of man flu,' said Hugh dismissively. He didn't want Rosie to feel too sympathetic towards Euan. After the night in the forest, Hugh and Euan had reached an uneasy truce.

Hugh had since avoided any situation where the three of them might be together. He still wasn't even sure whether Rosie and Euan were an item. He didn't want to ask. It was obvious that Euan felt some kind of claim on her, but did Rosie feel the same? Hugh didn't think so but it was impossible to tell. Euan had told him about all the places he had taken her. 'Just showing her the land,' he had said.

Hugh was conscious of Rosie's hand still resting on his shoulder. Did that mean something? – anything?

'Sorry, what did you say?' he asked, aware that Rosie was looking at him quizzically.

'I asked what you've got for me this afternoon,' she repeated patiently.

'Oh. Erm . . . I don't know.'

'No problem. I'll take a look in the files and see what Euan had in mind.' Rosie tripped over to the filing cabinet and began flicking through the dividers. 'Ah. Here we go.' She pulled out a bundle of cardboard files secured with a thick elastic band. 'Looks like he's earmarked these for me. See you later?'

'Perhaps we could –'

'Yes?' Rosie replied quickly, not giving him the time to finish.

The office phone rang. Hugh picked up the receiver and gave her a look as if to say he would speak to her later.

Rosie flashed him a bright smile and left the room. Hugh looked helplessly at the letter he was attempting to draft, all hope of concentration gone as he listened to the voice on the phone.

Rosie took the scenic route to Lowdale Farm, bouncing the Land Rover through puddles and potholes, singing as she went. Everything was bursting with life; somehow it gave her hope of what was to come. Summer wouldn't be too bad, she thought as she dropped over the hill and in to the valley. Getting past her first wedding anniversary had felt like a milestone. The darker anniversary of the climbing accident was lurking round the corner. As she drove, she thought of Hugh, of that night in Kielder Forest. As she replayed it in her mind, she kept coming back to the embrace. Somehow, it had felt like more than a friend showing his concern.

The accident edged its way back in to her mind. Rosie now felt differently about it. In some ways she and Mara had already confronted it with the arrival of the police report. It would still be an emotional day but when Rosie thought about it there was no sense of dread, just sadness.

It felt normal, healthier. She smiled as she swung the car through the entrance at Lowdale, the gate standing open for her. Aelred would put her improved state of mind down to his self-help book, which had been pressed into service as a permanent wedge for the leg of the coffee table in their lounge. At least she could tell him honestly that it had been useful.

Rosie slid the Lowdale file out of the bundle and jumped out of the car, grinning at the prospect of Callum and Joel's latest hoodlum behaviour. At this rate, Kate's hair would be completely white by the time they reached eighteen. She sauntered across the grass towards the rambling old farmhouse, admiring the beautiful yellow roses just beginning to climb the latticed trellis framing the front door. She headed straight for the back door, knowing the kitchen was the hub around which the family orbited.

'Hello?' Rosie tapped on the door and walked in. She was met by a divine smell of freshly baking bread wafting from the oven. The kitchen was unoccupied. She went to the foot of the stairs and called up. 'Kate? It's Rosie.' The house appeared to be empty. Rosie checked her watch. Five minutes past two. The twins would be at school, of course and Danny might have an exam today, but Kate and Lucy would normally be here at this time. 'That's weird,' said Rosie, feeling an irrational pinprick of fear. She quickly checked the downstairs rooms, then went back outside. 'They can't all be out,' she reasoned. 'The door was unlocked and the oven's on. Where are they?' Something was wrong.

'Rooooo-ssiieee!' The cry carried on the wind, faint but clear. Rosie shaded her eyes and scanned the horizon. Relief turned her legs to jelly as she saw Kate and George strolling across the fields with Lucy skipping along between them. George was swinging a large wicker basket, a tartan rug rolled up under his arm.

A picnic. Rosie laughed at her over-reaction. She gave Lucy a big two-arm wave and gestured back at the house to show the Hardys she was going inside.

She was still chuckling over her stupidity when a sound brought her up short. A low moan came from the threshing barn that stood parallel to the house. It was the sound of a creature in pain. She walked over and leaned in through the open door, listening hard. There it was again, coming from the shadows.

Cautiously, she moved in the direction of the noise, wary of approaching an animal larger than she could handle. She found him hiding near an old tractor wheel, curled up on a pile of potato sacks. His head lifted, tortured brown eyes searching and finding hers.

Rosie backed away in panic as she saw the blood.

'No,' she breathed. '*No!*' The next instant she was out of the barn, sprinting towards the Hardys, arms stretched wide. 'Kate!' she yelled, her voice hoarse with terror. 'Get Lucy into the house! Don't come out.' The trio stopped dead, Kate instinctively lifting Lucy into a protective embrace. George let the basket and rug fall.

'What is it?'

'Come with me, George.' Rosie seized his arm and tried to drag him forcibly towards the barn. She caught sight of Lucy's terrified face and made an enormous effort to leach the fear from her voice. 'Hurry. George, you *must come*.' She tore back to the barn without waiting for his reply. George looked at his wife.

'Do as she says. Get indoors. Stay there.'

Back in the barn, Rosie fell to her knees. The sacks were stained with blood. 'Hold on,' she gasped. 'Just hold on.'

Danny lay with his arm cradled to his chest, blood pouring steadily from the gashes in his wrist as his heart unwittingly pumped on. His head lolled on the ground, his eyes unfocussed.

'Son?'

'Take the sleeve off your shirt,' Rosie ordered George. They had to stem the blood somehow. George stood there, unable to respond.

'*George!*' Rosie leaped up and ripped the sleeve off. She snatched up the abandoned kitchen knife and stabbed into the fabric, tearing the sleeve in two. Then she prised Danny's arms away from his body and wrapped the makeshift bandages round the wound as tightly as she could, ignoring his cries of pain.

'Danny,' she said clearly, 'we're going to hospital. You must hold on until we get there, do you hear me?' He was sliding towards unconsciousness. An ambulance would be too late. Rosie's fist closed over her keys.

'What can we do?' George asked as he just stood there.

'Get him to the car. I'll drive.' Staggering into motion, George lifted his son. Blood trickled down his arms and chest as he strode out of the barn, Rosie sprinting ahead to start the engine. She had a glimpse of Kate, white-faced at the kitchen window, as George bundled their eldest son into the car, then she rammed the gear stick into first and they were away.

The car careered down the country lanes, taking the corners wide and at speed. The sound of George's weeping filled Rosie's ears.

'Why, son? Why?' he repeated over and over as they sped towards the hospital.

Please God, let us be in time. We have to be in time, Rosie prayed hard, meaning every word.

'I'm sorry, Dad,' Danny whispered.

It was the longest journey of Rosie's life. Even though the roads were empty, the minutes dragged . Danny slipped in and out of dreaming, crying, asking his father to forgive him. Rosie prayed every mile that he would live. George sobbed as he held his son.

'The College didn't want me Dad . . . none of them wanted me . . .' Danny said again and again as his father held him with the same love he had done when he was new-born.

By the time the Land Rover skidded to a stop outside Accident and Emergency at Alnwick Infirmary, she felt she had aged a hundred years. Rosie hurled herself from the driving seat and threw the passenger door wide to give George a clear run.

He half-jumped, half-slid from the vehicle and stumbled through the sliding doors, Danny hanging limp in his arms. Nurses came running from every direction. Voices gave clipped, concise orders. Danny was taken from his father's arms and rushed away.

George followed, escorted by another nurse. 'Please don't tell anyone about this Rosie,' he whispered before disappearing round a corner. Rosie was left in the waiting area, her breath coming in heaving gasps. She was aware of someone guiding her to a seat, pressing a cup of water into her hand. She mumbled her thanks and closed her eyes. There was nothing she could do now but wait.

She had no idea how long she waited. Units of time became meaningless, every minute, every second a lifetime. She was roused by a hand on her arm. A dumpy nurse was beside her, kind eyes smiling out of a round, red face.

'Mr Hardy is asking for you.' Rosie followed the nurse to
the cubicle where Danny lay, either sleeping or unconscious.
A junior doctor bent over the bed, checking the lines that
fed into his arm.

George sat by the bedside, his face damp with sweat and
tears. 'He's OK,' he said brokenly. A chair was produced and
Rosie sat down beside him. 'They had to take him to theatre, but they managed to stop the blood. He cut through a
tendon.'

'Do you want to call Kate?' she asked. 'I'll stay with
Danny.'

'In a minute. Doctor wants a word first.' Rosie started to
get up as a second doctor entered the cubicle but George
grasped her arm. 'You've a right to hear it,' he said gruffly.
The doctor pulled up a third chair and sat down.

His head was shaved, his eyes sharp behind black-rimmed
designer glasses. He didn't look old enough to be in charge.

'Everything's going to be fine. There's some minor damage to the flexor tendons on the left wrist, but it is not severed. If he'd cut deep enough to hit the radial artery it could
have been problematic, but he was nowhere near.'

'Right,' said George, sounding fazed. 'That's . . . that's good
then?'

Rosie felt taken aback by the doctor's businesslike detach-
ment. He might have been discussing the weather. It was
almost callous. *I suppose they'd go insane if they allowed
themselves to care about everyone,* she realised. *You can't
absorb other people's pain.*

'We'll keep him in for observation,' the man continued,
'and he may need a psychiatric consultation to assess his

current state of mind. All things being equal, he should be home in forty-eight hours.'

'Thank you, doctor.'

'Dad?'

'Danny!' George darted to the bedside. The doctor nodded politely to Rosie and stepped beyond the curtain, drawing it closed behind him.

'Son, why did you do it?' George asked, his eyes filling with tears. 'What could be so wrong? You've got your whole life ahead of you.'

'No, Dad,' Danny said, his voice trembling with exhaustion. 'I can't go to medical school. They didn't want me.'

'What? But what about Cambridge, Nottingham? You said . . .'

'They rejected me.' Tears of humiliation rolled down his cheeks. 'You and Mam were so proud, telling everyone you met . . . I couldn't tell you I'd been knocked back.' Danny turned his face away. 'Now everyone will know.' George laid his hand tenderly on his son's head.

'About medical school, yes.' Though spoken to his son, Rosie knew that George's next words were intended for her. 'But not about this. Please don't tell anyone Rosie – not even Hugh . . . please.'

'No one will hear of it from me,' she said. 'No matter what. That's a promise.'

George bowed his head. 'Thank you.' Rosie backed out of the cubicle and walked quietly away, her feet dragging with weariness.

❀ ❀ ❀ ❀

Rosie drove first to Lowdale Farm to check on Kate and the children. That done, she headed for Earleside. When she reached the turning point for the Dower House, Rosie spun the wheel and steered the Land Rover along the track. It was past six o'clock now. The working day was over. Besides, the thought of driving up to the house to file her paperwork and trudge down to the Dower House on foot was more than she could stomach after the day she'd had.

'I'll get up early and return the car first thing,' she decided. She stumbled into the sitting-room and fell into the nearest armchair.

'Is that you, Rosie?' Mara's voice floated down the stairs.

'Yeah, I'm home,' Rosie called back.

'I'm just having a bath, I won't be long.'

'OK. Give me a few minutes, I'll make supper.'

'Bless you.'

There was a knock at the door.

'Go away,' Rosie groaned, walking to the door as slowly as possible in the hope that her wish might be granted. Hugh was waiting outside. The worried frown on his face cleared when he saw Rosie.

'You're all right,' he said.

'Um . . . yes,' said Rosie, unable to see where this was headed. It seemed rather an obvious statement. 'Come in. What's up?'

Hugh followed her into the sitting-room.

'I waited at the office for you to come back. When it got to six, I started to worry.' Rosie pointed him to a chair and collapsed back into her own.

'I'm sorry,' she yawned. 'By the time I got through visiting everyone on my list, I was so beat I came straight home. I was going to bring the car up early tomorrow.'

'The Langhams called from the Old Mill,' Hugh said casually. 'They were expecting you at four-thirty and you didn't show. What happened?'

Rosie thought fast. An excuse. She needed a good excuse. 'Oh, shoot,' she said, picking her bundle of files off the floor and making a show of sorting through them. 'I must have missed their file. Hey, look, it got slipped inside the Stewarts' folder.' She chose a file at random and waved it at Hugh. 'No wonder I couldn't find it. I'll call them tomorrow morning.'

'I don't think it was urgent, but if you didn't go to the Langhams, where have you been? You look done in.'

Rosie dropped the file and raked her hands through her hair, playing for time. Where could she have been? 'Don't be mad,' she said hesitantly. 'I went to check on Euan.'

'Oh?' Hugh looked tense.

'I'll make the time up, I promise,' Rosie babbled. 'I was a little worried about him after what you said earlier on. Flu can be pretty nasty and he lives on his own. I just took him some food, bits and pieces to keep him going while he's stuck in bed, you know?' She rolled her eyes comically. 'It was quite a chore, actually. I never thought a grown man could be so whiny.'

Hugh laughed. 'I won't tell him you said that.'

'Thanks.' Rosie smiled at him. *I think I've got away with it.* 'Listen, why don't you stay for supper?' she said. 'It's not much, just pork pie and some vegetables, but you're welcome to join us.'

'I'd love to.'

'Your mission is to cheer me up,' she said. 'I can't take any more whining.'

Hugh pulled Rosie to her feet and ushered her into the kitchen.

'Something to cheer you up,' he mused, attacking a pile of carrots with the peeler while Rosie chopped some potatoes. 'Have you heard the story of how Mara and Mrs Drummond became best friends?'

'No,' said Rosie, her interest immediately sparked. 'Is it funny? Mara's never mentioned it.'

'She wouldn't. It is funny, but not to Mara.' Hugh chuckled. 'Her father had fairly radical ideas for his generation and decided to send Mara and her brother Robert to the local village school instead of to boarding school. He saw it as a social experiment. That's where Mara and Mrs Drummond met. They didn't get on at all.'

'They didn't?'

'No. What happened was . . .' They worked side by side as Hugh talked, so close that their shoulders brushed together whenever one of them moved. Rosie stole a glance at Hugh, his face full of humour as he unfolded the tale.

I'd like to do this with you forever. Her knife slipped on the potato she was chopping and nicked her finger. Where had that thought come from?

'. . . so Mrs Drummond bet Mara she couldn't swim across the river and Mara was so stubborn she took the bet and jumped right in. The entire class was watching on the bank, so she couldn't lose face. The problem was: Mara couldn't swim. Mrs Drummond dived in, saved her life and they buried the hatchet on the spot. They've been best friends ever since but Mara's never lived it down.'

'I can't believe it,' Rosie giggled. 'No wonder she never told me.'

'And I'll thank you not to be having fun at my expense, Hugh Fenwick,' snapped Mara, appearing in the kitchen in her dressing gown and slippers. 'I heard what you were saying.' She wagged a finger at him. 'Shame on you!'

'Sorry, Mara. I was ordered to cheer this beautiful lady up. I had no choice but to spill the beans.'

'Ha,' said Mara sourly. 'You had no right. And for the record, I could swim perfectly well. I lost my footing and panicked, that's all.'

Rosie's lip wobbled as Hugh pulled a face at her. She bit the inside of her cheek hard to keep her laughter in.

Mara stumped to the fridge and took out a bottle of milk.

'Rosie, I'm dead on my feet. I think I'll give supper a miss, if you don't mind. I'll just take a glass of milk and go straight up to bed.'

'Are you sure? How about I bring you a tray up?'

'No thank you, dear. Rest is all I need. And a little respect where it's due,' Mara added sharply, jabbing Hugh in the ribs on her way past. He planted a kiss on the top of her head and tried unsuccessfully to look remorseful.

'Goodnight, Mara.'

'Bugger off.'

Mara sat on the stairs for a long time, sipping her milk and listening to the laughter ringing out in the kitchen. Her stomach rumbled painfully when she eventually tiptoed up to bed, careful to take her empty glass with her. It wouldn't do for them to know she'd been eavesdropping.

She felt a twinge of regret as she curled up in bed. Pork pie was her favourite. Rosie and Hugh's voices carried up through the floorboards, accompanied by the distinctive clink of wine glasses raised in a toast. Mara burrowed further under the blankets, grinning broadly. *Rosie and Hugh*? Mara thought. On balance, it was well worth it.

Chapter 23

Steel Traps

Rosie pulled up and parked awkwardly on the narrow terrace. The Range Rover looked bulky amid the other cars.
She checked the address again and walked slowly down the
road, counting the door numbers. A fat man in an old Ford
stared at her as she walked by. Rosie smiled, the man nodded, picked up his newspaper and watched her walk on
down the road.

Euan's house was the last on the neglected street. The
walls were pebble-dashed in grimy white. The paintwork on
the window frames was flaking: weatherworn and sun-
peeled. Flanking the path to the front door was an unkempt
verge, the grass several inches high. Rosie felt as though she
was in the wrong place as she pushed the waist-high gate
aside and approached the house. She raised her hand and
tapped on the curtained window-pane set into the door.

'Euan?' She tapped again, a little harder this time. A
muffled call came from inside the house. Rosie glanced at
her watch. It was past noon. She didn't mind running
errands but this was really eating into her day. Still, Hugh
had said this was important and doing it meant one less

thing for him to worry about. She smiled to herself at that thought.

A minute later the door opened and Euan peered out, disheveled and sleepy in grey sweatpants and a T-shirt.

'Rosie . . . what are you doing here?' he said as if she was the last person he ever expected to see at his house.

Rosie held up the file. 'You forgot to sign off the accounts for June.'

'Couldn't it wait?'

'Hugh says not.' Rosie waited but Euan just stood there, scratching his chest through his T-shirt. 'Are you going to invite me in?'

Euan looked wary. 'Uh . . . yeah, OK,' he mumbled. He reluctantly backed away from the door and beckoned her in.

Rosie stepped over the threshold, clutching the file to her chest. The plastered walls were painted stark white and the place felt cold. She scuffed her feet on the doormat, pushed the door closed with her hip and followed Euan down the hallway past a staircase so steep it was almost vertical.

'Late night?' she asked.

'Can't a bloke sleep in on his day off?'

'Hey, I'm kidding,' Rosie said lightly.

Euan led her into the kitchen.

'Sorry,' he grunted, indicating the dirty dishes in the sink and the crushed beer cans piled on the breakfast table. 'I wasn't expecting visitors. Have a seat.'

'No – no worries.' She didn't know what she'd been expecting, but it wasn't this. She looked about for somewhere to sit down. The whole place felt grimy. The wooden spindle chairs clustered around the table were piled with old newspapers, discarded post and half-folded washing. She looked to Euan but he was lifting plates out of the sink in order to fill the kettle. Rosie shifted a pile of post to one side and perched awkwardly on the corner of a chair. She laid the file down on the table but snatched it up immediately as a patch of spilled beer seeped into the cardboard.

'Here you go.' Euan slapped down a mug on the table so that the liquid sloshed over the rim. 'Sugar?'

'I'm good, thanks.' It was tea. Pale, milky and disgusting. Rosie lifted the mug and wondered how long she could politely avoid drinking it. 'Did you have some friends over last night?' she asked, nodding at the empty cans.

'No, just watched a movie and had a few beers.' He gulped his tea down and stretched out his hand for the file. 'Let me see that.' Rosie handed it over and watched as he leafed through. 'Yeah, I see. Tell Hugh I'll have it back to him tomorrow.'

Rosie inched herself further onto her chair, feeling awkward.

'Um, I think he needs it today,' she said apologetically.

'Tomorrow,' Euan said firmly so she knew he was not going to change his mind. 'I work my backside off for that man at this time of year. It's my day off.'

He glared at Rosie, daring her to answer back. Rosie raised her mug to her lips, trying to hide her discomfort. Euan was normally so smart and cheerful, a little crass maybe – a flirt definitely – but this? He was so ragged, unshaven and so not like Euan. The house was uncared for, dirty and not what she expected. Rosie could sense that she wasn't welcome.

Euan stood up. 'I'm going to make some toast. Want some?'

'Sure,' answered Rosie, relieved to be moving onto a safer topic of conversation. 'I'll just use your bathroom, if that's OK?'

'Turn left, it's at the end of the hall,' said Euan over his shoulder. 'Ignore the mess. One slice or two?'

'Two please.' Rosie got to her feet and walked to the door. She stumbled and caught herself against the wall. Her hand came away damp. Everything about the place was unpleasant. Rosie wanted to be out of there, in the car and safely away. Now she had to stay and eat toast or she would appear rude.

Rosie turned into the hall and saw two doors, slightly off-set on opposing walls. She chose the one on the left and tugged it open to find a walk-in storage cupboard crammed with junk. Rosie closed the door automatically and started to turn away, but something stopped her. She re-opened the door, found a light switch on the inside wall and flicked it on. Hearing Euan whistling as he crashed around in the kitchen and her pulse hammering in her ears, she looked inside.

The cupboard was filled with a selection of coiled ropes, traps and row upon row of lamps with different coloured lenses. She remembered what Hugh had told her: blue for deer, red for rabbits. Some of the ropes were stained with old blood. A shotgun lay on the floor. Rosie felt her stomach turn as everything fell neatly, horribly, into place.

'Jam or marmalade?' Euan called.

'Coming . . .' Rosie started to panic. She had to get out without arousing suspicion.

'Rosie?' She spun round. Euan stood in the hallway.

'I – I . . .' she stammered. 'I got the wrong door.'

Euan nodded and advanced towards her with slow steps.

'Close the door, Rosie,' he said in a low voice. She obeyed instantly. 'Good girl.' He kept coming, walking right into Rosie's space. She was forced back against the door. There was nowhere for her to go.

'I didn't see anything.' Rosie said as she glanced down the hall. She thought of running. The front door seemed a long way away. Euan followed her gaze.

'I don't think so.' He placed his hands either side of her on the wall to block her in. Sour beer breath filled Rosie's nostrils. She stared into his face, trying not to show her fear.

'It was you.' Images flicked through her mind. The pub lunches, the fruitless hunting parties, Euan casually explaining that the poaching ring must have an informant. 'You – all along.'

Euan held up his hands in mock defeat. 'Guilty as charged.' He half laughed, half looked like the Euan she had got to know – before his face contorted and he slammed his hands back against the wall. Rosie flinched. 'The question is,' he continued, pushing his face unbearably close to hers, 'what are you going to do about it, Rosie?'

His eyes bored into hers. Rosie turned her face away. She could feel his breath, hot and stale on her cheek as he gripped her wrist.

'I – I won't say anything. I promise. No one will hear it from me.'

'You expect me to believe that?' He grabbed a handful of hair and pulled her head back, forcing his mouth onto hers.

Rosie clamped her mouth shut, recoiling from his tongue and his teeth. He bit into her lip and pulled her closer towards him. She tried to kick out but Euan had his full weight against her, pinning her to the wall. Rosie gasped as the breath was driven out of her.

Euan pulled back, but kept hold of her hair. 'I've wanted to do that for a long time.' He licked his lips, leering at her.

Rosie tasted blood in her mouth.

'Hugh knows I'm here,' she said desperately, guessing what Euan wanted. 'He'll come looking if I don't go back.'

'Hugh is an idiot. I've been running this operation right under his nose for over a year and he doesn't suspect a thing.' There was a wild look in his eye. 'Besides, you were in on it too, Mrs Whitton.'

'I wasn't.'

'Oh, yes you were,' Euan hissed. 'All those pub lunches? Playing the merry widow for me while I struck the deals before Christmas? You were the perfect cover, my little American sweetheart.' He smirked. 'I told people you were in love with me.'

'I had no idea what you were doing. I thought you were being a friend.'

'Think the police would believe that, do you? You're in it up to your neck, you stupid cow. You were a pretty alibi. And if anything else came of it, well, that would have been a bonus.'

'Alibi? That's all I was to you?'

'And nice to look at – especially in those tight jeans.'

The smell of burning toast prickled Rosie's nostrils and caught the back of her throat, mingling with the taste of her own blood. She coughed.

'What are you going to do with me?' Rosie hated how pathetic her voice sounded.

'One thing springs immediately to mind.' His smile was more of a snarl. How could she not have seen this in him before? Euan pulled her away from the wall and twisted one arm up behind her back. 'Why don't we go upstairs?'

'Get off me!' Rosie started to struggle, tears pouring down her face. Her wrist screamed in pain as Euan twisted her arm even harder.

'Please God, no,' wailed Rosie, knowing that no one could hear her cry and no one would come.

'Shut up,' Euan snarled, forcing her down the hall ahead of him.

Suddenly he stopped.

'What was that?'

There was a tapping noise. Euan slipped one hand over Rosie's mouth.

'Hello? Anyone at home?'

Rosie felt Euan's grip on her arm tighten. 'You stupid . . .'

The front door creaked open. Rosie obviously hadn't shut it properly behind her. Two uniformed police barged into the hallway. Euan released Rosie and she sagged towards the wall.

'Stay where you are.'

Rosie sank to the floor 'Thank God,' she sobbed. 'Thank God.'

She was barely aware of Euan lunging between the officers, the shouts, the sounds of a scuffle. She took a deep breath before she felt herself seized by fresh hands. She didn't have to say anything, but anything she did say may be taken down and used as evidence . . .

❀   ❀   ❀   ❀

Rosie shivered again and shifted on the tubular metal chair.
The interview room at the local police station was small, cold
and unfriendly. But then, it wasn't intended to be friendly,
Rosie thought. The formica-topped table was bare, apart from
a Styrofoam cup and a small black cassette player used for tap-
ing interviews. She could see the spools turning in their deck.
Her gaze travelled across the table to the podgy hand of the
officer sitting opposite her. She had seen him before. He was
the man from the old Ford outside Euan's house.

He tapped his chubby sausage-like fingers silently on the
table, his wrist bulging from the cuff of his shirt. It looked
painfully tight, Rosie thought absently, looking up into his
face. He stared impassively back at her.

His companion, a thin-faced, mousy-haired female officer
with anxious eyes, cleared her throat and pushed a large
brown envelope across the table to Rosie.

'Showing the suspect photographic evidence B12,' she
said, over-pronouncing each word for the benefit of the tape.

Rosie opened the envelope and pulled out a handful of
photos. 'What are these?'

'Suspect is examining the evidence.' Rosie leafed through
the pictures. Her eyes widened as she perused the shots of
her eating and drinking in various pubs, laughing at Euan
across the table, getting into his car.

'These are from months ago,' she said feebly. 'Before
Christmas.'

'Yes,' said Sausage Fingers, leaning forwards in his chair.
'Just about the time when poached venison sales peak on the

black market. Bit of a coincidence, that, wouldn't you say?'

'Can you confirm that you are the woman in these pictures?' the female officer cut in.

'Of course it's me, but look, it was just a few lunches. Euan was showing me the area.'

'That's not what Mr Turnbull says.'

'He's lying.'

Sausage Fingers sat back in his chair and folded his arms. Rosie slid the photos back into the envelope and handed them over without a word. She tested the inside of her lip with the edge of her tongue. It tasted metallic. *God . . . get me out of here*, she thought desperately. She had to stay calm. There was no proof of her involvement. How could there be? The clock on the wall read ten minutes past four. Mara would be getting anxious.

'Where were you on the afternoon of May the eighth?'

Rosie gawped at him. 'May the eighth? I've no idea, it was weeks ago.'

'Let me jog your memory,' he said sarcastically. 'It was a Tuesday.'

'Tuesday afternoons I'm out visiting tenants,' Rosie said automatically.

'And there are records of the times and dates of these visits?' prompted the woman. 'In other words, you can provide an alibi?'

Rosie frowned. 'I – yes. Why is it necessary?' May the eighth, May the eighth . . . it did ring a bell, but why?

'Mr Turnbull was absent from work that day and a large quantity of poached venison was seized by our colleagues in

South Wales on May 9, just one day later. Northumbrian deer. One of the carcasses still had its tag markings. Careless.'

'The chap who bought it described a man fitting Mr Turnbull's description,' said the woman. 'He's prepared to testify in mitigation of his own offence.'

'Well, great,' said Rosie. 'I hope he rots in jail.'

'I'm not sure you understand,' said Sausage Fingers, laying his palms face-up on the table as though revealing a winning hand of cards. 'There was also a driver.'

Rosie felt her mouth go dry as the date finally clicked in her head. May the eighth. Danny Hardy.

'Mr Turnbull says it was you.' This was said with an air of triumph. *You've got to tell them*, urged the voice in her head.

'No way,' said Rosie aloud, remembering the fraught journey to hospital and George Hardy's stricken face as he begged for her silence.

"According to our information, the exchange took place a couple of hours drive from here," said the woman. "Neutral ground. Set off after lunch, back home by supper time, nice and tidy. Was that how it went?"

Tell them, hissed the voice. *Don't stitch yourself up.*

"No way," Rosie said again.

The woman raised her eyebrows. 'You have an alibi?'

Rosie lifted her chin and stared defiantly at the officers. 'Call Hugh Fenwick,' she said with a confidence she didn't feel.

Both officers looked crestfallen at this unexpected declaration. The woman stopped the tape.

'Interview suspended at 16.22, DC Laskey leaving the interview room.'

Sausage Fingers picked up his Styrofoam cup and noisily drained the last of his coffee. He got up to put the cup in the wastepaper bin, then returned to his seat. Rosie could feel his eyes on her. She turned her head to stare at the clock and determinedly kept on staring as the minute hand revolved slowly, too slowly. She prayed Hugh would be able to make this right somehow.

After more than an hour, the door opened and the female officer appeared. She beckoned her colleague into the corridor. Rosie leaned back in her chair, straining to catch their hasty conversation. Seconds later Sausage Fingers re-entered the room and gestured to Rosie.

'You're free to go.'

'What?'

'For now.'

Rosie got to her feet unsteadily, pulling her jacket from the back of the chair. This was too easy. 'You're not going to charge me?' she said suspiciously.

'I'm not saying that,' he answered, resetting the cassette machine and scooping up the envelope of photos. 'But it's your word against Turnbull's. We've checked your alibi and it's solid. It seems there are people willing to vouch for your character in court.' He shrugged, as though the fact was of little importance. 'It bodes well for you, but you're not in the clear yet. We may call you back for further questioning.'

Rosie was too tired to care. All that mattered was that she was getting out of here.

'Could I please make a phone call? I need a ride home.' Rosie thought Aelred might come for her, or Charlotte. Their numbers were in her mobile phone somewhere.

'No need,' said the officer, leading her into the corridor. 'There's someone here for you already.'

'There is?' Rosie followed him into the reception area.

Hugh was leaning against the front desk, chatting to the duty sergeant. At the sight of him, Rosie let the strain of the last hours overwhelm her.

'Hugh.' He turned and caught her awkwardly as she stumbled towards him.

'Let's get home,' he said. Rosie let him lead her outside. His car was parked haphazardly by the police station, one wheel skewed up onto the pavement. Hugh took his arm from around Rosie, pointed his key fob at the car and flipped the locks. 'Get in.' The words sounded distant and curt.

Hugh drove in silence for about five minutes and then swerved the car into a taxi rank.

'Did we forget something?' Rosie snuffled, blowing her nose on a sodden Kleenex.

'No.' Hugh switched off the engine and rounded on her, ignoring the flashing lights of the waiting taxi he'd just cut up. 'Why did you do it?' he said fiercely.

Rosie was confused. 'Hugh, I didn't. You know I didn't.'

'What I know,' said Hugh through clenched teeth, 'is that you were missing all afternoon on the eighth of May. When I asked you where you'd been, you told me you'd gone to Euan's home to check on him.'

'Did you tell *that* to the police?'

'I told them you were with me,' he said irritably. 'Going through one of the tenancy renewal agreements.'

'I can't thank you enough, Hugh, really, I . . .' Rosie tried to take hold of his hand but recoiled as he shrugged her away.

'Where were you? The truth, Rosie. I've just lied for you in there.'

Rosie twisted the Kleenex between her fingers. 'I . . . I . . .' *I can't tell him. I can't tell him.*

Hugh pulled her round to face him. 'Were you with Turnbull? I need to know.'

'No. I swear it. I never saw him that day.'

'Then where?'

Rosie closed her eyes, trying to keep the tears in.

'I can't tell you,' she whispered. 'But not with him. I promise.'

There was a long, painful silence, broken by a sudden click. Rosie felt her seatbelt slide off her shoulder. Hugh leaned across her and opened the passenger door.

'You're lying,' he said flatly. 'Get out.'

'Please trust me.'

'Just get out.'

'Hugh?' Rosie clutched at his arm.

'For Mara's sake, you can stay at the Dower House, but find yourself another job. And stay out of my sight. You disgust me.' He dropped a twenty pound note into her lap and jerked his thumb at the waiting taxis.

'I won't go like this,' Rosie said stubbornly, tears trickling onto her cheeks. 'Not until you listen to me.'

Hugh refused to look at her. 'Either you get out, or I drive you back to the station and turn you in,' he said evenly. 'Your choice.' He put the key into the ignition and switched the engine on. Rosie tumbled out of the car without another word. Hugh reached over and slammed her door before roaring off.

Rosie stood alone on the pavement, tears streaming down her face and the twenty-pound note balled in her fist. She had misjudged everyone and nothing was what it seemed. Worst of all, she could see no way of making things right. How could Hugh think her capable of such a thing? She thought of Danny and George Hardy – they could help.

'I won't do it,' said Rosie, shoving the money into the pocket of her jeans. 'Hugh wants to believe I'm guilty? Let him.' She marched towards the taxis, trying to scrub the hurt from her face as she went.

Chapter 24

Lammas

Rosie sat at the kitchen table in the Dower House, poring over the *Northumberland Gazette*. A well-chewed pencil lay in the central fold of the paper, waiting to be put to use. It had been waiting like this for several days now, poised hopefully over a variety of newspapers. It had all been to no avail.

Sighing, Rosie turned the paper over. There were no jobs, but the weekly crossword on the back page had a first prize of twenty-five pounds. That would be better than nothing. She gave an involuntary shiver and rubbed at the gooseflesh bubbling up on her forearms. In August, the kitchen seemed to operate its own unique weather system irrespective of the outside world. The temperature ranged from cool to freezing. It must be twenty-five degrees outside, she thought, looking at the bright scrap of blue sky visible through the top panes of the little window above the sink.

Hugh would be in his element. She hoped he wasn't trapped indoors doing paperwork on a day like this.

Mara appeared in the doorway.

'Why don't you come and sit outside for a while, Rosie? It's lovely out here. Mrs Drummond has brought some homemade lemon ice cream down.'

'I'm all right, thanks,' mumbled Rosie, looking at the newspaper in an attempt to seem busy. Mara waited for a few moments but Rosie kept her head down.

'If you're sure, dear. By the way, there's a magazine for you. Mrs Drummond has finished with it.' She waved the August edition of *Hello*! It could have been a blank sheet of paper for all the response she got. 'I'll leave it just here,' Mara said, putting it down on the empty stool.

Mara made her way back to the front yard, where a small circular picnic table and a parasol were set up beside two striped canvas deckchairs. Mrs Drummond was reclining in one of them with her eyes closed against the glare of the sun. Her stockings were rolled down to her ankles, revealing stout white calves marred by the occasional blue bulge of a varicose vein. She opened one eye and squinted up at Mara.

'Any joy?'

'None,' replied Mara, easing herself down into the other deckchair. 'I'm so worried about her, Ellen. She's been like this for weeks.'

'Five at least. But what else can we do? The girl just won't snap out of it.' She struggled into a semi-upright position and took her bowl of ice cream from the table. 'It's this police business with Euan, isn't it?'

'No,' said Mara shrewdly. 'That's upset her dreadfully, of course, but it's not that. I think it's Hugh.'

Mrs Drummond sucked the ice cream slowly from her teaspoon, savouring every morsel. She glanced furtively towards the Dower House.

'Word is, she didn't resign, Mara,' she said in an undertone. 'The staff are saying Hugh sacked her.'

'That makes no sense. Rosie has been categorically cleared of any deliberate involvement in that poaching scam. Hugh was her alibi. Why would he sack her?'

'I didn't say it made sense,' Mrs Drummond grumbled. 'But that's what people are saying. What has Rosie told you?'

'Oh, not much. Something cryptic about a promise and Hugh not respecting her integrity. She wants a change, apparently.'

'Rosie hasn't got a dishonest bone in her body,' answered Mrs Drummond through a mouthful of ice cream. 'Hugh knows that.'

Mara helped herself to some ice cream and balanced the glass dessert bowl delicately on her lap.

'I'm not sure that he does,' she said, carving a modest spoonful from the frozen lump. 'As odd as it sounds, I think he suspects Rosie of being involved somehow.'

'Then he's a fool,' grunted Mrs Drummond.

'A fool who hasn't darkened our door since the day Euan was arrested.' A wasp came to hover over Mara's dish and she batted it away with her spoon. 'Things were going so well between them, Ellen. I had hopes of . . . well, I don't know anymore . . . Something.'

'They did seem to be very . . . *comfortable* with one another,' said Mrs Drummond with uncommon tact. 'I hate to see

Rosie like this after everything she's been through. All this moping around. It's not like her. She's lost her spirit.'

A sudden cry from inside the Dower House made both women jump. Mrs Drummond dribbled ice cream onto her blouse.

'Rosie?' called Mara sharply. 'Are you all right?'

Rosie staggered from the Dower House like a sleep-walker, her eyes wide and unfocussed. She was holding Mrs Drummond's magazine at arm's length.

'Look,' she choked, shoving it into Mara's face. 'Look at it.'

'OK Rosie. Calm down,' said Mara soothingly, taking the magazine. 'Ellen, your reading glasses – I can't see a thing.' Rosie began to pace up and down, plucking at her clothes while Mrs Drummond dived into her handbag and produced two pairs of glasses. The older women spread the magazine onto the table and examined the double page article.

'I don't see the problem,' said Mrs Drummond, utterly bemused. 'Model marries multi-millionaire business tycoon? So what?'

Rosie made a noise, somewhere between a laugh and a sob. Mara was speechless.

'It can't be,' Mara wheezed as if she was about to breath fire. 'Valentina . . .'

'But it *is!*' cried Rosie, unable to contain herself. 'The nerve . . . She doesn't care, she . . .'

'I know.'

'And we . . .'

'Please calm down,' begged Mara. 'It's a shock, but –'

'I can't bear it!' Rosie snatched the magazine from the table and beat it against the wall. 'I wish . . . I wish . . . I . . .'

But Mara and Mrs Drummond didn't discover what Rosie wished for, as she sank to her knees crying loudly and choking uncontrollably.

Mrs Drummond was stunned. 'Mara, do something before the girl does herself an injury. Quick!'

Mara prised the magazine from Rosie's fingers and eased herself down beside her. Rosie was rocking backwards and forwards on her knees, her body convulsing with each brutal sob.

'Ellen, fetch Rosie's mobile from the kitchen. Call Father Aelred.'

'Are you saying she's possessed?'

'Don't be ridiculous, Ellen,' snapped Mara, aware that Rosie's tears of rage were not even beginning to subside. 'She's just upset. Hurry.'

Mrs Drummond launched herself up the steps.

Mara stood. 'I'm here when you're ready,' she said softly returning to the deck chair. 'Take your time.' She knew Rosie's anger and violent grief would eventually give way to calm, but there was no hurrying these things. Mara could wait. From her glossy pose on the centerfold of *Hello!*, Valentina smirked out at the world.

❀ ❀ ❀ ❀

Hugh sat on the terrace in the Aldersons' carefully landscaped garden, rocking gently to and fro on the old-fashioned wooden porch swing. A scalloped canopy in terracotta formed a hood over the swing, affording some shade from the afternoon sun.

The padded seat covers matched, of course. Charlotte lay a few feet away, artfully sprawled on a sun lounger in white Capri pants and a yellow sleeveless blouse, her face hidden by an enormous white hat. A bottle of industrial strength sunblock sat on the paving stones by her half-finished novel and glass of Pimms. Hugh prodded the bottle with his foot.

'I don't know why you bother sunbathing, Lottie,' he yawned. 'You must be bomb-proof with that stuff on and on the one day of the year you can sunbathe in Alnwick.'

'Don't be objectionable darling, it's beautiful here all the time. Anyway, I need the vitamin D.' She raised her head and lifted the hat a couple of inches so she could glare at him. 'So do you. I've never seen you look so peaky.'

'Nonsense,' boomed Alastair, puffing up the wide steps of the terrace with a loaded tray. 'The man just needs a couple of large daiquiris. That'll pep him up in no time.' He put the tray down with a clatter and mopped his brow. 'Just the plain ones today, I'm afraid. Charlotte polished off the strawberry liqueur last weekend.' His wife reared up and threw a flip-flop at him.

Hugh smiled despite himself.

'I'm driving, Alastair. Lottie can have my share.'

'My body is a temple,' said Charlotte loftily. 'I'll drive you home, Sweets.' Alastair caught Hugh's eye and mouthed *hung over*.

'I heard that,' snapped Charlotte without opening her eyes. Hugh burst out laughing.

'You two are amazing,' he said, accepting a glass from Alastair. 'Cheers.'

Alastair took the seat beside Hugh on the swing. They swayed gently backwards and forward. Hugh reached out and pulled a sprig of lavender from the shrubbery. He shut his eyes and wafted it under his nose, inhaling the calming scent. A water feature burbled away in the background, overlaid with the sound of birdsong and the occasional hum of a passing car.

Rosie's face materialised in his mind as he had last seen her, blotched with hurt and tears. She was a liar, Hugh reminded himself for the thousandth time. He crushed the lavender and tossed it away. She was a liar and that made him a fool. It left a bad taste in his mouth.

'Have you seen Rosie?' asked Charlotte, with her unerring knack for picking up on his thoughts.

'No. And I don't intend to.'

Alastair cleared his throat uneasily. 'You know, Hugh, I just can't believe she's guilty. She's such a sweet girl.'

Hugh said nothing, aware that Charlotte was watching for his reaction. 'Have you considered that Rosie might have been telling the truth?' Alastair continued. 'Perhaps she wasn't with Euan that day.'

Hugh gave a short bark of laughter. 'The evidence is fairly compelling, Alastair. Euan said she was with him. Rosie had already told me she'd been with him that afternoon. If that was a lie, then what's the truth? What could possibly have been so private that she couldn't tell me?'

Alastair took a sip of his daiquiri. 'I don't know,' he admitted. 'It does look dodgy, I'll give you that. But a confidence is a confidence, Hugh.'

'Not under these circumstances. I'd just lied to save her skin and she couldn't even be honest with me. The whole thing has to be a fabrication.'

Charlotte removed her hat and narrowed her eyes against the sun as she stared up at him. 'But that's just it, Hugh,' she said slowly. 'If Rosie was guilty, why give her a false alibi? Why?'

'OK! OK!' said Hugh uncomfortably, squirming under Charlotte's scrutiny. 'I thought she was innocent at first, too. I knew Rosie wasn't with me on that day and I remembered what she'd told me about visiting Euan, but I . . . I kept thinking there had to be another explanation.' He made a sudden movement with his arm, slopping rum over the rim of his glass. 'Hoping, really. But there wasn't.' He covered his eyes with his hand. 'And I couldn't bring myself to turn her in. I can't believe I'm such a fool.'

'Enough,' said Alastair to Charlotte, moving swiftly to top up Hugh's drink. 'We're on his side, remember? Give the poor man a break.'

'Sorry, Sweets. It was just . . .'

'What?' asked Hugh, knowing what she would say.

'You looked well together. She made you smile.'

※   ※   ※   ※

Mara and Ellen Drummond sat in their deckchairs outside the Dower House, like anxious relatives awaiting news from the operating theatre. On the picnic table, the ice cream bowls had been replaced by a rapidly filling ashtray and a pot of over-stewed tea. A packet of custard creams was propped against the parasol stand. The shadows lengthened and stretched across the fields as the afternoon slid into evening. Mara pulled her cardigan more snugly round her shoulders.

'Another drink, Ellen?'

Mrs Drummond stirred sleepily. 'Bit early still.'

'I meant tea,' said Mara patiently. 'But it's half past six. Have whatever you like.'

'That late?' Mrs Drummond looked up at Rosie's bedroom window. 'They've been in there for hours.'

Mara glanced at the photo of Valentina, now callously smudged with tea stains, biscuit crumbs and cigarette ash. Mrs Drummond followed her gaze. 'I didn't know it was – you know – *Her*. I thought Rosie was having a breakdown.'

'Perhaps she is,' Mara replied. A note of fear shook her voice. 'One person can only take so much. Everyone has their breaking point.'

'No, no.' Mrs Drummond hurried to reassure her. 'You were right. Rosie's just upset. Anyone would react that way, seeing that gold-digging tramp flaunting herself for all the world to see. It was the shock. She'll be right as rain in a couple of days.' She stood up and put her arm around Mara's shoulders. 'Come on, let's go inside and see what we can rustle up for supper.'

Shortly after seven o'clock, Aelred entered the kitchen and found the two friends sitting down to a hot chicken salad. 'May I join you for a moment?' he enquired.

'Of course, Father. You don't need to ask,' said Mara, reaching under the table for a third stool. 'Will you eat with us?'

'No, thank you. I'm expected at the Priory.' Aelred sat down with a weary sigh. 'A drink would be much appreciated, though.' He smiled his thanks as Mrs Drummond poured him a glass of water. Rarely had he felt more in need of a gin, but it seemed inappropriate to ask.

'How is she?' asked Mara.

'Resting. She's much calmer now.'

Mara hesitated. 'I don't want to pry, Father,' she began.

Aelred smiled kindly at her.

'Not at all. We've had a long talk and Rosie got a lot of things off her chest.' He chose his next words with care. 'She's emotionally exhausted, obviously, but that will mend itself, I think, with time and space . . .' he trailed off. 'Better that she talks to you herself.'

'I'll take some supper up,' offered Mrs Drummond.

'Good idea.' Aelred drained his glass and stood up. 'I must be going.'

'Of course.' Mara pushed her plate away and walked him to the door. 'I can't thank you enough, Father.'

'It was no trouble. It's a privilege to spend time with someone like Rosie. I've never seen such loyalty.'

'It's the one thing I could never understand. Rosie hardly knew me and yet she chose to stay. She could quite easily have gone back to New York and started again. In all this time she has nursed me, humoured me and, if I'm honest . . .' Mara paused and thought. 'I haven't done a great deal for her.'

'More than you think, Mara.'

'When James was killed, I thought that God had raised a hand against me. Now I can see that He sent me Rosie. I know what I have to do.'

He shook Mara's hand. 'Good night.'

Mrs Drummond was hovering at the foot of the stairs with a tray of food.

'Shall I?' she queried. Mara held out her hands.

'Let me, Ellen.'

Mara tiptoed into the bedroom and found Rosie lying on her back with her eyes closed. She had kicked off her trainers. One big toe poked brazenly through a hole in her stripy socks. The sight was so typically Rosie, it brought a lump to Mara's throat. She was still so young. Mara set the tray down on the bedside table and leaned over her daughter-in-law.

'Rosie?' she whispered.

'I'm not asleep.'

Mara smoothed Rosie's hair off her face. 'Would you like some supper?'

Rosie opened her eyes.

'No, but I'll try,' she groaned. Mara helped her to sit up and started to fuss over the pillows, plumping them this way and that. 'I'm not ill, Mara,' Rosie said, lifting the supper tray onto her lap.

'You're not *well* either.'

'I'll be fine,' Rosie said stubbornly, concentrating on chasing a cherry tomato round her plate. Mara perched on the edge of the bed and pushed her hands into the pockets of her cardigan.

Rosie had lost weight, she realised, seeing the jut of her collarbone above the neck of her T-shirt. She was naturally pale but her skin was almost translucent, the flesh caving in beneath the arch of her cheekbones. Her eyes were dull and puffy with weeping.

As Rosie lifted her fork to her mouth, Mara saw that her wedding ring hung loosely on her finger, sliding down to graze her knuckle when she lowered her arm. Hollow. That was the word for it. Rosie had given everything, kept nothing back for herself. Now, *nothing* was all that remained.

Mara remembered Aelred's words. 'She'll mend, with time and space . . .' She took a deep breath.

'Rosie.'

'Pardon?' Rosie looked up from her supper.

'Do you want to go home?'

Rosie put her fork down, a confused look on her face. 'We are home.'

Mara took her hand. 'I'm talking about your home. America. I know you won't go without me,' she rushed on, squeezing Rosie's fingers as she tried to interrupt. 'So if you want to go, I'll come too.'

'Leave . . . leave Northumberland? Start over?' Rosie's eyes filled with tears.

Mara nodded. 'Wherever you go, I go. Wherever you live, I live. That was the deal,' she said, quoting Rosie's own words back to her. 'It's your turn now.' She kissed Rosie gently on the forehead and moved quietly to the door. 'Think about it. Perhaps there are reasons to stay as well as reasons to go. That's for you to decide. The offer is there.'

Rosie dumped the supper tray on the floor and flopped back onto her bed. Leave Northumberland? She hadn't even considered it. Suddenly ideas were raining down around her, soaking her brain with possibilities.

They could stay with her parents until they found a little place of their own . . . Mara would get a temporary visa . . . there'd be the issue of extending it but her Dad might be able to pull a few strings . . . she'd be able to get a decent job . . . her mother would be deliriously happy . . . with Mara there it would be a new start, not slipping back into the old life she'd outgrown.

And yet . . . leaving England . . . the memory of Cameron . . . Oxford . . . Hugh . . .

The place had gradually worked its way under Rosie's skin. She was a hybrid now, neither British nor American. There was no guarantee that she would fit in any more, however hard she tried. What if she were unhappy in the States? And Mara was getting old, she might not handle the dislocation of moving abroad. If they left, it would be a definitive goodbye. There would be no return journey. What should she do?

'I'd still be with you,' said Cameron as she began to dream. She could see his face even though he stood far away.

'I know you would,' Rosie murmured.

Rosie could see his lips move but could not hear him speak. He faded in her mind as he turned and walked away. It was as if he was moving on to another world. Rosie woke suddenly and stared up at the ceiling, as if hoping to find instructions written on the crumbling white plaster. Reasons to stay and reasons to go.

'Where do I belong?' she whispered the words like a prayer.

Chapter 25

Harvest Antiphon

'You're really going to go through with this, aren't you,' said Mrs Drummond, caught between horror and admiration. Mara didn't look up from her work.

'Keep polishing, Ellen. The silver needs to be sparkling for the ball next week and there's a mountain of the stuff here. It looks like a dragon's hoard.'

It was no exaggeration. The entire table in the estate kitchen was covered with an assortment of cutlery and serving dishes.

'Don't fob me off, Mara Whitton. Answer me. Do you honestly intend to move to America with Rosie?'

'You know I do. It will be an adventure.' Mara scooped up another fork and began to polish it vigorously. 'I hoped she would choose to stay, I don't deny that. But I have to respect her choice. Rosie deserves this.'

'If only Hugh knew you were leaving. Even he would come to his senses, I'm sure of it.' Mrs. Drummond sucked her cheeks in. 'Stubborn. They're both too stubborn.'

Mara smiled at her friend.

'It has to be a secret. Hugh can't find out. Let's make the best of it, Ellen. It will take Rosie a little while to settle in and find an apartment for us. You've got me for a few more weeks at least. And there's the ball to look forward to.'

Mrs Drummond's face took on a crafty expression.

'So there is. I wonder if . . .'

'No, Ellen,' said Mara firmly. 'That evening is going to be complicated enough already without throwing one of your cunning plans into the mix.'

'Why don't you hear me out first?' said Mrs Drummond, sidling around the old pine table to sit beside Mara. 'I've never told a soul, but Mrs Fenwick left me something to pass on when the time was right. She told me to keep it until Hugh found the right girl. I think it's now or never.'

'Ellen, you're making no sense.'

Mrs Drummond whispered every detail of her plan in Mara's ear, breaking off periodically to check the kitchen door remained closed. Mara's eyebrows climbed higher and higher up her forehead as she listened. Finally Mrs Drummond stepped back. 'So what do you think?'

Mara sat back in her chair and considered the information. 'It's a long shot. In all honesty, I don't think it'll make much difference. It might even cause a fight.'

Mrs Drummond poured herself a generous malt. 'It *is* a long shot. But if it's the only one we've got . . .' Mara shook her head doubtfully. 'Come on, Mara,' she wheedled. 'What have you got to lose?'

Mara threw her polishing cloth down.

'Oh, very well, Ellen. One last roll of the dice, for old time's sake.'

'For old time's sake,' echoed Mrs Drummond solemnly. Then their faces split into huge grins and they high-fived over the mound of cutlery like naughty schoolgirls. 'I feel like Mrs Danvers . . .'

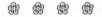

Without Euan's guiding hand on the tiller, the preparations for the ball were haphazard to say the least. By lunchtime on the day itself, chaos was threatening to overwhelm Hugh. He stood in the doorway of his study and faced his irate house-keeper, tugging at his wayward hair.

'Mrs Drummond,' he said, the strain of courtesy evident on his face. 'I'll say it one last time. I do not care what colour the balloons are. I have no interest in the art of napkin fold-ing. I will eat whatever the caterers put in front of me and I don't give a flying –' he caught himself in time, ' – care a bit whether the ceilidh band does three performance sets or three hundred. Is that clear?'

'Crystal.' Mrs Drummond's face was rigid with affronted dignity.

Hugh pinched the bridge of his nose and took a few deep breaths.

'Now,' he said quietly. 'I'm going to go into my office and make a phone call. If there is a God, help will shortly arrive. Otherwise . . .' he cast around for another solution. There wasn't one. '. . . just do the best you can.'

'Fine.'

Hugh shut the door with a bang, grabbed the phone and made his S.O.S. call. 'Lottie? It's Hugh. Look, it's a total dis-aster here. Can you come?'

'Of course, Sweets. I'll be right there.'

'Great. When you get here, find Mrs Drummond, she knows what needs doing. I'll see you tonight.'

'But —' there was a sharp click. Charlotte looked at the receiver in bemusement. The dialing tone flat-lined in her ear. Hugh *never* hung up on people. 'Alastair!' she hollered. 'Get the car.' Oblivious to the panic he had induced, Hugh settled at his desk and buried himself in the accounts.

❀ ❀ ❀ ❀

Slowly he became aware of a noise — an insistent knocking at the door of his study. Hugh raised his head and stared muzzily at the crumpled pages on the table. The ink on the topmost page was badly smudged, the figures almost illegible.

He swore quietly. How long had he been asleep? The knocking came again.

'Hang on, I'm coming,' he called, stumbling to the door. George and Danny Hardy were waiting patiently in the corridor. Hugh ran his hand through his hair and hoped he didn't have ink stains on his forehead. 'George,' he mumbled. 'Come in. What can I do for you?'

George beamed at him.

'Nothing at all, Hugh.' He entered the room, his son half a step behind him. 'We're just on our way home. Been helping set the marquee up for tonight. Mrs Alderson asked us to stop by and let you know that everything's under control.'

Hugh gave a sigh that was half relief, half tiredness. 'Thanks, George. I appreciate it.' He waved his hand at the chairs on the other side of the desk. 'Have a seat.'

'Thanks, but we've got to get back, or we won't be dressed and ready in time. It's six o'clock already.'

Hugh was aghast. 'Six o'clock? Seriously?'

'Time flies when you're having fun, eh?' joked George, nodding at the pile of papers on the desk.

'Something like that.'

George turned to Danny. 'Come on son. Let's be off.' He walked to the door, but Danny remained where he was, shifting nervously from one foot to the other. 'Danny, come on,' George said impatiently. 'Your mam will be waiting.'

'Something on your mind, Danny?' Hugh asked, seeing the agitation in the boy's face.

'Is it true what they're saying, Mr Fenwick?' he burst out.

Hugh smiled quizzically at him. 'I don't know. What are they saying?'

'That – that you sacked Rosie from her job.'

George took a couple of steps back into the room.

'Danny.' He whispered the warning.

Hugh shook his head. 'It's all right, George, I don't mind,' he said, his eyes on the boy, who was now beetroot with embarrassment. 'Why do you want to know?'

Danny bit his lip and looked from his father to Hugh, clearly determined to say his piece but afraid of the consequences.

'Because you'd have no right to be sacking her, Mr Fenwick,' he said in a rush. 'She's – she's a brilliant person.'

George reached his son's side and seized him by the elbow.

'Danny! Apologise to Mr Fenwick. It's none of your business how he runs his affairs.'

Hugh's jaw dropped as the normally mild-mannered teenager tore his arm free and squared up to his father.

'It is, Dad. If Rosie's been treated badly, it *is* my business and yours too.' He faced Hugh defiantly. 'She saved my life.'

'Danny, no,' George pleaded.

'She what?' Hugh was completely flummoxed. 'George, what's this about?'

George Hardy mumbled something incoherent and tried to take hold of his son again. Danny folded his arms and stepped away.

'Tell him, Dad,' he raged. 'I don't care if he knows. Make him change his mind.'

George gazed at his son, a mixture of pity and fierce pride in his eyes. 'OK, Danny. OK.'

'Let's sit down,' said Hugh, struggling to get a mental grip on the situation. 'Take your time.'

George moved slowly to a chair and sat down, his weathered face overlaid with guilt. Danny sat beside him, his eyes downcast.

'The lad's right,' George said hoarsely. 'Rosie did save his life.' He passed his hand over his eyes. 'Dear God, I'll never forget that day.'

'What happened? George?'

'Well, it was the eighth of May,' George sighed. Hugh snapped to attention.

'Did you say the eighth of May?'

George nodded. Hugh gripped the arms of his chair and listened as he'd never listened before.

The grandfather clock in the entrance hall struck the half hour as Hugh sprinted past it, up two flights of stairs and along the upper corridor. He crashed into his bedroom, kicking the door shut behind him. The reverberations were so strong that a picture fell from the wall and landed face down on the carpet. Hugh tossed it onto the bed. Broken glass crunched beneath his boots as he hurried to the wardrobe and began pulling out items at random.

His dinner jacket was definitely in there somewhere, he'd had it dry-cleaned. Shirts flew through the air, hollow arms flapping like weirdly shaped birds that crash-landed in a great mound on the bedspread. Hugh spotted the dinner jacket right at the back, still sheathed in its dustproof polythene wrapper. He grabbed it and threw it on top of the pile. He checked his watch. He had thirty-five minutes . . .

Aelred bumbled around his small room at the Priory, humming softly to himself as he put the finishing touches to his outfit. He looped a thick black leather belt about his waist and cinched it securely. Then he removed his dressing gown from its peg on the door, revealing a little-used three quarter length mirror. He examined himself carefully. The formal white habit hung in heavy folds, the hem just clearing the floor. Aelred revolved slowly on the spot, twisting his head round like an owl to check the rear and side views. The hood was nicely draped over his upper back and there were no noticeable stains, though admittedly the light was fairly dim.

White was such a damnable colour for an outfit, Aelred thought ruefully, as he always did on these occasions. It was the sort of thing the vocations' directors declined to mention when one was considering which order to choose. At least he only had to wear it on formal occasions and there was no doubt he scrubbed up rather well.

'Better than the Jesuits, anyway,' he muttered. 'Scruffy beggars make no effort at all.' He opened the old sash window and stuck his head out, peering up and down the road. No sign of his lift yet and it was starting to rain. A light drizzle misted his face. 'Drat.' Aelred pulled his head in and cleaned his glasses on the sleeve of his habit.

No doubt he'd be covered in mud by the time he'd tramped across the field to the marquee, but it couldn't be helped. He went in search of his hiking boots.

Rosie knelt on her bedroom floor, folding the last of her sweaters into a neat square. She laid it in the suitcase and attempted to close the lid. There was a full inch between the two rows of teeth on the zip. Rosie stood on top of the case and bounced up and down a few times to squash everything down. Then she sat down on the lid and tried again, straining as she tugged the fastener slowly round. This time it went a quarter of the way around before it snagged on the hem of the green cardigan Mrs Drummond had knitted her last Christmas. Meanwhile, clothes were bulging out on the other side of the case.

Don't do this to me. Painstakingly, she worked the zip free of the cardigan and eased it back round the lip of the suit-case. Immediately the lid sprang up and the clothes seemed to double in volume before her eyes. Rosie collapsed against the bed.

She never had this trouble when she just shoved every-thing in, but Mara had insisted it would be easier if it was all folded. Rosie rubbed her eyes tiredly. Everything about today was turning out to be difficult.

Mara popped her head round the door. 'How are you get-ting on?' Rosie gestured wearily at the gaping suitcase. 'Ah. Let's have a little look.' Mara bustled in carrying a large, shal-low box which she deposited on Rosie's bed. She knelt down by the case. 'Now then.' She refolded two sweaters, tweaked a couple of items and pressed the lid down with quiet authority. The zip realised the game was up and whizzed smoothly round at the first attempt. She straight-ened up and brushed the dust off her skirt. 'There you are, dear. Folding is the key. Just take what you need and the rest will be sent on.'

'But I – oh, never mind. Thanks.' Rosie eyed the box next to her. 'Is this to go too? I'm not sure I'll get that on as hand luggage.'

'No, no.' Mara's eyes twinkled as she chuckled. Rosie looked at her suspiciously. Mara looked supremely pleased with herself. It was worrying.

'What is it, then?'

'Open it.'

'Mara, I really can't carry anything else.' Rosie lifted the lid and delving through layers of waxy paper and scented tissue wrapping. 'Wow.' She lifted out a diamond tiara and matching necklace and held it up to the light. 'It's . . . incredible.' The stones were exquisitely cut, with heavily boned silver claws to keep them in place. 'This is vintage, isn't it?' Rosie said reverently, swishing the necklace gently from side to side.

'Nineteen-fifties. I think it will fit, don't you?'

'I can't – you haven't . . .' Rosie was speechless. The tiara and necklace were in priceless condition. 'It must be worth a fortune.'

'It's borrowed, not bought. From a friend, for one night only.'

'Who?'

'It doesn't matter who.' Mara stepped forwards and laid her palm against Rosie's cheek. 'I want you to enjoy this evening,' she said. 'When you've gone, people will look back and remember how beautiful you were on your last night in Northumberland.'

Rosie couldn't speak past the lump in her throat. There was only one person whose opinion mattered on that score and he couldn't stand the sight of her. Tears burned in her eyes as she hugged Mara.

'Thank you. I'll wear it for you.'

Mara smiled into Rosie's hair and whispered a silent prayer.

❀   ❀   ❀   ❀

'Damn it!' Hugh hopped across the carpet in his shirt-tails, clutching his right foot. He fell onto the bed and turned his sole up for inspection. There was a piece of glass embedded between his second and third toes. The cut was bleeding copiously.

Instinctively, he dabbed at it with a corner of his dress shirt and swore at the sight of the spreading stain on the crisp white cotton. He hopped back into the en suite bathroom and pulled open the mirrored storage cabinet above the sink. Blood dripped onto the lino as he grabbed a chunk of cotton wool, tweezers and a box of plasters and balanced his foot awkwardly on the bath.

'This needs stitches,' Hugh thought. Too bad. There were more important things to attend to. Tweezers in hand, he approached the cut.

❀   ❀   ❀   ❀

A silver Mercedes crawled up the narrow street towards the Alnmouth Priory, squeezing between a double row of parked cars. Miraculously, a space appeared on the left.

'Pull up here, Alastair. Put your hazards on.' Charlotte reached across him, flicked the appropriate switch and sounded the horn.

Alastair sighed. 'You know, darling, I did offer to let you drive.'

Charlotte looked impatiently out of the window. 'Don't be ridiculous. You always drive.'

'I know, but it seems rather pointless, don't you think? I just sit in front of the steering wheel and you tell me what to do.'

'Do behave, Alastair.' She glanced at him. 'And don't sulk. It's embarrassing.' She sounded the horn again. 'Where is he?

We're going to be late.' She relaxed as Aelred's head appeared in one of the first floor windows. 'There he is. Marvellous. We can still make it if you put your foot down.'

'Now *that* would be a first,' said Alastair.

Aelred was clipping his leather mobile phone case to his belt like a gun holster when the horn sounded.

'Right. Time to go.' He looked at the two items lying on his bed. Ideally he would take both but only one would fit in the phone case. 'Decisions, decisions,' he dithered. The horn sounded again. Aelred ran to the window. 'On my way,' he called. He snatched up the hip flask and strode out. His phone lay stranded on the bedspread, the display light blinking sadly.

❀   ❀   ❀   ❀

Mrs Drummond let herself into the Dower House.

'Everyone ready?'

Mara emerged from the kitchen in a long-sleeved velvet dress in midnight blue. It was stunning. 'Won't you be a bit hot in that?' said Mrs Drummond.

'Ellen, one of these days I will swing for you, so help me. You're as bad as James was. Just tell me I look nice and leave it at that.'

'Obviously you look nice. I was just saying –'

'Well just don't. You look lovely, incidentally. Pink suits you.'

Mrs Drummond smoothed the heavy crepe gown self-consciously over her stomach. 'Thank you,' she said coyly. She moved closer to Mara and dropped her voice to a whisper. 'Is she wearing it?'

'See for yourself.'

Mrs Drummond gasped as Rosie appeared on the narrow staircase. 'You look like a fairytale princess,' she breathed.

Rosie wrinkled her nose. 'Not Cinderella, I hope,' she laughed. 'Glass slippers are so not my thing, but the tiara and necklace . . .'

Mara and Mrs Drummond exchanged glances.

'Please, not the trainers,' begged Mara. 'Not this time.'

Rosie grinned. 'Would it really matter?'

'Yes!' the women shrieked.

Rosie lifted the primose tulle skirts of her gown, revealing a pair of flat ballerina style pumps in black leather. 'It's the best I could do,' she said. 'I think I chucked my old heels away after the ball last year. No one can see my feet anyway.'

'Those will do fine,' said Mrs Drummond. She smacked her hands together briskly. 'Now, Rosie. Down to business. Suitcase?'

'By the door.'

'Tickets and passport?'

'In my flight bag.'

'Train ticket?'

'Same.'

'Travelling gear?'

'Excuse me?'

'You can't fly back to New York looking like Marilyn Monroe,' said Mrs Drummond, rolling her eyes. 'You need a change of clothes for the journey.'

'Good point.'

'I'll do it,' said Mara, intercepting Rosie before she got to the case.

'OK,' said Mrs Drummond. 'The ball starts with drinks at half-past seven. That gives you an hour to see the people you want to see.' Rosie nodded, her mind running through the list of friends. So many people had shown her kindness over the last year. It was selfish not to come clean and say a proper goodbye, but it would hurt her too much. They might beg her to stay and then there would be a scene and Hugh would come striding over and order her to leave and . . .

'Rosie!' She jumped as Mara snapped her fingers. 'Pay attention. Your taxi is booked to leave from here at nine o'clock sharp. You need to be out of there and in the trap by eight-thirty, no later. That gives you half an hour to get back to the Dower House, change and go. You're sure no one else knows?'

'Well, I told Aelred,' Rosie confessed. 'But he's sworn to silence.'

'Was it under the seal of confession?' demanded Mrs Drummond.

'Leave off, Ellen,' Mara interrupted crossly. 'We're not in a James Bond film. He's a priest, for goodness sake.'

Mrs Drummond was taking her part in this far too seriously. 'I'll have a word with him,' she said darkly. 'Now, after you've gone, Mara and I,' she looked over at Mara, who was busily repacking the contents of the suitcase, 'will give it a few days and then put the word out. Agreed?'

'Agreed,' said Rosie.

'Right. It's ten past seven. Let's move out.'

They trooped out into the yard and climbed into the trap, Mara and Mrs Drummond side by side in the front, Rosie perched awkwardly in the back amid a sea of tulle. She closed her eyes and inhaled deeply, trying to draw part of Northumberland into herself.

Hugh would be busy at the ball tonight. All she had to do was keep her head down, be polite and get out of there. No confrontations, no arguments. *No Hugh.* Rosie stamped on the thought before it could take root. He had been all she could think of and now leaving would end all that . . . she hoped.

Mrs Drummond snapped the reins and slid along the bench towards Mara.

'With any luck, Hugh will see what he's missing and we won't have to go through with this wretched scheme. Mind you, based on his recent behaviour, I'm not holding my breath, are you?'

'Have a little faith, Ellen. It's not over yet.'

❀ ❀ ❀ ❀

Hugh hobbled down the stairs, wincing each time his injured foot struck the ground. The grandfather clock rang the quarter hour. Seven-fifteen. Hugh limped down the front steps and started towards the marquee, bracing himself for the social onslaught.

He raised a hand in greeting as Alastair's Mercedes swept through the gates and pulled up in a spray of gravel. It would be awful in there. Everyone would want a piece of him. Hugh squared his shoulders determinedly. All he had to do was circulate, shake off the hangers-on and find Rosie. No arguments, no confrontations. Now he knew the truth, nothing else mattered.

Chapter 26

The Yield

Rosie threaded her way through the crowded marquee, flitting from group to group in what she hoped was a light-hearted, sociable manner. Her initial instinct was to skulk around the edges of the tent ready for a quick getaway, but she quickly realised that she would be less noticeable behind a constantly moving screen of people.

Every few steps she felt a hand on her shoulder or a tap on the arm and turned anxiously, only to find another friend or acquaintance with a smile and a compliment for her outfit. Agreeing to wear the vintage jewellery had been a mistake. She wasn't blending in.

Hugh entered the marquee and, as he had feared, was immediately swept up into meeting and greeting. 'So good to see you . . .'

'Terribly sorry to hear about that business with young Turnbull . . .'

'Fantastic yield this year, over the odds with the weather . . .'

'Kind of you to invite us again . . .'

The voices overlapped, faces blended into one another. Hugh mumbled random pleasantries, smiling blindly and shaking each extended hand, his eyes searching the room for Rosie. He caught sight of Charlotte and tried to mouth the question, but suddenly a group of people on the far side of the marquee broke apart and he got a glimpse of Rosie in his mother's tiara and necklace. She looked breathtaking.

'How . . .?' Hugh began to push his way towards her but she was aware of him and quickly slipped out of sight. Where had she got his mother's jewellery? 'Rosie, wait!'

Hands reached out to clasp his own as more guests planted themselves in the way. Rosie was gone and gone and gone again. Every time Hugh wormed his way free of one group of guests, he was instantly sucked into another.

Everyone he asked seemed to have seen Rosie but no one could pick her out in the crowd. As time wore on, Hugh felt his temper begin to fray. He had to find her.

Aelred loitered by the punchbowl, swaying gently in time with the music. With one hand, he ladled another measure of the fruity liquid into his glass as he slipped the hip flask back into his mobile phone case with the other. Someone grabbed his sleeve from behind and a voice hissed, 'Gotcha.' Aelred choked on his mouthful and turned to find Rosie snorting with laughter. She thumped him helpfully on the back.

'Sorry,' she said, without a trace of repentance in her face. 'I couldn't resist.'

Aelred wiped his mouth on the sleeve of his habit and glared at her.

'It's all very well swanning around like the Queen of Sheba, but you can't creep up on a chap like that. It completely spoils the effect.'

'I thought it was a great effect.'

'My point is, it's not ladylike behaviour,' Aelred said piously. 'What time is it, anyway? Shouldn't you be doing your disappearing act about now, before the meal starts? Hugh's on your trail, you know. I think he wants a word.'

'A word?'

A strange look flitted across Rosie's face. Was it hope or panic? Aelred couldn't tell. 'Calm down,' he said, refilling his glass and adding a generous splash from his hip flask. 'I said I hadn't seen you.'

Rosie's eyes were over-bright and tense. Hardly surprising when one considered the hare-brained scheme she'd set in motion, Aelred mused. Women were such odd creatures. The circumstances were awkward, to say the least, but surely it would be easier to say a straightforward goodbye and leave?

'I'm leaving now,' Rosie said tightly, as though she'd heard his thought. Her eyes never left the shifting throng. 'I've come to say goodbye and – and thanks for everything.'

Aelred swept her into a great bear hug. 'Dear girl,' he said gruffly. 'Are you sure you know what you are doing?'

'I'm not sure I know anything anymore,' she said tearfully.

'Take care of yourself. I shall miss you.' He set her down and pulled a face to make her smile. 'Oh, now you're leaking. You'll spoil your make-up. Here.' He produced an almost clean handkerchief from beneath his habit and presented it to Rosie with a little bow. Rosie mopped her eyes carelessly, smearing mascara across her cheeks. 'There, that's better. Much more like your normal self.'

Rosie managed a wobbly smile. 'I'll see you around.'

'Are you on speaking terms with Him yet?' Aelred pointed to the roof of the marquee.

'Just about . . .'

She picked up her skirts and hurried away, fighting more tears. When she reached the doorway, she glanced back and found Aelred still watching her. They gazed at each other for a long moment, each trying to communicate the things that neither had said. Then Aelred raised a hand in farewell and Rosie disappeared from view.

'Thursdays won't be the same without you,' Aelred murmured fondly.

On the other side of the marquee he glimpsed Hugh trying to extricate himself from the clutches of a red-faced landowner and his wife. He was beginning to look rather angry, Aelred thought. Perhaps it was better this way after all. Rosie had endured so much. She needed peace, not conflict. Right now, Hugh looked as though he was spoiling for a fight.

Duchess stumbled up to the Dower House, puffing and blowing, unused to the fast pace Rosie had set. Rosie leapt from the trap before it had come to a stop and began peeling her dress off as she ran up the steps. Inside, she checked the clock and saw that it was already eight-fifteen. Time was running out.

She stepped out of the ball gown and draped it carefully over one of the armchairs, then hastily pulled on the jeans, T-shirt and sweater that Mara had laid out for her. Her trainers were still packed. She eyed the suitcase for a moment before deciding to make do with the ballet pumps. Lastly, she took the necklace and tiara and placed them carefully back in the box. Mara never did say who they were from. They were on loan for one night only and now, that night was over.

She took up position by the window but turned her back on the view and gazed sadly about the room. The Dower House was silent – accusing.

'I can't stay,' she said aloud. She had lingered too long at the ball in the irrational hope that someone might realise something was amiss and demand an explanation . . . even make her stay. The someone she'd worked so hard to avoid, perhaps? It was a ridiculous thought. Nobody knew she was leaving because she'd planned it that way. No more good-byes.

It still hurt to pull up the fragile roots she had put down into the Northumbrian soil, hurt more than she had imagined now the moment was upon her. She thought of Hugh and tried to savour the last glimpse she'd had of him. Better to leave than to be thrown out against her will. Brooklyn had been home to her for many years. It could be home once more.

'I can't stay,' she repeated, as if speaking the words would make it true. Rosie walked slowly around the sitting-room, trailing her hand over the backs of the chairs, feeling the scratchy, lumpy texture of the rugs and throws against her palm – who would have thought you could miss something so hideous?

She touched the curtains, skimmed the mantelpiece with her fingers (still dusty) and traced the pattern on the wall-paper. She stared into the empty fire grate. They hadn't given it a proper clean since the spring. Bending low, she scooped up a handful of coal dust.

'Ashes to ashes,' she mumbled, staring at her blackened hand. Her soul ached with the burden of mourning. 'In the sure and certain hope.' It was never going to end, Rosie thought dully, turning her hand over and watching the ashes drift through the air in slow motion, like tiny charred snowflakes. Cameron . . . Fraser . . . James . . . Oxford . . . Northumberland. Hugh. Hope crushed by reality. Despair encircled her, talons poised. Rosie raised a hand to ward it off. 'I can't stay,' she said a third time, her throat clogged with tears.

She jumped at the sound of a car horn. It was time. Rosie lifted her battered leather jacket from its peg by the door and picked up her case. She took one final look round the room. The silence reproached her. 'I kept my promises,' Rosie said defiantly. 'I kept them all.' So why did she feel so wretched? Mustering all her strength, she closed the door on what might have been and stepped towards the taxi.

'Alnmouth Station, please.'

❀   ❀   ❀   ❀

Aelred sat quietly on a high stool by the portable bar, swinging his legs and staring vacantly into his glass. He didn't see the women bearing down on him until it was too late. Mrs Drummond clamped a heavy hand on his shoulder.

'Has she gone?'

Aelred nodded. Mrs Drummond sagged theatrically against the bar and put her head in her hands. 'That's it then,' she said. 'I really hoped it would work.'

'It did work,' Aelred pointed out. 'Rosie left quietly, all according to plan.'

'Not *that* plan. The other one. Plan B.'

Aelred raised a bushy eyebrow. 'I'm afraid you've lost me.'

Mara stared across the room, searching for Hugh.

'I thought he was a bigger man,' she said quietly. 'He's a fool to let her go.'

'Men,' spat Mrs Drummond, signalling the bartender. 'They're all fools. Whisky, please. Straight up. A double.'

Aelred felt honour-bound to defend mankind against this sweeping accusation. 'In all fairness to the man, he doesn't actually know Rosie's leaving. And furthermore, from what I've observed, he appears quite desperate to find her.'

'You're not trying to tell me he couldn't spot her, standing there like Cinderella in his own mother's tiara and necklace?' scoffed Mrs Drummond, downing her drink and slamming the glass onto the bar.

'On the contrary, but, look.' Aelred gestured to a spot on the dance floor where Hugh's head was just visible amid a tight ring of people. 'They're like bees round a honey pot. The poor chap doesn't stand a chance. He's the host, what can he do?'

The two women stared at one another, seeing the flaw in their brilliant plan.

'He's right,' said Mara. 'On top of which, Rosie didn't make it easy for him.'

'Exactly,' said Aelred. 'She didn't want to be found.'

'She doesn't know what she wants.'

'True,' Aelred said. 'But we ought to respect that.'

'But she loves him!' cried Mrs Drummond in despair.

Mara shook her head. 'You can't force a happy ending, Ellen,' she said sadly. 'Love doesn't work that way.' She hugged her friend and gave her a consoling smile. 'We'll be sitting down to eat in a few minutes. Why don't you go and find our table?'

Mrs Drummond heaved an enormous sigh and shuffled off, looking for once like the old woman she was.

Mara turned her sharp-eyed gaze onto Aelred. He shrank back, suddenly gripped by the uncomfortable sensation that she could see inside his head. She took a step towards him.

'Did Rosie swear you to secrecy, too?' she asked casually. Aelred nodded. Another step. 'Under the seal of confession?'

'Technically, no. But it was in confidence.'

Mara took another step. Her shrewd eyes were boring into him, testing his mettle.

'Are you familiar with the term, "for the greater good"?'

Aelred had an inkling of what was coming next. Mara was right in his face, her hands on his shoulders, pinning him back against the bar.

'Yes,' he squeaked, praying for deliverance. 'But, ah, we can't force a happy ending, can we? It would be unethical.'

Mara smiled sweetly.

'Quite right. So let's think of it as a theoretical exercise. What you're about to do is create the right conditions in which a happy ending could, *theoretically*, occur. That's not forcing anything. It's simply generating the possibility of happiness as one potential reality among many.'

Aelred shuffled on his stool. This woman had a dangerously sharp mind.

'And if it doesn't make any difference?'

Mara shrugged her shoulders. 'Then Rosie made the right decision.'

Aelred considered his options. 'You do it.'

'That would be meddling.'

'I'm a priest. It's too risky. Look what happened to Romeo and Juliet when the clergy got involved.'

'That priest was a Shakespearean twit. *You* –' Mara poked him hard in the chest with her forefinger, 'are a very clever man.' There was a brief, silent tussle of wills.

Aelred lost.

Hugh was sandwiched in a heated debate between George Hardy and Mrs Ludlow, chair of the local Women's Institute, on the merits of traditional dry-stone walling when Aelred ploughed up to him through the crowd.

'. . . don't you agree?' said Mrs Ludlow, tapping Hugh on the arm.

'Pardon?' Hugh turned a blank face towards her, lost from the conversation, still scanning the room for Rosie. She had completely vanished.

'I said, don't you agree?' Mrs Ludlow repeated. Hugh felt something inside him snap. 'Actually, I couldn't care less,' he said.

Aelred dived forwards and seized him by the arm.

'Do excuse us,' he panted, nodding meaningfully at Mrs Ludlow. 'There's an urgent question regarding Aquinas's theory of primary and secondary causality. It needs immediate attention.'

He put his head down and towed Hugh away, not releasing him until they stood in relative seclusion by the abandoned welcome table. Aelred looked longingly at the dregs in the punchbowl.

'Aquinas theory of . . . of what, Father Aelred?'

'I'm not good under pressure. It was the first thing that came to mind.'

Hugh had never seen the Franciscan look so flustered.

'Look, never mind that. Have you seen Rosie?'

'Yes.'

'I need to speak to her.'

'Why?'

'Because . . .'

'Ladies and gentlemen,' Charlotte Alderson's voice boomed over the sound system, 'please make your way to your tables. Father Aelred Faulkner will now say grace.'

Aelred raised his eyes heavenwards.

'O God, come to my aid,' he muttered. 'Or at least stop hindering me. Right, you,' he gave Hugh a shove and gestured at the top table. 'Go and sit down. And for the love of God, pay attention.'

'What? Father, wait . . .' but Aelred was gone, jogging over to the stage where Charlotte stood waiting with the microphone. Hugh limped to his table and threw himself into his seat. Alastair was already comfortably installed with a bottle of scotch. Judging by the flush in his cheeks, he had clearly wasted no time getting into the party spirit.

'You all right there, Hugh?' he asked, jovially.

'No. I've never been less all right in my life.'

Alastair quickly pushed his own glass over to Hugh. 'Get that down your neck. We'll soon have you cheered up.' His eyes widened as Hugh knocked the whisky straight back and immediately started to gag. 'Crikey,' Alastair said, thumping him on the back. 'I think we'll be needing a second bottle.'

On the stage, Aelred cleared his throat and made the sign of the cross, largely for his own benefit.

'For what we are about to receive,' he began, 'may the Lord make us truly thankful. And . . .' he added swiftly as every mouth in the room formed the 'ah' of Amen, 'we take this opportunity, Heavenly Father, to remember absent friends.'

Three hundred mouths once again fell open on cue. 'And also *soon-to-be absent friends*. Particularly, O Lord,' Aelred went on, watching his hard-earned reputation dissolve before his eyes, 'particularly friends who may feel they have been wrongly judged –'

'Is he drunk?' hissed Alastair. Mouths were hanging open for real now as the Franciscan rambled on.

'– and who might, even as I speak, be embarking on a lonely journey –' Hugh was suddenly bolt upright in his chair. Charlotte stepped forwards to take the microphone from Aelred, but he sidestepped her and carried on, eyeballing Hugh fiercely. '– American friends . . . far from friends *and those who love them*.' Aelred took another breath but faltered as the full force of Charlotte's basilisk glare struck him. 'Er, in Jesus' name. Amen,' he gabbled as she seized the microphone.

Hugh turned to Alastair. 'Car keys!'

'Pardon?'

Hugh slapped his palm on the table. 'I need your car. *Now*, Alastair!'

Cringing in the shadows at the side of the stage, Aelred watched the keys arc through the air, saw Hugh's hand fly up and catch them as he headed towards the exit. Aelred raised his habit to knee height and pounded after him.

Outside the marquee he found Hugh, with both youth and desperation on his side, already halfway across the field. 'Hugh!' He bellowed. 'Wait!' The younger man glanced back, hesitated, then slowed to a jog, allowing Aelred to make up some ground.

'Am I too late?'

'I don't know,' Aelred wheezed as he drew level.

'Can you drive?'

'Yes.'

'Good. I've been drinking.' Hugh tossed him the keys. 'The Merc.'

Aelred felt a thrill of pleasure. He'd never driven a Mercedes before. Hugh pulled ahead as Aelred stumbled over the cobbles in the courtyard.

'Hurry, Father!' he shouted. They dived into the car and Aelred stabbed the key into the ignition. He swung the car into a clumsy reverse manoeuvre.

'The Dower House?' Hugh guessed.

'Too late. She'll be on her way to Alnmouth Station.'

'The ten o'clock train?'

'Seven minutes past ten to Newcastle. Taxi to the airport. Flight to Heathrow and on to New York.' Both men glanced at the digital display on the dashboard. It was eight fifty-five. Aelred floored the accelerator and the car flew through the gates like a bullet.

❀　❀　❀　❀

Rosie stood in a daze on the pavement outside Alnmouth Station. The taxi driver lifted her suitcase out of the boot, set it down beside her and waited expectantly. Rosie stared at the entrance sign, her body making small, jerky movements forwards and back as though receiving conflicting impulses from her brain. Stop. Go. Stop. Go.

'You alright, lass?' The driver took her gingerly by the arm. Rosie started.

'Oh. Excuse me.' She fumbled for her purse and pushed a random selection of notes into the man's hand. Taking a double-handed grip on her suitcase, she walked towards the station entrance.

'It's too much,' the driver called after her.

'Keep the change.' Rosie didn't break stride. She couldn't afford to turn back, even for a second, like Lot's wife fleeing Sodom and Gomorrah.

'Except you're running from something good,' said the voice in her head.

Rosie ignored it, bumping her case down the steps to the platform. 'Figments of my imagination don't get a vote.' She sat down on a bench and burst into tears.

❀　❀　❀　❀

Only someone with total conviction in the promises of eternal life could drive like this, Hugh thought, flinching as Aelred sent the Mercedes swooping around another blind bend at speed. He clutched the edge of his seat with one hand and kept the other hovering over the hand-brake.

'What's the plan?' Aelred cried excitedly, half-turning in his seat.

'I'm not – watch the road!' yelled Hugh as the Mercedes drifted out of lane and into the path of an oncoming Range Rover. Aelred wrenched the wheel, narrowly avoiding a collision.

'Whoops,' he said cheerfully. 'You were saying?'

With admirable restraint, Hugh suppressed his gut instinct to fling himself bodily from the vehicle and tried to marshal his thoughts. Closing his eyes significantly reduced the fear factor.

'There's no plan. I'll just tell her I'm sorry and there's no need for her to leave.'

'That's it?'

'Pretty much.'

'No offence Hugh, but that wouldn't make me stay. I don't know much about romance, but I know Rosie and, believe me, that's not going to cut the mustard.'

'What else can I say? It's the truth.'

'No, it isn't!' Aelred, thumped his fist on the wheel. 'Own up, man! *Carpe diem!* Stand up and be counted! *You love her!*'

There was a long pause.

'Yes. I do . . . I love her,' Hugh admitted. 'But –'

'But nothing. You love her. You tell her.' Some distance behind them, a siren wailed. Aelred checked his rear view mirror and saw a police car closing on them, its lights flashing. 'Oh, no.' He hit the brakes. Hugh looked back.

'I don't believe it.'

The patrol car pulled up behind them. Two burly officers emerged and approached the Mercedes. Aelred stared straight ahead and spoke out of the corner of his mouth.

'When I get out, put your foot down and make a break for it.'

'*What?*'

'Do as I say,' Aelred hissed. 'There's no time. And take this.' He thrust something into Hugh's hands. The policemen were almost level with the car. Hugh stared at the hip flask as though it was a loaded gun. 'Put it out of sight, man. And don't look at me like that; I've only had a few sips.' Hugh stuffed it into his cummerbund as one of the policemen opened the door.

'Could I ask you to step out – oh, it's you, Father Aelred.' Aelred swung his legs out of the car.

'How are you, Joe,' he beamed, pumping the bewildered man's hand. 'I haven't seen you at church lately. Everything all right? How's your mother?'

'Er . . . she's fine thanks, Father.'

Hugh began to inch across the seat, his eye on the second policeman who was watching his partner, temporarily non-plussed. Aelred put an arm round the first man's back and steered him further into the road, using his body to block Hugh from sight.

'Good, good. And how's your little dog? Gemma, wasn't it? I heard it had an operation. How did that go?' Aelred prattled as he steered both men back to their car.

Hugh slid into the driving seat and reached for the ignition.

'It's Lula, Father. Gemma's me Mam. She had the operation.'

The Mercedes sped away.

'He's stealing your car, Father Aelred,' said the other man.

'No . . . Colum . . . he is in search of lost love,' Aelred replied as he punched the air.

❀   ❀   ❀   ❀

The station clock read ten minutes to ten. Doubled over on the hard metal bench, Rosie sobbed into Aelred's handkerchief, unable to stem the flow of tears. Involuntarily her mind took her through her whole acquaintance with Hugh. From her arrival at Earleside, clothes strewn along the hedges, the curt exchanges that followed, the night in Kielder Forest that nearly changed everything, then that whole business with Euan, to the last conversation she had had with Hugh. The disgust on his face as they had sat in his car still stung. How could she have been so sucked in by Euan?

She pulled out the cardboard wallet and checked her ticket with the station clock. Eight minutes to go.

How could Hugh think the worst of her? *But you thought the worst of him,* her conscience said. It was true. She had instinctively disliked him at Cameron's funeral. Her face flushed as she remembered describing him to Mara as 'a pompous ass'. She dabbed at her eyes with the handkerchief.

Overhead the clock struck ten and the world seemed to speed up while Rosie was stranded in a slow motion bubble. The train appeared on the horizon.

'The train,' she murmured as if she didn't want it to come. She hauled herself to her feet and tugged at her suitcase.

Doors opened, several people jumped down onto the platform, talking and laughing as they shouldered their way good-naturedly past the travellers waiting to board. There were mingled cries of welcome and farewell.

Rosie felt herself being handed up into a carriage, her luggage thrown in beside her. Then she was standing at the open door, the cardboard wallet in her hand. She looked up and down the platform, searching in vain for . . . who? The guard raised his flag.

Hugh abandoned the Mercedes at the roadside with its engine still running and hurtled into the station. He ran for the platform and bounded down the steps in time to see the last carriage fade into the distance. Hugh let out a yell and kicked the nearest bench hard, once, twice, three times. His voice echoed on the deserted platform.

A cold wind blew in from the sea. Hugh sank to his knees on the cold concrete and, to his own amazement, began to cry. Dry, painful sobs that tore at his throat. His whole body shook with the force of it.

A crumpled ticket driven by the wind rolled across the concrete where Hugh knelt. Slowly, he raised his head.

'Rosie?'

The breeze snatched at the shreds of airline tickets and scattered them along the platform like confetti. Rosie gave the tiniest of shrugs and a smile pulled at a corner of her mouth.

'I love you, too,' she said.

Epilogue

Benediction

The chapel at Earleside looked beautiful. Primroses and daffodils shone like sunshine against the sombre tones of wood and stone, vivid, like a shout of joy. The place was at absolute capacity, the guests squashed ten to a pew and the latecomers crowding along the back wall. There was an air of expectancy in the chapel as the elderly organist donned her spectacles and shuffled through her sheet music.

'Why is it always so cold in here?' Mrs Drummond grumbled.

'Put a sock in it, Ellen. At least we've got a good seat.' The man beside Mara gave a start of surprise.

He had never heard Lady Whitton be so rude to someone. It must be a side effect of the weather, he decided. The biting wind and harsh northern climate were bound to erode one's sense of delicacy over time. He shuddered at the thought of winter in this place. Despite the cold, the man removed his overcoat and leaned across Mara, offering it to Mrs Drummond. 'Take this, Madam,' he said. 'I should hate the cold to spoil the service for you.' Mrs Drummond blushed and accepted the long grey coat, draping it round her shoulders. The man inclined his head. 'Very becoming, Madam,' he said with precisely the right degree of sincerity. Mrs Drummond felt rather breathless.

'Well, I – er – thank you,' she stammered, blushing even harder as he smiled.

'I'm impressed,' Mara murmured to him. 'It's not often you see Ellen Drummond lost for words. I salute you, Abbott.'

'It was nothing, Madam,' he said. Mara looked at Mrs Drummond's pink cheeks and uncommon attention to posture.

'On the contrary,' she replied, making a mental note to keep an eye on them at the reception after the service, 'I think you'll find it was quite something.'

A flurry of activity in the chapel porch made the guests turn in their seats.

'Here they come,' said Mrs Drummond excitedly as Hugh entered the chapel with Rosie at his side. Gasps of admiration rippled through the congregation as they processed slowly to the front of the chapel.

'She's beautiful.'

'Look at that smile.'

'Those eyes.'

'Stunning.'

Pride radiated from Hugh with every step as he held his baby daughter up for all to see. Abbott surreptitiously wiped his eye as Hugh handed the child to her mother with a kiss and encircled them both with a protective arm.

Aelred stood ready by the font; Charlotte, Alistair and Kate lined up beside him as godparents.

'We are gathered here today to celebrate the baptism of Naomi Rose Fenwick.'

Little Naomi kicked and squirmed in Rosie's arms, more interested in snatching the glasses from the funny man's face than in becoming a Christian. Seeing this, Aelred removed the glasses and immediately handed them to the child, smiling as she closed her chubby fingers around one plastic arm.

'Aelred!' Rosie hissed.

'What?' he shrugged. 'I know the script. Don't worry, they were only a fiver.'

'She's only sixteen weeks,' Rosie said, vainly trying to wrestle the glasses from her daughter's grip. Naomi roared in protest and began sucking one of the lenses. Hugh lifted her out of Rosie's arms and held her up to his face.

'Naomi, no,' he said sternly. The child struck him on the bridge of the nose with the glasses and gurgled.

'She's so like her mother,' said Aelred.

Rosie turned to find Mara and laid the baby in her arms. 'Without you Mara, this would never have happened.'

Mara held the child close to her and smiled.

'Without the Lord, patience and Mrs Drummond's whisky.'

❀　❀　❀　❀

The pilgrimage of guests walked across the fields to the Harvest marquee. Hugh had spared no expense for the baptism of his first child. Tenants and villagers gathered; everyone mingling together as the champagne blessed them all.

The band played in the afternoon sun as the children raced on donkeys and whirled in the Ferris wheel.

Mrs Jacobs hovered at Rosie's side, watching both her daughter and grand-daughter carefully. Naomi appeared to be quite happy, charming young and old alike, but the crowd and the noise were beginning to take their toll on Rosie.

'Come on,' Hugh said simply. 'Let's find a quiet spot. You need a rest.'

'I'm fine. I don't want to miss the celebration.'

'It'll still be here when you get back.' He held out his hand and Rosie went quietly, Naomi crowing triumphantly on her hip. Mrs Jacobs turned to her husband in astonishment.

'Did you see that? She didn't even try to argue with him. She was . . . *reasonable.*'

Dan Jacobs put his arms round his wife and kissed her. 'She's still our Rosie,' he said with a grin. 'Just a grown-up version.'

The little family sat on the grass a safe distance from the marquee, Hugh's coat serving as a groundsheet. Hugh folded Rosie and Naomi into his arms, his chin resting on Rosie's head as they looked out over the land, enjoying the simple pleasure of the day. 'You know,' said Rosie. 'If someone had shown me the path my life would take, I'd never have believed them. Not in a million years.'

'Plus, you'd have run screaming for the hills,' Hugh said, laughing into her hair.

'I would.'

She was silent for a long time. The choices were visible now, the moments when her future had hung in the balance, waiting for the scales to tip. The day she met Cameron; staying with Mara; choosing to risk happiness and finding Hugh.

'What are you thinking?' Hugh asked after she had been quiet for some time.

'It could all have been so different.'

'Do you regret anything?' asked Hugh. It wasn't a barbed question.

'No.' Rosie tipped her head back and looked up at her husband. 'I made the right choice.'

'Keep on making it,' he said fervently, bending his head to kiss her.